# SUGAR SKULLS

# SUGAR SKULLS

LISA MANTCHEV
GLENN DALLAS

This is a work of fiction. Names, characters, organizations, places, events, and incidents are either products of the author's imagination or are used fictitiously.



Published by Skyscape, New York

www.apub.com



ISBN-13: 9781503949713
ISBN-10: 1503949710

Book design by Sammy Yuen

Printed in the United States of America

*To Mom and Dad, who never said it was impossible . . . They just said, "Keep working."*

—G. D.

*For Terry Pratchett, who taught me it was all right to go for the joke.*

—L. M.

# CHAPTER ONE

## M

Three blocks away from the club, two stories up, I'm staring at the Wall and counting down, waiting for the shift from twilight to dusk.

*Three . . . two . . . one . . .* As the last flickers of holographic sunset fade, the stars wink into view, speckling the fake horizon.

Of course, nobody streetside is watching for it. The newest crop of recruits wanders around the Odeaglow, dazzled by all the neon-splashed debauchery. As I make my way down to ground level, across ledges, down fire escapes, and through back alleys, I see them everywhere. Streaming into the nightspots. Waving a wrist in front of a vending machine for a hit of glim. Pairing up for another evening of physical and chemical delights.

There's nothing like the Cyrene nightlife.

I step into Hellcat Maggie's, trading the constant hum of the city outside for ambient murmurs and the breathy tones of speaker-buzz.

The shift eases my nerves ever so slightly. Speaker-buzz can herald great things.

Sidestepping an attractive pair of temporary blondes wearing more mini than skirt, I let my gaze stroll along their bodies, appreciating the show. One girl's hair colorshifts from ash to auburn, the other's to a light aquamarine. They stumble past me without a hint of acknowledgment, eyes glazed from a few hits of moondust. *Glad the fresh meat started off with something light.*

Normally, I'd never brave the front door of Maggie's during business hours, but with all the new recruits getting their first taste of prime-time excess, I'm just another face in the crowd.

The 'dusters slip outside, letting the city lights dazzle their chemically enhanced eyes. They're the first girls I've seen without the ghostly face paint or other overt signs of obsessive fandom. They'll be in the minority inside, from what Maggie has said about Sugar Skulls fans.

Maggie is all about them right now. I remember her pitch almost verbatim from her post on the Cyrano network, advertising the show: *Forget our usual fare. Forget all that DJ-spun techno generated in-city. The Sugar Skulls shatter the mold. This band is all-girl metal-infused technoglam, complete with lead vocals. There's nothing else like it in Cyrene.*

Since I ran a few extra errands for her this week in addition to the usual drops, she's passing me a ticket for the show. I *would* duck out on the invite, but I can't keep blowing her off. Losing Maggie as a contact isn't an option.

I make my way down the narrow corridor, from one staggered pool of light to the next, past the facilities and a few convenient shadowy alcoves, which will no doubt be seeing plenty of traffic later on. My fingers instinctively whisper-brush a curtain, grasping at memories of damp skin, the barest traces of shared moans, the heady hints of rapture.

I pull the curtain closed and walk away.

One dark corridor and a sharp left later, I taste the ozone in the air. I'm here. The double doors are propped open, and the static electricity spikes the hair on my arms.

Right now, for everyone else, dopamine is flooding their mesolimbic pathways and making everything fine and dandy. Nanotech scrubs out anything harmful but lets the recreational chemical goodness through unscathed. Like a soft blanket, these top-of-the-show highs envelop them in a thousand flapping butterfly wings of sensation.

Not for me, though. I ease up to the bar and order a #3, a double. Neat. Tastes like the inside of a vacuum cleaner bag but burns so good on the way down.

One quick drink, then I'll retreat to the safety of the rafters. *Out of sight. Out of mind. Above the fray.*

Less than a foot separates the pit from the bar area, but they might as well be alternate worlds. Everyone's already down there, the hive alight as they sample pills and eyedroppers and stimulants galore, expenses covered by a simple tap on a biometric scanner, small stipends of starter credits funding newfound vices. This preshow binge will pay off in spades a few minutes from now.

Especially if those new thrum-collectors mounted along either side of the pit are up to the task. In a few minutes, the show will kick off and the collectors will go to work, grids of lasers collecting every ounce of thrum generated as the crowd writhes and jumps and dances, fueled by a cocktail of music and chemistry. The free light show is just icing on the cake.

On cue, Hellcat Maggie saunters out of her private office, projecting an aura of easy confidence, but I can sense the tension all around her. She believes the Sugar Skulls are a Big Deal, and she'll be going over every aspect of the show with razor-sharp attention to detail.

Draped in a luxurious red silk dress far too formal for the occasion, Maggie is harshly thin, all sharp angles and careful craftsmanship to hold aging to a stalemate. At least she pays the club the same attention, constantly striving to keep pace with tech upgrades and the latest mods and fads. I help out wherever I can, doing odd jobs and maintenance work to ingratiate myself with her.

On her way to the back dressing room, she spots me at the bar and instantly changes course, adding an exaggerated little wiggle to her walk. I sigh, recognizing the intent behind that wiggle.

"Oh, hello, dove." Maggie's always careful not to use my name in public. She hugs my shoulders and kisses my cheek, a bit closer to my lips than I'm comfortable with. "Thank you for running those extra parcels for me today. You're a lifesaver, as always." Her arms slowly drift from my shoulders, but she lingers close. Her lavender perfume assaults my nose.

"Not a problem at all, Maggie. Happy to deliver more over-the-Wall tunes to the musically impoverished here."

"Which reminds me." She slips a prepaid card from her cleavage and presses it into my hand. The card's warmth is unsettling.

"Right. Thank you." I tuck it into my pocket. "So, what do you think of the new recruits?"

Maggie reluctantly drags her eyes away from me and considers the crowd: the fruits of Cyrene's most successful recruitment push to date. They can afford to turn people away now, cherry-picking those best suited to keep the city fueled and humming. "Corporate has high expectations for this lot. Tonight'll be a solid test. I bet we'll out-thrum the competition two to one."

*She's wagering the band will help her deliver.* "Anyway, thanks for the ticket. Can't wait to see if they live up to all your hype." The edge of the bar digs into my back as I lean away.

Maggie doesn't give an inch, her breath already haunted by wisps of high-octane booze. "You know, you're welcome to join me for the after-party. Little get-together at my place. You deserve a treat, always working so hard for me."

*Yeah, a little get-together that turns out to be just the two of us.* "Appreciated, but after this I should really get back and grab some shut-eye. Gotta be well rested for my runs tomorrow."

"Oh. Of course. Well, if you need anything, talk to Rete. He's at the Palace for the next week or so. He won't mind."

*Ugh, Rete. Her scumbag second-in-command.* I'm saved from discussing him further by a short double tap of static over the speakers. To the uninitiated, it's just background noise, but to the rest of us, it's Maggie's five-minute warning before showtime.

She scowls slightly before brushing the expression away with a flutter of her fingers. "Business before pleasure, dove. I'll catch you later."

She takes my wrist for a moment to punctuate her promise, before turning and stalking toward the back. Still wiggling.

*Better move soon. After one more drink.*

# V

The girl in the mirror is an undead supermodel in search of a catwalk. It's the handiwork of the new styling team Corporate brought in to deal with my hair and paint my face and glue sequins to my eyelids and shove in the black-light contacts after the old team quit.

Not that I'm admitting I had anything to do with them unceremoniously packing their kits and leaving before the last show. Better to point the finger at Jax.

In the group, Jax is "the crazy one." Damon recruited her a year ago, just before her eighteenth birthday, and she's driven every styling team we've had batshit insane with her demands.

"Spiderwebs," she decides for her face paint tonight, then points her index fingers at a case of skunk-striped bedhead so legendary, it looks like mice have nested in it. "Just don't touch the 'do."

There's a continuous rumble coming from the front of the house: newbies, fresh off the nanotech install and frothing at the mouth to get a taste of everything Cyrene has to offer. The mistress of ceremonies appears a few minutes later, hovering around the edges of my mirror like a moth about to get bug-zapped, makeup already settling into creases she thinks no one else can see. Hellcat Maggie drones on for a bit, her words painted in every shade of predictable monotony.

Eyes glued to the set list on her laptop, short hair spiked and pink, Sasha nods and makes understanding noises without really listening. Five months back, Damon pulled her from outside Cyrene, where everything is workaday business as usual, melting polar ice caps and recycling and talking heads, minimum-wage jobs and Wall Street assholes. She told me he offered a considerable chunk of cash to her poor-as-dirt family in exchange for a three-year contract capitalizing on her sound design and computer skills. Means Sasha got to leapfrog over a hundred thousand or more eager applicants all clamoring to get into the city, but instead of acting like a badass, she's more like a puppy that might pee on the rug.

She and Jax are the same age, but you'd never guess it, because Sasha is "the nice one."

And me? Well, I guess that makes me "the bitch." Like now, instead of joining in Jax's preshow pill binge or Sasha's obsessive run-throughs of the set list, I hug Little Dead Thing and wish everyone would just shut their cakeholes. He understands my mood, curling up in a tight fur-splotched ball in my lap, purring like a rusted-out lawn mower engine. Sasha dragged this sorry excuse for a cat in off the street a couple months back. He'd almost immediately started trailing after me, gratitude be damned, yowling at doors closed between us and shredding furniture when left behind at the Loft. Just easier to bring him along, a freaky little mascot who leaves hairs all over my robe.

But I banish him to a dark corner before getting dressed. Fuck-me wardrobe. Heels so tall, I prance instead of walking through the dim red lights in the wings. Corseted waist, narrow skirt, a thousand pounds of hand-sewn beads catching the light when I step onstage. The dress was a class-me-up gift from Damon: vintage and gorgeous and beyond expensive.

I'd taken a switchblade to it, because tatters suit me better.

Still miles away from comfortable, I try to draw a deeper breath than the corset allows, and it catches in my throat. I shouldn't be stressing. Tonight's just a warm-up for the big to-do at the Dome. Three days and counting. Have to test the set list and the newest energy-grabbing thrum-collectors Corporate's eager to roll out citywide.

Every time I blow up one of the old ones, it knocks me off the grid. Cue a mind-scrubbing and a nanotech reboot. I'm tired of waking up as a brand-new Vee. I'd like to keep this version of myself, even if that means making nicey-nice with the equipment.

Anything to keep Damon off my back for a little while longer.

# M

From the bar, I watch roadies and techies in midnight black swarm the stage, running cables and hauling equipment for the band. On the left, a girl with hot-pink punk style and an enigmatic smile warms up a laptop and lovingly caresses the keys on a top-of-the-line Moog synthesizer. On the right, a dervish with an unkempt lion's mane and retro-goth Victorian flair barks orders at anyone who comes within two feet of her holographic mixer board and turntables. I dub the left one Treble and the right one Trouble.

Then my gaze falls front and center where *she* commands the stage despite a sapphire cloak of preshow lighting. I barely glimpse her face behind a curtain of raven hair. Streaks of wicked green and electric blue only highlight her two-tone mystique. Porcelain skin gives her the perfect palette, highlighting every brush, dab, and flourish of face paint. Her eyes are two black-rimmed blossoms, illusory sunken sockets wavering between bluest sky and deepest violet. Her nose vanishes beneath the dark makeup, shadows bending to her will. Her lips and cheeks are lined with more black strokes, completing the effect.

*Sugar Skulls, indeed.*

Her beaded black dress shimmers in the soft blue light, shredded beyond all reason, as if she lost a few dozen knife fights in the last twenty-four hours. She's adorned it with staples and buckles and all manner of punk rock regalia.

Whining feedback arcs from speaker to speaker when Treble and Trouble plug in their laptops.

Maggie steps into the small spotlight at the edge of the stage, reveling in her brief moment of ringmaster glory. "And here they are," she croons into the mic. "The Sugar Skulls!"

The overhead lights cut out, and the masses cheer in the darkness. Anticipation spikes as warm ambers, pulsing crimsons, and soothing blues scatter across the crowd. Swirling spotlights illuminate the pit. The emerald lasers of the thrum-collectors fan out, activated by the crowd's enthusiastic response.

Maggie is banished from memory as the girl stands at center stage, bathed in purest white.

# V

At some clubs, the spotlight's the ghost of a lover, already fading as the sun hits the sheets on the cold side of the bed. Other times—times like this, a club like this—it's bright enough to drain a dozen power banks. It tightens, sparks on the beads, and throws tiny reflections across the room like stars.

Sasha loads up "Drunk on You" and starts accessing threads of older songs, forgotten songs, conjuring the voices of dead musicians on the fly. No crystal ball necessary, just the Corporate music archives. It's the only way to get a taste of over-the-Wall music, percolated through a thousand programs and filtered by every piece of equipment we have; even then, it's in hacked-up bits and pieces, just like my dress. Jax mixes the threads together and brings up the volume until the stage starts to vibrate.

I lean forward a hair's breadth, close enough to almost kiss the microphone, focus my eyes on some random guy at the bar, and pull the first note from the dark space in the back of my throat.

# M

She looks straight at me. Gazes at me. Gazes *through* me.

The first note slips past her lips. It rolls over the crowd, and they're instantly hers, already amped and soaring higher. There's nothing quite like popping your Cyrene cherry, and a hundred newbies are experiencing it all around me as their nanotech processes the music, the drugs, the booze.

*I miss that.*

So it damn near knocks me on my ass when her words smash into me, and inside I unfold, like flesh-and-blood origami. Hands numb, mouth dry, blood on fire. I just stand there, rigid, muscles refusing to respond. *Can't move. Gotta move. Too exposed here.* But her voice runs through my veins like napalm.

For a moment, a long moment, an eternity of a moment, I'm lost. *This . . . this is impossible.* Flutters and tingles and frissons long absent, jolting me as dormant synaptic pathways are jarred back into service. If strings ran up my spine, she just plucked the high E, a fierce vibration that shakes me to my core.

She looks away, and quakes subside into mere tremors. I close my eyes, welcoming new sine waves of sensation for three sharp breaths, then open them again, back in control. Propping myself up against the bar, I abandon my drink to process the last few seconds.

All these months, there's been nothing. But just now? I felt it. I *feel* it. I pulse with life, lightning dancing across my skin as she batters the crowd with furious verses.

But I'm stuck on that first gasp.

One note. One word. She laid me low and resurrected me in one fell swoop.

*Who is this girl?*

# V

Wrapping the microphone cord around my hand, I really lay into the lyrics, jacking straight into the brains of the audience. The boys and girls slosh around the pit like iridescent-foamed water in a dirty fish tank.

Except for the guy. The guy at the bar with the piercing gaze and the messy hair and the look of a lost soul. I'm too far away to see the color of his eyes, and he isn't wearing anything worth noticing. Not the sharp edges of clothes fresh off the rack. Not the silver glint of a dozen facial piercings. None of the writhing subdermal implants or interchangeable magnetic tattoos that are the latest trends to hit hard and fast. At least, not any I can see from my vantage point. Black shirt and jeans that help him fade into the background. Dark blond, lacking all the bleach and color of anyone who spends any time in the sun or a salon. Even leaning back, every line of his body indicates a readiness to bolt.

I force my attention back to the pit, determined not to spare him another thought.

*Just another gig, Vee. Just another audience. Get through the song, already.*

## M

*Need to move. Need to run. Should run. Should get out of here.*

It takes supreme effort to tear my attention away from her long enough to acknowledge her partners in crime. Treble summons entire orchestras and metal bands from her laptop and synth with a few frenzied keystrokes. Trouble snarls with hungry delight as she channels torrents of sound with a pair of haptic gloves, manipulating the very notes midstream like an angry sorceress as holographic turntables whirl in the foreground.

But front and center, there's Her. She's a creature of myth, with Her siren song and Her banshee wail. The set's barely begun, but the hive's heart and my heart both beat to Her drum.

Our eyes finally meet again, and I'm thrown back into a surging sea. When that first note hit, I was a drowning man finally breaking the surface. This time, the current simply takes me.

Outside, I betray nothing. Cucumber-cool and casual, even as Her eyes narrow and Her gaze bores into me. My crippled nervous system allows little else to show. But inside, I'm a being of crystal, oscillating in perfect harmony.

Running is the last thing on my mind now.

# V

I should call a bouncer and have him ejected. Injected. Hauled off for a diagnostic and a thorough probing. There's something not right. Not right with him. Not right with the way he looks at me or the way the song pours into him like water into the desert.

I force myself to look away, to push through the next song. If it's not working for him, he'll leave, right? He'll go register a complaint with the main office, and they'll roll up to the Loft and ask a lot of questions that boil down to the same freaking one I have:

*Why isn't he responding to the music?*

Approaching the end of the set, the lyrics get rough around the edges, liable to rip if I lean into them any more than I already am. Everyone below me is frantic, writhing. Thrum output's still on the rise as the lasers scan the crowd, gather up the ambient energy, and funnel it away. Neat, clean, efficient—and why we're all here.

Except for the guy leaning against the bar. Separate from the others. Motionless. Gaze latched on me like he's dying and I have the cure in my pocket.

That's when I realize he's responding, all right. Just not the way I expected.

*Fuck the grid. I'm the one with the power right now.*

# M

The mood is shifting. The air is thick with it, the crowd buzzing and overstimulated, neurons firing and misfiring as the hive responds to Her rage, and She unleashes it. I swear, the ground trembles with thumping bass lines. She just might bring Hellcat Maggie's down around us.

Now Her eyes won't leave mine. She's no longer the eye of the storm; She's the storm itself, pounding the crowd and sweeping them along with Her.

# V

I'm pushing it. I can feel the stress building in the new thrum-collectors like a force field against my bare arms, my throat, my lips. It's too much for this crowd, too, their fresh nanotech already blitzed out and buzzing. I should dial it back. Get backstage. Take a handful of pills. Chill the fuck out.

It's been a year since the last blowout, the last blackout. Three hundred and sixty-five days of uninterrupted consciousness, flushed down the toilet for the sake of some asshole staring at me from the bar.

I twist the microphone out of the stand and launch into something new. To hell with the set list. To hell with Corporate-approved garbage. I find words that have been bouncing around in my head for so long that I can spit them out now, perfect and round. "It's all just screams and whispers, just prettied-up and dyed. Your fuck-façade all faded, a tarnished future bride . . ."

Somewhere behind me, Jax loses her shit.

"What the hell are you doing?" she shouts over the thumping rhythm that's our artificial heartbeat. "Break time! Sasha's gonna wet 'em, and I need a hit of silvertip!"

Despite the protest, she turns up every dial and pushes up every slide, fingers moving over the touchscreens with brutal efficiency. Sasha's already pulling in chants from sixteenth-century monasteries and screams recorded in hospital waiting rooms. I can feel the fluid in my inner ears pulsing.

I'm going to get a reaction out of our silent onlooker, even if I fall headfirst into a blackout.

So I let him have it, all the words and the anger and betrayal and despair I hold in my hummingbird heart. The rest of the crowd moans and sways, crashing into each other, molecules colliding. Hellcat Maggie shouts something at Sasha, then tries the headset, but all I get from my earpiece is crackling feedback that drives me hard into the next verse.

I lock eyes with the stranger, vomiting up all my dark, dirty guts for him to see. Below me, the flotsam holds itself upright. If these people were pleasantly giddy before, now they're stumbling drunk. A few fall and are dragged to the side by security. A couple kisses so hard that blood trickles from the corners of their mouths. A threesome in the back crashes into an alcove, tearing the velvet curtains from their brass rod.

I can't stop myself now. I close out the set with a crescendo that drives everyone and everything off a cliff and into glorious sonic freefall.

# CHAPTER TWO

## M

Her spell ends, still echoing in every fiber of my being, and its absence hits the crowd like a shock wave. Spotlights burst, punctuated by pop-pop-pops as hot glass shards cut through lighting gels and shower the band. A heavy crash follows as one of the thrum-collectors blows out and its emitter plate shatters against the floor.

People in the pit are frothing at the mouth, manic and terrified and roaring like beasts. It's like two hundred simultaneous nervous breakdowns or the worst trip in pharmaceutical history. This would be brutal enough for recruits with a few months under their belt; for the newbies, it must be damn near agony. I retreat in self-preservation and start working my way toward the double doors. I've never seen the hive like this.

The lights go out, plunging us into darkness. I can hear the chaos all around me.

Definitely not my scene.

# V

With howls and screams, they rush the stage, shoving at the barricade and the security detail, tossing the hired muscle aside like paper dolls in their gleeful rage. With my own berserker haze fading, I rock back, shell-shocked. When I wipe the sweat from my eyes, my hand comes away smeared with black.

"What was *that*?" Jax grabs me by the arm and hauls me backstage.

"Nothing. Just go!" I'm clinging to the grid, but I could topple off any second now; I can feel the energy snaking over my skin, in between my ears, threatening to bounce me.

Emergency lighting flickers to life around us, and my stomach clenches. I would puke up my dinner, if I'd eaten anything; instead I manage one good dry heave.

"You'd better fucking run!" someone shouts at me. Might be a bodyguard. Could be Hellcat Maggie herself. Doesn't matter, because I'm already skimming down the hall. A hand clamps down roughly on the back of my dress, but I duck and twist. The fabric gives way, exposing my back down to the crack of my ass, and beads rain down on the floor. I whirl around and face my attacker. I don't know who she is or why she's chasing me, but adrenaline brings my fist up to connect with her face. She falls back, taking down the three people behind her.

*A knife to my throat, trailed down my neck, along my shoulder. Blood. Screams of pain . . .* My *screams.*

It's like my finger's on the trigger, firing off shots from a memory gun.

*I don't want to remember any of this, damn it. The mind-scrubs are supposed to wipe out everything: Conversations, the faces of friends-turned-strangers. The way he smelled. The way he touched me.*

But I remember pain like that. I remember the blood . . .

Sasha stumbles into me and shoves me out of the past. "The back door's this way!" she gasps between harried steps, her arms full of equipment, wiring spilling out of her embrace and trailing behind her like a disemboweled octopus.

"Not without Little Dead Thing!" Instead of turning right, I veer left. Another left turn, and I'm back at the dressing room. The styling team already evacuated, leaving behind a debris field of sequins and translucent powder and bits of black lace. Pushing me to one side, Jax grabs a black nylon bag and crams her gloves and mixing console inside. Sasha reaches for her laptop case and tries to wrestle the cord-tangle into submission.

I end up flat on the floor, pulling an irate and hissing cat out from under the threadbare velvet couch. "Come on, love. Time to bail."

With the girls at my heels and Little Dead Thing in my arms, I twist open the heavy stage door. The dark outside surprises me—sporadic backup lights have activated down countless shadowed blocks—but the limo is waiting, engine running, headlights carving out an escape route. I clamber inside, the memories of screams and blood still fresh in my mind as I teeter on the edge of the grid.

# M

The music is gone, but Her voice remains. My bones resonate with it.

Trailing my hand down the length of the counter, I quickly retrace my steps, leaving the elevated bar behind for the chaos of the pit. People ricochet off me in the darkness, all grasping for something. Crashing through the crowd, I find one of the propped-open doors. Memory guides me down the halls.

There are still people in the alcoves, going at it. Unbelievable. *Too bad the grid's not up to harness the energy from* those *exchanges.*

Another collision with an addled fan sends me stumbling, and I grab the nearest thing in reach: a velvet curtain.

Not the same curtain—wrong club, wrong time—but close enough. *I don't want to remember this right now.* I tear the curtain free from its rings and hurl it aside, taking off down the hall. *Gotta keep moving. Maybe I can catch the Skulls before they flee the scene.*

I'm one of the first outside. It was blind luck that a few stumbling pit-dwellers made it out here before me. Some crouch against the wall, huddled together for comfort. Others brawl in the street or just stand around, in total meltdown.

*Something's missing.*

Buildings all around us are dark, shadows shaped by moonlight and the glow of distant, unaffected neighborhoods. No thrum-collectors to harness clubgoer energy, no substations to process it, no glass-globes transmitting wireless energy back to the citizens.

The hum is gone. It's been with me every second since I got back, but now it's gone.

*That's insane. She did all this. Who* is *this girl?*

Tearing ass around the front of the building, I sprint down the alley toward the backstage doors. The band must have slipped out the back during the melee.

I two-step up some crates onto the loading dock, just in time to catch the limo's taillights as it speeds off down the road.

## V

We left the speakers behind, but static still crackles between my ears. I'm breathing hard and clutching Little Dead Thing to my chest as the limo takes the first corner way too fast. Jax and Sasha end up on the floorboards with their equipment bags, and I slam into the door. Even though my chest just kept his head from getting bashed in, Little Dead Thing scratches the crap out of my cleavage trying to escape.

When the car slows down enough, I turn him loose. "Fine, you little asshole, go."

He picks a careful path across the seat, curls up in the corner, hikes a leg, and starts to lick his junk. Probably just to reassure himself that everything's where it's supposed to be.

Everyone else looks way more rattled. Sasha's still on the floor, cradling her laptop like a child with a janked-up toy, trying to get it to boot up.

"Come on, baby. Come on." She makes a low, grieving noise, a whine that probably only dogs and I can hear, then shouts with triumph when the screen bathes her in blue light. "Yes!" Leaning over to squint at the screen, she starts keystroking like it's the only way to get enough oxygen. "I'm up. Everything's still here, but my case is jacked and I can't access any of the remote files while the grid is down."

"What the fresh shit was that, exactly, Vee?" Jax demands again, hauling herself into the seat opposite me.

"Something I've been working on awhile." If I'm not careful, she'll boot me in the shins with one of those platforms, so I shift my legs to one side.

She aims higher and kicks me in the thigh instead, dislodging a dozen iridescent beads and putting a new hole in my skirt. "Not the song."

"It's not my fault. Maggie probably had the new collectors wired in ass-backwards."

"Nothing about her wiring or backwards ass explains *that.*" Jax jerks her thumb at the buildings on either side of the street. Windows that should be glowing white are as dark as black eyes punched into someone's face. The horrible orange emergency lighting reminds me of a cheap Halloween carnival. "You overloaded the grid, for fuck's sake. That shouldn't even be possible."

*Of course Jax took that personally.*

Her family—two dads, a mom, a couple of older siblings—are all bioenergy specialists. According to Jax, they were "part of Cyrene's genesis, theorizing a radical alternative to the usual clean-energy solutions. Not only that, but they assembled the original team that developed the thrum-collectors and brought the grid online." I can't eye-roll hard enough every time she says shit like that.

When push came to shove, Jax followed the family's scientific tradition in her own way, isolating frequencies and rhythms that trigger higher thrum production in clubgoers, making her one of the best DJs the city has ever seen. Cyrene might be her vice-infused playground, but it's also where she's honed the skills that brought her to Damon's attention in the first place.

"Obviously, there are flaws in the system." A factory specializing in throbbing sets up shop just behind my eyeballs, and I pinch the bridge of my nose. Headaches are standard after a show, but this promises to be a full-flare migraine. *Still, there are worse things.* "Maybe you should discuss it next time the family visits."

"This won't wait," Jax says. "Corporate's going to be up your ass the minute we get back to the Loft."

"She's right," Sasha adds, still 90 percent preoccupied with file recovery. "Damon's going to want answers."

With a scowl, Jax pulls out a flask and unscrews the lid. "He can get in line." She chugs the contents, not offering to share.

The second she pauses to take a breath, I swipe it out of her hand and take a deep pull. There's at least six kinds of liquor and some designer street drug mixed up in there. Tastes like lighter fluid mixed with broken glass.

*Maybe it can cut this voice from my throat.*

I hand her back the empty flask and rub my hand across my mouth. "I'll think of something. I always do."

# M

Instinctively, I start mapping my route. Stretch limos aren't exactly made for the back alleys of the Odeaglow, so the options are limited. They can take a left either two blocks up or three.

Mentally, I'm nine steps ahead of my body, scaling the surrounding buildings to nab the best vantage point. I crouch and jump down off the loading dock, but I only take two steps toward the fire escape before slamming into somebody. We both stumble back a few feet.

I'm first to respond. "Sorry, man, didn't see you th—"

I cut myself off. He's framed in the high beams of an SUV that just pulled up, and I recognize the uniform, not to mention the heavy-duty flashlight he bends down to retrieve.

*Crap. Should've expected this.* They were already out in force to assist the fresh meat. Factor in the blackout, and you're halfway to a greyface parade.

He smacks the flashlight against his palm a few times, and the beam keeps flickering. Must not bother to keep it charged. The power grid's usually so reliable that you can phantom power whatever you need from the ambient thrum.

"Hey, son, can't have you wandering around in the dark like this. Come on up front. We're getting everyone scanned, cleaned up, and home safe." He continues to smack the flashlight, and I can't take my eyes off it.

*If that has a nanotech scanner in it, I'm screwed.* "Oh, that's all right, I'm just fine." *Whack!* "Just hoping to grab an autograph . . ." *Whack!* "You know how it is . . ." *Whack!*

The beam flares and hits my face for a split second. Long enough to detect I'm off-grid.

"Hold it. Stay right where you are. We've got a runner!" he yells, alerting his pals to my unauthorized presence. I hear footsteps pounding toward us.

*I get one chance at this.* I shove him hard in the chest with both hands, knocking him two steps back and onto the uneven sewer grate. His legs go out from under him, and he topples backward.

I make a break for it as he hits the ground with a satisfying thud. Two quick steps up the wall, and I jump, grabbing the fixed ladder and scrambling onto the fire escape. Diving over a concrete barrier, I tuck and roll into the parking garage next door. I hear the commotion below: The staticky blare of walkie-talkies, snippets of "mobilize," "secure perimeter," and "bring him in." The crunch of boots arriving, the ominous whine of stun batons going live. These won't be keep-the-peace greyfaces; these'll be the hardcore Facilitators brought in to handle threats to the city itself.

I run, and I don't bother looking back. I don't know what all of them are carrying, so it's best to put as much distance between them and me as possible.

Bathed in the sickly orange of the emergency lighting, I race down three rows of cars and scan the ceiling for a telltale gap between this level and the next one up. *There.* I run toward the nearest truck, hopping up the front bumper, over the hood, and onto the roof. I leap, reaching for a small ledge built into the rafters, and snag it with my fingertips.

Tires squealing against asphalt means they're on their way up. *Gotta move faster.*

I lever myself onto the ledge and hop up and over the security wall, tumbling onto the rough flooring of level three. Rolling clear of the nearest cars, I get back to my feet and stumble right into the path of an approaching SUV.

*Damn, these guys are fast.* I break left and head for the outer ring of cars, hemmed in by yellow lines and the concrete retaining wall of the garage. I can't help but think of Her and that vicious voice as I charge over a parked station wagon, cross the barricade, and hurl myself out into open space.

Legs tucked, arms out, I soar. Untouched. Untouchable. Master of my own fate. Beholden to no one and nothing.

*Except gravity.*

My arc peaks a third of the way across the alley, and I do some quick math midflight. My target's twelve or thirteen feet out and about four feet down from the takeoff point. A few seconds later, I tumble onto the warehouse roof, rolling to my feet with a gasp. *More like five and a half feet down.*

I dash across the roof, doing my damnedest to ignore the worrying pings of whatever they're shooting at me.

*Keep going, gotta keep moving—*

Impact. My calf spasms, and I snag my foot on a length of sprinkler pipe I should've been able to dodge. Just barely, I get my hands up in time to prevent a full faceplant, and the calluses on my right hand rip open. With my left, I check my leg, finding something small and definitely foreign.

A dart. *Shit.*

Tearing a strip of cloth from my tank top—undershirts are a must on the run—I wrap up my hand. *Can't leave a blood trail.*

I scramble to the roof's edge and over the side, sliding down a drainpipe section by section. I hit the street harder than intended. *Dammit. Misjudged the landing.*

A tranq dart won't put me down like most people—*thank you, fubared brain chemistry*—but it'll sure screw with my balance and depth perception.

*Gotta hurry.* Darting out into the street, I baseball-slide across the hood of a sports car as the driver slams on both the brakes and the horn. I'm across the street in a flash, whipping down side roads and back alleys, hoping to lose the greyfaces in the maze of urban shadows.

A few minutes later, there's no sign of them anywhere. I race out of an alley and into the street, dodging a speeding coupe with no lights on, refusing to break stride as I run toward a tall chain-link fence.

I plant one foot on the fence and step up, using its natural give to get my other foot on the wall beside it and spring upward, pinballing between the fence and the wall. Losing momentum, I grab the top of the fence one-handed and toss myself over, kicking off the wall for good measure. I clear it, barely, landing on the ever-reliable heap of garbage bags outside the Carlisle Building.

Down the pile and onto my feet, I take off down the side street, muscles slower to respond than I'd like. *Must've upped the dosage in the dart. How thoughtful.*

I crouch between two parked cars, virtually invisible. A big-box delivery truck is speeding from the other direction. Time to hitch a ride.

As the truck passes, I charge, leaping for the tiny offload platform, grasping for the rear handle bolted to the back. My foot slips, and my shin slams against the edge of the platform. I bite my lip hard to keep from crying out. Looping my left arm through the handle, I hug it tight, holding on for dear life as I try to get my feet back underneath me.

After a block or two, my right foot finally finds purchase, and I gratefully stand up. Resting my head against the cold metal, I close my eyes for a moment, the stinging of my bloodied shin radiating up my leg.

I open my eyes and glance at the passing scenery. Half a dozen blocks from leaving the blackout area behind me. Still a long, long way from home.

# V

Our limo glides to a halt in front of the Carlisle Building. Fancy digs don't pout in the dark, even during a blackout, so it's running on backup generator power. The doorman opens the front door for us with a murmured, "Evening, Miss Vee. Miss Jax. Miss Sasha." He pauses before adding, "Little Dead Thing."

The cat's still pissed, but at least he's riding my shoulder now and not trying to eat me. I have him by the scruff, just in case. He's on the last of his nine lives, and the traffic just behind us won't be as forgiving if he tries to bolt again.

Jax is right in front of me. She's going to catch it if Little Dead Thing jumps, but that doesn't seem to be her primary concern. Ignoring all the discreet brass placards that warn people not to smoke in the lobby, she pulls out a bundle of silvertips and lights one up. Her first major exhale manages to nail me in the face, and I teeter in my heels trying to avoid the second.

"Would you please message a med team?" Sasha murmurs in passing, a power cord still trailing behind her.

"Already did, Miss Sasha," the doorman responds.

Just goes to show that I'm forever under surveillance, even in my ivory tower. I've been living here since Damon "discovered" me. For a second, I can't dredge up how long ago that was, and I have to count back.

*Nineteen now, fourteen when I came in, so five years.*

Between the mind-scrubs and seshes of nanotech rehab, there's precious little I remember before waking up in the penthouse and Damon handing me my medical file. Apparently, that's our thing. I glitch off the grid and he shoves me back on. I go all jigsaw-puzzle brain, he gives me back my name and my voice. Even now, I don't remember anything pre-Cyrene. No friends, no family, but I sense that it's no real loss. If someone had ever loved me . . . really loved me . . . I know I would remember that.

*That's how I know for sure that life outside the Wall was utter shit.*

Tiny colored dots appear at the edges of my vision—never a good sign—and I forget to be impressed by the ornate foyer before we're in the elevator, and I lean back against the mirrored wall. Up we climb, up to the heavens.

Everyone in Cyrene sings for their supper in some way, from the newest arrivals to nightingales in pretty gilded cages. The more energy we generate for the grid, the more credits we accumulate, the fancier our accommodations, our clothes, our food, our drugs. Five years ago—

*Was it five?*

*Fuck.*

—I'd been singing in a club, I think. Not onstage, just goofing off with that night's group of riprap pals, trading lyrics for drinks. I remember a business card appearing in front of me alongside a shot of Pennyroyale. Lucky fucking me, one of the few things that *does* stick is the memory of looking up at Damon for the first time. Even after all the mind-scrubs, that first moment of seeing him is still seared into my brain.

Except now . . . now there's another memory, another face vying for my attention.

*The blond guy at the bar.*

Remembering him shoves me a little closer toward unconsciousness. Even with my eyes closed, I can feel Jax staring daggers at the side of my head. She's still torqued off about our conversation in the car. That I hinted something was wrong with the grid, a flaw in her family's work, rather than take any responsibility for it going down.

But when I open my eyes, it's Sasha's fleeting gaze flicking over me, because she doesn't want me to catch her looking. She stares down at the floor, frowning at the carpet, and I can guess what she's thinking.

Damon's played me the recordings, previous versions of me singing. It might as well be a stranger; there's no connection at all to the songs beyond my voice. *Those songs aren't mine.* If I need another mind-scrub and a nanotech reboot by a Corporate medical team, this Vee is gone. My connection to the Sugar Skulls songs? Gone. The band implodes like a dying star, and Sasha's family stops getting that monthly subsistence check.

Can't be a comfortable way to live, keeping a wary eye on me at all times. Some nights I bet Sasha wishes she could zip-tie my hands together and lock me in the closet.

I jerk my chin at her. "I'm sorry about what happened at the club. It was . . . stupid."

"You didn't do it on purpose," she hastens to say, although I'm not quite sure if she's trying to reassure me or convince herself.

We hit the top floor. Before Jax can close the apartment door, Damon exits the second elevator with a security detail behind him, crackling radios indicating their greyface counterparts are pursuing someone.

*Freshman orientation really went to shit tonight. Wonder what poor asshole had the misfortune to trip their radar in the middle of a power outage.*

The security team numbers a modest four tonight: two men, two women, all in dark suits and sunglasses. As always, I struggle to see beyond the bland features and nondescript hair that mark all the past-their-primes in Cyrene. Over-21s are few and far between here, working maintenance jobs, operating within strict caregiver parameters that keep the recruits producing as much energy as possible for the grid. Very few—like Hellcat Maggie—register as individuals. Mostly they're a blur, background filler in an old black-and-white movie.

Damon manages a bit better than that. Tonight, he's wearing an expensive navy blue suit tailored to perfection. Despite the late hour, his tie is still tight at the throat, the starch in his shirt still standing at attention. Under the fabric, there's the suggestion of old-school tattoos, a throwback to the days when he was raising hell as one of the under-21s in Cyrene. When his jacket comes off, I get a better impression of shapes and lettering through the cotton, but nothing definitive. He never rolls his sleeves up around us—part and parcel of maintaining that professional demeanor spit shine.

Knowing the nature of the beast, I strike before he can. "A year since I had an episode, and some douchebag in the audience triggered me. Migraine City. I'm lucky I didn't pass out in the middle of the set." I drop Little Dead Thing on the floor and watch as he skitters off in the direction of the kitchen and the nearest can opener, a patchwork tumbleweed of calico and tiger stripes.

Damon steps to the center of the room, making calm adjustments to his cuff links; a small gesture, but even Jax stays quiet. "I just spent three hours reassuring Corporate and their select guests that we're locked and loaded for the Dome. That these new thrum-collectors are going to push us far beyond covering Cyrene's energy needs. That energy production will outstrip consumption three to one. That we're only a few days away from rolling in investment capital and moving ahead with building more cities based on the Cyrene model. And right about the time they cracked open the champagne, the call came in that you cocked things up at Maggie's."

He reaches out and snags me by the arm. Some girls get off on being bossed around, but some previous version of me didn't and stopped sleeping with him. Well, that and Corporate found out we were banging. Apparently, at their insistence, I'd broken it off. This go-around, I have zero inclination to shag him, but it's still a relief to have an official excuse to keep Damon at arm's length.

We'd reassured each other that it wouldn't affect our working relationship.

We're both good liars.

When I try to pull away from him, he carefully lowers his voice to the Damage Control setting. "You're lucky you're still on the grid." Then he steers me to the couch.

It's new. White and impractical and velvet-ridiculous, but I love it anyway. I had the apartment made over last month, and the interior decorator took the term *carte blanche* literally. Everything feels sanitized, the metal sleek with silver-shine. The colossal fireplace crackles around the clock, the violet and blue and green flames offering one of two spots of color in the room. The other is a life-size photograph hanging over the hearth: the Sugar Skulls in full hair and makeup but very little clothing. I remember that shoot. Hard to forget freezing your ass off for hours while a photographer shouts at you in a language you don't speak. Corporate uses it for publicity shots now, so I get to see mostly naked versions of myself plastered all over the city.

The city. Beyond a floor-to-ceiling wall of windows, most of Cyrene shimmers. The playground is still lit up like a dance party: some kind of couture show in the Cordray District has high-intensity halogen spotlights scanning the sky. The nightclubs and restaurants are seeing a steady flow of traffic. There's the twinkle of strobes off the hyperglass penthouse dance floors of Club Aurora in the distance. The business district is down to night-lights because the paper-pushers have clocked out for the day, but the manufacturing district runs 24/7 to keep up with the demand for nanotech-tuned narcotics and booze.

In eerie contrast, the blackout area still shrouds the Odeaglow. Even more disconcerting, there's a gap in the endless starry horizon, a hole in the Wall's standard projection. The Wall keeps publicity hounds, prying eyes, and anti-Corporate interests at bay, the citywide equivalent of velvet ropes and burly bouncers. And who can blame them for trying to get in? Everything here is glitter and music and eternal, invincible youth. No one picks black-and-white Kansas if they can live in the Emerald City.

*No one but that sucker, Dorothy . . .*

"Is everyone all right?" Damon cuts in, keeping his hand over mine as he redirects a bit of his attention to the other girls. "How about you, Jax? Any injuries?"

"Few broken ribs, maybe a concussion, but it can wait until you're done dealing with the princess." She drops down in front of the fire, blocking the flames from view and courting not-so-spontaneous combustion.

"She's joking," Sasha quickly adds. "We're all fine." She then finds the corner where the windows meet the wall, slides down until her butt hits the marble floor, and opens her laptop again. The light from the monitor bounces off her pink hair and painted cheeks. Her lips move as she reads through the crash information, locating backup files and checking to make sure the new song I belted out on the fly etched electronic grooves in a virtual wax cylinder. Corporate's going to want a copy of that recording for the morning news blast. It's her responsibility to make sure they get what they want.

"Fine? You don't know that. I could have internal bleeding." Jax's makeup is already flaking. When she scratches her cheek, more sequins litter the white carpet.

I would protest, but the pain that receded during our adrenaline-fueled escape crashes into me full force. Pressing my fingers to my temples, I bring my knees up and try to make myself smaller, like the migraine might not find me if only I can hide fast enough.

"Could you identify the person that triggered the attack, if you saw him again?" Damon has his phone out, no doubt accessing Corporate databases, profiles, mug shots. Finding the face he wants, he holds the screen out to me, but all I can make out with unfocused eyes is a blue-white blur.

"I can't tell if that's him or not," I manage to say before things start to go black around the edges, paper held over an open flame. Sweat gathers along my forehead.

*No need to set me on fire, I'm already burning.* I always think in poetry right before keeling over. *This is it. I'm going to glitch out on my own fucking couch.*

Damon gestures to one of the bodyguards to turn down the lights as he reaches out to steady me. His cool hand finds the hot spot at the base of my skull. "Hold on."

The pressure in my head builds, and I'm already shaking. "Hurry."

"Try to breathe through it," he suggests, still supporting my neck, trying to keep the broken flower on its stem. With the other hand, he reaches into his breast pocket for a sleek, black case. Inside, elastic loops hold glass cylinders in place, a pharmaceutical cocktail bar on the go. Keeping one hand on me at all times, he loads up something to take the edge off.

I barely feel the injection. Barely notice as Damon picks me up and carries me upstairs to the master suite. Over his shoulder, I catch a final glimpse of Jax's scowl, of Sasha's enormous eyes peering over her laptop.

"Get some rest. We'll speak again in the morning," Damon says to me. An order, not a request. I hear him moving about the room. The sound of the dresser opening, then closing.

The bed is a soft little nest for his songbird, and I drift off into the darkness with one last thought:

*This face paint is really going to fuck up the sheets.*

# M

I scale the last few feet of scaffolding to my cozy nook beneath the Arkcell Bridge and collapse gratefully to the floor, banged up, bloodied, and all sorts of exhausted.

My eyes immediately lock on to the bed. It's a two-person field cot, topped with an unzipped all-weather sleeping bag. Right now, it looks like the comfiest damn thing in the world.

I rode the truck as far as I dared, trying to shake off the worst of the tranq before hitting the streets again. The hum gradually returned as I left the blackout behind, but there were a few more squirrelly landings and confidence-shaking stumbles along the way.

*They're getting smarter, but they haven't nabbed me yet. Going on six months now . . .*

Six months. Six months under the radar. Pride morphs into disbelief as I think about the months of running and hiding, of chasing down leads and following the trail. Months of scrapes that won't heal and scars that linger. Months since the happy highs and paradise juices.

Months since Trav and Zane and Rina and . . . us.

I drag myself over to the metal security door built into the wall—a modified tool cage left over from the bridge's construction—and unlock it, swinging the door open. Pushing aside a half-stocked tool chest, I reach for the small safe nestled in the corner of the vault. I slide my thumb over the reader and hear the two-beep confirmation. There's a click, and I pull the handle, checking my stash of prepaids before adding Maggie's latest contribution to the stack.

*A few hundred credits. Enough to keep me going. For a little while longer.*

Closing up the safe, I bust out my well-stocked first-aid kit and tend to my wounds. My shin is pretty mangled; I pick bits of filthy denim out of the gash and give it a splash of disinfectant before stitching it up and slapping on a bandage. I rewrap my hand with clean gauze, and stash the kit in its usual spot.

Crawling into bed, I close my eyes and pull Lara into my arms. Curling up with her, her body close to mine, my hands caress her, finding my favorite familiar places. My fingers instinctively brush along her neck, before stopping at just the right spot and strumming a few comforting chords. In my muzzy state, I play "Bryn's Lullaby" for the first time in what feels like forever. For the first time since the last time. Between velvet-curtain memories and tranq-dart haziness, past and present overlap in my thoughts.

But I don't sleep. I lie there all night with Lara cradled close, listening to the hum and dreaming of stolen moments in an alcove with that very strange girl with the deadly pipes.

# CHAPTER THREE

## V

When I wake up, the master suite is casket-dark. Damon must have closed all the blinds and pulled the curtains across the length of the room.

*That or I'm dead.*

Except I can still feel my pulse, thumping away without mercy. After that, the inventory list reads like a postbender highlight reel. If it was just a hangover, my nanotech would have taken care of it. This . . . This is residual blah from the heavy-duty tranq Damon used to keep me on-grid. Dry-mouth that tastes like something crawled in there to die. Eyelids scraping like sandpaper over eyes that roll loose in their sockets. It's hard to breathe, but that's just Little Dead Thing sitting on my chest. I move him to one side and reach out to flick a finger over the window controls, opening the curtains half an inch.

*Uuuugh. Even that tiny amount of light is too much.*

I take a minute before sitting up, only to discover I didn't sleep in my stage gear. Damon traded the corset and beaded dress for one of the plain cotton T-shirts from the dresser. They're V-necked and three sizes too big for me, because they're not usually *for* me. At a glance, you expect them to smell like aftershave, except they don't, because the ones that get borrowed go straight down the garbage chute.

Turning ever so carefully, I slide my legs out of the twisted sheet to let them dangle off the side of the bed. My legs are bare. He went through the effort of taking off my fishnets. Panties are also missing, but he's nothing if not thorough.

Glancing at the mirrored side of the room, I see the faintest reflection of my own face. The real me, not the glammed-up stage-ready vixen. Damon must have wiped off my makeup, too. My mask stripped away, you wouldn't recognize me on the street, which makes it easy to go out without being mobbed. Sure, the hair is pretty crazy, especially now, matted up in the back and in a wild tangle on one side, but it's nothing a hat can't hide. My eyes, without the black-light contacts, are darker than I remember. Brown? Hazel? I'd have to look closer, but I have no desire to get up.

In quiet moments like these, without the rest of the band, without the lights and the fans and the neon trappings, I try to remember who I am.

Except this morning, I'm just a shadow on the sheets.

I reach for the glass of water on the nightstand and hazard a sip. There's a small pile of pills in a silver dish; I manage not to choke when I swallow them in one go. The glass makes a *clink!* when I set it back down, and that's immediately followed by a knock at the door.

It opens a second later.

*So much for the new keycode I programmed.*

"You're awake." Damon stands in the doorway, framed by distant light. Today's suit is gray, the shirt a soft white, the tie muted pastel stripes, like he's trying to be considerate of my frayed optic nerves by keeping the colors quiet. Also means he left at some point to change his clothes. "How are you feeling?"

*Like asscrackers.* "Fine. I'm awake. Here, and not the medcenter. That's a good start."

"True." He steps into the room and closes the door behind him. Accessing the control panel on the wall, he brings the lights up only enough to navigate the room without bumping into anything. As he crosses to me, he lifts a sturdy upholstered chair from its spot against the wall and places it next to the bed. When he sits down, at least a foot or so separates us, but authority rolls off him. "Are you well enough to discuss last night?"

*So we're sticking to formality this morning. Good to know.*

I fold my legs underneath me and tug at the hem of my T-shirt, thankful I don't have to reach for the blankets just to cover up my thighs. It's hard to swallow, so I take another sip of water. "Yeah."

He glances back at the door. "Would you like me to ring for some tea? Coffee?"

"No," I croak. "This is fine."

His hand is already reaching inside his jacket for the med case. "Hair of the dog?"

Oblivion sounds good, but . . . "Not just yet." I promise myself that the moment he leaves, I'll run the hottest bath on the planet. Slip inside it and stay there until I'm the color of a cooked lobster.

"Tell me if you change your mind." Instead of extracting the medical paraphernalia, he pulls out his phone and offers it to me. "Are any of these gentlemen the one you saw last night?"

I thumb through the photos, dismissing each with lightning speed until one particular blur trips my sensors. It's an official Cyrene photo ID, and it's definitely the guy from the club. Sure, his hair is shorter, brighter. He's actually smiling. Blue eyes, the sort of blue that's easier to describe as what it's *not* than what it *is*: not an electric blue, not like the ocean, not tempered in any way by green or gray. His face is clean shaven where it had promised stubble last night. This shirt is black, too, but off-the-rack new. There's a silver chain visible at his throat, with interlocking metal rings that are solid enough to look masculine without veering into heavy metal territory. The name at the bottom of the screen reads—

*Micah.*

"That's him," I say with a nod.

Damon doesn't reveal any flavor of surprise as he takes his phone back. When I think about it, emotions like that aren't really part of his range. No room, what with all the research and prep work and nonstop PR spin and damage control.

*Especially that last one.*

"You're certain," he says. It's not a question. "Where was he?"

"Leaning against the bar."

"Was he dealing? Circulating through the crowd, maybe taking advantage of all the new faces to pass along a few little green tabs?"

"He wasn't doing *anything*. Just stood there, staring at me." *With those fucking too-blue eyes of his.*

"Makes sense. We didn't find anything at Maggie's, and none of the recruits who needed medical attention tested positive for anything illicit." Damon doesn't sound happy, though, and I get why when he takes the questioning in a different direction. "Was he holding something? A device maybe? Thrum-detector? Anything that struck you as odd?"

I give a shake of my head that I instantly regret. "No, nothing. Why?"

After a long moment, Damon finally answers. "Corporate's concerned. There are certain parties that would be more than happy to see the new thrum-collectors tank and the entire project declared a failure. Everything we've worked for, flushed away. All of the people in that file are suspect because they've left Cyrene and can't be tracked down out-of-city."

"Spies?" It's hard not to laugh, but his expression strongly suggests that I suppress my amusement. "You think people are sneaking into Cyrene to steal . . . what, exactly? Technology? Like scientific espionage?"

"Wouldn't be the first time," he says, deadly serious. "So tell me anything else you remember about him."

"Just that I knew something was wrong the minute we launched into the first song and he didn't move." I twitch with the memory of Micah's stillness. "I pushed it as hard as I could, trying to get a response from him—"

"And overloaded the grid." Damon leans back in the chair, steepling his fingers, looking merely contemplative as though we're discussing something far less worrisome than an energy malfunction of holy-fuck proportions.

A malfunction I triggered by acting like a grade-A diva. "Sorry."

"Don't apologize, Vee," Damon says as he stands up. It's the first time he's used my name in a month. "Could've been just the reaction he was hoping for. But it was an excellent test of our emergency response teams, plus Sasha copied the recording for me last night. It's already available for download and racking up some serious sales numbers."

After another long moment that I don't even attempt to fill with a response, he adds, "Just don't do it again."

# M

My little slice of privacy shudders under the onslaught of the morning commute. Horns become the roars of tamed beasts lumbering on the bridge overhead. I imagine great mechanical monsters stalking the city instead of the glorified go-karts and fuel-efficient delivery trucks I know are actually there.

I sit up too quickly and my body aches in protest, still pissed at me after last night's unexpected workout. Before anything else, I slip Lara back into her case and zip her up tight and secure her in my makeshift vault. Locked away all cozy and pristine, she's my one indulgence among prepaids, bandages, and protein bars to keep me going.

Now standing, for better or for worse, I hop from one foot to the other, testing things out. No twinges, no pain, no soreness beyond my shin. *Good. Didn't tweak anything on the fly.* My usual runs are good exercise, but I rarely have anyone in hot pursuit.

I can hear the patter of rain against the tarp running the length of the warren, masking it from unwelcome eyes and holding the elements at bay. Without it and the safety rail that anchors it in place, there's nothing between me and a sheer drop to the rocks below. The digital microfiber camouflage plastic is a welcome change of pace from the stone and concrete that surround me on three sides, plus above and below. Add a lamp, a few storage bins, and you've got yourself a certified hermit's retreat, or a low-rent prison cell.

Closing my eyes, I try to lose myself in the percussion of the rain, but lurking behind it, the hum is back in full force. Rain or shine, day or night, it's always there, an omnipresent sign that phantom power flows across Cyrene. The hum seems to climb in register whenever I stare at those glass-globe emitters that top every building and dot every landmark. On the Mixolydian scale, it's an F. Not piercing, but unnerving. Your hair should stand on end when you hear it. Mine did, before I got used to it.

No one else notices it; it was one of the first things I asked Maggie about when I came back to Cyrene, but she'd never heard anyone mention it. My own personal white noise, I guess. Every waking moment alight with energy-turned-hum, as if the entire city is trying to find the perfect word, a magic word with powers beyond imagining.

I ditch my club clothes, tossing my button-down onto the heap bound for the laundromat. One leg shredded, my jeans are a no-go, so they're relegated to the everyday-wear pile. I gear up for the day's errands, grabbing boxers, track pants, T-shirt, and socks. Lacing up my sneakers and tossing on my hoodie, I close my eyes, listening to the staccato of the raindrops. *Rain is good. Won't be suspicious to have my hood up.*

Flipping up the fragments of canvas that cover my strategically placed peepholes—see-through black netting from an old tent—I ensure the coast is clear before climbing down and hitting the street.

*Time to get moving. Lose myself in the job. Shake off thoughts of greyfaces and sugar skulls.*

First stop: the drop site on Wynn Avenue, to nab any return parcels for Maggie.

I do runs for the Hellcat a few times a week as an off-the-books courier. Sometimes it's just information, supplies, or cash runs, but most of the time, it's thumb drives loaded up with the latest songs and classics alike, anything you can't get in-city. Over-the-Wall music, like over-the-Wall booze, is pure. Unmodified. Everything in Cyrene is engineered to maximize thrum production, so naturally, there's a healthy market for so-called connoisseurs, audiophiles, and anyone else looking to buck the system with minor indulgences. Maggie's hookup ensures new tunes to complement Cyrene's newest pharmaceutical delights. The job keeps me in essentials and gives me a convenient excuse to explore some of the darker corners of the city.

I keep my pace slow on the main streets, a casual jog, nothing that might draw attention, nothing out of place amid the bustle of business-as-usual. I kick on the afterburners along the side streets to make up some time. With that bullshit dose of tranq out of my system, I'm light as vapor and smooth like liquid mercury.

Halfway down Wynn, I stop in front of a maroon door, otherwise unmarked, and double-tap the nearby grate with my foot. One shrill buzz later, the door swings open. A small brown parcel waits patiently on the floor for me. I snap it up and tuck it under my shirt.

Normally, I'd take the long way down the Jobalign, through the business district, and loop back around to Hellcat Maggie's, but after the near catastrophe last night, I better keep my distance and do some recon first.

Doubling back down the street, I head for Sidri's Place. The dive bar to end all dive bars, Sidri's is the last refuge of the jelly-kneed and frazzle-brained. Every bad trip ends here, every neon junkie booted from the clubs stumbles through these doors.

It's a pit. They don't even have the Cyrano network here, so you better have a prepaid on you.

It's the only place in Cyrene dodgy enough to make me wish my nanotech still worked. It's also the only place where you can get the sweet and lowdown in two minutes flat for the price of a single stimshot.

One of the locals, a slack-jawed tweaker named Prozzen, fills me in. "Word on the street is, the greyfaces buttoned the club up tight. Right after the blackout hit. Cleared everyone out. Hellcat Maggie's is closed."

Since he's a little more awake after his stimshot, I try for more info. "Hey, have you seen Ludo around here? Elfin-looking kid with too many piercings?"

Prozzen shakes his head, harder than he intended, based on his pained reaction. "No, man. If I see him, should I let him know you're looking for him?"

I decline his offer. "He knows I'm looking. That's why he's ducking me. See ya, Proz."

With Maggie's shuttered for the time being, my only move is to swing by her apartment and see where things stand.

On my way out of Sidri's, a riot of color catches my eye, and I pump the brakes.

It's her. *Her.*

Front and center once again. Decked out in full Sugar Skull splendor . . . and very little else. Treble and Trouble are there, too, with tresses dressed and faces painted, and a brain-incinerating amount of flesh on display. Strategic hand-placement prevents all the secrets from showing, but the tangle of supple limbs and desperately touchable skin is more than enough. The splashes and smears of body paint, meant to evoke lingering touches by bandmates, are highlighted by colored extensions in their hair, and practically glow against the empty black background.

My eyes dance across their oh-so-inviting forms and alight on Her lips. Those lips that work magic, that spew fire and anger and bend worlds to Her will. The memories flood in, sensations of heat and perfection and a living, breathing supernova . . .

I pull the poster down—no touchscreens or digital billboards at Sidri's, none of that high-gloss tech—and an identical one sits underneath.

*Their street team is good.*

I duck into an alley and look again, before folding the half-sheet up and tucking it into my pocket.

Three days. Three days before She hits the Dome and unleashes that siren song once more.

Shaking my head, I reluctantly push thoughts of Her aside. *Not why I'm here. Back to work, Micah.*

# V

Damon leans against the wall, scrolling through reports of last night's ridiculousness on his phone. "Damaged thrum-collectors, spotlights, speakers . . ." He pauses, looking up at me with minor disbelief. "Did you punch a fan in the face?"

I shrug. "She grabbed me first. It was self-defense."

He sighs, transferring credits to the girl's account before calling down to the kitchen for food and caffeine. "I don't want to give you any more injections on an empty stomach. You need to try to eat something."

"I guess I'm hungry." It's a lie, but I'm not missing an opportunity to make him jump through a few hoops. "Some of those pastries from the bakery on Ahriman, maybe, before a double stimshot."

He raises an eyebrow but knows better than to push back. To push me. The girl with the voice. Damon's explained the numbers until my eyeballs rolled back in my head, but it all boils down to leverage, the single bit of it I have with him and Corporate. They need me and what I can do onstage to take Cyrene to the next level.

"Not a problem," he confirms a second later, except his voice is a bit tight when he adds, "Anything else? A puppy small enough to shit in your purse, maybe?"

"Little Dead Thing would eat a tiny dog," I answer. "And I'm too important to carry a purse."

"That part you have right." He reaches out to tuck a stray curl behind my ear, playing lion tamer. "Just like you know this is make-it-or-break-it time. For the band. For us."

*There it is.*

I eyeball him good and hard. "There is no 'us' Damon. There's you, and there's me."

"So you've said." Three bitter words as his hand falls to his side. "Repeatedly."

I keep going, right over the top of him. "There's working together—"

"Except you're not even managing *that* right now," he snaps back, the muscle in his jaw ticking because I've called him on his bullshit. "The closer we get to the Dome gig, the more you ignore that we have to be a team. Every fucking step we've taken in Cyrene, we've taken *together*. Then you run off half-cocked and put us in a state of emergency last night—"

"Emergency, my ass. You said you handled it—"

"Yeah, I fucking did, just like I always handle it." His vehemence surprises me into buttoning my lip long enough for him to finish his thought. "So now I've got Corporate breathing down my goddamn neck, not just about you, but about the shithead who egged you into blacking out a significant chunk of the Odeaglow, ruining our field test."

I let my thoughts slide back to the unreachable stranger, melting just a bit against the memory of him. When my brain catches up with my body, I try to defuse the situation. "Relax, he was probably just—"

"Just what, Vee?" Damon's face tightens. "The guy you ID'd glitched off the grid nine months back using illegal street drugs. Fried his nanotech and his brain. He should be a vegetable, and instead he's back here." His steady gaze bores into me. "Just what I needed, right? Another goddamn responsibility, catching this guy when we have no way to track him."

"Somehow I doubt that will slow you down much," I say. What Damon wants, he usually gets. The only question is how long it will take. "Then what will you do?"

"Hand him over to the medcenter and have him scanned for bio-recorders and other implanted tech, just in case he's something more than a bottom-feeding 'jack peddler." He looks me over, like he's assigning me a price tag. "But if he sought out you and the band for a reason, I doubt he'll be able to stay away for long. Not when he's had a taste of what you can do."

I smile without humor. "You're a pusher. A dealer in a nice suit." He stiffens at the accusation, but before he can protest, I add, "And I'm the drug you're dealing."

"That's hardly complimentary to either one of us, Vee—" He takes a step toward me, then thinks better of it.

*Smart boy.*

I'm tired of this conversation, tired of thinking, tired of hurting, and tired of him. I wish he would leave, but I don't have the energy or the balls to kick him out just now. Damon's phone pings and saves me the trouble. He checks the message, then says, "There are a few things that need my attention. Do you want another painkiller before I go?"

*They work better on an empty stomach, anyway.* I pull my sleeve up for an answer.

# M

The rain falls in sheets now, clearing the sidewalks of the usual vendors and midday millabouts. Even taking the unnecessarily long way around doesn't eat up too much extra time.

Maggie's home address isn't common knowledge for good reason: it would ruin her Hellcat rep for clubgoers to see her swapping dank for swank, trading the joyful decadence of her place for a high-end apartment building for over-21s. With flower boxes for every window and ivy ringing the doorways, it's postcard pretty, even from across the street. The scene is marred only by the two raincoated greyfaces stationed just outside the main lobby. They stick out like bland thumbs, old before their time, surrounded by youth but drained of it. Like refugees from cheesy crime vids, they lack that futuristic SWAT vibe of the Facilitators.

Thankfully, the curtain of water streaming off the Isambard Hotel's hideous green-striped awning keeps them from spotting me.

I head down one block, splash my way across the street, then take my time circling around back.

*No way of knowing how thorough they'll be. The rear garage is definitely out. If they're smart, they'll have somebody inside the side service entrance, checking delivery boys and anybody else unfortunate enough to use it today.*

With two quick steps, I plant my feet on the brick face of the building and spring skyward, grabbing the bottom rung of the fire escape's ladder. It doesn't give an inch—rust and lax maintenance will do that—so I scramble up with ease.

Two flights up and a surefooted dash across the ledge, and I'm outside Maggie's living room window.

If you didn't know any better, you'd swear the place looked fine. But I do know better. Before I made the Arkcell my haven, this was home for a few weeks. Since then, I've caved on a dinner or two here and there, when I couldn't duck one of Maggie's loaded invites.

Maggie has one rule: a place for everything and everything in its place. But a few things *are* out of place. Knickknacks shifted. Pieces of furniture out of position. They must have gone over every inch with a fine-tooth comb and an arsenal of scanners, detectors, and whatever else beeps and whistles and boops when it finds something they want.

There's no sign of Maggie. Either The Powers That Be took her in, or she bolted before they could drop the hammer on her. Those are the only options that make sense.

*But why? Why case the place so thoroughly? The black-market thumb drives and booze? That's pretty low priority to justify closing down the club.*

*Was it the blackout?*

*Was it* me*?*

The deep breath I've been holding comes out as a defeated sigh. *Dammit.*

One last thing to check. I slip back across the ledge and onto the fire escape. Maggie's bedroom window. Shades perpetually drawn. She always calls it "where the hellcat comes out to play."

I never pushed for elaboration.

My hand runs along the window frame until one of the bricks shifts slightly. *Bingo.* Pulling it from the wall, I find a white envelope sealed inside a plastic baggie to keep the rain out: Maggie's just-in-case instructions. Once I've stashed them in my pocket, I carefully replace the brick.

I glance down, making sure the alley is clear before hustling down the fire escape and dropping back to the ground.

Letting the rain wash away any trace of my visit, I calmly and casually stroll down the backstreets of Cyrene, stopping only to liberate some more copper wiring from a construction site on Lattimer Street, prime real estate on the outskirts of the business district. Ducking behind a dumpster, I slip off my drenched hoodie and slip the coiled wire over my head and under one arm, letting it rest across my chest like a skinny bandolier, before layering up once more and heading for home.

This is where paranoia serves me well, my eyes jumping all over, trying to see everything at once. Forever vigilant. But it's hard to focus. Try as I might, I can't get that girl out of my mind. I hear the crinkle of the poster in my pocket. I see Her in shadows and road signs and street art. Hell, even the hum reminds me of the speaker-buzz at Maggie's last night.

*Three days. Three more days.*

Three more days with Her voice ricocheting inside my head. Three more days of raw, blood-fresh memories coursing over my strip-mined soul.

I'd forgotten . . . I'd forgotten what it felt like to glide like that, beyond shadows and shapes and off into endless sensation, where gravity's shackles fall away and you whirl on updrafts of chemistry's great bounty . . .

She stole it back for me, for just a moment. And then she was gone, and the world turned back.

I shake my head slowly, as if I can gently jostle the pieces into place, and realize how close I am to home. *Be smart. Be safe. Stick to the job at hand.*

Sprinting away from the bridge, vaulting benches, and scaling access ladders, I cut loose and make the Odeaglow my own personal jungle gym. If anyone managed to track me this far, following me through this would buffalo their day something fierce.

*Twist scramble through, then double back.* Once I've erased all doubt from my mind, I jog back toward the bridge. Scaling the slick scaffolding and familiar tangle of stone and metalwork, I slip past the heavy tarp and into my lovely little refuge.

Hoodie on a hook to dry, copper added to the growing pile, I sprawl out on the floor, laying my recent acquisitions out in front of me. Wynn Avenue parcel, otherwise unmarked. Envelope from Maggie's, with "DOVE" written on the front. The poster, unwrapped once more, sinfully alluring and utterly mystifying.

I choose the envelope first, tossing the plastic baggie aside and dumping the contents into my hand. It's a meager haul: a prepaid, a business card, and a sheet of paper folded once. The first is no doubt an emergency fund to keep me in essentials until further notice. The second is a simple white card, the swirling logo of Cyrene Medical Services on one side and eight digits written in pen on the other—the access code for a medical supply depot in town.

*That could definitely come in handy.*

I stash the prepaid with the others in my safe and pocket the business card. Unfolding the sheet of paper, I find a list of coordinates and times and a few words from Maggie, hastily scribbled, far from the measured precision of her usual handwriting.

> HERE ARE YOUR DROPS FOR THE NEXT FEW WEEKS. GIVE ALL OF MY PARCELS TO RETE. STAY LOW. BE SAFE. DON'T BE STUPID.

She always ends her instructions with "don't be stupid," but she's never underlined it before. *Hmm.*

The parcel is next. I quickly note the shape, size, and packaging details for later, then slice it open. Two thumb drives and a note with a date, time, and serial number. *The usual. This one is clean. Maggie's streak continues.* I grab a fresh shipping envelope and packing tape, slipping the paper and music inside before sealing it up neat as before. Rete'll never even know.

Thinking of him further sours my mood. The more I learn about him, the slimier he seems. But Rete can wait. I'd rather pay attention to something more pleasant, so I pick up the poster, finding myself eye-to-eye with Her again.

Using a few pieces of duct tape, I stick the half-sheet to the metal door of my storage closet. I step back and stare. In a gentlemanly way. Then in several ungentlemanly ways.

With great effort and more than a little regret, I turn away, closing my eyes and breathing deep. Thinking of Her and the club stirs up those old memories. *Unwelcome memories.*

My eyes snap open, and I bend down to retrieve a bucket of metal pegs, a hammer, and a swatch of carpet from the corner, where I'd left off in the midst of my latest endeavor. Using the carpet to deaden the pounding, I drive a peg into a crevice between two stone blocks, burying it in the surrounding rock. Then another. And another. A dozen more times, the pegs are driven home in specific positions on each wall, a near-perfect grid pattern.

Satisfied, I put the hammer and chunk of carpet beside the door for later, and I select a length of copper wiring from my stash. Unspooling it, I get down to work, with a haunting hum and a heavy downpour as my soundtrack.

# CHAPTER FOUR

## V

Little Dead Thing perches on the side of the bathtub, carefully arranged into the perfect rectangle I think of as a kitty-loaf. He stares down his crooked nose at the water. Innate distrust radiates from every ugly patch of fur.

I sympathize, but bip him anyway with one wet toe before letting my leg drop back into the water. The skin on my chest is flushed pink. The water is hot, but not hot enough anymore, so I drain a few inches and then top off the tub. Have to balance out the fact that I opened a window just so I could listen to the rain.

Fat drops bounce off the roof. I can hear them pinging off metal, off concrete. That's the weird thing about living in a penthouse, I quickly realized after moving in. Thirty floors up, I can see everything, but I can't touch anything. The world is out of reach. I'm shut up, shut in.

But then there's the sky. Blue, black, or gray. Moon and stars. It's up there, nothing between me and it except open space. I think that small knowledge is the only reason I can still breathe without screaming.

I settle back into the tub, my limbs loose with the painkillers still snaking through my system. With the worst of the migraine gone, this is a welcome high instead of an obligatory one. I can relax, naked spine pressed against warm white marble. Sink down until my lips are covered. Blow tiny lemon-scented bubbles, every one of them a word to a song I haven't written yet. I don't even have to think about shaving, thanks to Damon's preference for smooth skin and four seshes of all-over electrolysis. The scratches that Little Dead Thing's claws left on my chest last night are also gone, courtesy of my nanotech.

There's something more, though. Something else that's missing. I trace the skin on my hand, the inside of my right wrist. *There should be scars . . . there. Vertical lines from an ivory-handled switchblade.* My fingertips slide up to my forearm, where the memory of a dark tattoo wavers under the water. A skull, but not a sugar skull. A rose. A dagger. Gothic lettering that turns to livid bruises . . .

The memory bleeds around the edges, disappearing as the locks disengage and one of Jax's big-ass buckled boots kicks in the bathroom door.

"Get out of the tub, wench."

I glare at her through my bangs. She's dressed head to toe in black mesh. Always on display, always another step closer to after-show debauchery. "Is Damon back?"

"Nope." Jax leans over and fishes out the plug, then flicks me in the face with her dripping hand. "We're going out."

"We're . . . what?" I blink, trying to follow her reasoning and wishing I could pull the water back over me like a blanket.

She straightens up and huffs her rat's nest of hair out of her eyes. "The grid's patched back together. Corporate's trying to make up for lost thrum, so they opened a new hookah den at the Palace. I'm jonesing for strawberry cough, and I'm sick of looking at the same four fucking walls every night. Get dressed. We're going."

"You can go. No one's stopping you." We go through this routine every time, varying the amount I make Jax work for it. But tonight, I mean it. Every bit of me aches, and I'm tired of voices in my ears and commands being issued like I'm a goddamn greyface lackey.

"Not by myself!" She chucks a towel at me.

Bubbles slide off me when I stand up. "The last thing I want right now is to get manhandled by a hundred toked-up potheads when I don't even smoke."

"No one said you had to smoke, Princess. We all know how you feel about those precious pipes of yours." Jax grabs me by the wrists and shakes me in a way that says I'm pretty much forgiven. "Come on. I deserve a night out. We all deserve a night out."

I lose my grip on the towel. "Meaning you want to get laid."

"Ding-ding-ding!" She tugs on me again. "Damon's had us on lockdown for a month, and it's use-it-or-lose-it time. You can sit at the bar and sip some liquid neon and make rude jokes at my expense. Just don't make me go alone. I need company. And I need someone to pour me into the car after I score."

I see the dimple tucked into the right corner of her mouth: a sure sign of trouble to come. "I don't know . . ."

"What is there to know?" Sasha flutters in the doorway, an agitated bumblebee. Seriously. She's wearing a canary-yellow shirt over black leggings, striped knee socks, and a headband that reminds me of disco ball antennae. Not a damn thing about it says Palace-wear, which means she's sitting firmly in Camp Stay-at-Home. "You're not in any shape to go clubbing."

"It's not that—" I start to argue, but she nods like I agreed with her.

"Anyway, Damon wouldn't like it. He said you needed rest."

I glance at Jax.

She raises an eyebrow at me. "That's right, Princess. He did say that."

"Of course he did." Shifting my gaze, I stare at my reflection, the picture filtered by the steam hanging in the air and the mist clinging to the mirror. Damp strands of unnaturally black hair tangle over my bare shoulders. My cheeks are flushed as pink as my chest.

And I realize again that I look nothing like Vee-the-rock-star. Minus the makeup, you'd never know it's me.

Normally, if I'm going to thumb my nose at Damon, I make damn sure he knows it. But I'm not in the mood for shallow victories tonight. "I'm sure nothing would make him happier than knowing we stayed in tonight, braiding each other's hair and eating cookie dough out of a tube."

"I'll get the cookie dough!" Sasha says, blissfully oblivious to the fact that we're doing no such thing.

# M

I slump to the ground, finally, gratefully. Fingers ache and arms throb from hours and hours of painstaking work.

There was just enough copper to finish, after weaving the wire across the walls and ceiling of the warren in increasingly finer lattices. Secured to the numerous pegs hammered over the last week or so, as well as taped in precise latitudes and longitudes on my tarp weathershield, it should be perfect. I sit there for a few moments, flexing life back into my fingers and admiring the elaborate gridwork all around me.

*There. Any lingering doubt about trackers in my prepaids or other intrusions . . . successfully banished. Better than a tinfoil hat for keeping Big Brother out of your business. Thank you, Mr. Faraday.*

My eyes scroll past the checkerboard pattern that defines almost every inch of available wall space before landing on the poster of the Sugar Skulls. I embark on a futile staring contest. Just looking at Her summons up wisps of Her voice like smoke from a bonfire, and a shiver rolls over me.

I blink first, of course, and my averted gaze falls upon the parcel, awaiting delivery. I pick it up and sit on the cot, glancing toward Lara. Rete's pretty much the last person in the world I want to do business with. But I don't know where Maggie is or when she'll be back, and I need to keep the information flowing. For now, all roads lead to Rete.

Grabbing my guitar and slipping onto the bed, I lie back and let my fingers stroll across the strings. These days, I play only for me. There are no appreciative claps from friends or playful cheapshots when I flub a chord, just the twang and strum and gentle melodies. The tension in my shoulders fades, dripping down my arms and off my fingertips as Lara soothes my frustrations with the sudden change in management.

Instinctively, I play the opening chords of "The Third False Dmitri" and half smile, remembering the old tale someone told me of multiple pretenders to a powerful throne.

*On that note . . .* Carefully bundling Lara up in her case, I return her to the storage vault.

I flip up one of the cover flaps on my tarp and peer outside. Night's fallen while I've slaved away, but the rain remains.

Rete's only legitimate job is bartending at a few of the lamer clubs in town. Basically boxes with speaker systems, most of his haunts are glorified energy collectors, nothing more. But some nights, he tends center bar at Palace of Wonders, the music-and-medication emporium du jour.

Maggie said he'll be there all week. *Maybe the Hellcat got a message to him before pulling the disappearing act. Or being disappeared.*

In either case, it's a start. I make a quick meal of some protein bars before tossing my T-shirt and track pants onto an ever-growing pile—*gotta make a laundry run soon*—and pulling on a clean pair of broken-in 550s and a fresh button-down.

One rain-hampering hoodie later, and I'm a ghost.

# V

With the grid back online, it's like goddamn Mardi Gras out here. The sidewalk in front of the Palace is crammed with pleasure-seekers, new recruits, energy junkies, strung-out sex fiends . . . and us. The only condition I placed on this evening was anonymity. No line-jumping or name-dropping, so we stand huddled under an umbrella for almost an hour before the doorman sees us.

Which doesn't mean "recognizes the Sugar Skulls" but "notices three nearly naked hot chicks" freezing our bits off.

"About damn time!" Jax mutters, throwing the dripping umbrella into a dark corner and leaving it for lost. We cruise past a row of promo posters for the Dome concert, each one bathed in a pool of colored light.

Everywhere I turn, there I am.

Jax is still bitching that I nixed the face paint, but even without crazy stage makeup, she isn't going to have a problem getting attention now that we're inside. Back at the Loft, she traded her catsuit for a dress made of shredded netting and promises, then topped it with a cape that looks like she skinned Little Dead Thing's littermates.

Sasha's right behind her, wearing her discomfort like a suit of medieval armor, if armor resembled acid green overalls and a sequined tube top. "Are you guys sure you want to go dancing? There's a diner right down the street that serves pie all night."

"This place serves pie all night, too," Jax says, towing Sasha down the dimly lit hallway and throwing a smirk over her shoulder at me. "Right, Vee?"

"It's been a while since I've been here," I counter easily. "Maybe their menu's changed."

I almost feel bad for Sasha. Her family back home suffers from the sort of ass-backwards fundamentalism that frowns on anything that makes you feel good. That they hit a tide low enough to send their daughter into a "den of sin" like Cyrene speaks volumes about their desperation.

*But that's Sasha's cross to bear, not mine.*

I shrug off my coat and feel the air hit my bare back. It would be highly optimistic to call what I'm wearing a shirt. It's more like three or four dozen silver chains linked together over a piece of sheer lining, a jingle-jangle peekaboo number that would give Damon a simultaneous hard-on and heart attack, if he ever saw me in it.

*With luck, he won't.*

It's paired with a flared miniskirt that shifts and sways with my smallest movement. I skipped the contacts and pulled all the colored extensions out, but left the bath-damp curls so my hair is a glorious tangle down my back. It tickles as I walk, but it will come alive when I dance. Music rattles the walls, the bass line settling into my bones and my blood.

I'm ready to burn the place down.

Slamming through a set of double doors, we're on the edge of the action. A dais in the center of the room showcases a troupe of professional ass-shakers and a shirtless god in well-tailored black dress slacks and a gold circlet crown.

"Look, it's Adonis!" Jax screams before letting out a long wolf whistle. Within seconds, a dozen people turn to peer at us, but this isn't stage adoration or fan worship. This is eye-fucking. This is assessing potential pleasure levels according to what I'm wearing and how I'm standing and who I'm standing with.

Jax quickly rounds up a group of likely prospects, an even split between wide-eyed newcomers and laid-back regulars, and heads to the bar to open a tab. That leaves me to corral Sasha into a booth, wondering if she's going to relax enough to enjoy a single moment of our stolen freedom. A waitress stops by with a nanotech scanner; a wandwave to access our available credits would alert Damon and Corporate, so we slip her one platinum prepaid card from Jax's special stash to cover the bill and a second to keep for herself. That nets us a wink, a smile, and a complimentary round of liquor and pills.

*Pay to play, that's how it works.*

Our nanotech will still shut down any unpleasantness that might result from all the casual sexual contact. STDs and pregnancy aren't a concern in Cyrene. It's one of Corporate's biggest selling points.

A shot of Pennyroyale washes down three pretty pink pills. I don't actually like the hot-buttered lighter fluid taste of it all that much, but it's the most expensive thing on the menu, and I'm told I have standards to maintain. Across the room, Jax shares a hookah full of strawberry cough with a pair of androgynous twins who are a regular hookup. She's the only one who knows which is the sister and which is the brother, and she's not telling. The one time I'd asked her, she told me if I wanted to see the surface of Mars, I could put down my own goddamn rover. Flanking them is a dude with a colorshifting 'hawk and a cybergothette with baby-fresh nanotech.

"Vee—" Sasha protests, fiddling with her glass.

"Don't start. I'm going to enjoy myself tonight, so you might as well have what fun you can." I push a second set of pills at her. "Swallow the green one first. It'll take the edge off."

She holds the appetizers in her hand, staring down at them with her usual frown. "Someone should stay lucid. Our trackers are off, and all our security is back at the Loft. They think we're watching videos in your room."

"Yeah, and they could ping our nanotech any second now and turn up to spoil the fun."

A boy with hair like a metallic waterfall slips into the booth on Sasha's other side and flashes a welcoming grin at her. "Hey there."

I hold my breath. The only thing Sasha likes better than her pajamas and cookie dough is pretty goth boys. This one has a dozen visible piercings and, my guess, at least three more we can't see.

Sasha turns the same bright pink as her hair. "Hey."

*Young love. Always so eloquent.*

I nudge her with my foot under the table, give her knee a reassuring squeeze, then slide out of the booth to afford them some privacy.

"Have fun, you two," I admonish with a tiny finger-wag. Sasha looks from me to Pretty Goth Boy, pops the green and the white, and waves me off.

I down a second shot and head toward the dais. The thrum-collectors at the Palace are newer than most, but the lasers are violet instead of next-gen green. They stroll across my skin, absorbing heat and the first wisps of arousal.

*Give me a few minutes . . . I'll be feeding a lot more into the grid.*

I'm halfway across the floor when Adonis sees me headed for him. The first of the pink pills kicks in as the next song cues up. Suddenly, I'm listening to my words seducing the entire room. "Screams and Whispers." The one I made up on the fly at Hellcat Maggie's. The one I composed on the spot for him.

*For Micah.*

The second pink pill drops into my system as Adonis's hands find my waist. "Evening, gorgeous. Killer song, isn't it?"

"You have no idea," I shout over my own voice.

"Ever seen them live?" His mouth is against my ear after he pulls me to his chest. "I could take you. They're playing the Dome on Friday."

The third pill hits its stride, and I forget to be annoyed with him. Forget he's talking about me. The Sugar Skulls? Just a band. Their music? Just noise. "Fuck them. What else are you offering?"

"You want something special?" With a slow grin, he reaches into his pocket and pulls out a packet of tabs. Peeling one off, he offers it to me.

"Applejack?" I hesitate. Illicit shit, the kind Damon suspects Micah of running. That stuff isn't Corporate-engineered or approved; it's over-the-Wall contraband, and there's no way to tell from one batch to the next how strong it's going to be.

*Damon will crap himself if he finds out.*

*Maybe I'll tell him, and maybe I won't.*

I smile up at Adonis, ducking my head and licking the tab off his thumb. For a split second, it feels like a square inch of flypaper is stuck to my tongue, then it melts into green apple and acid and chemicals.

When he kisses me, he tastes like it, too, and everything is sticky and sweet and perfect.

# M

*Wow, the Palace is packed to the rafters and then some.* There's no slipping past the front-door bouncer or the delivery-side security on a night like this. Instead I take the scenic route, scaling the neighboring hardware supply outlet and blue-skying across the alley to the Palace's rain-slicked roof.

I land on both feet, but such leaps of faith come with a tax, so I tumble forward and shed that excess momentum, rolling back onto my feet and dusting myself off.

The roof pulses with pounding bass lines. I listen for the revealing rattle of a loose hatch and strike gold on the far corner of the building. Prying up the skylight, I gaze down into the writhing sea of flesh, the heady scent of sex and artificial pheromones already hitting critical mass.

Slipping through the window and onto the rafters, I pull the skylight shut behind me and spidermonkey my way to the nearest catwalk, dropping in on a couple in the midst of petting so heavy, I'd call it pawing. They don't even spare me a glance. *Works for me.*

It takes a few minutes to weave a path to a spiral staircase and down to the dance floor. Easier to crowd-surf across the room than push my way there. Unfortunately, that's not an option. The crowd is so thunderously addled with chemical comforts that they'd fold like pamphlets under my weight.

I shove, elbow, and fight for every inch of territory, and finally make it to the neon-trimmed bar. When I manage to flag down Rete, he slams both palms on the countertop, the universal symbol for "get your ass over here and help me out." *Already giving orders.*

It would take forever and a week to crawl my way to the swinging gate that separates the drunken rabble from their beloved booze, so I take two steps back—just barely, considering the crush of the crowd—and charge forward, planting my hands on the counter and leaping upward, almost doing a handstand before dropping feetfirst onto the raised plastic mats behind the bar. The few patrons that actually notice look impressed. Then thirsty.

I turn toward Rete and immediately wish I hadn't. Maggie's second-in-command is a fingerpoke to the visual cortex. Jeans with flared legs, more fashionable than utilitarian, so not at all my style. Long sports jersey over an electric blue undershirt, and the just-audible buzz of freshly applied magtats, though I can't see them. Underneath his broad-brimmed cap are a mountain range of cheekbones and chin, with two brown valleys for eyes.

He puts me to work mixing drinks: two Desevros on the rocks; several party cocktails that are more drug than drink; a small bathtub's worth of some whiskey variant called minksack; three Blasters; and a shot of Sex on a Park Bench. Nothing I haven't served before.

After the rush, we steal a quiet moment and duck in the back, ostensibly to restock. It's the perfect opportunity to do a little fishing.

I pull the parcel from my back pocket and hand it over. "Any word from Maggie? I went by the club and her place, and nothing."

Rete tucks the packet into a case full of something orange and viscous before straddling a neighboring crate, obviously glad to be off his feet. *A runner gone to seed.* "Not a word, not a peep. Like she evaporated and fluttered away to the clouds, man."

"And you're more than happy to step in." Rete and Maggie share each other's distribution networks, though I've never gotten a look at what he's moving. This might be my chance.

"Hey, Mr. Quick, it's all for the greater good. You just let me handle the supply side, and everything will be golden. Dig?"

*Ugh.* "Sure, I guess."

Rete ignores my lack of enthusiasm. "That's the spirit. Do you need any Rivitocin to keep the greyfaces away?"

*He doesn't know I'm off-grid, so I don't need it. But the less he knows, the better.* "No, I'm good for a while yet."

"Cool, man, cool. Keep in touch. I might have a few additions to your itinerary." He offers his hand before I can press for details. "This awkward bit of small talk was a delight. See you around."

I nod, ignoring the handshake, pissed I couldn't get more out of him. After I carry two cases out to the bar for him, I launch back into the mob scene in search of an exit. Even the chaos of the Palace is preferable to shadow games with Rete.

I begin scanning for the right cover. The skylight trick only works as a way in, so I need a decent-sized group looking for some fresh air, and I can slip out with them.

Before someone spots me first.

# V

It practically takes a crowbar to extract myself from Adonis's grip. Every time I move one hand away, another materializes, holding on to my waist, running down my back, sliding a finger along the edge of my skirt.

*Fabric ripping. Fingers wrapped around my neck—*

My throat starts to close with panic until I realize that I'm imagining it.

*Remembering it?*

The applejack is fucking with me, that's for sure.

"What's the matter?" Adonis murmurs into my mouth.

"Nothing, I guess." I expect the words to slur a bit, but they run together like water into a drainage ditch. "I need—" *Shit. What do I need?* A minute ago, I wanted to climb on top of him. Then the drugs had me imagining the overture to a fucking assault. *Three seconds to catch my breath ought to even this out.* "I need to visit the ladies' room."

"Don't go yet," he complains, dark eyes trying to memorize my face.

*Fair enough. With all the new faces, he could lose me in the crowd in a hot second.*

"I'll be right back, I promise." I kiss the golden god one more time to seal the deal, but before he's quite done, I pull away and duck into the crowd.

The music transforms the dance floor into a mosh pit, elbows and arms jostling me from all sides. I ride the tide toward the bar and smack into the only guy in the room not dancing.

"Sorry about that," I purr into his chest, then look up.

The guy's face comes into focus, and it's him. *Him. What's his name? Shit. The guy . . . from Hellcat Maggie's.* The drugs in my system ate his name for breakfast, but I'd recognize him anywhere. Just like before, he's trying to fade into the shadows. Unlike every other writhing, grinding, sweating body on the dance floor, he doesn't want to be noticed. He isn't part of the scene. He isn't moving to the music. He isn't high on anything.

*He isn't on the grid.*

Before he can bolt, I grab his wrist. My other hand locks on to one of his belt loops. "Where are you headed, love?"

His eyes jump from my hand on his waist to my eyes, but except for a raised eyebrow, he's still stone-faced. He mumbles something about "important" or "urgent" or whatever, but all I hear is "I'm late, I'm late, for a very important date."

"You . . . don't remember me?" I peer at him, the sharp pain in my chest shifting from disappointment to relief.

*Not a spy, then. Or the worst one in history, if he can't recognize Clark Kent without his glasses.*

Which makes him just a guy. And I'm not that girl with the voice, I'm just a body. A warm body. Shit, a really hot fucking body, liquid gold running through my veins. I can feel the sweat gather in the small of my bare back as I lean into him. "Really?"

He steps back and bumps right into the wall. His hands are rough and callused, trying to pry mine from his belt loop, but he's going at it gently. The next time he speaks, I get every word.

# M

"I'm sorry, believe me, I wish I did remember you." A pause. "I have a hard time believing I wouldn't remember you."

Okay, there are distractions, there are *distractions,* and then there's this girl, glistening with sweat and radiating pure, unadulterated sex.

Her barely-there shirt offers tantalizing glimpses, her untamed ringlets of hair bouncing with every movement, begging to be grabbed and pulled and caressed.

She presses her body close to mine and flicks her tongue across my lip before I can protest. Not that I do protest, because while part of me wants to, plenty other parts of me are more than thrilled with the recent turn of events.

As her knee slips between mine, she smiles, triumphant, in control. Her hand moves from my wrist to stroke my neck possessively, trusting that I won't push her away.

I don't. I won't. Because, truth be told, it's nice just to be touched again. To be *wanted.* My hand drifts along her arm, fingertips tracing the soft skin until I bury my fingers in her hair, pulling her mouth close to mine.

With our lips almost brushing, I mutter, "I still don't remember you."

Her answering smile is downright wicked. "You will tomorrow."

# V

I'm plastered against him like one of the sixty billion posters that Corporate's hung all over town. The music's getting louder, more distorted, the high end a shriek and the low a steady, throbbing bass line that reverberates in my chest. It's been years since I was just another girl at the club. Just another set of lips to kiss and just another riot of fucked-up tangled hair he's more than welcome to twist his fingers through. Just another set of wants and needs and aches.

*He doesn't need to know my name to touch me.*

Better, really, if he never knows. That way, when the Facilitators pick him up at the Dome, he won't connect The Girl in the Club to The Girl with the Voice.

Maybe she's the girl he really wants, but I'm the girl he gets tonight.

I take a step back, bringing him with me like it's a tango and I'm leading. There's a bank of velvet-curtained alcoves not ten feet from where we're standing, and a little privacy would be nice right about now. I tow him to the one on the end, push him inside when he hesitates at the entrance, follow him in. There's a tiny bench and a mirror. The sconce on the wall burns bright and blue, painting my skin with frost.

It's only an illusion, a less flashy version of the thrum-collectors. I can feel myself burning up. By now I must be sparking enough energy to power the entire club on my own.

One good yank, and I manage to rip his shirt open to the waist. Buttons fly in every direction and disappear into the darkness. He starts to object, but I'm already kissing his chest, mouth roaming over pale muscles and scars and ink. I bury my nose in the scents of clean sweat and soap and an unexpected metallic tang.

*New pennies. He smells like new pennies.*

I haven't seen or held a coin like that in years, but I'm already past that revelation. The moment my lips touch his in earnest, everything inside me implodes.

# M

My shirt's open in a flash, and her lips are on me, her tongue tracing hot little swirls along my skin. My arms close around her, one hand still buried in her hair, the other stroking along her spine, fingertips trailing along the exposed skin, and she shivers despite the warmth radiating from her.

She's a whirlwind, a hungry, passionate, desperately fuckable whirlwind, and I'm swept up in her wake.

The only furniture in the room is a little bench against the wall, since you need the space for couples, trios, and other gatherings of willing bodies. I sit down quickly, pull her closer, my hands on her ass as she climbs onto my lap, straddling me. Her afterthought of a shirt brushed aside, her chest against mine, I can feel her heart pounding like a speaker about to blow out.

Grabbing two fistfuls of my hair, she yanks my head back, exposing my neck. She chuckles as she kisses along my jawline, then bites . . . not too hard, but not gently, either, like she's marking me as hers.

Her hands run down my neck and across my chest, her fingernails grazing my skin, one hand resting on the tattoo emblazoned over my heart. She pauses a moment and whispers the top name aloud—"Bryn"—before her mouth meets mine again. My eyes slam shut as I lose myself in her lips, her tongue, her little gasps for breath before she dives in for more. Our hands roam and grasp and tease, but it's all background to one endless, ravenous kiss. She's insatiable, a five-story drop, and I take the plunge, succumbing to gravity and falling falling falling with her.

She tastes like hard liquor and candy and sex and longing and . . . something else. Every brush of her tongue against mine makes it sharper, until it's all I can think about, until even the promise of a gorgeous girl against me fades.

*Apples. She tastes like apples.*

*Fuck. No.*

I tense up and pull away from the kiss, and for the second time tonight, I think I've surprised her. She leans close as if to kiss me again, only to purr in my ear, a rolling seductive sound that gives me shivers.

But the spell is already broken.

*Velvet curtains. Bryn. Apples.*

*Someone in the club is dealing applejack.*

"Did you take something? Did you take little green translucent tabs of something?"

Her warm breath finds my ear once more. "I'm sorry, love, I only had the one. But I can get more, enough for both of us, and—"

"Where? Where did you get it?" I shout with a fury that startles us both.

She leans back and takes a moment before answering. "From Adonis. The guy on the dais. He gave me a taste while we were danc—"

"I need you to listen to me." I stand up, awkwardly dragging her to her feet, and I grab her face with both hands. Locking eyes with her. Hazel. Clear. No ruptured blood vessels, no discoloration. Doing quick calculations in my head: skin temperature, time elapsed since she took the tab. If something bad was going to happen . . . *It would've by now. Lucky girl.* "Take anything, anything you want. Sample anything else in the whole place and get as blissed out as you like, but please, please don't ever touch that rancid garbage ever again. It will fuck up your soul."

She looks baffled by my spur-of-the-moment plea. I'm sure I would, too, in her place. I pull her close and kiss her again—a gift for me, an apology for her—and then I bolt.

Making a beeline for the illuminated dais at the center of the Palace of Wonders, I have no problem spotting him, even if we've never crossed paths before. Shirtless, crowned, grinding against a pair of waify young things wearing bioluminescent body paint and spaced-out smiles.

I hustle up the glowing side stairs and onto the platform, barging in on the soon-to-be threesome. "Hey, apologies, ladies, but I need a moment with His Majesty."

The glow-in-the-dark sexpots step aside, dazed eyes already looking for a new plaything, and he looks suitably pissed. But three magic words make it all better.

"I can pay."

He sizes me up—torn shirt with no buttons, half-mauled chest, dark jeans with a little bit of roof dust still clinging to the legs—and shrugs, gesturing me toward a side exit. "Fun inside, business outside."

We step out into the heavy mist of the alley, and the door shuts behind us. Standing with his back to me, he reaches into both pockets. From one, he pulls a handful of silvertip sticks and a lighter; from the other, a stack of green-tinted tabs, individually wrapped and ready to share. "What's your pois—"

I don't give him the chance to finish, charging him as he turns and slamming him against the opposite wall. His head bounces off the brick. I'm ranting away in my head, bordering on raving.

*That's for the girl in the alcove and Bryn and Rina and every other person you've torn to pieces with this fucking life-ruining shit . . .*

He collapses to the ground, drugs still in hand, and I lean close, almost snarling. "Where'd you get this? Huh? Who's your supplier?" I snatch the whole stack from him, cracking one tab open and sparking the lighter beneath it.

The applejack flares up in an instant, burning hotter than I expect, and I drop it into the garbage can against the wall, dumping the other tabs in after it. Each one bursts into flame with a *whoosh*, incinerated in seconds. *This is some potent shit.*

I turn back toward the scumbag dealer. "Who keeps you stocked? Is it Re—"

He punches me in the leg, and pain arcs through me. I crumple to the ground in a heap, twitching.

*Fuck. Took too long.* My hand still clutches the lighter tight, the nerves frozen and nonresponsive. I can't even speak.

Standing now, he kicks me in the gut, hard. He leans down and smiles, showing me the glowing set of knuckles on his hand. *Brights. Should've known.* Then two furious kicks to the chest, punctuating them with "should kill you for that" and "wasted all my best shit." I'm still so rattled by the shock from his modified knucks, I can't cry out. I wheeze, trying to get my breath back, and he gives me three more kicks, just for good luck, I guess.

The security door swings open, and His Majesty instantly steps away from me. Blinded by the light from the doorway, I can barely make out the shape of the bouncer. "What's going on out here?"

Slick as bacon grease, His Majesty goes into spin mode. "Guy wanted a hit of riprap and got a little aggressive, that's all."

"Should I bring him inside and call the greys?"

*Fuck.*

But saving his own ass saves mine by accident. "Naw, let him sleep it off in the alley. You know how these little tweakers can be."

Curled up in pain, I'm in no position to argue. I just lie there on the cold, damp asphalt as he spits in my face and struts through the security door. It slams shut behind him, and everything goes dark.

# CHAPTER FIVE

## V

The curtains are open. The rain is gone, leaving the sky a perfect blue. Sitting up in bed, chin resting on my knees, I can't help but think of him, of his eyes. They're that same shade of blue.

*Where the hell did you go last night, Micah?*

"Morning, gorgeous," says a distinctly male voice from somewhere near the pillows.

I glance over at Adonis. Thin sunlight slants over his bare shoulders, proving he's every bit as nice to look at in my bed as he was last night on the dance floor. The more I study him, the more certain I am that I've seen his face on cologne billboards and in coffee ads.

The man's multitalented, I'll give him that.

"Sleep well?" I ask. We were a tangle of arms and legs and more interesting bits until just an hour or two ago, so it's more a polite conversation starter than an actual question.

Hooking an arm around my waist, he pulls me back against him. I slide through a damp spot in the bed and make a mental note to stuff everything—sheets, blankets, maybe even the mattress—down the garbage chute when he leaves.

"I could use another few hours," he murmurs into my hair, guiding my hands down to convince me he's telling the truth. "What do you think?"

"I think I'm hungry," I say, not lying and yet willing to go without food a little while longer.

"That's the applejack," he says as he kisses his way down the side of my neck, lifting up the mad tangle of my hair. "It's epic stuff, but it leaves you feeling a little used up." A bit lower. "Admit it. You're probably ravenous."

"Well, yeah, as a matter of fact—" My breath catches when he locates a sensitive spot. "I thought that was because of last night's extracurriculars."

It's pretty amazing that I feel as good as I do. The drug metabolized out of my system without any repercussions: no headache, no dry mouth, no regrettable decisions staring at me from the bed. Energized, even, and I've never been a morning person. Maybe if I say please, I can score a few more tabs from my lovely friend.

Even if I ran into Micah again, I sure as hell wouldn't be getting any applejack from him. Judging by his reaction, he'd rather stone-cold starve than peddle . . .

*That rancid garbage.*

I shake off the warning, because he was obviously mistaken. To hell with him and his terrifically crappy manners.

"Any way I could get some more of it?" I ask Adonis. "The applejack, I mean?"

"I'm fresh out of stock for the moment. Swing by tonight and I'll fix you up. In the meantime . . ." He nudges me back onto the sheets and lowers himself on top of me. "I think we can find some way to keep you happy."

Looking up at him, I realize I'm up for another round, as well. Why not? He's easy on the eyes, built like a god, and he sure as shit didn't abandon me hot and bothered and *alone* in an alcove last night. I run my hands over the taut muscles of his back, fingertips skimming over a deep set of scratches that give me pause. "Did I do that to you?"

His abs contract as he turns to peer at his back in the mirror. "There are plenty of marks that are yours, but not those. Hazard of the job, working shirtless. Got shoved into a brick wall while you were in the ladies'."

I don't bother mentioning that I never made it to the bathroom. Thinking about Micah and the way he bailed on me pisses me off all over again. "Someone jumped you?"

"Don't worry, gorgeous. It was just a fucked-up little tweaker with a shitty chest tat. I kicked the shit out of him." Adonis laughs and presses another kiss to my shoulder. "A word of advice: never get someone's name inked on your skin. No one wants to read the notches on your bedpost."

*Bryn.* It's my first thought. My only thought. Another girl's name scrawled on Micah's chest, marking him as hers. But it's ridiculous to think that he bailed on me to pick a fight with a guy in an alley.

*Isn't it?*

Maybe I'm mistaken. Maybe my instincts are jangling for no reason. "The guy who jumped you . . . Was he blond? Medium height and wearing—"

"A shirt someone had shredded," Adonis finishes for me with a frown. "Yeah, you know him?"

"We're not on a first-name basis." *Mostly because he doesn't* know *my first name.* And all of this pretty much nixes Damon's theory that Micah's some kind of ninja anti-Corporate spy. Anyone interested in stealing thrum technology isn't going to tangle with a lowlife dealer in an alley.

I spare another glance at Adonis, chewing on the inside of my lip before asking, "You kicked the shit out of him?"

"Literally. Dropped him with my Brights and booted him a couple good ones in the ribs." Blasé as fuck. He's not showing off for me, which has me even more worried.

Without nanotech to help him heal, Micah could have broken bones and internal bleeding that will kill him slowly. Painfully. He could be dying under a fucking bridge, for all I know. There's no way to track him down, no way to check on him.

When Adonis goes in for another kiss, I duck my head and bounce out of the bed. Pulling two shirts from the dresser, I toss one at him. When he raises an eyebrow, I offer the only explanation that will get him neatly and cleanly the hell out of my room. "If we're going to have any more fun, I need to refuel. I get really creative after pancakes, I promise."

"All right." He eyes the cotton tee like it's something he found on the floor of the club, then shrugs, pulls it on, and reaches for his pants. "But after food, we're locking the place down, and I'm keeping you here until it's time for me to go to work."

I make a noncommittal noise as I slip into my own shirt and a pair of black boyshorts. When I deactivate the door locks, an extremely pissed-off Little Dead Thing streaks into the room. His angry yowl sends Adonis dancing back several paces.

"What the fuck was that thing?" he asks, hurrying to catch up with me.

The poor bastard has no way of knowing I've already left him in the dust.

# M

Between the alley and my cot, I spend a long, long night curled up on my good side like an anguished question mark. My eyes drift in the soft lamplight between Lara, tucked away safe in her case, and Her, on wild display.

But I still taste the applejack girl on my lips, smell her in my skin, my clothes. Traces of her presence tickle my senses.

*Forget her. You burned that bridge with style, bud.*

It took a long while to get to my feet after His Majesty's beatdown. Beyond my injured body and wounded pride, there was the heavy blanket of guilt that settled over me when I thought of the girl in the alcove. I tried to check on her, slipping back inside after the bouncer took pity on me and opened the security door. But there was no sign of her anywhere.

This morning, I console myself with the thought that she's okay. Probably spotted a more accommodating partner and forgot me entirely in a matter of seconds.

A few more minutes pass as I stare at one girl and remember another, killing time before doing what needs to be done. *Priorities.*

Now the part I've been dreading. With a deep sigh, I sit up and wish to all gods everywhere that I hadn't. My arms wrap around my ribs protectively. Maggie's advice rolls through my forebrain—*Stay low. Be safe. Don't be stupid.*—and seems all the more apropos at this moment.

I take my time standing up, unfolding like an old roadmap until I'm fully upright. *Wish I'd had the energy to check for cracked ribs last night. Hours slumped on one side couldn't have done them any favors.*

Unlocking the door to my closet, I pull out my first-aid kit, along with a well-thumbed medical text cribbed from an ambulance a while back. Nanotech is all well and good, it'll keep you going, but traditional medicine still has its place.

*Especially for a dangerous thug like me.*

I laugh softly and instantly regret it. Flipping open the text, I skim the section on injuries to the chest. Tentatively, I run my fingers over each rib, looking for anything out of place. It sucks, it sucks so bad, but between a cursory touch and a few deep breaths, I'm convinced I haven't cracked or broken anything.

*They're just bruised as hell.*

I grab a roll of bandages, the widest I have, and wrap it around my ribs, fixing it in place with tape and checking the expansion of my chest with painfully deep breaths along the way. The text doesn't recommend this, but admits it'll alleviate some of the pain. I'll risk pneumonia for better freedom of movement. I'm gonna need it.

Some quick, light stretches later, and the pain is tolerable. I strap a few insta-cool gel-packs to my ribs for good measure, and gear up for the day's errands. *Forget the distractions, forget the Voice and the Palace and all that. Back to the routine. Clothes aren't gonna wash themselves.*

A few minutes and a glance through the peepholes later, I pull the tarp aside and toss my enormous sack of laundry over the railing, then carefully climb down to ground level and retrieve it. Wincing slightly, I heft my laundry bag over my shoulder and head out onto the streets.

Living the dream.

# V

Busy with Adonis, I missed the memo that I was hosting the after-party, though it's technically Jax's gig with Sasha catering. Palace refugees are scattered over every surface of the living room, and I have to step over a dozen snoring bodies to get to the kitchen. The breakfast nook is crammed to bursting with people in various stages of nano-recovery. Wearing a yellow silk kimono robe she hasn't bothered to belt, Jax sits on the counter, ass planted between bottles of juice and half the contents of the liquor cabinet. Sasha's at the stove, wielding two spatulas and slinging short stacks. That's her thing, the morning after a spree. She's still in her green overalls for practical reasons, but the tube top has disappeared.

"About time you were up," Jax drawls into her drink, allowing her gaze to trail over Adonis's impressive musculature before adding, "again."

He smiles easily at her before snagging a seat, a full plate of food right out of Pretty Goth Boy's hand, and me. Without asking, he situates me in his lap and offers me the fork. "Get to work, gorgeous. We have a plan, remember?"

Given that the primary directive of his plan is currently pressed against my backside, I can hardly say no. I have no intention of returning to the bedroom with him, but that doesn't stop me from teasing him with an evil wriggle. "Trust me, stud, I remember everything you said back there."

*Absolutely everything.*

I settle myself more firmly in his lap, but only so I can pay better attention to my breakfast. Apparently the applejack turned me into a morning person with a truck driver's appetite, because I pack in enough pancakes for three people. Adonis gives up waiting for me to share and asks for another plate, which I also help clear. Taking advantage of the moment when he's distracted by a coffee refill, I slide to the floor. One quick trip around the counter and past the tiny redhead standing alongside Sasha, and I edge my way up to Jax.

"Nice work bringing him home. I'm surprised you can still walk a straight line." She's still dishing out the snark, but Jax is way more relaxed than she was yesterday.

*If Damon was as smart as he is ambitious, he'd loosen up her leash just a smidge.*

"Careful now, you almost sound jealous." Under the guise of mixing orange juice with two shots of Samurai, I pull up a menu on the kitchen vidscreen, access the Cyrano database, and dash off a text message. Closing the window with a wave of two fingers, I ignore her and take my drink back into the living room. The state of the furnishings is enough to simultaneously break my heart and turn my stomach.

*Not just going to burn the sheets and the mattress. Couches go, too.* I step in something with my bare foot and wish I'd remembered to put on socks. *And the rugs.*

Adonis catches up with me at the bottom of the stairs, unaware that he's interrupting a mental redecoration of the entire Loft.

"You're a hard one to keep up with. Ready for round two?" His smile should melt me into a pliant armful, but all I can think about is Micah in a gutter somewhere. Micah, bruised and battered and coughing up blood.

When the expected knock comes at the door, I open it without sparing Adonis a single glance.

Six Facilitators duck inside, a coordinated blur of boots and gloves. They grab Adonis, hauling him out of the apartment as he struggles and shouts, "What the hell?" until one of them swats him upside the head with a heavy hand. Adonis jerks as the electricity discharges with a flash, then goes stiff as a board. Some sort of a shock gauntlet, a Corporate-approved version of Brights. I'm feeling vengeful enough to hope they have a lot more kick than the ones Micah met last night.

In the midst of all this, Damon enters the Loft and pushes the door wide open. "Anyone who wishes to avoid similar treatment should gather their things and depart."

The rest of the partygoers grab their clothes and duck out behind the security team in a steady stream that seems to last an eternity. Jax follows them around, protesting.

"You don't have to leave. I just ordered more booze and a pound of strawberry cough!" She turns her glare on me, then shares it with Damon when he closes the door on the last straggler.

"Productive evening?" he asks with a perfunctory glance around the room.

"Not as productive as today was supposed to be." Jax throws herself on the couch, ignoring the splashes of acid-orange liquor and the lacy underwear peeking from between the cushions. "What the hell are you doing here, buzzkill?"

"I was headed over anyway, but Vee messaged a request for a cleanup crew." He takes one step onto the carpet, peers down at his highly polished black dress shoe, then backs up to the marble. "Street-drug dealer, you said?"

"Pushing applejack at the Palace last night," I answer, sitting on the stairs because it seems the safest place for now. "You can transfer the finder's fee to my account whenever you get the chance."

"Sure. And Corporate won't question the delay between him offering you the drugs and when you called us in."

"They shouldn't." I indulge in a stretch that I learned from Little Dead Thing. "Not with the energy the two of us generated for the grid in the meantime."

Damon refuses to take the bait. "You three must have missed the reminder I sent last night."

"W-what's going on?" Sasha stammers, wiping her hands on a dishcloth as she ventures out of the kitchen. Pretty Goth Boy and the Redheaded Mini are right behind her. The former looks like a cornered raccoon as he eyes the closed door behind Damon. Unfazed, the latter makes her way out, blowing a kiss and tossing a wink over one shoulder that Sasha valiantly ignores as she adds a nervous, "We missed a message?"

Jax answers from the crack of the couch. "Did it say something along the lines of 'Dear girls, I'll be in around noon to crap on your day'?"

"Close." Another knock on the door, but this time it's the fashion minions. "You have scheduled appearances this afternoon to promote the concert. Hair and makeup now, into the broadcast studio by three."

"Fuck you," says the sofa cushion.

Pretty Goth Boy finally makes a harried exit as the styling team fans out across the room.

"I want another cleaning crew brought in," I throw over my shoulder as I head for the master suite. "This one for the mess."

Damon's already dialing the number. "You worry about your wardrobe and leave the rest to me."

# M

*Why oh why didn't I do my laundry yesterday?*

With a half-choked grunt of pain, I drop the bag into a wheeled basket and reserve some machines near the back, putting it on the prepaid I snagged from Maggie's place. I push my cart leisurely along racks and racks of identical off-white machines, scanning for any sign of Ludo after striking out at Sidri's. But no luck. Nothing here but clothes swirling and swishing or tumbling and somersaulting en route to warmth and cleanliness.

Three machines loaded and running, I close my eyes and take a slow, deep breath—as deep as the bandages will allow—holding it for a few seconds, then exhaling. Repeat. And again. And a few more times. I feel a twinge with every breath, something I better get used to, apparently.

The book recommended I do this every hour to make sure my lungs won't collapse. Seems like a small price to pay for continued lung function. It'll be a different story when I run.

The vidscreen behind me blares as someone unmutes it. I hate those things, I really do. The constant squawking of talking heads. News blasts advertising credit-for-thrum activities. High-voltage promotions for the latest companies to cut exclusive deals with Corporate and set up shop in Cyrene.

The sound kicks out for a moment between each channel, and those brief silences become my favorite beats in an otherwise intolerable piece of street music.

Finally, the "what'll we watch for the next twenty seconds" contest is over. "And in two days, they will headline their biggest show to date at the Dome downtown."

A dulcet voice responds with a few playful notes. "Oooh-oooo-oooh, yeah."

I whirl around in surprise, midbreath, and it turns into an unpleasant coughing fit that brings tears to my eyes. It's Her. It's them. The Sugar Skulls, laughing at their impromptu performance just now. Sure, the makeup is a little different, with tiny press-on jewels instead of the sequins, the outfit a blue-black variation on a very tempting theme. But it's Her, unmistakably Her.

I stare unabashedly at the screen, drinking in every pixel, every frame. The gentle swish of her hair that trails a second or two behind each movement of her head. Impossibly amethyst eyes rising from the depths of kohl rims. Ghostly white makeup that almost glows under the studio lights.

*There goes the slim chance of forgetting her anytime soon.*

"They're here live to promote their upcoming show . . ."

Broadcasting live. In the studio right now.

A studio *six* blocks from here.

My legs respond before my thoughts, carrying me partway to the door before I toss the prepaid to the attendant. "Give me the works, I'll be back! No lavender!"

*Promotion means public appearances. Which means a chance to see Her again. Just a look. A look and a few notes live. No harm in that, right?*

I rocket down the sidewalk, hell-bent on catching her. My lungs already ache, subsisting on half breaths as I race for the studio. *Worth it.*

# V

Jax and Sasha clamber into the back of the limo, leaving a trail of feathers and sequins in their wake. The area behind us descends into chaos, with riggers and techs moving as fast as they can to pack up equipment we're going to use at the mall.

Damon stands between me and the car, coordinating the security team, cherry-picking the best of his guys to ride shotgun in each vehicle and others to drive ahead and behind. All the while, he's fielding calls, following up tips, and whittling down leads. Hunting for Micah every spare moment, no matter how brief.

*Is that what this sudden rash of promotion is for? A trail of bread crumbs for Micah to pick up?*

I have plans of my own and pause in front of Damon, teetering in my heels. "Last night's catching up with me. I'm going to need something to keep me going." I slowly lean against him, careful not to get any makeup on his suit.

There's a pause in which I'm certain he holds his breath, and then one of his hands finds its way to the small of my back. The corset I'm wearing today is more like body armor than clothing, the antithesis of my shirt from last night. There's no bare skin available for touching, yet I can somehow sense the heat from his fingers, his wrist, as his arm tightens. He's holding me up. I can feel the barest whisper of movement in my hair; he must have given himself permission to breathe again.

I almost feel bad that the only thing he's going to get for his troubles is a snootful of product.

"Whatever you need," he says, voice low and controlled, like he's trying to throttle the words. "We've got a lot more to do today, and I need you on your game."

Turning into his chest, I slide my hands under his coat, making sure he can feel my fingernails through his shirt. "Thanks."

One of the guards calls to him; I disengage even as he takes a deliberate step away from me. Before he can say anything, I duck into the limo, no doubt affording him a glimpse of bare thigh and black garters under six layers of bruised-raspberry crinoline.

"What's with the spontaneous bump and grind?" Jax demands, looking like she can't decide whether to be amused or nauseated.

"I thought Corporate didn't want the two of you . . . uh . . ." Sasha trails off, making vague hand gestures when she can't find a polite way to finish the sentence.

"Corporate's not the only one who doesn't want us 'uh-ing.' Just putting in a formal request for a pick-me-up." I quickly turn Damon's phone to vibrate and tuck it into a hidden pocket of my skirt.

# M

*Pace slowing. Breathing labored. Pain . . . manageable.*

I expect to burst onto the scene outside the studio, but there's no sign of the Skulls, their entourage, or the crowd that populated the area a scant few moments ago. Where throngs of screaming fans, a phalanx of media cams, and the machinery of fame should be, there's nothing but an empty husk of a stage.

A few members of the studio's private security force mill about, but otherwise, zilch. The whole scene's a ghost town, abandoned en masse, leaving a baffled quartet of people who really shouldn't be allowed to carry batons or stun-tech of any kind.

Still, I keep my distance. I need to catch my breath before I start moving again, and having some wannabe greyface open fire because I sneezed at an inopportune time isn't really how I want to go out.

The stage is already disassembled, the day's business returning to normal. In ten minutes, everything will be gone, all evidence of the event banished to DVRs and recaps and retreads.

That's when it all comes together. *Of course.*

There's only one way they could've cleaned up from a crowded live event this efficiently: they didn't air it live. I raced six blocks to catch a prerecorded program, a set-up, a PR stunt. Any fans within earshot of the promotional push would've been here in a flash, the crowd padded out with recruits enticed by the promise of a few bonus credits for an hour's work. A dozen or so disappointed latecomers like me trickle in, providing some valuable camouflage as they message friends, telling them not to bother.

And now She's well ahead of me, cloaked in obsidian and glimmering with punk tinsel. The mysterious siren, just out of reach.

Thankfully, every loudspeaker and vidscreen between here and the laundromat blasted us with concert info and the details on the Sugar Skulls' surprise media blitz. Everyone in Cyrene knows where they're headed next: the Paleteni Mall Complex, clear across town. The trip here almost had me seeing spots, but I take off once more.

As I run, I ask myself the big question: *Why?*

I push forward, trying to ignore the pain. There's nothing pretty or fluid about my technique just now, no flair or pride in movement.

*Why are you running yourself ragged all over town for this girl? Is she really worth it?*

The rational mind asks questions like that. The rational mind considers the risks, lists the consequences, scorns the errands of fools. But the rational mind didn't feel what I did at Maggie's. It doesn't revel or weep or long for old sensations. It doesn't sing or cheer or soar or understand how a single song can come to define an entire year, or a person, or an experience.

The rational mind has nothing to do with this.

That vibration in my soul says *go*. So I go.

# V

I don't get my chance until we arrive at the shopping center. Bolting from the limo, I grab the two closest greyfaces and haul them down the gauntlet of screaming fans. "You guys are with me. Come on!"

"Vee!" Damon shouts. I can't hear anything that comes after that. Hard to think, much less communicate, over this level of noise pollution. No doubt he'll have us fitted with earpieces for the next junket, especially after what I'm about to pull.

Under the guise of signing an autograph for a girl crying liquid-eyeliner tears, I flick the latch on the barricade separating the kids from the carpeted entrance to the mall. The fencing twists on its hinges and crashes inward, pinning my handpicked guards to the ground. I take off at a run as rabid teenagers spill onto the carpet, like rubber balls bouncing out of an overturned bin. They catch up so quickly that I ride a screaming wave into the building.

For a few seconds, I severely regret some of my life decisions. I can feel pieces of my skirt tearing away. A buckle on my corset coming loose. Someone pulling one of the tiny silver skulls out of my hair. Souvenirs, I guess. But if I'm not careful, they'll shred me to nothing.

Twisting and ducking, I fling myself into an open supply closet. Leaning into the door with my shoulder, I manage to get it shut and locked. It's dark in here, the air reeks of hard scents like ammonia and bleach and plastic that burn as I try to catch my breath. I don't need to locate the light switch. When I rub my thumb over the screen on Damon's phone, it flares blue and then settles into a brilliant white.

This might be a safe place for the moment, but I have to hurry. Flicking through menus as fast as I can, I use Damon's privileged access to open the Cyrano database and type in four letters.

Three seconds later, I'm staring at Bryn.

She's like sunshine on water. Brilliant blond locks and blue eyes, her smile wide and mischievous and without a single secret. Tiny, according to her stats, from every possible measurement. Stepford adorable. I thumb down to get city of origin, medical history, recruitment information, but all that has been overwritten with red lettering:

**DECEASED**

*Fuck me. The girl who tattooed her name on Micah's heart is dead.*

I guess I'd thought maybe, just maybe, if I could track down Bryn, I'd be able to locate Micah. Make sure Adonis didn't do any permanent damage.

Best of intentions that, in hindsight, are nothing but ridiculous.

I get ready to close out the screen, except I realize it's not just Bryn. There are links to more names, ones I also recognize from Micah's tattoo: Zane. Rina. Trav. Except a security firewall activates, and I can't access more information without punching in a password.

"Jesus, Micah," I whisper, "what were you guys into?"

And then I remember his hands on my face, his eyes burning into me.

*Please, please don't ever touch that rancid garbage ever again. It will fuck up your soul.*

Applejack.

# M

I have to stop. Breaths are getting shallower. If I'm not careful, I'll start hyperventilating, maybe even pass out. A brutal stitch in my side throbs with every step, and I slump against the wall of a municipal building. I'm not even halfway to the mall, but it feels like I've been racing uphill for hours in a lead jumpsuit. At this rate, I'll never make it.

A trolley rolls past, too fast for me when I'm winded and wheezing like this. I stumble a bit getting upright again and walk back out onto the main road, glaring at every cab that speeds by. One more thing I'm denied off-grid.

Feeling exposed, I slip into a crowd gathered outside the neighboring market. I glance up and down the street and see people huddled around every vidscreen and newslink they can find, watching intently. *Guess the media blitz is working just fine.*

I let the crowd close around me as a news blast dominates the screen, and one of their airbrushed talking heads, all brilliant teeth and bronzed skin, does his thing.

"Reports of small-scale rioting have been reported at the Paleteni Mall Complex this afternoon as overexcited crowds slipped past security cordons. They're being managed by mall security and Facilitators, and once the issue is resolved, the Sugar Skulls' performance will go on as planned."

*Rioting before She's even sung a note? Impressive. I wonder if that's Her doing or Trouble's.* I smile, despite the lingering pain from the chase.

It'll take a while to get the crowd under control in a media-friendly fashion. *There's still time. Time to catch the show, time for her to pluck those strings inside me again.*

Parting the crowd with excuse-me's and pardon-me's and hey-buddy-do-you-mind's, I push my way to the corner where several fellow vidscreen watchers are flagging down an approaching trolley.

Normally I'd avoid it—scanner-free or not, confined spaces are not the fugitive's friend—but it's the only way I'll make it to the mall in my condition. And luckily, today fortune favors the impulsive and injured.

*Ludo. Finally.*

Guarding my ribs, I brush past a few straphangers and sidle up to the sullen-looking elf, slightly pointed ears accented with cartilage piercings galore, decked in ripped jeans and a leather jacket one size too big. Reliable customer for most of the dealers in town, legit and otherwise. Plays dumb, but knows plenty. And he's been ducking me for a while now. I even changed laundromats so I'd have an excuse to "bump into him," but until now, no dice.

I slap his back with one hand, and he practically hits the ceiling. "Hey, Ludo, long time no see."

"Hey, Mi—my man . . ." He catches himself. Eyes darting around, looking for an exit, his hand tightens on the leather strap overhead, as if he's considering taking a chance and swinging to freedom.

I lean close and whisper, "I know what you're thinking, but don't. There's two off-the-clock greyfaces near the front end, and they'll definitely notice. And you're carrying, I know you are, so you don't want their attention. Same reason you won't give me any trouble, right?" He nods, keeping his mouth shut, so I add, "Good. Now talk."

"The guy. You're not gonna find him. He's dead." Ludo shrinks away slightly, anticipating punishment for telling me what I don't want to hear. Frustration rolls over me, and I close my eyes for a moment. "Two kids I know from the Pyxis got his old place when they came into the city. Said they had to wait two extra days for 'remodeling and fumigation.' You know what that means."

*Means somebody died there, and it wasn't pretty.*

Pressing Ludo for the address of the apartment, I file the info away for later. *At least it's something.* Then I slip a prepaid card into his hand and hop off at the next stop. The mall looms large in the foreground.

My eyes jump from the plaza to the retreating trolley and back again. *I should've followed Ludo, dragged him off, and shaken him down to be sure. That would've been the smart move. That's the reason I'm in Cyrene.*

And yet, here I am. With just a few blocks to go.

I give my ribs a conciliatory pat, grit my teeth, and take off down the street. If it wasn't for Her, I wouldn't have bumped into Ludo. At this point, I don't know if this is luck or fate, but the dominoes are falling, and I'm going to see this through.

*Paleteni Mall, here I come.*

# CHAPTER SIX

## V

It takes a good five minutes for the racket beyond the door to die down. Standing there with my ear pressed to the metal, I get a crick in my neck and start cursing everything that brought me to this exact place, this precise moment in time.

It's a short list that starts with Damon and ends with Micah.

When I'm fairly certain the crowd is clear, I tuck the phone as far down the front of my corset as I can without dislodging a rib and flip the lock. I can see daylight through the crack—

"Well, I'm busy right now." Damon's voice pierces my temporary sanctuary. "For fuck's sake, I'll call him back once the Skulls are off the stage."

The second he turns around, I burst out and lead with "Those crazy glimheads almost killed me" and pair that with wide eyes and a heaving breath or two. My brain races ahead of the words, trying to figure out how the hell he found me so quickly, at least until I spot the phone in his hand, pinging my nanotech.

*Of course he has a backup. That goon with the aviators always has one in his pocket. Damon probably held out his hand, snapped his fingers, and had it replaced within three seconds.*

Worse news is that Damon's not buying the innocent routine; I can tell by the way the muscles in his jaw jump as he swallows words he'd dearly love to spit at me. But he's walking a tightrope, too. He has to keep the talent safe. Has to keep it happy. Has to get it shiny and slick and on the stage, because he's answering to Corporate.

Still, his grip on my elbow isn't gentle. "We've reined in the crowd."

*No thanks to you.* He might as well have said it out loud. The implication ricochets between us, unfriendly fire.

"Fantastic." I force some strut into my step.

The area alongside the stage is safeguarded by a human barricade of Facilitators, subtly armed. Damon isn't taking any more chances, I guess. He hands me three pills: two red, one white.

"As requested."

I barely swallow the pick-me-up before he nudges me toward Jax and Sasha, who are geared up in their own way. Sasha's got a minisynth slung over one bare shoulder like a guitar, a poor replacement for her beloved Moog. A small side table has her laptop wired in with her favorite touches. It'll do, not that Sasha would complain either way. Jax, on the other hand, has yet to shut up about the "glorified ironing board" rig she's got, a foldaway combination turntable-and-mixer that she'd rather surf than play.

She only checks her bitching long enough to nudge me with her elbow. "Next time you decide to start a riot, Princess, give me some warning and I'll help."

Already jacked into the sound system and primed, Sasha gives us both a dirty look. "That's not funny, either of you."

Ignoring them both, I throw myself into the lights, into the energy already pouring off the crowd, into the opening notes of "Screams and Whispers." Losing myself in the song, I can forget about everything else. Everyone else.

Except for the ghost of a guy in an alcove.

*Goddamn it.*

That's when I start to shake.

# M

I close in on Paleteni Mall, an oasis of high fashion and god-awful cuisine. The garish windows catch the sunlight and spit it back out in a dozen different hues, looking for all the world like a rainbow crashed and burned in the middle of downtown.

Once I hit the parking lot on the outskirts, I stop dead in my tracks when the speakers adorning every streetlight crackle as one. Then a voice steamrolls me, echoing across the asphalt like the wail of a widow.

> It's all just screams and whispers,
>     just prettied-up and dyed.
> My fuck-façade all faded,
>     a tarnished future bride.
> Coal-black eyes and heart to match,
>     no artifice, no joy,
> His desires just as sinister,
>     my precious lovely boy . . .

She flips one lyrical switch and I'm lit up, coursing with Her voice in my veins. *She's on. Boy, is she on.* But it's not enough to keep me frozen in place—guess I have to be up close and live-in-concert for that—and

I charge across the parking lot, the ache from my mistreated ribs either gone or just tossed aside by the sonic assault.

Cars and people and the rest of the background detritus blur as I move, my eyes locked on those enormous sliding doors. All the while, her lilt and cadence and emotion surge within me, drawing me in, luring me closer. Her words blast pains and shadows and doubts to pieces behind me, and for a brief moment, I shed the last few months and race, renewed, toward the source.

# V

I build the crowd's energy as carefully as a house of cards, one note stacked atop another, everything in perfect balance.

That's the good news. The holy-shitballs-fuck news is that the pick-me-up isn't working. Asking for it hadn't been a complete lie; every bit of last night's escapades was catching up to me, threatening to grind my face into the dirt if I didn't get three steps ahead of it.

The pills Damon gave me should have been enough to bliss out a complete tweaker, but they dropped into my system and evaporated like droplets of water in a red-hot skillet. Nothing.

No. Not nothing. The end of my nose is going numb with cold.

*Just finish the song.*

Lowering my voice to a croon, I bring everyone back down to earth as gently as I can. No point in generating a frothing rage-monster here . . . I need to save that trick for the Dome. I catch an approving glance from the wings: Damon, arms folded over his chest, frown still cutting his forehead in half, but relief beginning to dawn on his features.

It irks the living shit out of me.

Taking three steps back, I hand the microphone to Sasha. She stares at it, puzzled, but before she can say anything, I take a running start and launch myself off the front of the stage.

The crowd catches me and I surf it, accompanied by cheers and laughter and screams of "We love you, Vee!" all the way to a set of double doors. I curtsy to another roar of approval before ducking outside and making a mad dash for the limo parked around the corner. Still running, I pull Damon's phone from its hiding place and toss it just ahead of me. The screen shatters under my heel, but I don't look back.

By the time the others join me in the car, I have my legs crossed, my breathing under control, and a nonchalant expression cemented into place.

"That was quite the exit," is all Damon says.

I don't answer. *Cold inside, so fucking cold.* When I exhale, I leave frost on the window.

"We'll go back to the Loft and get you ready for tonight," he adds, checking the screen on his replacement phone. "You're hosting a cocktail hour for the VIPs coming in for the concert."

I slide down in my seat, pressing my face hard to the upholstery.

"Of course we are," Jax mutters.

A defiant "Fuck you" follows that, and everyone is surprised that it's not Jax's voice, but mine.

# M

I'm forced to slow down as I jog down the mall's main thoroughfare, toward the show and the voice and the throng crying out in delight. And even when the music swells and Her voice fades, Her words still radiate inside me, staving off the aches and pains of the day.

I hit the back of the crowd, just in time to watch Her leap into the audience, borne aloft like royalty as they clamber to touch Her, and She floats along with the ease of a cloud, awash in their adoration. "We love you, Vee!" they cry over and over.

*Vee.* They love you, Vee.

She drops to the ground on the far side of the mob, and with a flourish takes off through the doors. All that time and effort, hoping to feel that same soaring high that I felt at Maggie's, and it's gone in a flash.

Vee's hold on me slips, and the ache of my ribs returns. *No time for you now, gotta move.* I sneak back the way I came, evading the security guards, hoping to loop around and catch her. Ask her how, *why* her voice affects me this way. To understand, even a little bit.

Closing the distance between us, I burst out the main doors and hop the railing, my ribs very unhappy with the sudden jolt.

She's already in the limo and waiting for her bandmates. A swarm of mall security and private guards spill out the double doors, and Trouble and Treble—along with some suit-wearing tool, their manager most likely—drift down the stairs behind them.

I'm three, maybe four car-lengths behind, and I know the guards will spot me before I can get any closer. *Damn.*

I break left across the parking lot, anticipating the limo's intended path out of the mall complex, letting my inner GPS take over.

*They'll take the west gate—it's the nearest exit—just to create separation from the fans. If they take a right it's all back streets until you hit the Wall, so they'll hang a left. Then at least three blocks before a street that will accommodate the limo.*

I'm across the road as fast as my lungs will allow, and I glance back in time to see their car turn left out of the west gate. *So far, so good.*

Down the alley, I race along the next two blocks, catching a glimpse of the limo passing one street over. I turn right, behind one of the processing substations topped by another of those glass-globe behemoths, into the heart of the Odeaglow.

*Gotta get higher. They're closing in on one of the city's main transport hubs, and I could lose them easy.*

I push harder, scaling two flights of fire escape before I lay eyes on the hub. Their car, surrounded by high-end security, rolls down along Highmore and into the maze of apartments and private residences at the far end of the district.

The convoy moves out of sight, but I haven't lost them. I know that area better than most people. And hopefully, with their press tour over, they'll ditch a little of their greyface deadweight.

Clutching my ribs each time I pause to catch my breath, I purposely slow my pace, minding every jolt when I jump back to the asphalt. Night is quickly falling over Cyrene, and that's in my favor as I walk with purpose from street to street, not far from Hellcat Maggie's.

I comb the neighborhood, looking for stashed-away stretch limos and out-of-sight SUVs. Nothing jumps out at me until I see the army of waiters and hired hands working to diminish the traditional pile of garbage bags in the alley adjacent to the Carlisle Building. The next two blocks are dominated by expensive cars of all makes and models, some with ice-blue halogen headlamps still aglow, having just arrived.

*Pay dirt.*

I press against the chain-link fence separating me from the hustle and bustle of soiree planners. The guy in the suit, the band's Corporate-issued handler, is calmly giving orders as the hired hands flutter around him like crisply dressed moths, under the watchful eyes of at least a dozen Facilitators.

I cast my gaze upward, toward the glowing penthouse suite of the Carlisle Building. After all that, this is as close as a party-crasher gets.

*Or so they think.*

# V

For the next hour, the Loft is the touchdown point of our personal tornado. The styling teams collide with the cleaning crew hauling out the last of the ruined furniture. Hired help weaves through everyone, loading in rental chairs, high glass tables, arrangements of flowers, crate after crate of liquor and food.

There's swearing and yelling from everyone involved, though Jax manages to screech down the house when she can't locate her electroshock dress and matching boots. Someone finds them in the back of her closet, and then her screams are reserved for the poor asshole trying to brush her hair into some semblance of submission.

Sasha disappears into her room, emerging in short order like a docile pink butterfly. Her only acknowledgment of the last twenty-four hours is the heavy eyeliner, a ring-around-the-eyes reminder of Pretty Goth Boy. She takes it upon herself to set up the audio equipment, pulling pieces as necessary from the studio space in the back.

And me? I'm the poster child for good behavior, a silent statue as everyone buzzes around me, worker bees around their queen. Fresh face paint. New dress delivered from an uptown showroom. I eye the burgundy burned-out velvet, the silver-green leaves twisting through the fabric, in love with the design but afraid to touch it. Afraid my fingers will burn cold through the blossoms and kill them with frost.

*Fuck, I'm freezing.*

I still can't feel the end of my nose, despite the fact that I turned the heat on high, and everyone else in the room is sweating through their clothes. The stylist wrestling my hair into a thousand impossible curls keeps wiping her face on a towel, but all I can do is bite my lip and try not to shatter into a billion pieces of ice.

She finishes by wreathing my head with blood-red roses: real flowers, raised in a greenhouse somewhere, coaxed to life only to die so they can decorate my head. The weight of them bends my neck forward. A thorn pricks my scalp and draws blood, but I deserve it.

"Everyone out," comes the quiet order from the bedroom doorway. The stylist grabs her combs and brushes. The dressers bail out behind her. Footsteps cross the room, and then Damon kneels in front of me, his expression carefully blank, his voice admirably modulated when he adds, "They're arriving already. I need you to get your shit together."

"I know." My teeth are chattering now.

"You know who's downstairs, right?"

*Every higher-up from Corporate, plus investors. Very important people with very deep pockets who may very well fund a string of Cyrenes, if we pull off the gig at the Dome.*

*Very important people who only give a shit about me as long as I continue to be their bright shining star.*

*The moment this star falls, I'm dead to them.*

"Yes, Damon, I know." The cold steals my voice, so that it cracks on the last word.

That seems to decide something for him. Without breaking his steady gaze, he reaches into his pocket.

I'm the one who looks down, barely able to make out the small plastic bag, the single green translucent tab. The promise of heat glows bright in Damon's hand, and though every bit of me is screaming on the inside, I reach for it.

He sucks in a breath when my fingers brush over his wrist in search of salvation. "Oh my god, Vee—" He starts to protest, but I'm already ripping the bag open.

The applejack dissolves on my tongue and melts all the snow inside me by the time I close my eyes, count to three, make a wish. When I open my eyes, everything comes into focus. Edges are sharp again, hot knives all around me.

When Damon pulls me to my feet, I wonder why I don't cut right through him.

"I'll get you through this concert," he mutters, "and then we're cleaning all the crap out of your system. We just have to keep you going until Friday."

When I kiss him, I leave a perfect heart-shaped blotch on his cheek. "Whatever it takes, right?" I don't wipe it off before leading him to the door. "Come on. It's time to throw the meat to the lions."

# M

The Carlisle is at least three stories higher than any apartment building in the neighborhood. So if, say, you wanted to peek in on the high society rabble glad-handing and schmoozing in a rock goddess's penthouse suite, your best option would be the soaring edifice known as the Cyrene Clocktower.

And if your ribs allow for it, there are some monstrously large gears inside that make for easy climbing.

Perched on one of the maintenance catwalks that grant interior and exterior access to the Clocktower, I can see half the city from up here. The various districts are aglow with their hedonism-fueled lights and vidscreens, but my eyes are locked on a particular floor-to-ceiling window of a particular penthouse.

I wish I had binoculars on me. Then I could see more than the distant blacks and grays of tuxedos and business suits strolling about the ultramodern furnishings, all hard angles and glass tops. There are occasional flashes of other shades, cerulean blues and emerald greens, the gowns and formalwear of wives, girlfriends, husbands, boyfriends, and hangers-on of both sexes.

The girls themselves must be lost among the monochrome monotony, their flair and style tempered by the presence of Corporate.

I can't see Vee, but I can picture her, draped in crimson elegance that suits her despite her objections. Fielding questions and compliments with equal aplomb, but desperately counting down the minutes until everyone's gone.

*She's a caged songbird. Why hasn't that occurred to me before?*

In a place like the Carlisle Building, she'll be on 24/7 lockdown. If I want to see her again, hear her again, and possibly steal a moment's attention, I'll have to brave the Dome somehow.

*Which is an insane idea. Sneaking into the Dome would make today look like child's play.*

I settle in for a bit, scanning the penthouse, hoping to spot her. Hoping against hope that she might somehow spot me. A flash of brilliant red catches my eye, flickering between the masses of black-clad interlopers.

I lift my hand, a first overture she can't possible see. Her voice finds me, though, lyrics from the mall rolling over me, warming me despite the evening's chill.

# V

With the applejack in my system, I burn hot and bright enough to make everyone believe I'm the most charming bitch in the universe. But offering my hand and letting dozens of people kiss me on either cheek tests my last bit of self-control.

*If one more person touches me, I might just scream loud enough to shatter all the windows.*

I have to keep it together, hold up my end of the bargain. Sasha manages the music while Jax entertains a few of Corporate's teenage tagalongs with wild-ass stories and that pound of strawberry cough she ordered this morning.

Damon has me on a short leash, introducing me once again to the men and women who own my soul. He remembers every one of their names. Asks the visitors about their accommodations and jokes about the Cyrene-withdrawal they'll suffer after returning home. Smiles and shakes hands and eases me along, careful to keep me moving so I don't burn a hole in the carpet. Every time we pass the bar, I exchange an empty glass for a full one.

Doesn't matter what I'm drinking; everything tastes like apples. And just about everything reminds me of Micah. When I catch a glimpse of blond hair and blue eyes, I think it's him and feel the floor drop out from under me . . .

Of course it's someone else.

*Don't be an idiot. Micah won't come within ten miles of this building, not with security swarming everywhere.*

The attractive not-Micah approaches, but Damon's right-hand lackey cuts through the crowd, a seven-foot-tall wall of muscle effectively blocking us off from the rest of the room. You can tell this is an important event because they've managed to pry his aviators off for once.

"There's someone here to speak with you," he tells Damon. "He's out in the hallway."

Instead of barking back, ten kinds of pissed, Damon scowls and checks his phone. The second-long flash of the screen tells me he's let ten calls and as many messages roll to voice mail. "Go up to your room, Vee. I'll be right there."

Without a moment's hesitation, I take the unexpected chance to escape, to catch my breath. Drifting up the stairs on a cloud of applejack and Pennyroyale, I hear the unmistakable strains of Damon's ire—*I have enough on my plate already. It's handled!*—because the front door is standing ajar—*We've tripled security and upgraded everything to your specifications. It's buttoned up tight!*—but one teetering step at a time I put it all behind me—*Stop bothering me. Just go home to your lab and get back to work.*

His voice fades out, dialed all the way down to nothing as I retreat to the bathroom. It doesn't feel nearly far enough. I can't breathe, and it has nothing to do with my dress or the climb up the stairs, so I push open the window. Boost myself off the marble sink. Out to the ledge. Up onto the roof. There are easier ways of getting up here, but this is my way.

The night air slams into me, cutting through the thin layers of red, tempering the applejack heat building up inside me. I skirt AC and heating units, tiny piles of debris and bigger piles of bird crap until I reach the ledge on the other side.

Facing the Clocktower, I watch the minutes pass, every one of them fresh and sharp as a razor against my skin.

*Where are you tonight?*

The taste of him is tangled up with the drugs still candy-coating my mouth. Funny, you'd think Adonis would be in there, too, but he's long banished. When footsteps fall behind me and hands find my bare arms, I know without turning that it won't be the person I'm looking for.

# CHAPTER SEVEN

## M

Spending half the night in the cold didn't do my ribs much good, but as I bandage them up for the busy day ahead, I have no regrets. In fact, I feel energized, raring to go despite any number of unforeseen complications that will no doubt leave me tenderized and ready for market.

At least I've got fresh clothes, free of lavender and unpleasant associations. I feel like a new man. A new man with the lung capacity of an elderly asthmatic. Nothing to be done about that, so I grin and bear it. I lace up my sneakers and gaze up at my Sugar Skulls picture.

*Good morning, Vee.*

It's strange, to have a name for her now. For days, she's been Her. The Voice. The Girl with the killer pipes, with the magic words. The Siren. More force of nature than woman. I steal one more glance at her and head for the exit, primed for a day of careful prep and recon.

As I climb down from my piece of privacy, I reflect on yesterday's madness.

*It's more by luck than skill that I managed to make it home without being spotted. I basically ignored everything I've learned in the last six months to chase her around the city in broad daylight.*

Would I do it again?

*In a heartbeat.*

But that doesn't mean it was smart.

*That kind of carelessness gets you caught, gets you hurt. Gets you killed. Gotta be smarter, play to my strengths.*

It's difficult, though, when the objective has changed. It was easy to run around Cyrene, hunting down leads and chasing bad guys. It was the mission. But now I'm risking all of that, tossing it aside.

*For her.*

Because deep down, I know yesterday was about more than hearing her in person again, more than understanding how her words slip inside me with such ease.

She kicked open a door I thought was locked tight and bricked over long ago. And I can't be sure where that door leads anymore.

I exhale, releasing a breath I didn't realize I was holding, before crossing the bridge at a light jog. There are occasional twinges, but nothing worrying. I feel better than yesterday, but I can't be certain if that's a sign of healing or it's just because I felt like freshly stomped grapes by the end of the day.

Either way, I'll take it as a win.

At a reserved pace, it takes longer than I'm accustomed to, but I finally arrive at my destination. Equipment is being processed through the Dome's loading area. With all the public transport around, there's not much call for parking spaces between those giant doors and the edge of the property.

I sneak up to the fence behind the loading dock. The place is positively electric with activity. Worker ants of every size, shape, and jumpsuit shade unload cases and cases of equipment from box trucks galore, all of them streaming in through the corrugated roll-up door. Plenty of it is what you'd expect: lighting rigs packed with color-scrollers, lasers, and strobes; pyrotechnic flares, mortars, and other setups; high-capacity thrum-collectors to make the most of the sold-out crowd.

But then there's the small fleet of black vans off to one side. I loop around, careful to keep plenty of distance between me and the Facilitators patrolling the Dome's perimeter. The greyfaces are using a side entrance, and I've never seen a band use the kind of gear they're hauling into the building: giant versions of those portable scanners at the Palace and other high-end joints, the ones that log your profile in the system.

*That could be a problem. If they can remotely scan for a nanotech signature or a concertgoer's energy output, they'll track me down fast, demisemiquaver fast.*

Okay, so all I have to do is get into the building without a ticket, bypass private security, Dome security, greyfaces, and top-of-the-line scanners, steal two seconds with Vee, and then get the hasty fuck out of Dodge. *No problem.* Maybe they'll have attack dogs, too; that would make this a good and proper suicide mission.

At least one thing evens the playing field: *none* of us know what Vee will do.

As I head out, slipping away from the Dome and back onto the main roads, I pull the business card from Maggie's envelope out of my pocket. They might have just what I need.

# V

Humming along on the applejack's clean-burn, I'm out of bed in time to watch the sunrise with a cup of coffee in hand.

Damon offered not once but twice to stay when we'd come down off the roof. Radiating heat and light, longing for someone to touch me, to run their hands over every square inch of me, it would have been easy to say yes. An enjoyable way to pass the night. But there's no room in my head for him right now. No room for anything except a new song, brewing like storm clouds. The new song, and the mental slideshow of stolen moments in the Palace alcove with Micah.

Hard to believe I chose to sleep curled up with pillows and memories, but it's true. With any luck, the song will coalesce into something worth singing by the time the sound check rolls around.

I have more time than expected. After two late nights, I have to pry Jax out of her bedroom. It's a scene of total chaos and destruction, with a wall-to-wall carpet of tangled limbs and exhausted teenagers. Damon joins me at the door; I think he's pleased she showed Corporate's precious children such a good time. Hard to tell for sure, because he won't meet my eyes this morning. He's wearing a different suit, but I have the suspicion that he brought it with him and slept here, either in the guest room or the studio space.

*I broke whatever trust there was between us with the shenanigans at the mall. I'm under surveillance now.*

"Sleep all right?" His query is polite, but under it are other questions I don't want him to ask.

"Well enough," I say, already headed for Sasha's room. Jax grumbles behind us, threatening to cut off our favorite appendages with rusty saws as payback for waking her up. She steps on arms, legs, and worse as she stumbles to the door.

Sasha, as it turns out, snuck someone back into the Loft. Seeing as I expected her Pretty Goth Boy, the curvaceous form and copper hair of the Redheaded Mini come as something of a surprise. She and Sasha curl around each other, two kittens in a basket. I hesitate to wake them, if only because very few in this world get to sleep with that sort of blissed-out peace on their faces, but Damon doesn't share the sentiment.

He slams the lights to full and starts throwing clothes at them. Sasha jumps out of bed like she's been shot in the ass and is dressed before the Redheaded Mini sits up on her elbows and drawls, "You've got my Cyrano link. Use it."

She's gone by the time we head into the elevator, and the ride to the Dome is quiet. Jax wears sunglasses and sucks down her second electrolyte-replenishment pack. Sasha smiles to herself, humming under her breath. *Smitten.* The kitten is smitten, with all the adorable squishiness of a child bounding across a rainbow-strewn field of daisies.

*And over a girl, no less. Shows how much I actually know about her.*

*Let her have her love song. Not all of us get to sing something that special.*

But Damon's temper is already approaching boiling point. I can tell by the way he keeps checking his phone for messages—probably from the same Corporate dipshit riding his ass at the party last night—that we're in for a screamfest of colossal proportions the moment something goes wrong.

Once we're inside the building, Jax and Sasha head straight for their gear. All our stuff is already in place onstage, but everything has to be adjusted. Equipment tuned until it cycles the music through the systems without a single hiccup, pause, or glitch. They won't need me for a while yet, so I get parked on the sidelines with a cup of tea and a stern warning to stay put.

"Rest your voice," Damon adds. "I need you at one hundred percent for sound check."

"Not a problem," I tell him, wrapping my hands around the cup and appreciating the heat of the ceramic. "Go put the universe in order."

With a last dark look in my direction, he disappears into the sea of black-clothed stage ninjas. Sipping my tea, I watch them load in extra thrum-collectors, banks of video equipment to broadcast the concert live across the city . . . and more. A swarm of greyfaces bring in energy readers and ID scanners, placing them at every entrance.

The moment Micah steps into the building, he's going to be the only dark spot in a spectrum of thrum output. Easy to spot. Easy to bring in.

*Stay away, Micah. Just . . . stay away.*

I shudder, then realize the tea in my cup has gone cold. Everything is cold. I count back and realize I didn't even make it twenty-four hours this time before burning most of the applejack out of my system.

*Damon was in a hurry. He probably got a weak tab off some street dealer. That's the only way to explain it . . .*

"Vee, get your ass onstage!" Jax yells. "You're up."

I set the mug down and take the stairs as quickly as I can. Three steps up, my depth perception wavers. One heel finds a hole in the metal grating, and I pitch forward.

Damon's there to catch me before I crash face-first into the stage. The moment his hands meet my skin, he knows.

"Fuck." It's all he says. All he has to say.

I twist away from him and run for the microphone. "What do you want to start with?"

"'Screams and Whispers' is loaded in," Sasha says, checking her screens, "then transition to 'Little Dead Thing.'"

I nod and wait for the synthesizers and computerized downbeats to take over. Stage techs test the projection screens behind us: clips from old monster movies, footage from our other concerts, still photos of various Sugar Skull makeup variations that slowly morph into real skeletons. The light show kicks into high gear, firing green and pink and orange beams of light out into the audience. I jump when the first of the pyrotechnics fires off, missing my intro.

Everything fizzles to a halt, leaving us in the half dark, projections frozen, light beams wavering, golden sparks dying on the floor.

"What the ever-loving fuck, Vee?" Jax glares at me, cuing the music back up to the proper place. This time, I hit the first note but mess up the lyrics in the second chorus.

By now, Damon's pacing in the wings, having a low and very serious phone conversation that ends when I try to start the song for the third time and don't get out a single note. Before I can call for a reset, he has me by the elbow and tows me off the other side of the stage.

"Take a ten-minute break," he barks at the girls. "I'm going to get this sorted out."

My feet barely touch the floor as he hustles me along. "Damon, I'm fine," I say, trying to reassure him, but it's all lies, lies, lies. "I just need to concentrate."

"Like hell. You never miss a cue. You *never* forget lyrics." More furious tapping against the touchscreen. "I was afraid of this."

Even before we hit the dressing room, I'm a broken-down windup doll. He sets me on the chaise, covers me up with a furry gray blanket, and checks his phone again. No telling how much time passes before there's a quiet knock at the door. A muttered conversation between Damon and three Facilitators.

A golden jungle cat pads into the room, his smile all teeth.

"Hey, gorgeous," Adonis says. "If you wanted to see me again, all you had to do was ask."

"She burned through the tab you gave me already," Damon mutters.

*Not a weak-ass street dose, then.*

I won't give either one of them the satisfaction of looking away, but I'm still the first to blink.

## M

I make a quick run to the Eadlin District to hit up the north-side supply depot for Cyrene Medical Services. The code on Maggie's business card grants me a few minutes' access off the books, and once the card is scanned and shredded, I've got the run of the place.

Stocking up on the necessities—bandages, antiseptic, gel-packs, anti-inflammatories, the works—along with a few special items that could come in handy tomorrow, I'm in and out in less than five.

*Good.* I try to spend as little time in the Eadlin as possible, since a good chunk of Cyrene's central authorities and other higher-up mucky-mucks haunt its streets. I keep my head down and my pace slow but steady, since I'm too deep into the district proper to hightail it somewhere safe if things go all shit sandwich on me in a hurry.

But soon enough, I'm back in relatively safe territory, headed off the beaten path toward a brick-and-mortar storage shed of Maggie's, tucked away among the city's maintenance garages and material depots.

I stroll to the roll-up steel door and knock twice. The door flies up and back, and one of Rete's boys—a fuck-ugly kid built like a fire hydrant—waves me in before closing the door behind me. The screech of poorly maintained casters rips through the place, and even Fire Plug winces as he releases the chain.

Making a beeline for the back wall, I realize I'm not alone. The warehouse isn't exactly sprawling, maybe half a soccer field long, a little narrower, and I hear him behind some pallets before I see him. In the back corner, hunched over a few plastic-wrapped crates of over-the-Wall whiskey, is another runner, scrawny yet scrappy. Someone whose name I've never bothered to learn. And he's here for the same reason I am.

Rivitocin.

Scrappy has the injector to his neck, and with a soft hiss, he doses himself. Closing his eyes and clenching his fists, he steels himself for the proverbial ton of bricks about to fall on him. And does it ever. His muscles start twitching, limbs flailing as the Rivitocin races through his system, disrupting his nanotech and temporarily kicking him off-grid. The perfect way to move around the city without pinging sensors all over Cyrene, it's another valuable over-the-Wall import.

Obviously I've never needed any, but no need to spread that knowledge around. After Scrappy recovers from the injection and heads out, I ask Fire Plug to grab me a quick restock: six doses of Rivitocin, plus injectors.

*Always good to have a plan B.*

Once he's out of sight, I wander a few pallets over into Maggie's meager stockpile and pull out two sets of stun-knucks. *Brights. A little scuffed but usable.* I've already tucked them into my messenger bag by the time Fire Plug returns, handing me two thin, black cases. I stash them in my bag as he heads over to the door and pulls it open for me. I thank him on my way out, grateful for a Rete-free supply run. With two more errands to go, I don't have the time, patience, or restraint to deal with him.

My head down once more, I set a measured pace for my next stop.

# V

Adonis leans easily against the makeup table, arms folded over his chest.

*At least he's wearing a shirt this time.*

I want to bolt for the door, but it's only a fleeting daydream. I'm frozen in place, unable to uncurl my fists from the blanket, unable to clear the crystal cobwebs from my head.

"She slipped the leash at the mall, and I'm pretty damn sure she started that riot," Damon tells my new watchdog. I might as well not be in the room for all the attention they're paying me right now. "I can trust her about as far as I can throw her."

"Meaning not at all," Adonis says with a mirthless laugh. "Yeah, I'm well aware that she'd stab you in the back, midfuck if it suited her."

Damon goes very still, then gets right up in Adonis's face. Only then do I realize my keeper is a good three inches taller than the golden god. Factor in the sheer authoritative presence, and it might as well be six.

"You're only here because I was told it was safer to give her applejack from the same source to minimize variables," Damon says very slowly. "For the next thirty-six hours, your only purpose in life is to keep her functional. The second you fuck up, you're headed out of Cyrene in handcuffs." He pauses, looks Adonis up and down, then adds, "And if something happens to her . . . If she ends up dead? I'll see to it you tragically OD in a gutter, hollowed out by the filthiest combination of street drugs imaginable. Is that understood?"

Adonis isn't smiling anymore. "Got it. Keep the songbird singing, at least until tomorrow night."

Damon glances over at me as his phone pings madly in his hand. There are probably a dozen technical malfunctions he needs to sort out and at least as many PR fires he needs to put out. When he finally stalks to the door, he shoots off a parting "Get her up and running. You have ten minutes" before slamming it shut behind him.

Adonis detaches himself from the makeup table and crosses to me, crouching in front of the chaise like he's about to make a sacrifice.

"Don't t-t-touch me . . ." is all I manage between tiny, frosted exhalations.

"Sorry, gorgeous, I'm going to have to," he mutters, fingers finding the pulse at my wrist, gaze shifting to the clock hanging on the wall. "You're a special kind of special. I've never seen anyone react to it like this before."

I thought about the migraines, the mind-scrubs, the reboots. "S-s-special doesn't begin to cover it."

"Hot and cold, that's just how you run." He shrugs as his attention slides back to me. "I thought we were having a good time. Guess I disappointed you somehow, since you called in your boyfriend and the greyfaces."

"Damon's n-n-not my boyfriend."

Adonis smiles down at me again, but this time, it's not feral. Not calculating. Far from it.

*Fuck. He feels* bad *for me.*

"Whatever you say, gorgeous. Tell me the sky's green and the Wall's a foot high, if that makes you feel better. You just have to keep breathing. Making pretty music. If I can get you through tomorrow night, I get a clean record and more credits than I can spend in two lifetimes." Shifting so that he's sitting next to me on the narrow chaise, he checks my pupils. Runs a hand down my arms. "I have to admit, it shocked the shit out of me when I found out who you are. When they dragged me out of your apartment, I just figured I banged a piece of ass that belonged to Corporate."

"You did." By now, everything is soft and hazy and gray, like he's pulling the blanket up over my face and shoving it down my throat. I hear Adonis swear under his breath, feel his muscles bunch and shift as he reaches for something.

I'm almost at the bottom of the rabbit hole by the time the applejack hits my tongue.

## M

*Bridge, sweet bridge.*

Between my supply run to the warehouse, hitting up the construction site for more copper, and a quick visit to a clothing store in the Odeaglow, I'm loaded for bear by the time I return to the underbelly of the Arkcell.

And while I've taken it easy in comparison to yesterday's high-speed detour, the weight of the day's bounty is more than making up for a fairly leisurely pace. My breaths are getting shallower, and it feels like a small, mean-spirited xylophone player is working over my ribcage from the inside.

I look up at the tarp concealing my little hideout, and the plan instantly forms in my head: climb up, grab a length of rope and a pulley from my storage closet, rig it up to a piece of plywood, and voilà! An open-air dumbwaiter in a matter of minutes. Lower it to the ground and climb down after it. Load it up, climb back up, unload the day's purchases, and break it down again. *Easy*.

That's what Rational Mind would do. Exhausted Mind looks at the expected up-and-down-and-up again and says, *fuck it*. Then he unhooks the strap on his messenger bag, slips it through the handles on everything else he bought, hooks it back on, and soldiers on up into the warren.

Stashing everything in the storage closet, I retrieve Lara from her case, lock the vault door, and settle gratefully into bed. While the hum serenades me as always, it's Vee's voice in my head as I close my eyes. Wishing her good night, I curl up with the guitar, my fingers coaxing unfamiliar rhythms from Lara's strings.

For the first time in ages . . . for Vee . . . I start composing something new.

# V

We make it through the second attempt at a rehearsal just fine, running each number twice, smoothing transitions, then testing the thrum-collectors on a group of contest winners gathered in the pit just below the stage. The kids practically vibrate out of their skin with the joy of being there, getting an early glimpse, a little taste of what's to come tomorrow. It's well past midnight by the time the greyfaces corral them into an interview room where they scream hysterical praises to the sky.

I watch them go as the last of the music fades from my system. Adonis is next to me within seconds, hustling all of us off the stage in the opposite direction of the camera crews.

Jax starts to argue. "I don't see why we have to go straight back to the Loft—"

"Get in the goddamn car," he barks, not taking any of her shit.

"Fuck you, too!" she flares, ducking into the limo with a scowl that should have burnt him to ash. Sasha's right behind her, not offering a peep of protest.

I don't process much of the car ride. Things get progressively blurrier, so that I'm only aware in the vaguest possible way when we hit the front door.

Adonis packs me up the stairs. "Stay with me, gorgeous." With one hand, he whips out his phone and pulls up a contact, waiting for someone to pick up before settling both of us on the bed. "She's already crashing, Damon. There's no way she should have burned through that tab so quickly." There's a pause and then he adds, "Yes, it's from the same fucking batch. Something else is wrong."

The pause that follows is filled with ice. Ice, and a spark, inspiration fueling my new song, red on white, blood on snow. Let Adonis and Damon wring their hands over burnouts and doses.

*I'm gonna sear the sky with my words—*

Another dose of applejack hits my system, and I jerk like I've been punched. Reeling, I scramble away from Adonis. Slam into the wall. Slide to the floor.

He's panting, wide-eyed, like he just saw a ghost. "We're going to have to keep you up all night. If you fall asleep, you could flatline."

"Fine by me." There's a thousand and one ways I can fill the time, beginning and ending with blue-eyed dreams. There's no way in hell Micah's going to chance the Dome. But he'll be watching the broadcast. Everyone will. And I want this new song ready in time.

# CHAPTER EIGHT

## M

In the predawn quiet, I slip out onto the streets of the city, getting an early jump on my increasingly ambitious to-do list. The first item, and the only one requiring me to leave the warren: drop a message for Niko in the usual spot. Niko handles part of Cyrene's ever-changing real estate holdings, so he can use the address I got to confirm or deny what Ludo told me about the supposedly dead applejack dealer.

I'm hoping Ludo's wrong and there's still a chance I can get my hands on the guy.

The brief field trip is a solid test for how I'm healing. Everything hurts a little less than the day before. I make it to the drop and back in good time, no seeing spots or threat of hyperventilating. *Good. I don't need any unwelcome surprises at the Dome later.*

As soon as I'm home, I look around and survey what to do next. My eyes find Vee's poster, and I smile. "Am I crazy? Am I crazy for going through all this just for the chance to see you? To talk to you? To be there when you unleash those pipes on the world?"

I don't really expect a response. Even if I am crazy, I'm not *that* crazy.

*Just crazy enough to talk to a poster of her.*

"I have to tell you something. There was this girl at the Palace a few nights ago. Superconfident and floating on a cloud of this vile designer street-shit called applejack. She came right up to me and pushed me into an alcove and . . .

"I wished she was you." I feel a weight in my gut, like I'm confessing to a crime. I guess I am. "Man, what a shitty thing to think, to admit. She was gorgeous, no lie, and she knew it, too. Wearing not much more than you in that poster.

"Another time . . . another place . . . even a few days ago, before I saw you at Maggie's, she would've been a dream come true. But I just kept wishing she'd stop pursing her lips and flatten me with a note like you did."

As I talk to her, my hands work overtime, gathering supplies and preparing for the evening's impending insanity. A pile of finished Sugar Skulls T-shirts to my right attests to how long I've been at it. I survey the scene all around me, imagining it from her eyes.

*I bet she'd let the mess slide.*

"What do you think, Vee? What will you think if I actually get five minutes alone with you? I'm pretty sure you remember me, but would you care if I showed up again?"

Now that I've started, I can't stop. The words tumble out, blurted like unintended poetry. "You shot straight through me and out the other side like it was nothing at all. You came through an unguarded window and have been padding barefoot through empty rooms ever since, leaving your footprints in the dust.

"I've been listening to your footfalls for days, and honestly, I wish I could listen to them for eternity. But tonight, I'm turning around. I'm risking looking back and finding you just a ghost, a delusion, a figment of my lonesome imagination."

Even to a picture of her, I fear I've said too much. More than I've said to anyone in months.

I look away, pull the set of Brights from storage, and get to work cracking them open. The wiring inside is pretty simple, thankfully. I'm no engineer.

"This part is gonna suck like a night at Sidri's." I glance at Vee and steel myself for what's to come. Retrieving my old silver chain from a small bin next to my bed, I loop a piece of wire through one of the links before putting it on. Then I run the length of wire down my back, hook the other end into one of the Brights, and slip the stun-knucks into the left pocket of my jeans.

The other one I tinker with for a few minutes more before closing it up, satisfied, and stowing it in my hoodie. I overclocked it so it will shed more energy than necessary. *But this* . . . I pat the one in my pocket twice, and the jolt stuns me for a second. "Owww." This one triggers an involuntary emotional response. Between the two of them, I should show up on their scanners.

*Hopefully.*

I double-tap the one in my pocket again, and the low-level unpleasantness dissipates.

Turning to the half-sheet once more, I look Vee in the eye. "Wish me luck. No matter what happens, at least I'll get to see you soon."

I continue stashing supplies into various pockets as I gear up and get dressed. It's almost showtime.

# V

Adonis has circles under his eyes. It would almost be funny, except I can't stop singing long enough to laugh. Micah's song spirals through my brain on a never-ending loop, the first verse picking up where the last chorus leaves off. I hum it under my breath, scratch the words into my skin.

> What would I give for just one taste of you?
> What would I trade to fall straight into you?
> I would burn this city to the ground.
> Down, down, down to the ground.

Every few hours, Adonis shoves another tab of applejack into my mouth. Then every hour. He breaks out in a sweat as the window between doses gets shorter and shorter. When I start to go cold again, he has to administer CPR to get me breathing again.

"Just an excuse to kiss me," I tease him as I race out of the room. Have to stay ahead of the music. The lyrics will slam into me, crush me, kill me, if I rest for a single second—

"Vee, you need to sit down."

I toss a glance over my shoulder, evilly pleased to see that Adonis looks ragged around the edges. Dogging my every step from my suite to the kitchen, he tries to keep me hydrated and fueled up.

The food's a lost cause. Even the electrolyte packs are coming back up now.

Damon shows up right when I'm puking a pink watermelon concoction into the kitchen sink. Adonis has one arm looped around my waist, the other hand holding my hair back. There isn't anything left for Damon to grab, but it looks like he wants to snatch me out of the golden god's arms.

"I said I needed her functional," Damon says, but my babysitter cuts him off.

"I'm doing the best I can—" Adonis doesn't have a chance to finish defending himself, because now I'm throwing up straight stomach acid, then going limp.

There's no such thing as mercy here,
And the space between us grows ever wider,
Come taste the sugar on my lips,
Your precious girl, you won't deny her.

"She's supposed to be in makeup by now," Damon says. The words crackle in and out like speakers on the fritz.

"She *was* in makeup, until she spewed what little food I got into her all over the stylist." Adonis turns on the water and splashes some of it into my face. Cold trickles work their way down my neck, into my shirt. "And fuck you if you think you could have done any better. This was supposed to be an easy little nursing gig. I've been messaging you *all day*. Where the hell have you been?"

"Doing my goddamn job," Damon says, bringing me a kitchen towel. He tries to dry me off as he's pushing the hair from my face. "I've got Corporate to answer to, investors to impress, the lab guy up my ass—" Getting a good look at me, he can't help the strangled noise that comes out of him. "Holy fuck, have you seen her eyes?"

Adonis tilts my head back and swears again. Scooping me into his arms, he heads for the master suite, for the bathtub. He's already filled it with cold water and ice cubes. Without hesitating, he drops me in.

I sink to the bottom, barely feeling the cold, my skin melting the ice like it's nothing.

What would I give for just one taste of you?
What would I trade to fall straight into you?

Two sets of strong hands heave me back to the surface—*Hands on my wrists, on my throat, over my mouth . . . Skull. Rose. Dagger . . . Back the fuck up, man, you knew this was part of the deal*—I gasp for air, startled into remembering the existence of oxygen.

His shirtsleeves wet up to the elbows, Damon snatches a towel from the rack and starts drying himself off. "She has to be onstage within the hour. Give her another tab and get her in the car. We'll take care of her face paint at the Dome."

"Are you shitting me?" Adonis kneels next to the tub. He pulls me against his chest, sliding me out of the water and into his lap. We're both soaked. He's freezing.

I'm burning.

> I would burn this city to the ground.
> Down, down, down to the ground.

"It'll kill her," Adonis says.

"It won't. She's stronger than that. And we'll take her straight to the medcenter the second the concert is over."

Adonis looks down at me, about to argue.

"Come taste the sugar on my lips," I croon into his chest. "Your precious girl, you won't deny her."

He shudders in response, eyes bleak as he puts another tab into my mouth.

# M

The transit hub outside the Dome is an absolute mob scene tonight, as expected. Two enormous snaking lines of hormone-fueled enthusiasm stream into the building, while small cabals are scattered beneath the streetlights, mixing up their preconcert cocktails in the hopes the high will kick in just as the band starts playing.

In simple black from head to toe, I easily blend in, lost in a field of aspiring and practicing gothdom. Meandering through the crowd, I distribute a dozen modified Sugar Skulls T-shirts to random members of the audience, all of whom are psyched to receive some free swag just before the show.

Dodging the watchful eyes and flashlight beams of a few random greyfaces roaming the lot—*they've saved their best and brightest for inside, probably*—I keep it gel-pack cool until I'm around the corner and away from the main doors. Stepping onto the bumper, then the hood of a delivery truck, I jog up the windshield, onto the cab, and then hop onto the body of the truck, sprinting as I leap for the eave of the great sloping roof that gives the Dome its name.

Crouching as I land, I breathe a quick sigh of relief before I start climbing. Between the natural adhesion of my fingers and the quality tread on my sneakers, I negotiate the trip with relative ease, looking for a recessed access point, a skylight, anything that will let me inside.

I sweep along the backside of the structure, away from the parking lot, just in case someone catches a glimpse of me. *Don't want anyone mistaking a ticketless interloper on a mission for your average, run-of-the-mill ticketless interloper.*

Finally, I spot power cables running from farther up the Dome to parked vans in the back lot. *Perfect.*

Sliding on my stomach, I follow the cables to a cracked access hatch. It's held open by the thick wires that'll channel all of that hormonal, drug-fueled thrum into usable energy for the city. I ease the hatch open more and slip down onto one of the gridded rafters of the Dome.

*Whoa. Much higher than the ceiling of the Palace.* I look down and let the vertigo pass. *Long way down. Fifty feet, maybe. Stay frosty.*

With great reluctance, I let go of the beam with one hand and double-tap my hoodie pocket, activating the overclocked stun-knucks.

Then I sigh again, wrap my right arm around the beam, and double-tap my jeans pocket, feeling the punch of the Brights as my neck muscles spasm. I seize up for a moment.

*Ow! Thought I was ready for it! Obviously wrong!*

I grab on to the beam with both hands and close my eyes, pushing the steady ache down as much as I can, getting ready to move. At least it's distracting me from my ribs.

I glance at the crowd beneath me, a mass of humanity like I—and the Dome, I suspect—have never seen.

And already, I can see plan A working perfectly. Facilitators fight their way through the crowd, trying to get a hold of the kids wearing my special Sugar Skulls shirts. I was right about the energy scanners; they must track your nanotech signature. And the copper wire that I cloth-taped inside the shirts is working like a small Faraday cage to block their signal, leaving conspicuous little black holes in whatever display they're monitoring.

*Sorry, folks. It's for a good cause.*

I gingerly make my way across the rafters, climbing three rows back and swinging from one to the next, monkey bars–style, until I reach a convenient space to climb down, dropping the last six feet and hustling for the pit. Most of the security guards and greyfaces I can see are either busy grabbing my decoys or manning various scanners. I close my eyes and concentrate on my breathing, which is a little labored.

*I think I'm okay. I think I'm okay.*

*I might be okay.*

Shivering for a moment under the onslaught of my improvised equipment, I push and shove until only the barricade and an open pathway for security stand between me and the stage. I pat the black plastic case in my hoodie pocket, grateful I didn't have to go to plan B. A dose of Rivitocin would've ruined someone's night, and quick.

*But I'm in. I'm here. And I think I'm okay.*

I turn expectantly toward the stage, hoping for a glimpse of Vee before the show. Hoping all these risks weren't in vain.

# V

The girl in the mirror isn't me. Her flesh is gone, the drugs painting it out of existence. Her sugar skull shows through, eerie in the brilliant light. Where there are usually swirls of red or pink or shocking green, there's only shadow. Her electric-blue gaze locks on to me, stripping away every attempt at artifice. Her hellfire burns through me, twisting and coiling in my veins with apple-flavored poison.

*Snow-white wicked thing, she wants me dead.*

I feel my robe slide from my shoulders, white silk and steel boning taking its place. The styling team banished, the golden god holds me up and Damon fastens the hooks, metal curving around me in another kind of cage. Every tug at the laces steals another tiny breath from my lungs until I'm paper thin, easily crumpled. After that, there's a neckpiece, fabric hands that clamp down on my throat and raise my chin to the heavens. Then spiderwebs of ribbon that connect the collar to the corset, crisscrossing bare skin, tying me down and up and into myself.

A gift he's going to let the audience unwrap.

There's very little to the rest of the costume, just thigh-high boots and the scrap of velvet passing for a skirt. Minutes later I'm standing in the wings between my guardians. Jax and Sasha are a techno-sorceress and a black swan ballerina. The preshow lighting shifts. I can hear the audience roar in response to the sapphire sea spreading across the stage.

Damon motions to Adonis. "Give her one more."

Adonis looks at me, sees the skull-girl looking at him, through him. She smiles. I smile. We're both smiling at him, and he is utterly terrified of us.

She pushes me, so that I lean into him. "Come on, now. You don't want to keep them waiting."

He can't manage a single protest, can't even take a breath as he dopes me up again.

The music crashes to life onstage, pouring out of the speakers, filling the ears of the screaming, frothing rage-monster in the pit. Damon hands me the earpiece, adjusts the mic.

The dead girl inside me is silent, but I mouth two words at him—*fuck you*—before she and I hit the stage together.

# M

The stage is bathed in blue, Trouble and Treble already in position with mountains of equipment around them, like mad scientists hosting a rave.

The incessant buzz of the Brights against my skin fades as I start to lose myself in the energy of the crowd. It swells with anticipation behind me, and I press my hands firmly on the security barrier, just in case the pit pushes forward. The last thing I need is to smash my ribs against the barricade.

*I'd probably fall and get trampled before the greyfaces even got close—*

An avalanche of sound rolls over me, sending my train of thought plummeting off a cliff, shoved aside by my first real glimpse of her in days. Vee, damn near marching onto the stage from the wings, owning it, commanding it. She's a beautiful nightmare, half shadow and half soul, and the horde responds like loyal subjects, crying and shouting her praises and giving her everything.

I would, too, if I could. Instead, I hold the barrier tight and let her first note throttle me into submission, lyrics swallowing me whole.

She tosses me into the stratosphere, and I'm all hers once more.

# V

The outpouring of energy causes all the lights to flare; the techs compensate for the spike in power and set off the pyrotechnic cannons for good measure. Orange-gold sparks cascade out of the tops of four towers set along the front of the stage. I weave a path through the blazing rain, already crooning the opening notes to the song I improvised at the Hellcat's. By the second line, the crowd is singing along with me. The entire world shares my headspace from those first moments with Micah.

A possibility cracks open inside me: he could be here tonight, leaning against a wall like it depends on him to stay upright. Never smiling. Never moving. Never taking his eyes off me until the greyfaces locate the black hole in the energy readings and haul him away. For his own good. For questioning.

Or worse.

*God, Micah, just stay away. If Damon will do* this *to* me, *I don't want to think about what he'd do to you.*

It's the only thought I can spare with a fresh dose of applejack screaming its way through me. Different this time, though, like holding a blowtorch against a piece of charred wood. There's so little left of me to burn. Everything inside is black, like my hair down my back, like the paint on my face. Under the lights, the white satin of the collar and corset glows icy blue.

The vidscreens behind me go to work. I can feel the hands of pretty skeletons sliding down my back and over my shoulders. A three-story version of myself holds a hand up to the skies, and ten thousand sets of hands reach back at her; over, under, around me, like the ribbons in my corset.

*Not a gift for the audience. A fly caught in a web.*

# M

She's fury incarnate, a phoenix midplunge, and she douses us in lyrical kerosene, licks the match alight, and sets us all ablaze.

But I can still hear a tiny voice in the back of my head, screaming for my attention. *Too exposed. You're a sitting duck. Move. Fucking move!*

It's hard to fight that voice, the paranoid little watchdog in my head, but I've worked too damn hard to get here. The only concession I'm willing to make is shoving myself away from the barrier and into the crowd, swaying back and forth along with their rapturous movements. I'm a stringless marionette, lucky to still be upright under Vee's honey-voiced assault.

Mired in the crowd, a thousand scents rise up: the metallic tinge of sweat, the suffocating mists of perfume and powder, the acrid stench of chemistry at work, and somewhere, a hint of rotten cider. But those are sensory gnats, easily swatted by the thunderous roar of the Sugar Skulls, launching into their next musical barrage.

She's relentless, spitting verses like a bonfire spits embers, as if time itself is her enemy. She's got the thousand-yard stare of the possessed, and each of us samples the demon inside her.

The crowd presses forward, and I barely manage to get my forearms up in time to save my ribs from the barricade.

*I might complacently crumble to dust before you ever know I'm here.*

# V

My gaze flicks over the dark blurs that are Jax and Sasha before I move down the set list. The crescendo at the end of "Screams and Whispers" makes for a nice transition into "Little Dead Thing." It's an old one, one of the first songs I wrote for the group.

Carve your name into my skin,
    I promise I won't cry.
You ask a hundred thousand times,
    but you know the reason why.
I'm just your perfect little dead thing . . .

My voice slides into the notes, like a party girl into a latex dress. The stage is turning tricks as well, the platform underfoot rotating up as I lower myself by inches, arching my spine as far as the corset allows. When the back of my neck hits the deck, four remote-controlled cameras swing overhead. Different angles, but they all want the same thing: the shot of the candle being snuffed out.

Holding out my hand, I offer my twitching fingertips to the audience, let every bit of life behind my black-light contacts fade into nothing. I'm still singing, but the refrain is coming from very far away.

"I'm your perfect little dead thing . . ."

# M

Ice runs through my veins as Vee writhes on the stage, erotic and tortured all at once. When the refrain hits, I plummet from the sky like a stone.

Bryn reaches out to me from the past, terrified, and Vee mirrors her every move. Two hands, grasping for something, anything. Two hands out of reach, my body unable to respond.

And each girl exhales, past and present, a soul-stealing wisp of apples.

# V

"I'm just your perfect little dead thing . . ."

I should be scared that the lies are becoming truth. That this isn't a performance anymore. When I exhale, it's corpse-cold. There's only one angel I want to come for me—

That's when I see him pressed against the barricade.

I blink droplets of sweat and distilled applejack from my eyes, but Micah's still there, just out of reach, looking up at me, his expression as unreadable as it was that night at Maggie's.

*It's not him, Vee, it's the drugs, giving you one last high before this fire goes out.*

The song's over. Buoyed by the screams and clapping, I somehow find my feet. Stumble back to the wings for water, sugar skull hallucinations swapped out for visions of blond-haired, blue-eyed boys who may or may not be real. Adonis steps into the dream-space only long enough to force-feed me another mouthful of poison. I twist away from the taste of it, but too late. Fireworks are already going off in my head, shooting down my neck. With a low scream, I reach up to claw at the collar.

"Get it off," someone says. "She can't breathe."

Not waiting for help, I dig fingernails into my skin. Bloody scratches. My neck. His face. Someone swears and stumbles back, clearing the path for a tail-twitching tigress done being caged.

With a snarl, I storm back out into the lights.

# M

Vee returns, renewed, and all I can smell is fucking applejack. She's saturated, drowning in it.

My fingers go white as they clamp down on the barricade, not to hold me up, but to hold me back. Facilitators patrol the gap between the stage and the pit. *Remember Maggie's advice. Can't afford to be stupid now.*

Vee stands alone. The specter of Bryn is gone but not forgotten.

I feel the ache creeping into my neck and shoulders from clenching my fists, the constant pinch of the Brights only making it worse. *If I don't act now, if I don't do something, I might not get another chance. She'll send us skyward again.*

I want that, I desperately do, but I want her, too. The dream and the reality. The girl and the voice.

She makes the choice for me.

# V

It wasn't a fucked-up strung-out hallucination. It's really him. Micah's here. Front and center, right in the line of fire from every possible angle.

The angel's come for me, lacking wings but flying straight through me like an arrow.

I would burn this place down.

*For him.*

"Do you guys want to hear something new?" I scream.

They answer with insane, gleeful drug-fueled cries that gather like a tsunami and crash into the stage. I stagger back a step, faking surprise.

"I'm sorry, was that a yes?"

The noise doubles and redoubles, sending a shudder through the building's bones. Dust and glitter fall from the ceiling, the apex of a pyramid about to collapse in on all the pharaoh's sons and daughters. Somewhere behind me, Jax pulls a rhythm that's enough to get me started.

*Let them keep up. If they can.*

"What would I give for just one taste of you? What would I trade to fall straight into you?" I lock eyes with him, so that he knows, knows this is his song, our song. I wrote it on my heart for him. "I would burn this city to the ground. Down, down, down to the ground."

# M

Her eyes meet mine, the world vanishes, and she sings. She sings like armies falling and stars decaying, like gods tumbling and hearts breaking. She sings, and we play tag with the muses.

All the while, her eyes never leave mine, and I know. I know I wasn't crazy. All this and a hundred thousand more half-baked schemes would be worth it.

*Us.*

She sings for me, but draws the rest of the crowd along like the Pied Piper with a lot more style and sex appeal. I'm only vaguely aware of the mob surging behind me and the security barrier inching closer to the stage. The Facilitators take a step back, just to keep away from the desperate hands of the mob.

Suddenly, my neck spasms with pain, and someone behind me cries out. With supreme effort, I turn away from Vee, my eyes finding the pissed-off glare of a serious moonduster as he touches the red welt on his arm candy's shoulder.

*Shit. She must have touched my necklace.*

It all falls apart. He pushes backward to give her some space, and the pit responds in kind, tossing him from side to side. More people join the fray. One punch. Then more. Moondust Junkie shoves me hard, and I slam back against the barricade, gasping. My ribs vibrate with agony.

I slug him in the mouth as I feel an electric pinch moving down my back. I reach for my necklace. *Fuck.* No wire. Must have dislodged it when I bounced off the barrier. *No more camouflage.*

Vee blasts off for the stars again, and I turn back. Even as she tears the house down, there's something new in her eyes.

Fear.

# V

I see the security team—the one filling the gap between the stage and the audience—take a step back. But it's the special-ops guys cutting through the crowd that I'm worried about. They're coming for him from all sides, blocking every green-lit exit lane.

Whatever Micah was using as cover, it's fucking gone.

The lyrics are a warning now. "There's no such thing as mercy here, and the space between us grows ever wider."

He finally turns back to me, but there's no way to tell him, no way to sing us both away from this place.

Unless.

*Yes.*

I launch into the next line, gathering up the unraveling crowd in my hands and pulling their hearts, their souls, their energy into me, a continuous circuit that builds on itself, threatening to mushroom cloud at any second. The applejack hovers somewhere in the middle, driving me, killing me.

"Come taste the sugar on my lips! Your precious girl, you won't deny her!"

Below me, they're screaming and pushing and shoving against each other. The first of a series of scheduled pyrotechnic explosions paints their faces with the same shadows as mine. Another blast, another shower of sparks, another wave of silver-gold light.

*We're all skeletons now.*

I hold my arms out to them and issue the command: "We will burn this city to the ground! Down! Down! Down to the ground!"

The answering howl overloads the already stressed thrum-collectors. They blow out one at a time, their hiss-and-fizzle the last thing anyone hears before the screams take their place.

# M

Vee unplugs the world, and the last thing I see is her swaying on her feet.

Then darkness. The pit goes haywire around me, and I throw a blind elbow just to give myself some space. There's an unpleasant crunch, probably more unpleasant for him than me.

A wayward burst of pyro goes off, and techs scramble around the stage.

*Fuck whoever's coming for her. Cram her full of applejack and send her out to perform? Gutless scumbags.*

I pull the set of Brights from my left pocket, wire and all, crank it up to maximum, and toss it at the two nearest greyfaces while I can still see. I hear the satisfying cry when it makes contact, but nothing else over the rising chaos of the pit. Hopping the barrier and tearing ass toward the stage, I leap up, sliding past footlights and fallen mic stands.

Another furious blast of pyro, farther upstage this time, and I see Vee, lying in a heap a few feet from me, hands clawing at the stage floor. I crawl over to her and pull her close. She's cold to the touch, and the stink of spoiled apples is all over her.

And yet . . . it's still her. This hauntingly lovely girl looking up at me. My heart pounds, blood rushing to my ears, and the chaos all around us has nothing to do with it. I'm dumbstruck, fumbling for words. "Vee, it's me. Micah. I'm Micah. From—"

"They're coming for you, love. Help me with this." She takes my hand and places it on the spot she was pawing at. There's a handle.

*A trapdoor. Brilliant.*

I wrench it open as a third flare of luminous phosphorous explodes from the stage, and I can see people rushing toward us. I hurl myself into the hole, hitting bottom quickly and reaching for Vee. She slips down into my arms like a rag doll, pulling the trapdoor shut behind her. I put her down before jumping up and flipping the lock on it.

*Won't hold for long, but every little bit helps.*

I grab Vee's hand, threading her biting-cold fingers through mine. We make tracks through the understage, slamming right into the back of the greyface stationed at the exit door. He whirls around, reaching for his sidearm. But I'm faster, pulling the other pair of Brights from my hoodie and tagging him in the neck.

He goes down twitching. I slap an adhesive patch from the medical supply depot under his chin. Vee looks at me, still dazed.

"Level-five sedative," I tell her. "Just in case."

She leans against me and breathes frost into what little air there is between us. "Micah—"

I kiss her, one stolen moment of bliss in this legendary clusterfuck, and wish desperately I could keep kissing her forever. But I pull back, my lips and hers sticking for a second, the cold bonding us together.

"Come on. I'll get you out of here."

I wrap an arm around her, and we run.

# CHAPTER NINE

## M

The power's still out. Vee clutches my hand tight as we dodge beams of approaching flashlights. With the emergency lights in the back corridors flickering, we stick to shadows and dark corners, racing scanners and guards alike.

I look back at Vee as we run. Even under siege by the applejack, she's hardly a damsel in distress. Her reaction time is slowed, but her instincts are sharp, her shaky muscles reinforced with inner resolve. Ferocity lurks right below the surface. In the midst of this insanity, I'm still a little awed by her.

We duck into a maintenance closet just in time to avoid a pair of shadows on the move. Their riot gear clicks with military efficiency as they pass the thin steel door.

*They must've had a few special-ops guys waiting just in case.*

The acidic stench of industrial cleanser dominates the tiny room. Vee huddles close, her shivers radiating cold in all directions. I pull His

Majesty's lighter from my pocket and spark it, casting the darkness aside with a gentle flickering of flame. Her eyelids are heavy, and her thigh-high boots might be the only thing keeping her upright.

Handing her the lighter, I pull the slim black case from my hoodie pocket and crack it open, revealing the silver injector and a single dose of Rivitocin. In the meager half-light, it looks like rosewater. "Vee, the applejack. It's killing you. Not in the slow-and-eventual drugs-are-bad way. In the serious-and-brutal raze-the-earth way. I have something that will help in the short term—"

"No more drugs." Her eyes are wild for a moment, but just a moment, as if the cold is stealing her fear along with everything else.

"Shh, shh, I know. Think of it as medicine." A brief pause. *How do I convince her?* "I need you to trust me."

"I do trust you." No hesitation, which speaks volumes after the way she's been manhandled tonight. She stiffens just a little, like she's bracing herself. "Do it."

Placing one hand on her cheek, I try to hold her attention. All the while, her lips are tantalizingly close. I suppress that thought and soldier onward. "This is gonna hit you fast, and it won't be pretty. But I've got you. Okay? I've got you."

She nods, her head lolling forward, then back.

*I'll take it.*

I press the injector to her neck and with the low hiss of a deflating tire, the soft pink liquid is in her system. I grab her, one arm around her lower back, the other under her arm and cradling the back of her head.

There's no way to prepare her. She starts shaking, vibrating in my arms as nerve endings fire like bottle rockets, muscles spasming at random. I wince as she bites my shoulder hard to keep from screaming.

It's the longest ten seconds of her life, I'd bet. It's a close runner-up to the longest ten of mine.

When the aftershocks finally subside, her skin is warmer, and there's some color beneath her china-white makeup. I step back as far as this closet will allow, and she stumbles. I catch her before she falls.

Vee leans against my shoulder as I open the door, just a sliver. The coast is clear, but she's in no condition to run now.

"You'll have to excuse my hands," I whisper, as I dip down and wrap my arms around her, boosting her over my shoulder. "You can be my lookout."

I pull open the door and make a break for it down the hall, as fast as my precious cargo will allow.

## V

I'm not sure what's worse: the world twisted upside down or my mind turning inside out. Whatever Micah shot into my neck builds a barrier between the applejack and my skitzy nanotech, walling off the killing cold, but it leaves my body at the mercy of the green-tinted poison.

By the time he's gone ten feet, the heat is building again, as steady as the rhythm of his sneakers hitting the concrete. Just like that first night at the Palace, edges sharpen and colors brighten. What little illumination there is in the hall flares in the space behind my eyes. The moment he steps out of the building, the chaos is like an explosion.

No lights anywhere; no emergency backups, not even a distant glow to indicate other districts might have survived the outage. The sky has burned to a crisp, leaving only star-embers to wink at us.

The grid is dead. I brought it to its knees with Micah's song, and my fans finished the job. Now every single one of those glorious little dead things is following my orders to burn Cyrene down, down, down. In the distance, the audience floods into the streets, crowds down the alleys, swarms the loading dock. They write on the walls of the

Dome with flames, break windows, throw debris into the path of the responding rescue vehicles. Greyfaces try to form a human barricade and are knocked aside within seconds.

*I'm burning, so we all burn.*

I raise my head in time to see the other Sugar Skulls hustled toward the limo by one of the special-ops teams. Jax pauses at the door of the car, equal parts taunted and tempted by the cries of the rabble-rousers.

*Damn. Now* two *riots I owe her.*

In stark contrast, Sasha's face is a study in terror, and she's got her hands raised to keep the world from crashing down on her head. Reaching out, Jax snags her around the waist and shoves her into the car before tossing a look of regret over her shoulder.

Not that she would get far, if she tried to join the fray. Damon is right behind Jax, barking orders and shouting into two phones at once. Even with the grid down, even in the midst of utter pandemonium, he's strong-arming everything under control and gaining the upper hand.

I shudder, willing Micah to turn away, to find a darker place to stand. *Even pitch-black shadows aren't enough to hide me from Damon . . .*

Heat licks over every square inch of me, and I want to tell Micah to put me down. To leave me here. To get the hell out while he still can. But I'm afraid he'll actually do it. Afraid of being without him now that we've finally latched on to each other, two people drowning in a sea of fucking anarchy.

I twist my hands in the back of his hoodie; for an answer, he clamps his arms down harder on my legs. Scanning the scene from left to right, he affords me a partial view of the fistfights, the improvised weapons, the flares of discharged Brights and shock batons.

Micah sucks in a breath. "Holy shit . . ."

# M

"It's like the end of the world out here," I mutter.

The Dome is a war zone, punctuated with overturned vans and skirmishes between fans and security. The emergency lights kick on, their grotesque orange glow creating small safe areas in the darkness.

The mob has fanned out in all directions, scattering greyfaces and guards as they try to corral and neutralize the rampaging horde, employing every nonlethal trick in their arsenal. It's the perfect cover, and I switch from "escape the building" mode to "make a hasty retreat," looking for anything that will get us moving faster.

Off to the right, down the only side street not clogged with screaming fans, someone scrambles in the direction of a parked motorcycle. *Perfect.*

I set Vee down gingerly, her legs a little wobbly but otherwise stable. A brush of her cheek rouses her attention. She already looks clearer than a few minutes ago, her eyes focusing on me with ease. I put one finger to my lips, then I bolt down the sidewalk, closing the gap between me and the shadow.

*Don't have much time. She'll be burning up soon.*

As the shadow hurriedly rifles through his pockets, I clamp a hand down on his shoulder, spinning him around. The moonlight hits his face just so, and I snarl. The bright red scratches are new, but otherwise it's the same face from the Palace, just a little less smug and a lot more surprised.

"Hello, Your Majesty—" My fist reacts before I've even finished, and I crack him across the jaw, the throbbing of my bare knuckles a fair tax to pay. My Brights are out soon after, and I bury them in his gut, crumpling him as the juice tops him off. He hits the asphalt in a well-dressed heap, and I check his pockets quickly, showing the tiniest advancement in my learning curve.

Keys materialize in my hand, and I punt him in the stomach. Just once, and not in the ribs, because *I'm* not a sadistic asshole.

I spin in place, ready to check on Vee, and she's right there, gearing up for a monster boot into His Majesty's ribs. I don't stop her. He obviously did something to deserve those scratches.

*Unbelievable. Scumbag manages to peddle his shit to the only two girls I've touched in a long while. Aren't there any other pushers in this town?*

I smack a sedative patch on his neck before we go. A night in the alley might do his attitude some good.

Straddling the bike, I let my weight settle on the seat, keys in the ignition, my hand finding the throttle. I remember plenty of nights spent ripping up the streets on Zane's glorified rocket. We'd all taken turns racing the devil.

*It was a lifetime ago, but hey—just like riding a bike, they say.*

I turn to Vee, and she takes my hand, slipping in front of me, facing me, almost glowing with the heat from the applejack. She hugs me tight, tucking her face against my neck, and locking her arms and legs around me.

Feeling her body against mine, it takes me a moment to remember how to breathe. *But she's right. If she was behind me and started to pass out, she'd fall. If she faced away from me, she could lean the wrong way and swamp us both. This way, if she starts to go, I'll know, and I can stop the bike.*

I run my hands along her back, hugging her in return, before flipping up the kickstand with my heel and lighting up the road.

We fly.

# V

After that, it's only wind. And Micah.

I cling to him, arms about his chest, legs wrapped around his waist. Tendrils of my hair stream over my shoulders, whipping him in the face. I'm afraid to let go long enough to catch them, ribbons on kite strings. The engine under us is a barely muffled roar, and the drug-heat is keeping pace with it, chasing me down narrow streets and narrower alleys. The night air on my bare, burning skin makes me want to howl to the moon. The tattered excuse for a skirt flutters away, a ghostly wisp of velvet swallowed up by the dark.

"Stay with me, Vee," he says. "Hold tight. If things start going black, if your blood feels like it's on fire, if you're going to let go, tell me and I'll stop. But otherwise, I need you to hold on tight. Lean with me. I've got you."

It becomes evident very quickly that Micah knows what he's doing. Every time he leans into a turn, he takes me with him just to the edge of falling. I can't hold him any tighter than I already am, and I'm biting my lower lip so hard that I taste blood. Forehead pressed to his neck, I try to concentrate on breathing without screaming. One count in, two counts out. *Laundry soap.* Two counts in, four counts out. *Clean sweat.* By the third inhalation, everything that I am has homed in on the scent of him, of sex, of his body responding to mine. Every fear forgotten.

I blame the applejack when I lick the side of his neck.

His response is a strained noise of protest that ripples through his chest. When I press my mouth to the space between his ear and his jaw . . . Well, I hear the groan that time.

"Take it easy, Vee, I need to concentrate!" He's shouting, but the words are torn from his mouth and tossed into the road behind us.

I should stop. That's the smart thing to do.

*Except we passed up every chance to do the smart thing back at the Dome.*

His eyes on the road, both hands on the grips, he's mine for the taking. So what if we're ripping through the dark streets, faster than the speed of light? Who cares if siren wails are chasing us? All of Cyrene could converge upon us at any second.

So I need to make every second count.

His cheeks and chin and neck are rough with light stubble. I rub my cheek against it, brush my lips over it. I swear I feel the heat burning through his shirt.

*His shirt. Is in my way.*

I can't exactly rip it off him this time, but I slide my hands under the fabric, up his back. I dig my fingernails into him when he takes the next corner.

"Vee—"

Hearing him use my name, my heart's the sun, and solar flares erupt through my chest. I'm pressed against Micah, as close as I could possibly get with our clothes still on, but it's still not close enough.

"Hurry," I tell him, except I'm not sure if I'm counting down to the moment I can get his pants off or the second my hummingbird heart will finally explode.

Finding a straightaway, he opens the throttle to full. Emergency lights flicker on, sporadic bursts of neon hurtling past us on either side as we blast through light and shadow. The grid whines to life all around us. The noose around our necks tightens just a bit.

And I want to taste his lips once more before we hang.

# M

I weave us through the obstacle course of downtown, abandoned vehicles dotting the road. With the grid down all over Cyrene, everything phantom-powered has stopped dead, and between them and the cars still running, we're practically slaloming to keep speed.

All the while, I feel her skin getting hotter by the minute. She's burning up, and the applejack's only partly to blame.

I want her just as much. Her touch, her presence instantly revises my definition of *desirable*. Even as she creeps ever closer to boiling up inside, she draws me in. Magnetic and intoxicating. My muscles tense, coiled like a spring as I muster every ounce of focus to keep us on the road.

Her body pressed tight to mine, ringlets of black hair flowing in the wind, her lips on my neck and hands grasping, fresh memories bubble to the surface. Remembering a certain girl with a shirt made of temptation and promises, the confidence of a goddess, and a body that demanded obedience.

And then she bites my neck.

I moan softly in her ear, my resolve weakening by the second. Thoughts of Vee and the girl from the Palace swirl in my head, the coincidences rattling my brain.

We blast through the streets like a meteor. *Almost home. Almost safe.* I make some quick calculations: how many doses of the garbage she probably had, how long since the Rivitocin shut down her nanotech, how long before the heat peaks and she crashes.

*We're cutting it close, we're cutting it really fucking close.*

Finally, the bridge appears in the distance, and I gun it, sure that we're leaving flames behind us in the road, the melted slag of asphalt bubbling in our wake.

Vee grabs the back of my head and plants one on me. Hard. It's passion and terror and attraction and desperation all at once. Her lips are like lava against mine, the air around us almost shimmering with heat. I kiss her back, giving her all of me, sacrificing breath and focus and even our getaway just to share this with her.

She kisses me, and it feels like good-bye.

Our lips part, and we both gasp for air. The Arkcell looms before us, and I cut the throttle and kill the engine, letting our momentum carry us down the little access road leading underneath the bridge.

I just hope we're not too late.

# V

Micah manages to get both of us off the bike without dropping it or me or falling himself. I immediately cover his mouth with my own, so his words come through piecemeal.

"Vee . . . I've . . ." I bite him again and he stumbles. *"Shit . . ."* He tears his lips from mine; it's like ripping a piece of paper in half. "I've got to put you down."

My response is something between a snarl and a whimper, but I feel cold concrete against my ass a few seconds later. Then he's dragging my hands off his neck, his chest, pulling them away from his hair, his shirt, prying my legs apart but only because he's determined to leave me here . . . alone . . . in the dark. He has my face in his hands, his fingers measuring the pulse in the curve of my neck, but there's nothing left to feel; it's all one continuous stream of heat.

"Fuck, just hold on," Micah says, but he might as well be shouting over the top of the train barreling down on me.

He vanishes from sight, and I curl up on my side and start to shake. There's a tiny rock under my cheek, one sharp point doing its damnedest to pierce my skin. I'd turn my head, but then I wouldn't be able to watch the grid coming back online, district by district. Beyond the bridge, lights climb up the tower buildings one story at a time, like champagne flutes filled to overflowing. I can't see the top of the Carlisle from here, but I can easily imagine the moment it flares with brilliant blue-white welcome. It's a dragon uncoiling as I die, pierced by poisoned claws, smothered in ash, hollowed out by the applejack. The sky is hazy with smoke, the world a hookah den, everyone choking on strawberry cough.

Three minutes, maybe four before the power reaches into this dark space with electric fingers.

I should be cold now that Micah's gone, but this shallow grave of concrete and gravel radiates my body heat back to me. I close my eyes and try to remember the taste of anything but apples. No one would pick that as a last supper, not that I had any choice. Trying to count back, to remember how many sticky green tabs Adonis fed me over the last twenty-four hours . . .

I lose track when I hit double digits.

The applejack isn't playing nice with whatever Micah shot into me like liquid lightning. The wall between the drugs and my nanotech crumbles, melts; everything inside me is molten, shifting. I can feel the exact second when the applejack taints the last resisting cell. Then even the ability to form a coherent thought slips out of my grasp.

*Today is the day of the dead.*

*I don't have ancestors, just the past versions of me.*

*So today is my day. I* am *the dead.*

The only thing holding me together now is my skin. There's nothing inside me left to burn; I'm a shooting star turned black hole. Some tiny, utterly insignificant version of myself clings to life, clawing at the ledge.

My lips part. One breath left in me. *Do I call for help? Do I call to him?*

The song was right. I *am* a pretty little dead thing. And the dead don't share their secrets.

# M

*Hold on, Vee.*

I scramble up the stone face and iron supports of the bridge in record time, cursing myself all the way. *So fucking stupid! If I'd just done it yesterday, she wouldn't be lying out there, vulnerable as a snowball in summer.*

Inside the warren, I kick a sheet of plywood that was leaning against the wall as I pass, letting it settle on the floor with a *whumph*, pushing the air beneath it out of the way. I grab the pulley and rope from my storage closet and tie the rope to the platform.

Once the pulley's hung, the platform plummets toward Vee, landing a few feet from her. I hurriedly climb down after it, before pulling her into my arms and onto the plywood. She's unconscious, barely breathing. *Oh, Vee, hold on, please hold on.*

I loop her wrists into the rope so she won't fall, then race up the bridge, tearing open my hand again as I clamber back to the top. Grabbing the rope coiled on the floor, I wrap it once around my wrist and jump.

Freefalling for just a second, I see buildings light up like paper lanterns, then the platform launches past me, carrying Vee up to the warren. The knot catches in the pulley and the rope tenses, halting my plunge a few feet from the rocks below. My hands move quickly, aching as I tie the rope off to a bent piece of rebar at the foot of the bridge and claw up the bridge's supports a third time.

I pull Vee inside and close up the tarp behind me, hoping against hope that we managed it all before the grid blazed back to life under the Arkcell. If we beat the odds, then the copper wiring along the walls will prevent them from tracking Vee's nanotech signature between doses of Rivitocin.

*If not . . . we gave it one hell of a shot.*

Cradling her in my arms, I set her down on the bed, putting one ear to her chest. She's still burning up. Too hot for just the applejack. The Rivitocin's worn off, and the nanotech is rallying. Rallying and killing her.

I grab my first-aid kit from the storage vault and slam it down beside the bed, flipping it open and grabbing another vial of rose-colored fluid. Pressing the injector to her neck, I dose Vee again, letting the applejack run its course without nanotech interference.

The lesser of two evils right now.

My ear to her lips, I feel the barest wisps of breath, and I heave a grateful sigh. *First battle of many. Won.*

I steal a moment to softly brush her cheek. *You poor gorgeous girl. I tried to warn you. I tried.*

I shed my hoodie and toss it into the corner before gathering my supplies. First things first: gotta get her temperature down. Her body's still riding the applejack high, hot as the sun and as prone to flare-ups; she's taken too much in too short a time. If she doesn't burn up from the overdose, soon enough she's going to crash, turning to ice again.

*I've got you, Vee. I've got you.*

# CHAPTER TEN

## V

Concrete and plywood fit together like puzzle pieces. Swathes of copper wiring around and overhead. Not on the ground anymore, but whatever I'm on creaks when I curl up in a ball and do my best to die. Ice-cold patches punch holes through the burning bullshit, adding to the agony.

Every performer can sense when it's time to clear the goddamn stage. I can feel the lights dimming. The curtains shutting . . .

Except Micah's right there with me, refusing to let me go. I can sense him, a blur of black against the metal grid surrounding us. Can feel his hands on me when he checks my pulse and shoots me full of the next dose of mind-searing reality. Wrapping my fingers in his shirt, I try to tell him to leave me the hell alone, but all I can manage is his name before the spasms kick in and I try to crawl out of my own skin.

*This isn't going to be pretty.*

Sweat-slick, my skin reeks of the drugs working their way through my system. Concentrated, oily evil oozes out of me, one second at a time. And each second lasts sixty, a minute spirals out like an hour.

*An actual hour of this is going to fucking kill me.*

The inside of my mouth is so dry that my tongue might as well be sand, but I don't have the words to ask for water, and my stomach clenches at the idea of drinking anything. Through the haze, I hear Micah telling me something, but the words are buried in concrete before they ever reach my ears.

# M

I'm untying the rope from the plywood and pulley when she starts coming around.

I try to make her comfortable. Gel-pack adhesives on her neck and chest to cool her down, a wet compress on her forehead. We'll try some water in a few minutes to stave off dehydration.

The stink of cider is everywhere. I'm saturated in it from the frantic ride over here, and she's sweating that vile shit from every pore. I force my gorge down and follow it with a protein bar just to put something into my stomach.

Vee writhes on the bed like an egg on a hot sidewalk, and I try to tell her what's happening, but I know only bits and pieces get through.

Finally, I cup her face with my hands—the black-and-white paint mostly wiped from one cheek—and steal her attention for a moment.

"Vee, listen. I have to go. If I don't ditch that bike soon, they'll trace it right back here, and then it's Game Over. I don't want to leave you like this, but I have to."

I put a bottle of cold water and an electrolyte pack atop the bin next to her, my ribs aching as I crouch down. "Stay put. I'll be back in a flash."

She looks at me for a moment, wrung out and haggard, in no condition to fend for herself, then gives me a tiny nod.

*Fuck. Great plan. Leave the girl drug-addled, alone, and thirty feet off the ground while you try to cover your tracks.*

I slip my hoodie back on, feeling the smear of some of her makeup on my neck. Tossing the rope to the ground, I climb down after it, unknot it from the rebar, and tuck everything behind some loose rocks for retrieval later.

The city's glowing again, the hum embracing me with gleeful smugness. *I'm baaaaack,* it murmurs.

I push His Majesty's bike up the hill and onto the road before starting it. Pressure builds behind my eyes as I ponder the variables: how long before someone finds him and removes the sedative patch, stirring him back to consciousness; how long before the scumbag activates whatever tracking tech he's got on this thing; how long before he and the greyfaces swoop down on me.

*Gotta ditch the bike far enough to keep suspicion away from the bridge, but close enough to make decent time coming back.*

I rip down the streets of Cyrene. A dozen blocks away, on the edge of the Odeaglow, I stop the bike and pull up my hood. There's a guy slumped on the stoop of an apartment building, lit up on something low-end like riprap. Just pleasantly buzzed and letting the world drift by.

I stroll up to him, tense muscles playing casual by practice and sheer force of will. "Hey, you live here?" *Any question will do, really.*

"Yeah, man. I'm like the king of this castle. Cool?"

"Cool. Well, congratulations. You just won yourself a free crotchrocket." I toss him the keys and take off down the street, my footfalls echoing as he yells in reply, "Thanks, man! The kingdom rejoices!"

*From His Majesty to his majesty.* I approve of the synchronicity as I sprint down the side streets, taking to the fire escapes and up-high hideaways, trying to set a new land-speed record. I've already left her alone too long.

# V

I try to count the minutes that Micah's gone, but I'm shaking so hard now that I can't do anything except try to keep my teeth from shattering against each other.

At the medcenter, they would have sedated me. Let me spend three or four days looped out of my gourd on extremely high levels of detoxifying drugs and all kinds of take-the-pain-away beauties. Then there would have been purification baths, scented oil, hot rocks, candles, trance music, green smoothies full of vitamins and minerals and magic fucking unicorn sparkles . . .

*I don't know where the hell I am right now, but this is as far from a spa as it gets.*

But there's water and an unflavored electrolyte pack nearby. My brain doesn't want either one, but my body does. With more effort than it would take to bench-press a car over my head, I sit up, reach for the pack, tear the seals off. I only manage a sip before I gag.

Slumping back against the wall, I pull my legs up and press my forehead to my knees. The boning in the corset digs into me in a dozen places, constricting, Damon's grip on me even now.

It doesn't matter if this place is at the end of the universe, he'll still be looking. Have his goon squad patrolling the streets. Waiting for my nanotech to ping on his phone, like I'm a damn incoming text message. Just another thing to check off his to-do list.

I just want my own room, my own bed, and Little Dead Thing curled up in my lap. How I can miss that stupid-ugly piece of shit cat at a moment like this makes me want to laugh and cry at the same time.

The tears burn, but I figure it's just another way to get the goddamn drugs out of my system, so I let them fall.

# M

Two rides on a Busa wannabe and I'm ruined. All the freerunning in the world can't make you that fast.

Charging down Ahriman Street, I spot security SUVs patrolling the bridge. Looks like a regular sweep, but I don't hold my breath. Especially with my ribs throbbing like this. Slowing to a stop, I keep my distance, watching the greyfaces escort inspectors to every glass-globe in sight. *Must be double-checking the grid after the blackout.*

But there are more than a dozen globes within spitting distance of the Arkcell and the neighboring roadways. My eyes scan up and down the street, looking for any gaps in their coverage. For now, the bridge is sewn up tight. *I can't get back to Vee from here.*

But they did miss something: the river.

I sprint four blocks, then climb down the embankment on Hallmark and dive into the water. The warm current carries me downstream, past the vans and SUVs, past the armored lackeys, and right up to the shore next to the bridge supports.

Thankfully, this isn't your average dirtbag-filthy city river. With four treatment areas in Cyrene, this water's cleaner than most of the alcoves at the Palace.

No one's around to see me crawl out of the water. I grab the rope and slip it over one shoulder before scaling the iron and stonework until, at last, I'm sopping wet but home.

Vee looks up, tears streaming down her face. She's curled up in a miserable ball against the wall, and I'm across the floor in two steps, crouching beside her. *I know the detox is bad, really bad, but is there something else? Is she hurt? Did I miss it?* I surreptitiously give her a once-over, looking for blood or bruising or anything amiss, but other than a few scratches on her neck that I've already tended to, there's no sign of any injury.

Taking her hand gently, I let her cry it out, knowing any of a thousand reasons could've sparked this, and hoping there's something I can do. I just sit with her silently until the tears subside. She pulls her hand from mine and rubs her face, leaving streaks across her cheeks.

I replace her cold compress with a fresh one, using the moisture left in the old one to begin removing her smeared makeup. Alabaster fades to pink under my care, and soon, the goth china doll is washed away, leaving the real Vee behind. Flaws, beauty, and all.

I touch her cheek, the wheels of coincidence finally clicking into place. *The black curls. The applejack. She called me "love" too.*

I smile despite myself. *Of course it's her.* The voice. The girl. The alcove. It was always Her.

# V

He's looking at me, through me, just like he did that first night at Hellcat Maggie's.

*The face paint. He wiped enough of it off to see who I am.*

I avert my face for a second, sticking a finger into each eye long enough to ditch the black-light contacts. My nose is still running—no one could ever accuse me of being a pretty crier—and I wish more than anything that he would speak first. But I'm the one who pulled this party trick on him, so I get to start.

"I should have said something." I look down at my hands, which are covered in snot and makeup and applejack sweat. If my face looks as bad as my hands, he's probably wishing he left me onstage at the Dome for Damon and Adonis to clean up. "That night at the club."

"Why didn't you?" Micah sounds a little confused that I shared my body but wouldn't share my name.

"I didn't get the chance before you bailed." Still humiliating, remembering how he bolted out of that alcove.

He takes a moment before responding. "I'm sorry, I really am. It was the applejack. I tasted it on you, and just lost it. That vile shit . . . I had to get rid of it. Get my hands on the dealer, stop it from hurting anyone else. Couldn't let it fuck you up. I liked—*like* you, am drawn to you, even not *knowing* it was you. I couldn't let it get you."

Thinking about the metric shit-ton of drugs screaming through me, I can't help blurting out, "You did a great job with that." The moment the words slam into him, I wish I hadn't said it.

Micah stands up, stepping away for a second. A long second. His sudden stillness raises the tiny hairs on the back of my neck before he simply says, "I know. I'm sorry."

*He just risked his life to save your sorry ass, and you're going to give him shit for not doing better? Nice, Vee.* "I should be the one apologizing, not you. God. You didn't ask for any of this. You didn't need the world crashing down on your head because of me." Thinking about it, about everything, I suddenly can't breathe. Reaching behind me, I give the white corset strings a tug. The whole thing is soaked with sweat, reeking with chemical afterburn. Damon double-knotted the fucking thing, and I'm trapped in it, just like a marriage, for better or for worse. "I need you . . . to . . . Fuck, just get this goddamn thing off me."

Micah's already in motion, swinging open the wide iron door and grabbing something off a shelf. He slips a small serrated knife from its protective sheath; the silver glint of it cuts loose something in my hindbrain, and I can feel metal sliding against my skin. Thin ribbons of blood crisscross my arms, my chest. *Stop fucking moving. You knew this was coming. Someone hold her the fuck down.*

I press my hands to either side of my head, almost recognizing the voices as I sink deeper in that pool. "Don't touch me."

"Vee?"

"Please . . ." Just the one word, plea and prayer both, because someone is there, turning my face toward his—

"Vee." A soft shake, so much softer than I remember. "I need you to look at me."

I don't want to, but I have to, before that knife slides over me again. Even when my eyes open, it takes a moment to realize where I am . . .

. . . who I'm with . . .

. . . and that I'm safe.

A shudder accompanies my next exhalation, and I lean forward. Without a word, Micah slices through the knot and half the corset strings. He pulls the rest of the laces free as I scramble out of my shiny white straitjacket. Air hits my skin, and everything is goose bumps. The livid red marks on my body tell the story of what we've been through tonight, but I can finally pull in a real breath. Filling my lungs to capacity, I exhale and push against the memories as hard as I can.

*That was someone else. A different Vee.* It's feeble, but all I've got right now.

I want to chuck the corset as far away from me as I can, but it's all I have by way of coverage. Weird, to feel like a giant prude when Micah has a Sugar Skulls promo poster hanging on the door, every bit of me available to his eyes. Never mind how many times I've run mostly naked from the dressing areas to the stage while three or four sets of hands rip off costumes and put on new ones.

My gaze slides down to the knife in his hands, which he promptly sheathes and returns to its spot. Crossing the room and rummaging through a trunk, he comes out with a T-shirt and nylon track shorts, and tosses them to me.

"Here. Might make you a little more comfortable." And then he turns his back to me, averting his eyes.

*Is he for real?*

"That's almost adorable," I mutter, pulling the clothes on as fast as possible.

"Didn't want something else to apologize for."

"Yeah, well, I probably owe you one, since you only went after Adonis because he gave me the applejack. He said . . ." I trail off, heat flaring inside me that has nothing to do with the drugs.

*Nice, Vee. Bring up the pillow talk you had. Want to tell him about the pancakes, too?*

Micah's shoulders go tense as he balls up his fists. "'He said?' Is that why he was at the Dome tonight? Because he's your scumbag 'jack-dealing cheapshot artist?"

"He isn't *my* anything." The accusation makes me sick to my stomach. When I close my eyes I can still feel Adonis's hands cramming another tab into my mouth whether I want it or not. "Damon brought him in."

Micah rocks slowly from one foot to the other. "Damon's the suit, I take it."

"Stuffed shirt," I say, eyes closing. "And he's going to track us down."

"Not here." With his back to me, Micah gestures to the copper grid all around us. "It's a poor man's Faraday cage. Blocks electromagnetic signals. It'll keep anything he's got from finding your nanotech here." Some pride creeps into his voice, despite the lingering resentment.

"That's . . . good to hear." I wish I could appreciate it more, except it's all sounding like a lot of blah-blah-blah techno-jargon, like when Sasha gets wound up over a new piece of equipment. Everything feels heavier, and my words are more slurred than I'd expected.

*Something's off. Way off.*

He finally turns around, and all the color drains from his face. He's at my side again instantly, Dr. Micah replacing the hurt-and-angry hero.

He places his hand against my forehead. "Take off all the cold packs. The fever peaked. You're gonna crash."

"You're quite the fortune-teller." Everything he said was true. I just didn't realize it would be like running full tilt into a brick wall. I don't even manage to get the first of the packs off before I realize it's a lost cause.

# M

*Fucking applejack.* I kept her from OD'ing by fire, and now she's smashing into a wall of icy withdrawal. I pull down the neck of her shirt and rip the remaining gel-pack from her collarbone. *Last thing she needs is more cold.* I lay her on the cot, shoving what's left of her outfit aside. She's unresponsive.

"Vee? Vee! It's going to be okay. I promise."

*Bedside manner first. Never be mean to the patient. Textbook.*

First, I grab an old-school syringe and load it up from the electrolyte pack. I swab her arm with the rubbing alcohol and give her the shot. Something to help her fight it off. Load up a syringe and repeat. She'll need as much as she can take. Withdrawal is a bitch on wheels. I check her pulse, and she swats my hand away. Pretty sure it was unintentional. Not 100 percent sure, though. I put one ear to her chest. Her heart's pounding, just like at the Palace.

*Focus, Micah.*

The next hour passes as I check her vitals, load her up with vitamins, get her to sip water when she's coherent enough to raise her head. It's a hit-or-miss procedure. She misses the bucket and hits me twice with the water and vitamins on the way back up, but her temperature drops three degrees from the applejack peak.

I hold off on the next dose of Rivitocin as long as possible, hoping she can grab some meager rest in the meantime. But I can't let the nanotech reassert itself until the applejack is out of her system, otherwise all this was for nothing. Loading up the injector, I press it to her neck and dose her. The tremors start instantly, and her body convulses in my arms.

*She's gonna hate somebody before all this is done. Hope it's not me.*

"God fucking dammit" is just the beginning of the stream of curses coming out of her. She grinds her face into the front of my shirt, so half of them are lost to my chest, but their meaning is pretty clear.

"Hey. I know this sucks—"

"No, you fucking do not know." With my sleeves still bunched up in her hands, she pulls back far enough for me to see that there's a trickle of blood working its way out of her nose.

"You need to shut up and stay hydrated." *I do* not *want to do this right now.* "And, for the record, this is a lot better than the alternative. So listen to me and drink the goddamn water."

I point the bottle at her face, and she begrudgingly snatches it from my hand, her hand still trembling. "Go fuck yourself, right off a fucking bridge." At least she's aware enough to drink it slowly.

*I know it's the drugs. I know it's* mostly *the drugs.* "Soon as we're done here, I'll get right on it." *Bedside manner, my ass.*

When her core temperature starts dropping, I grab a heavy blanket and bundle her up as best I can, like a suffering little bitchy burrito. It's hours before I can spare a minute to change out of the still-damp jeans and shirt I wore to the concert. My ribs throb from four days of abuse, and stripping away my bandages and used-up gel-packs is one more aching reminder.

We burn through my electrolyte shots and a lot more water, plenty of which comes back with a vengeance. We use up the Rivitocin as well, each shot rousing Vee in worse spirits than the last. She goes through three one-use toothbrushes, the kind that come preloaded with toothpaste, and throws the third one at my head when she's done with it. Face against my pillow, she spews vitriol until unconsciousness takes her once more.

In the resulting quiet, I realize we've been left totally alone. No sirens, no special-ops thugs. The Faraday cage is working like a charm. *I mean, I knew it would, obviously . . . But confirmation is still a pretty good feeling.*

And then, there's nothing more to be done for her, and I just sit beside her, praying it's been enough.

# V

When I wake up, I'm coiled in Micah's lap like Little Dead Thing. I feel about the same as that cat usually looks. I don't stretch. I don't move.

I don't want to wake him up.

He's out cold, head resting against the wall and mouth hanging ajar. Dark shadows carve out spaces under his eyes, and he snores a bit with every breath. I don't know how long either of us has been sleeping, but I have very clear memories of every horrible thing I said to him as the drugs worked their way through my system.

*God, Vee. You're lucky he didn't punt you out the door.*

I'm twisted up in the borrowed clothes, in the blanket he used to swaddle me, but it doesn't take much to ease a hand out, to push some of that blond hair away from his face. It's the first time I've seen him—really *seen* him—without club lighting or stage lighting or emergency lighting painting his features with unnatural color.

Somehow, for the first time since all this started, he's real to me.

I wait a moment to see if he jumps up like a ninja; I've seen him move, and it wouldn't surprise me if he rocketed off the bed and across the room in one leap. But exhaustion trumps everything else, because his breathing barely hitches before the soft snoring resumes.

*Good.*

It gives me the chance to stare at him without having to worry about how I look or where we are or what the fuck comes next. Hard to concentrate, when he's got one arm under me, and the other rests on my rib cage. His unbandaged hand is rough with calluses, and yet he'd been so gentle every time he'd touched me.

I can't resist running a finger along the inside of his palm; but even that tiny movement is like being skinned alive. I can feel *everything*, now that the applejack is out of my system. The world moves around me. Through me. Muscles are sore, and my bones are glass, but I'm not shattered. Not broken.

*Not yet, anyway. If Damon gets his hands on me, all bets are off.*

Micah said we were safe. I vaguely remember an explanation about the insane amount of copper crisscrossing around us. I hope he's right. I hope he's not sorry he brought me here.

It's odd, to feel hopeful about anything just now. For days, all I'd secretly hoped was that I would see him again. Have the chance to say something to him. And now he's here. I'm here.

And I don't have the right words, even if he was awake to hear them.

For once, I'm not trying to sneak out of the bed without getting caught. This time, I'm the one wearing the borrowed clothes. This is all new territory, at least for me. Looking up at Micah, at his shirt, I know exactly where Bryn's name is tattooed.

*Was she here, with you? She didn't look like a spitting-and-swearing kind of girl. So what the fuck are you doing getting tangled up with me?*

As though ready to answer that question, his eyes flicker open. Blue. Piercing blue, right through the heart of me. I should sit up. Put some space between us. But I'm only looking up at him and trying to remember which muscles it takes to smile. "Morning . . . I think."

"Probably." He pulls his arm from under my back, retreating, then rubbing the sleep from his eyes like a mountain giant waking from a thousand-year nap. There's gravel in his voice, too, which does unexpected things to my pulse. "How are you feeling?"

Hard to tell if that last bit is politeness or genuine concern. It's certainly an invitation to move off him, to assess my various bruises and scrapes, to escape his steady blue gaze.

If I sit up, if I pull away, he'll do the same.

And I'm not ready for that yet.

# M

She swallows hard before answering, "I'm fine. And sorry. I mean . . . I'm sorry about everything. Every single thing I said." Her voice lowers a notch before she adds, "And I'm really fucking terrible at apologies, so take that for what it's worth."

*She's okay. Push away the bitchiness and the cruelty and every outburst. Be grateful. She's okay.*

*Better than okay. She's alive, in your arms. Smiling. Lips begging to be kissed again, and for the first time. Vee.*

I run my fingers through tousled ringlets, rough skin occasionally snagging on her silken hair, my gaze dancing across her face.

"Accepted." And I pull her closer, letting her body slide against mine, squeezing her tight, her head nestling on my shoulder.

"Whatever you do, don't let me go," she tells the hollow spot at the base of my throat.

Closing my eyes, I stroke her neck with two fingers, just below her ear. "You think I went through all that just to kick you out when you're okay?" I pause, trying to find the words. "I'm so glad you're all right. You don't even know how much."

"You're crazy, you know that?" She's got her mouth pressed to my neck now, so the words are half spoken and half kissed. "I never expected to look down and see you standing right there."

"To be fair, I asked your poster if I was crazy to try that. But you didn't dissuade me."

"Not surprising." She glances at the mostly naked and glammed-up version of herself hanging on my door. "The girl in that picture doesn't give two shits about anyone."

I tuck one hand under her chin, lifting it so our eyes meet again. "The girl in that picture kicked a guy in the ribs, a guy who did the same to me a few nights before. I doubt that's a coincidence. The girl in the picture tossed the city's power grid into a meat grinder to save me." Our lips almost brush as I speak.

"I would do it again, too. Without hesitating." Her chin tilts up so that our mouths graze, then the whisper breaks into a smile. "Except I'd kick Adonis again. In the junk."

I laugh, pulling back ever so slightly. *Kiss her. Kiss her.* Every fiber, every instinct . . . hell, even Rational Mind is chanting it. "Vee, I—"

"Don't," is all she says before her lips find mine.

Fireworks go off in my brain. We're back in the alcove in an instant, stealing gasps for air between fervent kisses, desperate to keep the other right here, ours, for as long as we can.

We slide down onto the cot together, lips locked and ravenous, bodies close. Achingly, tantalizingly close. I try to be gentle with her, rolling her onto her back and pressing against her, letting her hair splay out around her. A goddess, reborn.

Vee's having none of the gentleness. Her hands run up my shirt. Her nails carve burning trails down my back. I slip my arms under her, burying my fingers in that untamed mane of hair, pulling it. She slowly comes undone beneath me, moaning softly, tilting her head back and offering her neck to me.

I kiss along her jawline, stopping to tease her with cool breaths along the glistening skin. Her body arches against me. An invitation. I inhale at the spot where her neck meets her shoulder, breathing in the musk of sweat with lingering wisps of something fruity, all those electrolytes suffusing her skin.

And she tastes better than she smells, if that's possible.

Impatient, she tugs at my undershirt and I lift my arms, my lips barely leaving her neck as the fabric flies past. Her hands roam possessively over my chest, my shoulders, my upper arms, and she licks me once, twice, before biting my neck. *Fuck me.* Her teeth graze my skin the next time. It's like she's doing her best to leave marks on me.

I wrap my hands in her shirt and pull it off to one side, exposing collarbone, shoulder, the top of her arm. When I return the favor and let my teeth scrape over her skin, she makes a throaty noise. Then she's sitting up, pushing me over, climbing on top of me. Her arched back is more than an invitation to slide my hands over her taut skin. Not waiting for me to undress her, she grabs the bottom of the shirt, whips it off, and tosses it aside. She rests her palms on my chest, her right hand covering my tattoo.

My eyes explore her, and she rolls her hips slowly against me, teasing or savoring, I'm not sure. She moves forward until her chest is pressed against mine, hotter than anything the applejack could offer. Our lips reunite, hungry. Her hair drapes down over us, curtaining our faces, blocking out the world.

It's just the two of us, finally giving in.

My hands roam her back, stroking along her spine and trying to banish the memories of long nights in that corset. I trace fingertip trails along her bare skin, mapping the geography of her body, rises and valleys, mentally marking every spot that elicits a gasp. Lips wander with abandon, my kisses fluttering across her collarbone and chest, tongue trailing over sensitive skin, swirling and lapping and reveling in every inch of her.

Vee's hands trace and tease the waistband of my pants, before a button and zipper undone bring us ever closer. Her body slides down the length of my own as she shimmies my jeans off and drops them aside. Her shorts join the pile seconds later. She finds her way back into my lap, promises made with every brush of a hand.

She presses her forehead to mine with a soft sigh. When her hands find my chest once more, I gasp, my ribs still tender, and she leans down to whisper, "Tell me if I'm hurting you."

Pulling her to me, I shake my head. "No, let me. I've got you, remember?" I roll us over and slide into her. Vee's arms and legs wrap tight around me, and the tiny noise she makes is just for me. My lips are against her ear, every breath and moan for her, only her.

# CHAPTER ELEVEN

## V

It isn't until later . . . much later . . . maybe three rounds later . . . that I finally understand what it means to be beyond the grid's grasp. Every spark, every movement, every breath stays with us, generating more heat, more energy. There's nothing there to collect it, to channel it into wires, to funnel it away.

It's ours, only ours.

Even resting with my head against Micah's shoulder, I can't keep my hands off him, and it shows. He's got scratches down his back and arms, splotchy bite-bruises across his chest, and an epic hickey on the side of his neck. I'd apologize, but we've each got our calling cards, and he gave as good as he got. My scalp is still a little tingly. *Funny, but I never would have taken him for a hair-puller.* He's got his fingers wound through it now, like he figures that's the best way of getting me to stay put.

*How long have you been alone, Micah?*

But I'm not going anywhere. The moment I step outside, Damon's going to be there to clip my wings. I thought getting away from him, from all of it, would mean I was finally free.

As far as we ran, I just ended up in another cage.

Sitting up far enough to rest my chin on his chest, I trace over the marks I've left on Micah. Even the worst of them will fade in a few days.

*Temporary. It's all temporary.*

Not like the name on his chest, a forever-mark. I don't touch it. Don't want to look at it.

*You can't start off asking him about Bryn. Pick something else. Pick* anything *else.*

"How'd you end up here?" Before he mistakes my meaning, I hasten to add, "In Cyrene, I mean."

"Oh, that's not much of a story." Micah looks down at me, stroking my cheek and smiling softly. "Small town just outside Seattle. Big family, kids all over the place at all hours, you know? Got into the usual trouble with my brothers and sisters and at school, but otherwise, pretty standard childhood. Mom worked insane hours as a nurse, trusting us to keep an eye on each other. I worked a lot of nights and weekends with my dad. He was a repairman, did odd jobs all over town."

It's not possible to move any closer, or I would. "So why not stay and help out?"

He looks away as he starts sorting through the memories. "I started to realize the stress having so many kids was putting on the family. Even though it was years off, I knew college was expensive. We didn't have the money for that. So I put all my energy into applying for a spot in Cyrene. I'd seen the flyers, all kinds of promises. Sign a contract, do a few years' service generating thrum for the city, and bam, job placement when my term's up and no cost to the family. There was no reason *not* to."

*Everyone else is fighting to get into Cyrene to party, and he was thinking three steps ahead of that. Just like he always seems to be.* "Was it hard, leaving?"

"To be honest, I doubt I was missed," he says. "One less mouth to feed. And there was no shortage of hands to help Dad out."

There's a wistful look about him; I can't tell if it's nostalgia, regret, or some combination of the two. I run my hand up and down his chest, trying to remind him I'm here, to distract him from melancholy thoughts. Preoccupied, he kisses my forehead, responding to my touch without thinking.

"I met Trav during the nanotech install. It was the first time either of us had been on our own, so we bonded pretty quickly as a survival instinct. Then in orientation, we met Bryn and Zane and Rina. Pretty soon we were inseparable. Five against the world."

Leaning over, he reaches into the small bin beside the bed, pulling out a photo, framed and everything. Paper, not digital. Old school. Micah holds it so I can see. They're clustered together in an alcove. All smiles. He points to each in turn.

"Zane. Our speedfreak. Rina loved speed, and Zane loved Rina, so pretty soon, Zane was all about moving fast.

"Rina. Our ambassador. She knew everybody, she could get us into anywhere. She was elegant and everyday, you know? Everybody loved her.

"Trav. Our science whiz. Most anything you needed, he could find it or jury-rig it. He would've loved what I pulled at the Dome . . . We used to run together, made this whole city our playground." The longer Micah talks, the rougher his voice gets. And the only one left is the one I need to know about.

"Bryn." The silence drops like an anvil before he rallies and continues. "Our flame. She drew us like moths. She . . . she . . ." He finally falters, and oh my god, the crack in his voice about breaks me.

"Everyone loved Rina. But you loved Bryn," I say.

I feel him nod his head, and he gasps for breath. "Trav, too. We both. Loved her."

*He can't say it. He can't say, "I loved her."*

I started this shitstorm of emotion for him, and I'm going to have to finish it. Like cauterizing a wound. "The applejack killed her, didn't it?"

"It killed all of us. I just didn't know when to go." He stares at the photo. Remembering. Suffering.

"Is that why you know so much about how applejack works?"

Micah nods. "I started researching it as soon as I was feeling better. Pharma isn't really my strong suit, but I tried to learn everything about the drug. It's how I knew about the Rivitocin."

*Shit. He thinks he could have saved her.* Should *have saved her.*

I grab his face in both my hands. Force his eyes to meet mine. "You saved *me*."

A breath. A moment. "Because I couldn't save them. Couldn't save her. Never would've known any of it." He gets up, and cold rushes in to fill the gap.

It's a shock, after hours and hours together. I pull up the blanket, wrapping myself in it. It's a poor replacement for him. "Micah, come back to bed. Please . . ."

I might as well have not said anything, because he steps toward the opposite wall, putting distance between us, distance between him and that photo.

"They were waiting for me in an alcove at Solfetara's, that little spot on Jaster? Nobody goes there anymore—bad vibes, I've heard—but it was a primo club back then. Anyway, I was the last one there. I'd promised everyone a big surprise. Something special. Something new.

"You know how it is. Drugs don't hit as hard after a while, even with the nanotech scrubbing you clean every night. Blasting up and down the city on Zane's bike, high on riprap and adrenaline, it seemed like we'd tried *everything*. Then we started combining Cyrene-approved stuff for kicks. Trav was an amateur street chemist, always trying to improve whatever Rina got a hold of. That tided us over for a while . . .

"But then we heard about a new designer street drug. An illegal drug in a city full of legal ones? We *had* to try that. It became a competition, a one-item scavenger hunt across the city. I managed to track it down first."

*Oh, Micah. It was* you.

"Bryn and Trav were kissing when I walked into the alcove." There's no jealousy or possessiveness in his voice, just measured concentration as he stands there, arms closed around himself. "I think she loved both of us and never wanted to have to choose. Neither of us pushed her to, either. The thought of losing her, even to someone we knew, someone we loved just as much . . . It was too big."

*Only a terrible person would sit here and hate a dead girl for what she put Micah through. Making him chase her. Making him share her.*

*Which makes me a* really *terrible fucking person.*

It takes every bit of control I've got not to reach for him right now. Not to be the one wrapped around him.

*I can't make him forget her. He has to find his way through this.*

"She bailed out of Trav's lap when I came in. Got a running start and took a flying leap at me. I dropped my backpack to catch her. She was so excited to see what I'd found for everyone, she beamed like the sun at noon. That was worth every ounce of effort right there. I picked up my backpack . . . God, if I'd just left it on the floor . . ."

He goes quiet for a moment. The story looms between us, a spell that could be broken with a single word, but I stay silent. "Everyone leaned in and grabbed a little green tab for themselves, Trav already rambling on about the new chemical delights he'd cook up with them. We counted down together, our usual ritual. 'One . . . two . . . three . . .' Zane and Rina fed each other their tabs."

Bile rises in the back of my throat, remembering Adonis doing the same to me.

Micah shakes me free of my own memories, his voice hollow and defeated. "It didn't take long."

It's like riding a goddamn roller coaster up an incline and knowing the track ends just over the next rise. I'm strapped in. There's no getting off this ride now. I can imagine the heat rising. A few blissed-out minutes. Everyone kissing and touching and groping everyone else . . . except Micah.

*He only had eyes for Bryn.*

"The mood shifted. It got so loud so fast. I felt the brush of her hand, and instead of moaning, I screamed. *Everything* hurt. I couldn't even form words at that point. I can still hear Trav crying out, 'It burns, it fucking burns!' He was scratching at his arms as his muscles slowed, his skin almost lobster red."

I remember the applejack heat, the simmering sensation of napalm under my skin, but it was nothing like this.

"I slumped to the ground against one of the alcove's benches. I could barely breathe, barely move. Staring straight ahead, all I could see was Bryn, crying. I swear the tears evaporated as they hit her skin. She reached for me. Cried out for me with her last breaths. I couldn't reach her, couldn't lift my hand. I watched the light fade from her eyes. She died needing me, and I just sat there, broken and useless. Fucking useless."

*It's not your fault.* I could say it, but he wouldn't believe it, and he might even hate me for trying to argue. "What happened after? Did you, I mean . . ."

"I don't know the details. Next thing I knew, I woke up at home. *Home.* Guys from Cyrene Medical had dropped me off, told my parents I'd need serious long-term care. Got them to sign something promising to keep quiet about the circumstances in exchange for a chunk of cash for medical expenses.

"Everyone was surprised I survived at all. *A miracle*, my mother called it." Micah's still looking somewhere far beyond where I'm sitting. "I was burned out inside, my nerves and nanotech fried. Mom took time off from work, nursed me back to health. Doing odd jobs with

Dad got my motor skills back up to par. But I became exactly what I'd tried to avoid: a burden on the family. Found out later Cyrene had rejected applications from two of my sisters. Could've been they didn't make the cut, but they blamed me for it, like I tainted the whole family."

He pauses, and I pounce on my chance to nudge him away from the worst of it. "But you got back inside. How?"

"Maggie got the ball rolling. We'd been to her place a bunch of times. Guess she somehow heard I was out of the city, tapped me to provide her contacts with over-the-Wall music."

That sounded like the Hellcat all right: reducing everything—and everyone—to dollar signs and assets.

"I convinced her to sneak me back into the city as a runner. I found someone else to keep feeding her thumb drives of the choicest tunes, so she could maintain supply. Plus Maggie didn't need to supply me with Rivitocin. I did odd jobs and maintenance for the club, too, whatever I could to ingratiate myself with her more."

Looking up at him, I realize that Maggie's motives were probably more than just business. What little I know of her, I doubt she'd overlooked the fact that Micah was young, fit, attractive, and beholden to her in every way imaginable.

"But why come back? You must've known it would be hard, damn near impossible to live here under the radar."

He runs his hand along the wall, stopping only to trace the lines of copper he's woven around the room. A cell within a cell. "I owed it to them. Zane and Rina, Trav, Bryn. Running for Maggie was the perfect cover. Plenty of excuses to wander all over town, keep my eye on the darker corners of the city. Find the guy who sold me the applejack and make him pay for what he did. Then maybe work my way up the ladder, find every scumbag in the operation, and turn them over to the greyfaces. Worth getting caught inside to make that shit go away . . ."

*It's punishment. Penance for what he thinks he's done.*

But I keep that thought to myself as I close the space between us and wrap my arms around his neck. Standing on tiptoe, every inch of me pressed against him, I wonder if even that's enough to pull him out of the past.

Micah's arms close around me, and he holds me tight to him. I can feel his tears trickle down, warm splashes against my cheek. He lets me drag him slowly back to bed, and we curl up together under the blanket. Two broken people with pieces to spare.

# M

I'm losing all track of time, being in the warren with Vee. Every moment is ours, and we're taking advantage, mind, body, and soul.

You live a certain way long enough, under pressure, under stress, underfoot, and you forget that it's not the status quo. I'd never talked about that night. Not with Maggie. Not with my family. Not with anyone. Just me and endless replays in my head. I realize I hadn't even spoken their names aloud in months.

I'm slowly relearning what it's like to be with someone. All the gentle touches, the stolen looks and smiles. How to make conversation, how to share. Not just the physical closeness, but all of it.

We left the world behind, but we can't ignore it for much longer. Vee's not used to this, deserves better than this. She makes the best of my cramped accommodations, but stir-craziness can't be far off. Sponge baths with recycled water aren't gonna get the job done forever.

I try to give her space, but here, that amounts to leaning against the opposite wall.

And I'm still working on the "making conversation" thing. It's hard to concentrate. A girl, untamed hair and all, padding around your place, wearing your clothes? *Super hot.*

I clear my throat. *Nothing idle. I'm not going to ask about the weather or something.* Taking the plunge, I ask something I've genuinely been wondering. "So, Vee. Is that short for anything? Or a stage name? I mean . . . What do I call you?"

She's sitting in the middle of my cot, pulling out long sections of clip-in hair that I'd never suspected weren't hers. By the time she's done, there's enough sitting on the floor to mistake for a cat, and the girl in my bed looks even less like the girl in the poster. Running her fingers through the remaining black curls, she twists them around her fingers and over one shoulder before answering. Even then, it's with visible reluctance. "I don't remember." She hesitates, then adds, "I've had something wrong with my nanotech from the get-go. Every time they reboot it at the medcenter, they have to do a mind-scrub, too. Just like clearing out a hard drive for a reinstall, I guess."

"Oh, Vee . . ." *Tread lightly, Micah. You don't know everything she's been through.* "How thorough are we talking about?"

"As far as memories go, I have this last year." Another pause. She looks down at her arms, tracing over the skin with her fingers, as if she's looking for something there, some vestige of a previous life. "A few pieces from before that. Nothing good."

"I can appreciate that. Plenty of times I've wished I could forget what happened. Wished I could have a single night's peace, a stroll without the weight of remembering." I take a shot in the dark, wondering how bad it was, but knowing it was bad enough to push her here. "Rough childhood? Bad family stuff?"

She looks up at me, eyes bleak. "I had some kind of tattoo. And scars. From a knife."

I cringe, thinking of her reaction when I freed her from her corset. And then I wonder if she was cutting herself for the release or being cut by someone else, tagged with ownership. Each is horrible in its own way. I think of her smooth skin beneath my fingertips, and all the hours of nanotech treatments and restorative surgery to remove the signs of physical abuse. Worse than I expected, worse than I would wish on anyone. So much worse than I'd ever wish for her. "What *do* you remember?"

"Voices. People holding me down and cutting me up. Blood. Lots of it . . ." The last bit wavers, like she's drowning in it. "Damon told me I volunteered for a mind-wipe when I signed up. Showed me the paperwork and everything." I can actually see the moment she gets a lid on the feelings and forces them back into some dark place inside her. "So let's just stick with Vee, all right?"

"You got it." No more tough questions for now. "So, Vee, what comes next?"

"Food?" She looks down at the clothes she's been wearing on and off since landing here. "A shower. I can use a fire hose, if you have one handy."

"Fresh out of those, though I've recently found a dip in the river to be quite refreshing." I'm trying to keep things light, but we've been living off protein bars and electrolyte packs for days. She deserves something that doesn't come shrink-wrapped or prepackaged. I need to make a supply run. "Um, can't help you with a shower. Unless we rig something up. Water and a funnel or something. One of those burn-unit bags for debriding skin . . ." I look to her, mid-ramble, and her horrified expression says that's a no-go. "Right, scratch that. Food, I can definitely do." Still some money left on Maggie's latest prepaid. "What would you like?"

"I don't . . . I don't have anything with me. Credits-wise, I mean—" When she flushes, it's up to the tops of her ears.

"Vee, no. It's okay. I've got this. I swear." She's still looking away, and I close the gap between us, stroking her cheek. "Hey, look at me." She does, still pink, and I whisper, "We didn't exactly give you time to pack. It's okay. Improvising is what I do."

"It's just . . . stupid." She's got her knees up now, chin on top of them, like she's trying to make herself smaller, take up less space. "I mean, a week ago and we'd be at my place, in my bed, with fucking room service coming out of our ears, and now I'm here, and a burden . . . I don't want you to feel trapped because of me."

I pull her close and kiss the top of her head. "I don't feel trapped, sweetheart. I chose this. You're not a burden, you're a guest. Not even a guest, more like a roommate, or . . ." *You're rambling again. Stop rambling.*

Too late. Vee's already pulling back far enough to narrow her eyes at me. "Then your *roommate* wants pancakes."

I spring up onto my feet, grateful for the free pass she just gave me, one that I in no way earned. "What roomie wants, roomie gets. I'll be back before the syrup has time to cool." I grab my sneakers, sitting down to lace them up. "Hey, do you mind taking a quick look, make sure the coast is clear? It's about time I revealed to you the exact location of my secret lair."

Vee hesitates, looking at the tarp and back to me. "Sure. Not a problem." Placing a hand on the safety railing and stepping up to one of the canvas flaps, she flips it upward, gazing through the netting and outside. She turns back toward me, wide-eyed. "How far up are we?"

I look up as I finish knotting the laces. "Twenty-five, maybe thirty feet?"

She turns back, one hand pressing against the tarp as she scans everything within view. "So, under a bridge, huh? What's it like being a troll?"

I smirk, standing up and crossing over to her. "Ha *ha*. It works for me. Good hours, no managers bossing you around. Toll fees could be better, though."

"Those I can pay, at least." She wraps her arms around my neck and pulls me in for a kiss, and I gladly oblige. One kiss becomes several, and I lift her off her feet, her legs instinctively wrapping around my waist. I turn and pin her against the wall, careful to avoid any of the metal pegs in the Faraday grid. She gasps as I press my body to hers, and just like that, pancakes are forgotten.

Between kisses, she manages single words. "Your." Kiss. "Bed." Lip bite. "Now."

I spin us away from the wall, toward the bed, and a piece of copper wiring comes with us, clinging to Vee like I've been.

*Oh unholy fuck no.* I drop Vee, thankfully onto my cot, and twist back around to the damaged wall, grabbing the bent wiring and desperately weaving it back into place. "Oh fuck oh fuck oh fuck." *One break in the lattice, that's all it takes . . .*

She knows this is bad. "How long do we have before they find us?"

I keep at it, a stupid, futile gesture, knowing they're already on their way. "Minutes, at most."

Vee pulls the tarp aside. Daylight floods the room. "Stay here."

And she's *gone.*

Racing to the flap, I see her scrambling barefoot down the frigid stone and ironwork. "Vee, no!" I start climbing down after her, the rocks slick from earlier rain. *She could slip, she could fall, she could—*

"Get out of sight, Micah!" She's a third of the way down when she misses a foothold, leg sliding out from under her, knee banging into the wall.

A few more feet, and I'm at her side, reaching for her with one hand while anchoring myself with the other. A breeze kicks up, sending her hair into her face. One more distraction. "Vee, please, come back in. If you fell . . ." *I'd never forgive myself.*

But she recovers, planting her foot and continuing down the sheer stone face. If I reach for her again, I'll do more harm than good.

I follow her down, feet hitting the ground just behind hers, and I barely dodge a rock she wings at me. "Stop following me, damn it!" She takes off toward the river, running along its bank, leaving footprints in the muddy sand.

I chase her around the bridge's foundation and into the shallow water. She stops, and I almost slam into her as she stands there, still as can be. I strain to hear the sound of whatever's coming at us over the hum—

"No sirens, no helicopters. I don't hear anything," Vee murmurs. "Why aren't they here yet?"

*She's right. The goddamn sky should've fallen down around us, and there's nothing. I don't get it.*

Cold wind whips around both of us again, and she shivers. I reach for her, and she takes my hand. I sweep one arm under her legs and carry her back to shore, my eyes darting around us, hoping our shouts didn't attract any unwanted attention.

She climbs back up to the warren, adrenaline-exhausted but still strong, and I follow her up, watching her form as she scales the wall. Back inside, we stand together in silence, waiting for the hammer to drop.

But it doesn't.

She holds her elbows, hugging herself. I'd do that for her, but there's something else I need to do first.

I dig around in the storage vault and pull out the scanner. "Your nanotech should've been pinging sensors far and wide as soon as the grid was broken. Which means . . ."

I run the scanner over her wrists, then over her body like a security wand. Nothing. "You're off-grid."

*This . . . this is impossible. Could the Rivitocin have done this? One or two doses shouldn't have been enough. But six in twenty-four hours?*

*I guess the why doesn't matter. She's free. Instead of this tiny cell, she has a whole city, hers to see with new eyes.*

Vee looks up at me like it's Christmas morning, and I'm Santa. "So, we can both go for pancakes?"

# CHAPTER TWELVE

## M

Vee pours syrup over her third stack of pancakes, and I can't help but smile as I watch her dig in with relish. I'm sure after days of protein bars and water, this seems like a feast.

I polished off my omelet and bacon a good five minutes ago, and now I'm leaning back, trying to enjoy a quiet moment before we venture out in public again. As I sip my orange juice, one elbow perched atop the cheap vinyl booth, I scan our surroundings once more, just for peace of mind.

A few kids, still in their club gear from last night. A gaggle of tweakers at the counter. A few older guys in jumpsuits, maintenance by the look of it, or janitorial maybe. No one's paid us any attention since we came in. That's part of the reason we're here.

It's also not far from the apartment Niko let us borrow. One of my few friends from the old days, and as a housing rep, a handy one to have. With people coming in as new energy sources, moving up to classier digs, and eventually leaving as productive members of society, apartments are always changing hands, and he managed to get us an hour in an empty studio before the new residents arrived.

The shower was meant as a treat for Vee, but it would have been a shame to waste water with two showers, so . . .

Yeah, we made it out with three minutes to spare.

She catches me looking, her fork poised over the plate, and meets my gaze. For a brief moment, she hesitates, like she's suddenly realized the absurdity of sharing breakfast in the eye of a hurricane, and I worry that simply being out like this might be too much for her, knowing Damon is looking for her.

"Hey, it's okay." I reach for her free hand and squeeze it to reassure her. "Take a deep breath. I've been coming here for a while. We're in no hurry. You're allowed to enjoy the food. No one is gonna chase us out."

She trades her fork for a coffee cup, still mostly full and heavy on the cream. "I think I'm good. For a few hours at least." Then, just before taking a sip, I see her smile, seemingly enjoying a touch of the mundane. "Shower and food accomplished, fearless leader."

"Very true, plucky sidekick." I turn my attention to one of the great glass-globe emitters outside, dominating a rooftop across the street. "Hey, let me ask you something."

Vee pauses with another forkful halfway to her mouth, despite her earlier statement. "Shoot."

"When I came back to the city without nanotech, I heard this . . . hum. Always in the background, like an air conditioner in summer. A constant *rrrmmmmm* . . . Are you hearing anything like that?"

Vee tilts her head slightly, considering. "During withdrawal, I definitely felt this constant pressure, like rushing water, but I figured that was just my body fighting the applejack. No hum, though. Sorry."

"No worries." The applejack didn't have the chance to alter her brain chemistry like it did mine, then. I mouth a silent prayer to whoever cooked up Rivitocin.

*Time to switch gears and have a little fun.*

"So where to now? You've got the whole city, what do you want to see?"

She slides around the booth until she's pressed up against me. It's comfortable, intimate . . . easy, even. "You tell me. I know the top-floor clubs, some very high-end restaurants, and the backstage areas of every venue in Cyrene. You can take me anywhere else."

I think for a second, and then smile. "There is one place I can guarantee the Sugar Skulls have never spent a single second."

Instead of taking another sip of coffee, she tilts her head toward the door. "Lead on, stringbean. I haven't got all day."

# V

There are a thousand playgrounds in the city, and all the ones I know by heart are expensive as fuck. No way Micah would take me anywhere someone might recognize us, anyway. Credits issue aside, we're not exactly dressed for the All Saints Club or the fusion restaurant at the top of the Tener Building.

We walk down Hawthorne Street, and I can see the Dome in the distance, the cordoned-off area still swarming with cleanup crew. Even from here, I can tell the damage was mostly superficial, and a good chunk of it was cleaned up during my recovery time in the warren.

*Whatever. All that's someone else's problem now.*

We pass boutiques I've shut down so I could sort through them without having to deal with the plebs. Everything beyond the glass is brilliant white light, black-clothed staff, freestanding geometric statues, unnaturally shaped couches.

I'd rather be out on the sidewalk wearing Micah's clothes. After our shower, I ditched the dirty V-neck and shorts for a pair of his jeans—they mostly fit in the waist, but I had to cuff them up twice—one of his long-sleeved undershirts, and a spare black hoodie. The sleeves keep slipping down over my hands, and I might have dragged my arm through the butter twice at breakfast, but everything smells like his laundry detergent, and under that there's something warm and definitely male.

Micah also took a knife to my concert boots, cutting them down to the ankle and covering the white leather with electrical tape so I didn't have to wear thigh-highs to breakfast.

*Handy guy to have around in a crisis.*

Right now, he's got his nose pointed toward Mercette Park. It's one of four in Cyrene, brilliant green squares plunked down like afterthoughts, walled in like prisoners. Speeding past them in the back of the limo, I only caught glimpses of restless trees, branches reflecting the season, pedestrians pouring in and out through the gated archways marked by enormous thrum-collectors.

*Today's a day of firsts.*

People stream past us, all of them in athletic shoes and the kind of clothes meant for bending and stretching.

"Something's happening in the park," I note as I slip on an old pair of Micah's sunglasses.

"Something's always happening in the park," he says. The flicker of a smile signals he's amused by my ignorance. "It's an energy-for-credits program Corporate uses to keep the kids busy during the day." Easily sidestepping several people intent on running us down, he weaves in and out of the crowd, not breaking stride or fumbling a single syllable. I follow in his wake, grateful for his fingers laced between mine. "Activities every day that generate easily harnessed energy."

I don't know what I was imagining, but group exercise wasn't it, and that just shows I've been living on the nocturnal circuit too long. "Like what?"

"It varies between more regimented stuff—calisthenics, martial arts, you know—and group competitions. Obstacle course challenges. An annual park-wide zombie run."

I'm not sure what seems more foreign: voluntarily running through the park during the day, or doing it dressed as a zombie. For fun. "That sounds . . . strenuous."

"It's supposed to be. They're *zombies*. It's life or death, Vee." He's teasing, and it's a wider smile than I've seen before. This tiny moment of normalcy really suits him, but I can't help wondering how long it's been since he had something normal. "Plus, it's a great way to stay flush in credits for a couple hours' effort. A few years ago, Trav and I finished first and second in the obstacle course, two and a half seconds in front of the pack."

He gestures toward the east end of the park, away from the gathering crowd. "We sprinted to those sets of high and low bars." There's a series of wooden hurdles of various heights and wide enough for two people to jump. More competition, more thrum output, if I had to make a guess. "Up and over the high ones and under the low ones. Piece of cake."

I watch Micah relax into the story, his expression and gestures growing more animated. These memories don't hold any despair or bitterness, just the thrill of movement. The way he's bouncing a little on the balls of his feet signals a readiness to sprint off to join in the games this morning. I stifle a smile, wondering if he even realizes he's doing it.

Describing the next two obstacles, he walks backward with his usual easy grace, and I have all the time in the world to look at him. I can't help but note the way the light slides over his face and tangles in his blond hair. I'm feeling warm, and not just from the sunshine.

"The last part, the worst part, was the cargo net. My arms were aching by the time I was halfway up, and that thing sways with every move you or the other guy makes." Two stories tall, it looms in the distance, hanging from a raised platform with a finish-line banner. It reminds me of a tree house, with a slightly rundown perch for the victor to cheer and gloat from.

"Trav was first to the top of the net, first to ring the bell and claim victory. But as soon as he did, he turned around to cheer me on. 'Come on, killer. What's it gonna be?'" Micah shakes his head softly, as if brushing off the memory. Then he looks up at me and reaches for me, taking my hand again. "The credits we won bought the five of us ten minutes in the zero-g room at Sarabande. It was awesome."

"Jax wanted to go there." No need to say that Damon had nixed the idea so thoroughly that she never brought it up again, not even to bitch about it.

"Jax . . . Is that Trouble or Treble?"

I can't help but snicker, because I don't even have to ask what he means. "Trouble. Big trouble. Which makes Sasha your Treble."

Micah studies me for a moment, reaching out to touch my cheek. "So, speaking of the band, why the Sugar Skulls?"

His finger's still moving, still tracing some kind of pattern on my skin. It takes me a second to realize he's recreating my makeup from the show at Maggie's with his fingertip. "It was my idea. Everything Jax came up with was horrifying, and Sasha couldn't even name the cat. Plus I had this image in my head pretty much from the second I woke up in the penthouse. Roses and skulls. I figured I should take whatever memory that was and run with it—"

Before I can follow that thought down the rabbit hole, someone slams into me from behind. Stumbling forward, I grab a handful of Micah's jacket and manage not to go down. I snarl over my shoulder at some dude trying too hard to look edgy. "Why don't you go suck a bag of dicks?"

When I turn to look at Micah, his eyes are on the stranger, staring daggers and swords and machetes and all sorts of other pointy objects. Slipping an arm around my waist, he pulls me close to him, away from the guy.

"Should watch where you step next time. Somebody could get hurt." Micah's words are polite enough, but there's serious bite behind them.

The guy holds his hands up, muttering apologies through a cheesy smile, claiming it was all an accident. He shuffles off, but Micah watches him until he disappears from view.

Then Micah turns to me, dialing down the tension in his voice and trying to sound casual. "Hey, do you want to go somewhere a little less . . . mob scene-ish?"

"Absolutely." The day is less bright, the shine rubbed off somehow as I nod and fall in step with him.

# M

I mentally kick myself as we leave the park. Mercette wasn't the most brilliant idea—too many people, too little control over the situation—but Vee deserved some sunshine.

The odds of Ludo just being there by chance: slim to none. *Little twerp was following me. Following us. Need to be more careful.*

I keep us moving at a steady pace, not frantic but motivated, just two busy city dwellers with places to go and things to do. Vee squeezes my hand tight, betraying her anxiety, but trusting me to take us somewhere less conspicuous.

I know *just* the place.

A few blocks away, the buildings scrape the sky, and the shadows deepen, creating dark valleys where prying eyes are less likely and far less welcome. This is the Cyrene I know by smell and touch; it's tattooed on the inside of my eyelids.

Vee draws closer to me, more baffled than concerned. "Where *are* we?"

My carnival barker act is the perfect opportunity to distract her from what happened at the park. I lay it on thick and theatrical: "We're half a block from one of Cyrene's most hallowed underground halls of music appreciation. A shrine to every badass lick, kickass chick, and dude most slick. Oh yeah . . ."

"Quite the hype-man," she says through giggles. "How long have you been practicing that?"

Caught mid-gesticulation, I wobble a bit, then lower my arm sheepishly. "The whole way here. Too much?"

Leaning close enough to kiss me, she bites my lip lightly. "Just enough."

We round the corner hand in hand, and Vee takes in the scene. It's one long alley, and every square inch of it, from asphalt to bricks twenty feet overhead, is covered in spray-painted tributes to the DJs who stir the drug-addled souls of the Cyrene faithful.

"Welcome to Taggarty Ave."

She follows the painted footprints of gods and monsters as she wanders from piece to piece, angels and devils of musical mastery rendered in a thousand styles, every drip and dab contributing to a visual buffet that could easily explode a lesser observer. TumbleKitty is there, the mistress of sound, and Spunfloss, and Mystikal Mark, and Grimastetia, too, all the remix masters of note.

Vee glows with delight. Taggarty Ave is hardly a hotspot, and your average glimhead would never find it. It's meant for us, the ones who boil and burn and soar on sonic candy.

But when she nears the end of the alley, that's when she beams, a rhapsody of light. That's when she sees one of the newest additions to the Ave: a Sugar Skulls piece, the only band on a wall dominated by DJs. Trouble and Treble weave notes like spells over our heads, with Vee front and center, lips parted as she blasts a microphone to pieces with her song.

*No sex, no gimmick, just the music.*

She pulls her hand from mine, letting go for the first time since the park. Reaching out, she stops just short of the wall, fingers outstretched. An inch, maybe two; that's all that separates her from the art.

But she's moved a world, maybe two, away from that life.

One of the street artists startles her out of her reverie as he touches up the wall behind her with a few dustings of amber aerosol. "Man, you must be a hardcore fan. You even got the mods to look like her." He gestures toward the tableau.

"Oh, y-yeah," Vee stutters, adding a timid, "super . . . super big fan."

Shaken by the near recognition, she takes a tiny step back, not realizing that her face is now right beside the painted tribute, highlighting every similarity. The artist takes a step forward, squinting hard at her.

I speak up, trying to extract her from the scene without being too obvious. "Pretty girl, dark hair, plus paint fumes? You're being too kind, man." I grab her wrist. "Come on, babe, let's jet. Dinner plans, right?"

Recovering quickly, Vee nods and joins my charade. "Oh, totally. Let's move."

I throw an arm around her casually and pull her close, but she can't help looking behind us one last time at the graffiti blaster, stenciling shooting stars onto a DJ made of the night sky.

"I know where we can go," she whispers.

# V

The Pyxis hasn't changed much since the ribbon-cutting ceremony. The Sugar Skulls were there that day in full pomp and splendor, and yeah, I had the gold scissors; no one trusted Jax with anything sharp, and Sasha kept trying to hide behind me, tugging at her hair because the styling team cut it so short. The entire time we were inside, Jax bitched that artificial night is "just flicking the damn light switch off," but there's more to it than that.

*Makes a good hiding place.* That run-in with the street artist rattled me more than I'd like to admit. "Hey, you look like her" is only one step removed from someone taking a good hard look and realizing I *am* her.

Paranoia sinks its fangs into me, and suddenly I'm feeling exposed. There are more people up here than I expected, most of them just taking advantage of the late afternoon lull. Groups loll on the grass, some on blankets, others partly hidden by the hedges marking the outer edge of a new interactive labyrinth. A short queue waits their turn to get in, and we make our way past them, shoes crunching through gravel. There are weird animalesque topiaries and deliberately crumbling Greek statues set at intervals on the walkway.

*Probably disguising security cameras.*

I resist the urge to give every one of them the finger. There's nothing about us that should draw attention, as long as I keep taking Micah's cues. He's still moving with easy grace. Not too fast or slow. And somehow managing to do it all without looking like he's trying. It would be irritating, if I didn't think it was hot as hell.

I pull back on his arm hard enough to get a half step ahead of him. "Oh, *excuse* me, sir."

Grabbing me around the waist, he lifts me off the ground. "Boy, the manners of some people," he says, packing me up the stairs as I fake-struggle in his arms. "Like everyone will just give them stuff if they stand around and scream."

"You don't seem to respond to screaming as well as you respond to other things," I mutter.

Micah's arms are still clamped around my waist, and he gets in one more good squeeze before setting me down. "Depends on the other things."

"That sounds like a challenge to me." Setting my jaw, I pull him through the turnstile.

*No one's manning the entrance anymore; that's good.*

*God, I'm even* thinking *like him now.*

The moment we set foot in the building, we run smack into a wall of cold. They're running the AC about ten degrees below what's comfortable, encouraging people to keep warm however they can. Beyond that, the central viewing room sports an arched ceiling with shifting star-projections. Perfect acoustics for hypno-trance music. The seats not only recline, but they dispense a variety of viewing enhancers like ticker tape.

Trouble is, in the months since the opening, it's apparently become a magnet for off-duty greyfaces as well as light-sensitive burnouts. I can count at least six over-21s gathered in one of the back rows, joking with each other, thankfully not paying a lot of attention to those around them.

*But still. All it's going to take is one of them looking over here and recognizing me. Or Micah. Then we're toast.*

Micah's pace slows, and he looks around, probably for convenient exits. But he doesn't know the layout, not like I do. I give his hand a little tug, and he nods without looking at me.

I draw him down a corridor that grows progressively darker, the sconces shifting from gentle white night-lights to the palest of blues to violet and finally to black light. Neon-green swirls on the walls, artificial fog on the floor, and you might as well be flying to Neverland. I pull Micah into the alcove second from the end.

I only take two steps before hitting a wall. The room is tiny, smaller even than Micah's storage closet. It's pitch black inside until he closes the curtain behind us, then everything lights up pale purple. Overhead, there are plastic bins of bioluminescent body glitter, tubes of glo-paint, flavored lick-and-stick patches. We haven't discussed his views on reindeer games, but I figure now is perhaps not the most opportune time for that.

Standing so close, I can feel Micah's heart pounding. His voice is steady as ever, though. "How long before it's okay to leave, do you think?"

"I'm not sure. We should probably give it a half hour for the greyfaces to clear out, just to be on the safe side."

The sprinkler overhead lets loose with vaporized moondust that drifts over us in a green-glowing mist, sticking to whatever skin is showing. One deep inhalation, and random spots of color wink in and out of existence. It doesn't hit anyone hard or fast, or Cyrene would still be charging for it. And I don't think it's doing anything at all for Micah.

*That's my job.*

He meets my steady gaze and pays it back with interest. Something inside me breaks, some little piece of armor slips away, and even if I wanted to stop it, I can't. Here, with him, it's all too surreal to stay guarded. I kiss him thoroughly before he can say anything. There's something about being on the run that puts a girl on edge. I'm suddenly desperate to hold him, to feel something other than the fear that Damon's onto us, that he's got the rope around our necks and we just don't know it yet. Micah matches me, kiss for frantic kiss.

*This is going all Romeo and Juliet too fucking fast for my taste.*

# M

After a long, circuitous trip along the side streets and back alleys of Cyrene, giving Vee her first real taste of evasive maneuvers, we return to the familiar stone-and-copper patchwork of the warren.

This isn't how I wanted her first day of freedom to go. All the near misses are taking their toll, and she nervously paces back and forth, running her fingers along the copper grid as she passes.

She's a fucking trooper. She really is. All this change, coming fast and furious, and she rebounds. Still floating. Still fighting.

*I think it's high time she got some sort of reward. A treat. Something meant for her and her alone.*

*I just hope she likes it.*

I take her by both hands, interrupting her ninth or tenth pass, leading her over to the cot. "There's something that helps me unwind. Maybe it'll help you, too. Here, sit down for a sec."

She flops down onto the bed, gorgeous even in exhaustion. When the iron door of the storage locker swings open, she looks up, tilting her head like a curious puppy. With Lara free of her case and draped over my shoulder, I step into view.

Vee's gaze drops immediately to the guitar. "I didn't know—" she says, but she cuts herself off. There's so much we don't actually know about each other that there's no point starting a list now. She curls her legs underneath her, making room on the bed for me.

A few strums of the strings, and one deep breath later, I settle in on the bed, my private stage for one supremely important ticket holder. Our eyes meet, and hers sparkle in the dim light.

*No pressure there.*

I tap Lara three times just below her bridge to set the beat, then let my fingers take over, teasing out a simple melody. I lick my lips, close my eyes, step to the waterfall's edge, and dive in.

> You came in through an unguarded window,
> Finding me alone in this dark and empty space,
> Creeping through my every waking thought,
> Quiet as a mouse, and vibrant as the chase.

I hazard a peek at her through clenched eyelids, and she's hugging the pillow to her chest. *I don't know if she's hiding behind it or putting something between us or . . .* My mind jumps to the most catastrophic conclusions, even as the rest of me continues.

Lithe as a cat, prowling through the rooms,
Footfalls in pools of thought and light,
You wander lazy avenues in mind and heart,
Oh, to amble there with you tonight . . .

I can't look. I watch my fingers, the strings, my eyelids, anything but her face as I warble such heartfelt, treacly bullshit to her. *Why did I think this was a good idea?*

But I must open my eyes, open the door,
Let in the wind and cold and brave the blame.
If this was just a fantasy, a dream,
Smoke and dirty ashes, not torrid flame.

My eyes alight on hers, those shimmering pools of golden brown that warm my soul and give me shivers all at once. *Okay, big finish. All or nothing.* I almost whisper the last verse.

I could've closed my eyes and listened,
Marked the eons by your gentle pace . . .
Instead I turn around and find you here
And marvel as you take the figment's place.

I stare at her, dark curls framing her face, lips slightly parted in the soft lamplight. I try to divine her thoughts, what she's feeling, but hopes and doubts alike dance across my forebrain. Either way, I don't want this moment to end.

I could've closed my eyes and listened,
Marked the eons by your gentle pace . . .

Her voice, melodious and smooth, joins me in the refrain, and we share the last two lines:

Instead I turn around and find you here
And marvel as you take the figment's place.

# CHAPTER THIRTEEN

## V

From the bed, I've been surreptitiously watching Micah for at least ten minutes. Yeah, I admit it, I was admiring the view. My awareness of him—the way he moves, the way he breathes—hasn't softened in our time together. If anything, it's sharpened. Cutting into me with every intercepted glance. Every easy smile.

Except he's not smiling just now. He should be rolling through his morning routine, peering out one of his spyholes to check the weather or tidying up our clothes, but instead he's just standing there, lost in thought.

It's unnerving, to see him so still.

Eventually, he pulls an envelope from the pocket of his discarded jeans and settles in on the floor, carefully unfolding the paper so as not to disturb me.

I prop myself up on my elbow. "What are you reading?"

He jumps. Looking equal parts startled and guilty, he folds up the paper one-handed, like he's about to hide it behind him. "I . . . I thought you were asleep."

"Micah, what is that?" We both look at the partly crumpled paper, and I wonder if he'll lie to me. Lie to protect me, or to protect himself.

"It's an autopsy report," he finally says.

I laugh at the admission, so ridiculous in the moment, but when he doesn't crack a smile, I stop, feeling like a complete ass. "Oh, I thought you were kidding."

"Niko passed it to me yesterday morning before our shower." He walks over to the bed and hands me the page.

I skim it, skipping over the grislier details. "Who OD'd?"

"The dealer. The one who sold me the applejack that killed my friends. In six months, I've found nothing, no trace of him. Just bits and pieces of the operation he dealt for. There were rumors he died before I snuck back into the city, but this is the first tangible proof." Micah slumps to the floor beside the cot, disappointment in his eyes.

My first instinct is to reach for him, but I hold back, still processing the new information. "You had this on you all day yesterday and didn't say anything? Not a peep?"

*And I had no idea that he was carrying a weight like this. Way to be observant, Vee.*

"I knew it was going to be bad, I just didn't know *how* bad until a few minutes ago." He licks his lips, considering his next words carefully before turning to meet my gaze. "I'm sorry I didn't tell you sooner. I wanted yesterday to be about you, a perfect day." He brushes the hair from his eyes. "Didn't really work out that way."

"You've been chasing this guy down for six months. That's probably a little more important than a day out and about." I can't make up my mind if I should be pissed he kept this to himself or hurt that he might not have told me at all if I hadn't caught him. Before I can decide, there's a sudden rush of tears. I try to rub them away before he can see.

*Angry* and *hurt. No need to pick just one.*

Micah's eyes follow every tear streaking down my cheeks, as if blaming himself for each one. "I haven't trusted anyone in a long time, Vee. Maggie has no idea why I'm really here. Can't trust the other runners. Niko knows a little, but not enough to get him in trouble with Corporate. It's been just me. I've gotten really good at keeping things to myself. I know that's no excuse . . ."

I put one hand on either side of his face. "I'm here with you. I'm in this all the way. And I need to know that you feel the same. No fucking secrets, Micah. Not between us. Not ever."

Nodding, he responds instantly, "I promise. No more secrets. You and me, two against the world."

"Good." Leaning closer to him, I stroke his cheek, and his eyes close, the simple contact comforting us both.

"Um, speaking of no more secrets . . ." Micah's eyes open. "That guy, in the park. I know him, and I don't think that little encounter was an accident."

My stomach ties itself into a knot. "What do you mean?"

"His name's Ludo. He's a regular at Sidri's, a real lowlife. Riprap, glim, whatever he can get his hands on."

"And he's following you because he thinks something is up?"

Micah nods. "Ludo knows I've been looking for that dealer. With him gone—and no luck with the list of drops Maggie left me—the only option is to keep working my way up the chain." He hesitates here, obviously with a target in mind. "There's a guy, another scumbag, who's handling the Hellcat's distribution. Probably has Ludo on his payroll. Could get me back on track. I could run a few drops for him, see if he's pushing Maggie's usual or something worse."

"*We* could run a few drops for him, you mean," I correct Micah. Knowing he's going to protest, I rush to explain. "I'm not going to hang out here while you chase after the bad guys. That dirty shit almost killed me. Hell, it could have been Jax or Sasha taking that tab off Adonis, and what then? No security detail with us that night, no fucked-up nanotech to kick them off-grid, no Rivitocin to keep them from burning up . . . They could have died." I push the blankets aside to sit up in the bed and wrap my arms around him. "I'm going to help you end this."

When Micah stands up, he takes me with him. "There is one key logistical thing we should take care of, then." He strokes my back up and down, leaving warm trails on my skin. "We need to set you up with some . . . ladygear."

I meet that perfect blue gaze for a moment, then burst out laughing. "Ladygear?"

He smirks but valiantly continues. "Well, technically, they're *unmentionables*."

I break away to grab the nearest blanket, wrapping it around me to cover up the bits drawing so much solicitous concern. "I don't want to use your credits on clothes, Micah."

The smirk fades, and he looks at me with genuine concern. "Vee, yesterday we were lucky. But if we need to run, if we need to scram in a hurry, I can't imagine you'd be all *that* comfortable at a dead sprint with nothing between you and my jeans, or without some front-bumper support."

Reaching out, he passes the last of his clean shirts off to me. My hands full of thin white cotton, I try not to wonder how many mornings we have before it all unravels. The longer this lasts, the more we overlap, the edges between us blurring until it's not *him* and *me*, just *us*.

I get a weird lump in my throat that I swear I'll swallow or die trying. "Bra shopping it is. Even if it's just an excuse to put on a fashion show for you . . ." I think about the Loft for the first time since detoxing off the applejack, suddenly reminded of the drawers and drawers of expensive lingerie. Matching sets of lace and ribbon, all of it neatly organized by color and stored with tiny perfumed packets. I'd worn it, sure. Shown it off to my fair share of people. But I'd never worn it *for* someone.

"Where's the best place to go?" Micah is digging out the last of the protein bars and water bottles and stashing them in his faded black messenger bag, so he doesn't see my face burning. Doesn't ask me what I'm thinking, thank god.

I pull on his jeans, suddenly hyperaware that there's nothing between me and his pants. "The Cordray District, probably. There are some big box stores, and it's less of a zoo than the mall." After jamming my feet into my cut-off boots, I reach for the hoodie I've commandeered and leave my hair to do whatever it's going to do. "Let's move."

He snags me by my back pocket, stage-whispering, "Don't forget that you promised me a fashion show."

# M

After a brief and memorable bit of lingerie modeling, not to mention several rounds of "Aren't you going to hold my purse?" "I'd have to buy you a purse to hold first!", Vee is properly outfitted with one item for the penthouse and a few options for the ground floor, and we make tracks for Maggie's warehouse.

Once we're within spitting distance of the building, I hold up a hand and stop us. Vee tips up her sunglasses and cocks an eyebrow.

"I know asking you to hang back would be pointless, but keep your head on a swivel. I haven't been able to pin anything on him, but I've got plenty of reason to suspect Rete is dealing applejack. So far, he's played it cool, stepping in during Maggie's absence, playing friendly manager guy, but that could change in a hurry, and I don't want you—"

"I know. Don't worry. I've got your Brights. If things go tits-up, you'll have to catch me or eat my dust."

I smirk, more for me than for her. "Okay. Let's get into character, then." In unison, we flip up our hoods and head for the steel door. Vee's sunglasses are back in place, and I swear there's a little bit of swagger in her walk.

*That or a rock in her boot.*

Fire Plug works the door for us, and we step inside. With Scrappy in tow, Rete's already crossing the distance from Maggie's little side office, ready to bump my fist or teach me the secret handshake or something. He's as big an eyesore as ever in maroon bell-bottoms, a pastel tank top, and a gold-rope necklace like a hangman's noose.

"Mr. Quick, quick as a cat, always a pleasure. And not alone, I see. What can we do for you this fine day?" Rete keeps his eyes on Vee, but her face is a mask, betraying nothing.

*Nice job, babe.*

"Here to work. I've run through the list of drops Maggie left for me. Any word from her?"

"Not a one, chum. No one's seen her since Corporate hauled her in, the night of the Sugar Skulls show at her place."

*Dammit. The longer she's missing, the worse Rete will get.* By the looks of it, he's already made the office his wannabe command center. "Well, I figure you'll have no problem putting me to work until Maggie is back in charge."

Rete pauses, as if he needs to take a second to size us up, the smug ass. He strokes his gold chain, like a supervillain petting a cat. "Of course, ace, of course. There's plenty to move, and you're a proven commodity." He turns to Vee. "You know, I'm always on the lookout for worthwhile talent. The strawberry here should be a great addition to the team."

*There's the sales pitch, already locked and loaded.* Vee shifts slightly on her feet, but says nothing, even as Rete reaches for her. She holds up one hand and he freezes when he spots her knuckle jewelry. After a long second, she flips the hood back herself. I know what she's thinking. *It's a risky move, but she's in, all in.*

I stay perfectly still, because if I don't, I'll belt the guy, whether he recognizes her or not. "No dice. The girl's not in play. You know what I can do, just give me a chance to do it."

Rete nods at her and puts up one finger. "Let me and your boy have a little confab in private." He escorts me toward the office built into the wall, and I look back over my shoulder at Vee. She looks too small for the space she's standing in, right up to the point that Fire Plug gets unnecessarily close, reaching past her for something on a shelf. Without so much as blinking, Vee clocks him in the jaw with the Brights. Fire Plug drops like a sack of cement and stays down. Scrappy wisely backs off.

"No touching," she warns him anyway, her voice thinner than usual.

Rete barks with laughter, unconcerned that someone weighing a buck-twenty and change just laid out one of his guys flat on the concrete.

I watch as Vee pushes the sunglasses back up her nose, shielding her eyes once more. Her hand trembles twice, three times, before she gets it under control.

The pain she doled out to Fire Plug was reflex. Instinct. The kind of dirty sucker punch used in a street fight. I think it even surprised *her*. Never seen her react that fast before now, and I guess I should be thankful that she didn't waffle me like that during the worst of her withdrawal.

Rete grabs my attention, tapping my chin from underneath. "Close your hatch, sport, or you're gonna catch flies."

I step through the doorway with him, and he lays it out for me. "This is how it's gonna be. You and the girl, both doing drops for me. Keep the good stuff flowing. She can get into places you can't. Charm people you can't. She's useful. So it's a package deal."

*There's a catch coming. Always a catch.* Vee's out of earshot. "Or?"

Spreading his hands wide, Rete playacts like he's surprised at my reaction. "Micah, come on. I'm not stupid. Maggie kept a separate account for all your runs. She gave you extra leeway. Protected you. Which means you *needed* protecting. Corporate must want you for some reason. Now, normally, I wouldn't give a squirt about that, but if you start causing trouble, why, it would be my civic duty to speak up, wouldn't it?"

*Fuck. He can raise the alarm before we're even out the door. We won't get ten steps from the building before Damon arrives with half the city's Facilitators.*

Rete smiles like a shark gave him lessons. "But don't worry. Me and the boys would take good care of your lovely piece of arm candy."

I meet his smile with stone-cold fury. I'm outmaneuvered. *For now.* "What's the play?"

He claps his hands once and holds them together. "Simple. Two drops today, all in good faith. Easy one for her, sky-high one for you. Everything goes well, we move forward like bestest best pals with more drops tomorrow. You miss one, you run, you duck us, we put the city on high alert. And we come looking for you ourselves. Clear?"

When I nod, he leans over to the desk and passes me a parcel wrapped in brown paper. Just like the ones I move for Maggie. I snatch it from his hands.

He smiles again, that same shit-loaded smile. "Welcome aboard."

I step away, eager to put as much distance as possible between me and that scumbag. But before I make it to Vee, Rete says, "Oh, pigeon, one more thing."

My shoulders tense up as I turn back toward him. He's got a clipboard in his hand and flips the pages with melodramatic flair. "Sure you're good on Rivitocin? You said at the Palace that you were all stocked up, but two days later you took six more vials." Rete's eyes bounce between Vee and me.

*I have to get her out of here.* "Just miscounted, that's all. Turned out I had extra vitapep shots instead, so I did a quick restock."

With a few mumbled words accepting my explanation, he sends me on my way. My jaw aches from clenching it. Vee hurries over to meet me, looking concerned but keeping mum. She's waiting until we're outside to talk.

Scrappy has to roll the door up for us because Fire Plug's still on the ground. Vee shudders a little when she looks at the prone asshole. At a jog, we put the warehouse behind us. A few blocks away, Vee grabs my arm hard and stops me.

"Micah."

When I spin around, she gets a grip on my elbows, holding me there. I meet her gaze, replaying her knockout of Fire Plug in my head, the question already halfway out. "Vee, what happened back—"

"Rete knows who I am, doesn't he?" she demands, gritting her teeth.

"He hasn't gotten that far yet." I shake my head, thrown by the change in subject. "*I'm* the one he suspects, enough to make trouble. And he wasn't surprised at all that I brought you with me. Usually, he's so paranoid that just showing up with someone would've set off alarms. He knew beforehand, had his recruitment speech ready. Ludo probably ran back to tell him right after we 'bumped into' him at Mercette."

*Little weasel. Though, if a tweaker like Ludo is hanging around, maybe I'm right about Rete running more than music and booze.* "If I had to guess, Rete probably thinks the extra Rivitocin and your sudden appearance mean I'm building my own crew to challenge him. That's why he wants you making drops, too. Claiming you as part of *his* crew, ensuring you won't be at my beck and call for drops of my own." When Vee squeezes my arms, I can't tell if she's angry or trying to comfort me. "I never should've brought you here."

"Like I gave you a choice." Flipping her sunglasses down once more, she shoots a look at me over the frames. "The more drops we make for that dipshit, the more chances you have to gather the information you need."

Knowing that she's right doesn't make it any less frustrating. "Then let's move. We need to get out of sight so we can check these parcels before we deliver them."

A few blocks down, we find a quiet alley shaded from view. The perfect spot to do a little recon.

I look over each package carefully, noting any marks or distinguishing characteristics I'll have to duplicate with my own supplies. Then I slice one open, check the contents—all illicit, but nothing that troubles my conscience—and reseal it in a new envelope I brought, complete with packing tape.

Vee grabs the next one and follows suit. The whole thing takes only a few minutes. She's a quick study.

"Tricks of the trade," she says. "I'll be a master by midday."

I bundle up our gear and hand her the first parcel. She opens up the envelope taped to it and looks at our instructions. There's a time, coordinates, and what to do when we arrive.

We take off down the street together. As Vee keeps pace with me, a weight settles into the pit of my stomach. Whatever happens, she's a part of this now, with all the ugliness and danger that comes with it.

*What have I done?*

# V

*Why the hell did I hit that guy?*

He was about as intimidating as a Chihuahua, had barely brushed up against me. I didn't even register hitting him until the impact traveled up my arm, then it was like the Sugar Skulls' hasty retreat out of Hellcat Maggie's all over again.

*I punched that girl in the face, too. My go-to move is straight to the jaw.*

I try to shake it off because we have enough to deal with at the moment. Following Micah, I'm expecting filthy back rooms, dark corners, and maybe . . . yeah, I'll admit it, the chance to step over a dead body. What I get instead is an alley on the edge of the Odeaglow. Access doors to three separate nightclubs open off to either side, explaining the reasoning behind the drop point. The area isn't remotely seedy, but it certainly isn't anywhere I've visited before.

"It'll be *fine*," I tell Micah again, trying to get him to let go of my belt loop.

"Take it slow. First few runs, you always move faster than you think. Breathe, move, assess. Then haul ass back here." He puts the parcel in my hand, and the paper is damp with sweat.

This seems like a lot of work for over-the-Wall music. I'm still game, but all of Micah's poise and grace evaporate as I approach my first drop. Even though he's keeping his mouth clamped shut, I can imagine him squeaking out advice every few footsteps. The muscle in his jaw jumps; he's clenching his teeth *and* his fist.

*I need to hurry, before a car backfires or a door slams open and he loses his shit completely.*

Walking—chin up, with just enough ass-shake to signal a *fuck off* to anyone watching—I trail one hand along the brickwork.

*Act like you're supposed to be here.*

Halfway down the alley, there's a series of multipaned windows, the glass soaped over, the molding frosted with bird crap. I count them off, stopping in front of the third set. The ledge under it is hollowed out. For a second, I wonder if I can really stick my hand into the recess, but a glance back at Micah tells me I have all of three seconds before he starts after me.

*Get it done, Vee.*

The bravado lasts until my hand clamps down on something fur-squishy, and I have to swallow what could've been the girliest shriek on the planet. Just next to the dead thing is a paper-wrapped packet. I pull it out, repressing the urge to wipe my hand on my borrowed pants, and stuff the other parcel in its place. Shoving the pickup into my pocket, I pull away from the wall and circle back around to Micah at a reluctant saunter.

He heaves a major sigh of relief. "You did terrific, babe. Really, really great. Really great. Just—"

"Thanks, love, but shut up." I grab him with my clean hand, trying to avoid thinking about whatever germs are already crawling up my other arm and devouring bits of my flesh. Headed out of the alley, I pick up the pace. He's going to think the adrenaline got to me, but I'll explain after I boil myself in hot water. "I need a restroom *now*."

He gestures down the street, brushing my contaminated hand as he points. "Take it easy. There's a coffee and stimshot place—"

I don't even let him finish the sentence before taking off at a run. "Come on. You're gonna need some soap, too."

Between gasps for breath, I explain what happened, and the line cutting down the middle of his forehead is replaced with crinkles at the corners of his eyes.

"No problem dropping a guy with a set of Brights," he teases, "but a dead mouse throws you off your game?"

A glance down at my hand reveals there's something matted under my fingernails. Fresh panic puts wind in my sails. "Fuck, fuck, ew, ew, fuck. Yeah. Yeah, it does."

Micah races to keep up with me, probably thinking this is my way of demanding another hot shower.

I'll just have to see if I can fit both of us in the sink.

# M

The first job was a gimme, and Vee passed with flying colors, checking the parcel, repackaging it, and making the drop in a marked mail slot a dozen streets away from our brief bathroom detour. The sky-high pickup, however, ups the ante. We have to be careful and a little lucky, because we're well into the Jobalign District, surrounded by over-21s, and we're headed up.

For nostalgia's sake, I'm guessing, one of the Corporate apartment complexes has a wooden water tower on the roof, about nine feet off the ground and twenty feet around. It's certainly not utilitarian. The only water this puppy has seen is rain.

I tell Vee she can hang back and keep an eye out for anyone too curious, but that suggestion gets rejected. Instead, she puts her newfound climbing skills to the test and scales the rickety fire escape with plenty of style. I keep glancing back, but every time, Vee pushes me to keep going.

Once she crests the roof's lip and climbs onto the dusty, gritty surface, I'm up and charging toward the tower. I vault onto a storage shed and sprint across its weatherproofed shingles, running the numbers in my head: six-and-a-half feet up, twelve feet across, and a full head of steam add up to a successful leap, so I go for it.

Sure, I could've climbed the water tower itself, braving splinters and gravity, but honestly, this way is faster. *And more fun.*

I glide across the distance, legs tucked like a cannonball, arms straight behind me like a comet's tail. At the last second, I reach forward and my hands catch the lip of the platform; buckling down, I manage to pull myself up and onto the tower.

*No time to gloat. Gotta find the packet.*

I check the drain faucet leading to the roof, then feel around the body of the tower until I hear a click, and a piece of the wooden wall swings open. Inside is a thick white envelope, taped shut. I stash it in my bag before scrambling over the side and sliding down one of the supports.

Vee hustles over the raised partitions dividing the roof into sections. "That was impressive."

I do my best to keep from posing with pride. Not sure how successful I am. As we make for the fire escape and work our way down the side of the building, I think about the packets we've gotten from Rete so far. They've all been run-of-the-mill drops. No swerves, no traps. Except for that power play with Vee, he hasn't tried anything.

*Somehow, that doesn't comfort me at all.*

# V

Micah and I take the long way back to Rete's. His two goons keep their distance this time, so there's no need to flash any knuckle jewelry. *Amazing how a simple set of Brights can change your whole outlook.*

The short and ugly one gives me the stink eye, a bruise already spreading along his jaw. *Whatever.* Stripped down on top to a grubby wifebeater, he's sprawled on a crate with a 72-ounce convenience store cup pressed to his face. Eyeing his tats, I realize they're old-school ink under the skin, not the newer magnetic ones that Rete sports. I trace over my forearms with my fingernails just hard enough to feel them through the cotton of my hoodie.

"*Puta,*" he mutters at me.

"*Pendejo,*" I fire back, another knee-jerk response.

His matchstick partner cuts between us and jerks a thumb at the office. "Rete's in there."

"You speak Spanish," Micah notes under his breath as we head toward the inner sanctum.

"Enough to be mouthy, apparently." I stick close to him, wondering what other surprises I'm going to pull today.

Not that we need any more complications. Inside, Rete's got his feet on the desk and his fingers steepled; no phone call, no papers, no distractions. No doubt he's been watching us since we came into the building.

*He probably has cameras set up all around the warehouse.*

"Punctual with a capital *punk*," he drawls. "Just how I like it."

I don't answer because there's no point in rising to cheap bait. The way he looks at me makes me want to take another shower.

Micah tosses the repackaged water tower parcel onto the desk. "As requested. Made the first drop, here's the second."

Rete sets the package aside for a moment, pulling two black cases from a desk drawer and sliding them toward us. "Here. I know you said you're all set on Rivitocin, but based on the runs you've made since your last pickup and your new shadow here, you're due for a restock."

*Like a dog with a bone.* He can smell something's off, even if he's not smart enough to figure out what, and he's not going to let this go. I decide to cut in before things get stickier. "Thanks, Rete. Very thoughtful of you." I grab the twin cases and stash them in Micah's messenger bag.

"Think nothing of it." Slightly upset I broke his rhythm, Rete flicks his gaze from me to Micah. "It is odd, though, that I can't find *anything* in Maggie's files about your 'tocin use."

Micah's jaw is tight, his voice measured. "Wouldn't know anything about that. Maggie handled all the bookkeeping."

Rete sits up, planting both feet on the floor and feigning satisfaction with the reply. "Of course, of course. Well, now that that's settled . . ." He turns and reaches for two packets on a nearby shelf, tossing one to Micah and one to me. Both have coordinates written on the envelope. "Errands for tomorrow. First one's a clean drop, second one's an exchange, and follow the instructions on the new package." Rete flutters his hand when he adds, "Oh, and drop numero three is person-to-person, and he likes his couriers pretty. You're up, strawberry."

Micah goes very still, his fists clenching as he looks to me. I shake my head, trying to be subtle. *I've got this, love.*

Rete leans forward far enough to scrawl an address on the water-tower envelope. "Don't leave quite yet, pets. Not done for the day. Going to have you run this, too." He reaches into his pocket and pulls out a thick stack of prepaids. Tossing one on top of the envelope, he jerks his chin at me. "There's a dress code at the club, and 'Teen Runaway' isn't going to cut it." He tilts his head to the side. "Something short to show off the legs, maybe."

If Rete keeps this shit up, Micah's going to knock his teeth down his throat. And while I'd appreciate such a thoughtful gesture, this guy's attempt at innuendo is honestly pathetic. Never mind that every snake who's slithered through the Cyrene music scene has tried at least once to play grab-ass with me, and that goes double for most of Corporate's execs. On an ordinary night, I would have handed Rete his balls in a bag.

Different tactics might yield better results. I start with a slow smile and follow that up with a hand reaching down to indicate midthigh. "About here?"

Rete's nasty grin widens when I raise my hand another inch. "Keep going," is his only suggestion.

I shrug. "The less fabric, the more it's going to cost. You have expensive enough taste to know that."

Without missing a beat, he tosses a second prepaid on the pile and barks a laugh. "Get her out of here, ace, before I decide to escort her myself."

Micah grabs the envelope, the cards, and me before I can so much as coo a good-bye to our greasy benefactor. I'm pretty sure my feet don't fully hit the ground until we're three blocks away.

"What was all that about?" Micah finally asks.

I don't mistake his concern and frustration for jealousy, but I still dig in my heels until he's forced to a stop. On tiptoe, I manage to gently kiss the end of his nose. "I just want the chance to pretty up a bit for you before we go to the club. Why not do it on that asshole's dime?"

The line of his jaw softens, making my hummingbird heart flutter. Micah still wants so badly to protect me, to take care of me, but—*unlike Damon*—he trusts me enough to handle things myself. "Vee, I just—"

"No worries. A girl could get used to someone giving a damn." I trade him my parcel for the second prepaid card. "Meet you at The Spot for dinner in an hour."

## M

I shadow Vee for a block before reluctantly stepping back. She's casual and cautious. She nearly spots me twice in the short time I follow her. *She's got this. Trust her.*

The truth is I do trust her. I just don't trust this city. With Rete's barely veiled threat, Ludo sneaking around, and the omnipresent danger of guards and greyfaces, I hate having her more than an arm's length away.

*But she deserves the break. From the warren. From me. From being chaperoned.*

I steal one last glimpse of her, then take off at a decent clip, Rete's other prepaid in my pocket and the parcels in my bag. It'll take some time to get back to the Arkcell, but it's a worthwhile side trip.

Missing the trolley by a few seconds, I book it for the bridge, making up some time by hopping fences along the back alleys of the Jobalign. I slow down before crossing into the Odeaglow and duck into the back entrance of Needle & Threads, my usual place for picking up club gear at a decent price.

For one night, at least, I can look the part of a guy who actually deserves Vee's time and attention. I bypass the bargain racks and remaindered wear and head for the front, zeroing in on the smoky gray dress shirt on the side rack. *Definitely my style, but a little high-end for running around Cyrene.* There's a matching darker vest and tie; I debate for a few seconds before picking them up, as well.

Fingers crossed I won't look like a total douche. Or like that asshat piece-of-shit manager of hers.

I snake a pair of passable dress shoes for half price and run the prepaid through the system, ringing it all up. Snagging the biggest shopping bag they have, I head for home, picking up the laundry along the way.

With only a minor complaint from my ribs—thankfully, they *finally* seem to be on the mend—I scale the stone supports and slip behind the heavy tarp. As I put down the bags, the silence in the warren surprises me. It feels empty without her. I sigh, and then smile, picking up traces of her in the air, a comforting ghost.

I stash away the laundry, pulling out a fresh pair of jeans for tonight before opening up the storage closet, grabbing a few tools, and settling in to work on a surprise for her. Only a few minutes' labor, but it's intricate, demanding patience and a steady hand.

Once it's done, I admire my handiwork, then quickly replace the tools, lock up the closet, grab my new duds, and head out, leaving behind the lingering wisps of her.

I snag the briefest of showers at the gym, successfully dodging both scanners and recruits who exchange workout-thrum production for credits and a bit more definition, then I hit a coffee shop close to The Spot and change into my semiformal gear.

*Not too shabby, if I say so myself.* A fingercomb of the hair later, I stroll nonchalantly toward our rendezvous, bag with the usual Micah-wear in hand.

# V

I head straight for the Paleteni Mall. An emporium of cheese, sure, but I need options and I need them fast. Ducking into the air-conditioned building, I force myself to move with confident ease, the same not-too-fast, not-too-slow, just-right pace that's served us so well over the last few days.

The building is surreal enough, with its glass cathedral ceilings, steel beams, and massive fountains, but I also have to contend with fresh memories of the riot, the miniconcert, crowd-surfing out the doors.

*That happened to someone else.*

It helps that no one's paying any kind of attention to me today. At most, I'm getting the occasional odd look for being so underdressed, but it's time to change that. The first three stores are a bust. Everything is disco-ball shiny, covered in sequins or shedding glitter. I have no problem with tarting up, but I doubt tonight's venue calls for anything that bright. Taking a cue from Micah's everyday wear, I need something in muted colors.

*That doesn't mean boring. Not by a long shot.*

By the time I hit store number four, I'm ripping through the racks like lightning. I don't know why it's stressing me out so much, the idea of spending the evening with him. We've been inseparable, living in each other's pockets. He's listened to me pee, for god's sake. But we've been living without expectations for days . . .

And now I have them again. That, and flutters in my midsection at the idea of dressing up. Showing off.

*For him.*

The promise of the perfect dress is halfway down the row. Short . . . Shorter even than Rete would have expected. Silky, the sort of fabric that puddles in the hand without crumpling. Pewter gray. I didn't realize until that second that I'd been looking for something that would remind Micah of the shirt I was wearing that night at the Palace. Not a speck of metal on it anywhere, but it's backless, too.

*No need for "ladygear" on top.*

I do, however, grab a pair of black lace panties. The perfect shoes are one department over: heeled sandals that remind me of gladiators in an arena. I head for the self-checkout line, zipping Rete's card through the machine and breathing a sigh of relief when the light turns green. Sliding everything in a bag, I check the nearest clock and let myself relax just an inch. Plenty of time left for finish work.

Heading for the exit takes me down the endless rows of cosmetics. Pausing at each counter only long enough to use a sample and then split before someone barges over to offer assistance, I manage to put on dabs of foundation, silver eye shadow, tinted cheek-slick, lip gloss. Getting the eyeliner and mascara on without drawing notice requires circling the same kiosk three times, but by the time I'm done, the mirror tells me good things.

I let the girl wielding the bottle of Millennium fog me a good one on the way out the door. After a pit stop and a quick change in the bathroom, a different person—one who's just as foreign as she is familiar—stares back at me.

*Fingers crossed that Micah likes what he sees.*

I blow myself a kiss, shove my hacked-off boots and borrowed threads into the empty shopping bag, and head out the door.

# CHAPTER FOURTEEN

## M

Arriving a few minutes early, I stake out an inconspicuous spot on the sidewalk near the restaurant. I give my outfit a once-over—sleeves rolled up just so, buttons buttoned, fly up—and god help me, I even do a breath check.

The deadline passes. Then a few minutes.

Then a few more minutes. *Cue the worrying.* I scan up and down the streets, ignoring the honking of cars and the ding of an approaching trolley as I keep my eyes peeled for Vee. The trolley rolls to a halt in front of the restaurant, and everything stops when she appears. All of my doubts, fears, and worries turn to smoke and drift lazily away.

She's a vision of slinky elegance, her whisper of a dress making all other dresses everywhere insanely jealous. With a few simple brushes of makeup, a new Vee emerges, one I haven't seen before. Not the one for the fans, or the one hiding out from Damon, but one she chooses for herself. I offer my hand to help her down, and she accepts it with grace, taking the few steps in her own time.

Vee's hand still in mine, I spin it above her head, and she obliges me by following it in a slow twirl that steals my breath. She beams, obviously having gotten the reaction she hoped for. I hunt for the right words, telling painters to abandon their canvases and poets that there aren't enough golden apples to offer or ships to launch in her name. But when I find my voice again, all I can manage is, "You look stunning. Absolutely stunning." I hope my eyes speak the words I can't.

With faux coyness, she replies, "Oh, yeah, I clean up pretty good." She smiles, kisses me softly, then leans even closer to whisper in my ear, "Your vest is doing unholy things to me, I have to tell you."

I take her bag in the same hand as my own and offer her my other arm. She accepts it with a smile and a tip of her imaginary hat, and we head inside, grateful for the subdued amber lighting that makes The Spot so ideal for those who prefer their privacy. Tucking our bags against the wall, we grab a corner table near the back, opting to sit on neighboring sides instead of facing each other from across the table. I hold her hand, enjoying the quiet simplicity of the moment. I haven't taken my eyes off her since the trolley arrived.

She breaks the ice. "So, not disappointed?"

"Absolutely not. In fact, I think you look almost perfect." I slip my hand from hers, loosening my tie and unbuttoning the first button on my shirt.

"Almost?" She places one hand under her chin, not realizing that she's pouting just the slightest bit. "What did I miss?"

Reaching up behind my head, I unclasp my necklace and draw it down, only to place it around her neck and reclasp it, brushing the skin of her neck as I do. "There, that did the trick. *Perfect.*"

Her hand flies up to touch the chain, to run her fingers along the smooth links. "I recognize it from your ID picture." The blushing that follows is visible even by candlelight. "I only saw it the one time, but I guess it made an impression."

For a moment, I'm speechless. *Those three days, wondering if she'd even remember me.* I smile at the idea of her hunting down my ID photo. "I know the feeling." When I take her hand in mine again, Vee runs her thumb along one finger. Her touch is electric, like she's still wearing my Brights. "I had to replace the clasp because it melted back at the Dome. But now it's fixed, and it looks marvelous on you. Everything does." With each word, my heart beats a little faster, my eyes dancing over her as she sits a few inches away.

The rest of dinner is a blur, punctuated by images of her, laughing and smiling in flickers like candlelight. I'm sure there was ordering, waiting, conversation, and actual eating, but in my head, it begins and ends with Vee's smile. If I could bottle this moment and save it, I would. Peaceful, relaxed, and effortless, the most amazing girl by my side. With every word, every little touch, she glows brighter, dazzling me endlessly.

I settle up the check and we head out, arms linked and with a bag for each of us. We leisurely make our way to Rete's last drop of the day. It's a few blocks off the trolley line, and Vee passes me my Brights from her bag, which I tuck into one of my vest pockets.

Down one more street, we knock on the third red door on the right. I hand the hulking doorman the playing card that Rete included with the parcel. *The two of clubs. Huh. I didn't think Rete was capable of that kind of subtlety.* The doorman nods, letting us past, and we descend the stairs into the club itself, which is retro in all the right ways. The center of the place is laid with parquet flooring, and old-school speakers ring the room, offering pops and staticky buzzes that feel positively dead-on. There's a coat-check room with lockers, managed by a perky young lady with tight curls and a pillbox hat. We gratefully hand off our bags to her and receive two small keys in return.

Vee turns to me in curious bemusement. "This isn't like any place I've ever been to."

I scan the crowd, looking for our contact, and spot the bartender across the way. He must be the hand-off. "I've heard rumors of spots like this, but never been to one. A slow-jams club."

Assessing the place, Vee immediately puzzles out its purpose. "There aren't any thrum-collectors here."

"Nope, it's completely off-grid. Just you and the music and whoever you bring." *A break from the frenetic beats and pulsing bass of the clubs. Totally brilliant.*

I tap her shoulder and we head for the bar. The barman, complete with white shirt and black bow tie, takes the rag from his shoulder and tosses it onto the counter in front of me. "What can I getcha?"

Vee shakes her head, so I say "Nothing for us, thanks" as I place both hands on the countertop, pushing the small parcel under the rag.

The bartender nods, snapping up the towel and package together. "Should be a good lineup tonight. Better grab a choice spot fast."

"That's the plan," Vee replies, grinning as she drags me to the parquet. "Let's see what kind of moves you've got on the dance floor, slick."

# V

I feel like I've been waiting all evening to get this close to Micah. He wears the clothes instead of the clothes wearing him, and that makes all the difference in the world. The easy way he rolled up his shirt cuffs, the open button at the collar. And the vest.

*Good grief . . . Some decently tailored fabric and five buttons should not be doing this to me.*

But they do.

The speakers are only just crackling to life when my shoes hit the dance floor. Fingers laced through Micah's, I pull him along behind me until we stand dead center under the vintage chandelier. The first few notes that wash over us sound tinny, hesitant, like they're broadcasting not only from someplace far away, but from another time altogether. Someone with a gentle hand slowly turns up the volume until we're awash in orchestral strains that are old as dirt. The low-and-slow notes of the song slide over me, making promises: a thousand more dances like this one; going to bed together and waking up together and taking care of each other.

Reaching up, I slide my fingers around the silver chain Micah gave me, each link a moment we've spent together, a look exchanged, a breath against skin, a smile . . .

*His smile.*

"Are you all right?" he dips his head down to ask, probably because I haven't moved an inch since the music started.

"More than all right." As I turn to face him, a spotlight hits a disco ball and a thousand stars appear. One of Micah's hands finds my waist. With the other one, he tucks my hand close to his chest. I lean into him, letting my cheek rest on his shoulder. Time stops for us as we sway, back and forth. There are words in my mouth, a song I'm not quite ready to sing. I mouth them against his shirt, trying them out, but unable to put any breath behind them yet.

*I love you, Micah.*

He kisses my forehead gently and holds me closer, as if he knows my every thought. This man, so broken, so mistreated, and still so tender with me.

I do my best to gather the memories of this moment: the harmonies in the music, the way his body is pressed against mine, the scent of him, every line of every muscle. But there's no way to memorize someone's soul.

*Where's this supposed to go, Vee? It's not some goddamn love story. Damon's probably doing his best right now to fuck your happy ending. It's just a matter of time.*

The song ends, like my thoughts killed it, but everyone around me is clapping, smiling, winding themselves up for the next number, which is still throwback but significantly faster. Some couples even know the steps to the swing and the jive. They jostle us from all sides, but Micah manages to keep up with the tempo and our competition as easily as he'd jump a concrete wall.

"I got this, babe," he reminds me, grabbing my wrist, twirling me out, bringing me back in for a sudden and unexpected dip. "I got you."

And he proves, over the next three songs, that it's not just empty talk.

Winded and thirsty, I run to get us drinks and use the opportunity to have a conversation with the bartender. A few minutes later, I'm headed back to Micah with two Manhattans. I hand him one glass and take a sip from my own. The butterfly flutters are back, and they don't abate when the glasses are empty, when I take his hand, when I lead him up a narrow stairwell off to the side of the dance floor.

"What's the plan?" His fingers are twined through mine, so I know the second they tighten briefly. Relaxed, but never too relaxed. Never unprepared for the ground to shift suddenly underneath him.

"Grand finale." The upper levels of the building feel worlds away from the club, the music muffled through wood and wallpaper. A mellow baritone croons about love being a kick in the head.

*You got it, buster.*

I open the door at the end of the hall and step back in time again. It's like a hotel room from a hundred years ago, all wood paneling and satin coverlet and a beaded ivory lamp shade radiating just slightly more light than a candle.

"Apparently there's money to be made offering off-grid overnight accommodations." I draw Micah inside and close and lock the door behind him. "I traded the rest of my prepaid, but . . ."—I hook a finger into the top of his vest and pull him closer—"I think it's going to be worth it."

He lets his eyes roll over my body, his hands sliding to my waist. "Best credits you've ever spent."

I loosen his tie and slide it off, undo his buttons one at a time. Drawing it out. Making him wait. Making him wonder. Shoes in the corner, dress tossed onto a nearby chair, I'm only wearing his necklace by the time we fall into the bed.

# M

Waking up in an honest-to-god bed with a gorgeous, ass-kicking, rib-kicking girl in my arms . . . I don't give the tiniest shit about Rete or Damon or any of that garbage. I pull Vee closer and revel in the thousand little sensations sparked by every brush of her skin against mine. I gaze at her enticing lips, lips with sinful knowledge, lips that bring me to the brink with mind-blowing ease, and I kiss her, long and slow.

I know the exact moment she starts waking up, because every inch of her skin flushes a faint pink. She stirs and peeks at me through a tangled curtain of hair.

"Good morning, temptress," I whisper to her.

She stretches against me like a cat in the sunlight. "You're easy to tempt." Her fingers tiptoe south, down my chest, over my stomach. I suck in a breath when she slides on top of me.

Except she keeps right on sliding, out of the bed, running for the shower, hair streaming down her back, calling out, "Dibs!" over her naked shoulder.

I follow her in with a laugh. "That was cheating."

"I'll make it up to you, I promise."

*Oh, I believe you.*

We do our best to empty the building's hot water heater, but eventually we have to come out.

"Game faces, right?" Vee says, wrapping a towel around herself.

I wish I could toss her back into the bed and keep her there all day, but I have to nod. "Gotta gear up for more drops. But this . . . this was worth every credit."

Her smile practically blinds me, and she opens the door, finding our coat-checked bags waiting for us. "The service here really is top-notch." Tossing my bag toward me, she affects a terrible fake accent to add a blithe, "Remember to tip them well, trusted manservant."

She's almost dressed by the time I've got my jeans on. "A glowing review from a fugitive and his incognito companion would probably be good PR for them. 'When I'm on the run from the greyfaces, I always choose Two of Clubs.'"

Once we're geared up like proper anonymous street rats again, we quit our single-night paradise, but not without one last, lingering kiss to celebrate. On our way out, I toss the bartender what's left on my prepaid as a thank-you. *A most definitely deserved one.*

A quick side trip to the warren to stash our going-out clothes—and get a look at the contents of our parcels—doubles as a good warm-up run for the day's drops. The first one takes us past Mercette Park, and I can see giant vidscreens set up at intervals along the main lawn. The day's participants are split up into groups, and everyone's studying a set of pictures on the screens.

There, bigger than life, are Cyrene ID photos of both of us. Vee looks incredibly young in her picture, *too* young to even be sixteen, the minimum age of a standard recruit, but it still blows her anonymity all to bits. The girl standing next to me is unmistakably the same one in the photograph.

*Shit.*

"I guess today's activity is 'fugitive scavenger hunt.'" Casually, I take Vee's hand and draw her down a side street, away from the park. Careful pacing. Not quick enough to draw attention.

Her heart must be pounding. But she's keeping a handle on it, forcing herself to put one foot in front of the other and not break into a run. *That's my girl.*

I meet her eyes as we move, our pace quickening as we make tracks toward drop number one, a vintage newspaper machine outside an apartment complex. "I know, I'll make this fast and then we'll jet through the other two, okay?"

Vee nods silently, eyes shifting like she's already plotting the route to the next one in her head. I go for the dropbox. It's an old pay-a-quarter, open-the-hatch-and-grab-your-paper number, but it's rigged not to open. Instead, the window flips inward and the package vanishes, like a magic trick. I stuff the parcel inside and make sure it drops out of view.

When I look up, I see two kids in matching red T-shirts working their way down the sidewalk, pushing back the hoods of everyone they pass and whipping off sunglasses in order to case the neighborhood face by face. Across the way, a matching pair of crimson douchebags works the other side of the street.

*Scavenger hunters? Already?*

Vee keeps to the shadows, but those tools are getting closer. I move in on the nearest greyface wannabe, planting two hands on his chest and shoving him on his ass in front of his buddy. "See what happens when you're too pushy?"

Even stunned, they recognize me immediately. I smirk, then turn and bolt down the street, giving them a one-finger salute and crying out, "The race is on, motherfuckers!" Anything to draw their attention away from Vee.

It works; the two across the street abandon their one-by-one search and join their humiliated chums in chasing me.

*Okay, playtime's over. Gotta ditch these guys fast.* Quick as a glim-addled bunny, I jump and roll onto a dumpster, grabbing the top of a window ledge and slipping feetfirst through the open window into someone's apartment. "Pardon me!" I cry as I run through the living room and out the door, tearing ass down the hallway and a flight of stairs before hitting the street again.

I'm across the hood of a parked sedan and halfway across the street before two of the hunters charge around the building and straight inside, probably expecting to cut off my escape.

*No such luck.*

I walk one block up, then double back around to meet a relieved-but-still-spooked Vee, who's already spotted an easy exit down an unoccupied side street, now that I've misled the best of the frat boys.

I take her hand in mine, and we slowly stroll away.

# V

Crouched in a doorway, Micah wants to ditch the rest of the drops and head back to the warren. As much as I want to duck back to relative safety, I have to play fucked-up voice of reason.

"We don't need Rete's goons after us on top of everything else," I say, tugging him back out into the street. "They might be dumber than dirt, but they'll track us down easier than some random kid trying to match us to a set of old pictures."

He stops for a long, long minute before finally nodding his head. I can tell he's not happy about this, but he's following my lead now. Trusting me.

*I hope neither of us regrets it.*

We end up at a postal depot in the Jobalign. The packet has a numbered card-key taped to the back and no further instructions.

Micah insists we circle around the back to confirm there's an emergency exit, then we hang out across the street to do a little recon, eyeing the entrance for at least five minutes. Only one person goes in and out that entire time.

"Seems safe enough," I venture, hoping Micah will agree.

"Mmph," is all he gives me for an answer, but the next second he tucks his hand into my back pocket. "Let's go."

Ducking in together, we get a good lungful of recirculated air. Passing burned-out vidscreens, we move in tandem along the far wall until we hit the back.

"*Fuck*," Micah says, because the emergency exit is blocked with crates and boxes. "Come on, we need to hustle." He's checking for other escape routes as we make our way to number 435, two aisles down and one over.

The mailboxes are retro metal numbers with access ports for the card-keys. I shove in the one off the packet and wait for the light to turn green. *Beep beep beep ZZZT.* The reader spits the card back onto the floor—access denied. I reach down to grab it and cram it back in. *Beep beep beep ZZZT!*

The ping from the front door announces that we have company. Micah shifts closer to me, muscles tensed and ready to move as a group of kids in retro-neon rocket past us in a mind-numbing, eye-watering blur. I know what he's thinking.

*These are awfully tight quarters for a clean getaway.*

"Giving you some trouble?" he asks, offering up a laugh that only I know is fake.

"Just a bit, love." I jam the card in a third time and hold it there. "Nothing another minute and a ton of dynamite won't fix." *Beep beep . . .* "Don't you fucking dare, or I'll kick you in." *Click.*

The door opens, and I pull one packet out and shove the delivery in. Now I'm holding a new parcel, still small enough for me to stuff into my pocket. The front door pings again.

"Window in the back," Micah says, already moving both of us in that direction.

I can't help but glance to the front, where a squad of greyfaces is already fanning out and heading down the aisles in pairs. A few more steps, and Micah boosts my ass up and out. Two seconds later, he hits the street next to me and we take off. Squeeze through a gap in a chain-link fence. Detour down an alley.

Even as I show Micah the shrink-wrapped package, I know there's nothing in his messenger bag to replicate that. "A sure sign that there's something janky going on with this one, love." I scan the label and tell him, "It's the same address as the first pickup yesterday."

"Six blocks, not even." His mouth tightens as he checks around the next corner.

"Let's get this done," I agree, surprised that I'm still keeping up.

He sticks to the back streets, keeping tabs on the traffic from a distance. Another squad of greyfaces at the end of Dimity Avenue sends us up a fire escape and over two rooftops. The closer we get to our destination, the unhappier Micah looks. We end up back in the alley where I grabbed myself a handful of dead rodent.

He slows to a halt, gaze flickering over the windows and doors. "Not the ledge this time."

I nod. "Supposed to pass it along in person." *To someone who likes strawberries.*

Micah reaches for my hand, gives it a squeeze, and lets go. "I'll be right here—"

"It's a drop, love, not the gateway to Hell." I smile just to reassure him; it isn't doing anything to quell *my* nerves, that's for damn sure. Pulling out the packet, I head off, stepping up onto the small cement porch, sticking close to the wall, and knocking twice on the numbered metal door.

No answer. I thump on it again and then peer back at Micah, wondering if I should try to open it or bail. He launches forward just as the door opens.

I turn back, relief changing to sick horror. Adonis reaches out with an explosive "Fuck!" and grabs me the second I try to run. It's too late to reach the Brights in my pocket.

*Stupid, stupid, stupid! I should have put them on before I ever knocked on the door.*

Adonis lifts me off my feet. Clamps a hand down over my mouth before I can take a breath to scream. Memories crash over me, ghosts of the guys who held me down and cut me up.

*Not the first time this has happened.*

My only tie to *this* time is Micah, moving at a sprint, his face a panicked blur before the door slams shut between us.

# M

At twenty feet, I spot him.

At fifteen feet, he grabs Vee.

At ten feet, he slams the door shut.

At five feet and a dead run, I vault over the wrought iron porch railing, kicking in the door with everything I've got. It crashes open, tearing away part of the doorframe with it. With my feet back under me, I'm charging again, in time to see His Majesty cry out as Vee sinks her teeth into his fingers.

*That was your second mistake. I'm gonna make you pay dearly for your first.*

As he cradles his hand, Vee breaks free of his grasp, and puts some crucial distance between her and Johnny Applespeed. I'm on him in moments, wrapping both hands around his throat, already squeezing hard as my weight slams into him, smashing us both through the glass table behind him.

Hemmed in by the warped metal of the former table, I press down on his windpipe, watching his face turn red. I'm a berserker at this point, completely losing the plot for a second.

Vee keens like a wounded animal, and my eyes instinctively cut over to where she's slumped against the wall. The druggie scumbag takes advantage, bashing me upside the head with part of the broken table. Rolling me aside, the coward fuck scrambles after her. I grab for his ankle, delaying him just long enough for Vee to snatch up one of the larger glass shards. Eyes wild, she lashes out, slicing across His Majesty's outstretched arm and then making a second pass across his stomach. He looks incredulous as he clamps a hand over the gut wound.

"You cut me, you fucking bi—" is all he gets out before I crash into him, bouncing his head off the wall. He crumples into a heap, groaning, but he's not the one I'm worried about.

"Vee." Blood drips off the piece of glass she's holding, a warning I ignore to slowly reach for her.

She wheels on me, improvised weapon clutched in her trembling hand. "You said you'd take care of me, Damon. You said it would all be all right!"

Oh god, the memories. She's not even *here* right now.

"Vee, please, look at me." I keep my words calm, measured. *Gotta talk her down. Gotta reach her, like I did in the closet at the Dome.*

Her eyes move frantically from side to side, chasing phantoms, her grip tightening on the glass until her palm bleeds. "You promised you'd take me home!"

As she gets louder, I get quieter. "Vee, look in my eyes. Vee, please. It's me. It's Micah."

I stand a few feet from her, just outside the range of the glass's razor edge, hands open, palms out. "You're okay. Look at me. Remember me. You and me, two against the world. *Please*."

She meets my eyes, then looks down at her hands, her blood mingling with the 'jack peddler's. The shard slips from her grip. "Micah?"

I step forward and take her into my arms. "Yes, I'm here. Always, Vee. I've got you."

I glance down at His Majesty. He's still down for the count, neck already bruising where I choked him, back riddled with tiny glass shards, forearm bleeding freely while he continues to grip his middle. *Even with the stab to the gut, he'll be just fine. Nanotech'll see to that.*

Pulling away from Vee, I lean over him. "I ever see you again, you're a dead man. Bank on it." And I give him one hard boot to the nuts, ensuring he'll be in no shape to follow us.

Vee grips my arms. "Oh my god, Micah, get me out of here. I . . . I *remember.*"

I grab the parcel—no way I'm leaving anything here with the likes of him—and we're out the door like we were never there. Except, you know, for the kicked-in door, the broken table, his arm, his gut, his balls, the teeth marks on his hand—

*And pieces of Vee's past.*

No time for Memory Lane now. We sacrifice stealth for speed as we race from the neighborhood, trying to put maximum distance between us and His Majesty. Vee matches me step for step, doing her damnedest to shake off our latest close call.

Making it back to the warren, stopping only to scan for prying eyes, we collapse on the floor beside each other, grabbing deep lungfuls of air in our copper-wrapped cell. The adrenaline of the day is slow to fade from our systems. Vee's fingertips brush mine, and I look over at her, knowing I have to ask the question, already hating the answer.

"What do you remember?"

# V

I'm covered in blood—Micah's blood, Adonis's blood, *my* blood. It's sticking to my wrists, crusting under my nails, part of the voodoo spell that unlocked my past. I can feel Micah looking at me, but from so far away. I'm on the floor, a *different* floor. Somewhere outside Cyrene. My skirt is ripped, wrists and ankles pinned. Every one of us sports freshly inked tattoos, but I'm the sacrifice on the altar. Other voices ricochet around the room. People cheering and catcalling, I think. *Stop fucking moving. You knew this was coming. Someone hold her the fuck down.*

Looking down at my arms, I finally understand the phantom marks that have haunted my skin. Why I'd hit that guy back at Rete's warehouse.

"It was an initiation," I finally manage to say. "In Los Angeles, pretty sure. A bunch of street kids were camped out in an abandoned house. No furniture or anything, just empty beer bottles and some crates in the corner. Might've been drugs, but I don't know. I . . . was new. They were supposed to be my new family, except I don't think you're supposed to gang-rape your family. There were four guys . . . at least four that I remember." *Oh god.* "And Damon. Damon was there. Waiting his turn."

It's only when he goes unnervingly still that I realize Micah retrieved his first-aid kit and had been attending to my bleeding hand. Holding my wrist in place, he drops his voice a notch "His *turn*?"

"I guess?" I can't actually pull up anything beyond seeing Damon standing off to the side . . . *Black undershirt, baggy jeans, dark ink scrolled over his forearms* . . . but maybe that's self-preservation at work. "At some point, I stopped feeling anything. I just wanted to die. Closed my eyes and prayed for it."

I shudder, pain echoing through every limb, and try to curl in on myself enough to make it all stop. Micah's arms slide around me as my head hits his shoulder. I'm shaking now, holding on to him like he's the only thing keeping me from shattering. He just whispers in my ear, over and over, "I'm here, Vee, I've got you," as if by sheer force of will he can become my touchstone. He cradles me in his arms, carrying me to the bed like I weigh nothing at all.

The memory gun loads image after image into the cylinder: surgical masks, concerned eyes, halo-light surrounding their heads. "I woke up at the hospital. The surgeons somehow made it clear through the morphine that I had seriously limited options for survival." Curled up against Micah's chest, I keep talking, because it might slip away from me again. "The choice came down to either dying or letting them install experimental nanotech. I couldn't even sign my name." Distinct as anything, I remember the smear of red I'd left on the pristine touchscreen. "They let me press my thumb to a datapad to give consent."

"What about your family?" Micah asks when I hesitate. "Some emergency contact the hospital could have called for you?"

"There wasn't anyone." Fresh tears at the realization. "Career foster kid, professional runaway. No one cared. Made it through the surgery, but it meant I was Cyrene property. Fourteen was too young to get recruited, but they found some legal loophole."

"How did Damon find you again?" Micah threads one hand through my hair, teasing the tangles out like he's trying to help me put everything in order.

"Ran across me in one of the night clubs." Everything I thought I knew was suspect now. Damon didn't randomly "discover" some new musical act; he tracked me down. Found his way inside just to come after me.

Then he did everything he could to keep me close. Under his thumb. The memory gun continues to fire, images slamming into me like bullets: Damon in a shiny new suit, taking me into a Cyrene recording studio; Damon bent over a mixing board, yelling at me through the intercom; Damon gripping my shoulders and shaking me hard when I flub the first take.

As Micah holds me close, my fingertips brush over the glass shards still stuck in his arms from taking down Adonis. Blood smears crisscross his shirt, but I'm not sure how much is actually his. "Forget about me for a minute. We have to get you cleaned up."

I shove off the cot and reach for the first-aid kit, ripping open an antiseptic pack and trying to wipe away the worst of the blood. Unlike the golden god, Micah doesn't have any nanotech to rush to his aid.

*Just me. Only me.*

He doesn't flinch, even when I douse everything with astringent. *Still so focused on me, stupid sweet boy.* Once I've wrapped him from wrist to elbow on both arms with compression gauze, I can sit back and reassess.

"I have to get your shirt off, love." I don't waste time trying to pull it over his head. Surgical shears are faster, and I'm able to toss aside the filthy cotton in seconds. *No puncture wounds on his chest or back, thank god.* I go to wipe everything down with a clean damp rag just to be sure, but he catches hold of my hand.

"Today was too much," he says. "Everything I do puts the people I care about in danger."

I swallow, trying to get rid of the horrible empty ache at the back of my throat. "That's not true and you know it."

His eyes focus for a moment. "Bryn and Trav and all of them died because I *gave* them the poison. Maggie's probably dead at this point because I haven't found proof of what Rete's been up to. What about you? What if—"

I slam my free hand down over his chest tattoo, pressing against it as hard as I can. "You lost them, but you have me. *You have me.*" He shakes his head, like he's ready to argue some more, and I ball my hand into a fist. "Their names are on your skin, Micah, but I'm on your fucking heart. Admit it."

He pauses, eyes darting as he hunts for the right words, or any words. Finally, a few stumble out. "So much it scares me. When I saw that piece of shit grab you . . . If anything ever happened to you . . . I can't lose you, Vee." His voice cracks as he admits, "I'm afraid I'm gonna get you killed."

I look him square in the eyes, remembering everything we've just shared. "Long story short, love," I say, "Damon's more of a danger to me than you could ever be. He won't ever let me go, and he'll go through you to get to me."

Micah holds me tight. "Let him try. I won't let you go, Vee. No matter what comes next, no matter where we find ourselves, I won't let anyone hurt you ever again." Even in a whisper, I can hear the force, the conviction behind his words. "Two against the world, right?"

I nod my answer, wishing I hadn't wasted my chance last night.

*You had all the romance ever going for you. You should have said it then.*

Instead I wrap my arms around him until I can't get any closer. "I really fucked up my timing. Remind me to tell you something tomorrow, all right?"

He kisses my forehead softly. "Sure."

Under the blanket, wrapped up in each other, it's a long time before either of us falls asleep, but every beat of my heart is telling him what I can't.

# CHAPTER FIFTEEN

## M

I slowly return to consciousness, haunted by thoughts of Vee's past. Half expecting to see her beaten and bruised, I open my eyes, grateful to gaze upon her as she sleeps. I can hear her breathing, feel the shallow rise and fall of her chest.

Right now, she's untroubled by scavenger hunters inside the city or vicious gangs outside. Right now, the weight of the world is off her shoulders, no worries about Rete's thugs or Damon or getting out of Cyrene.

*Let her enjoy a few more minutes' peace.*

Sliding out of her arms and crouching beside the bed, I tuck the blanket around her as she dozes. I slip silently across the floor and retrieve the shrink-wrapped parcel from the pocket of my discarded hoodie. *His Majesty was there to receive it. That can't be a coincidence.*

I weigh the package in my hand. *Doesn't feel like thumb drives, cash, or prepaids.* My fingers make short work of the envelope, ripping it in two. Don't need to worry about being careful after what happened at the last drop.

The tabs of applejack spill into my hand, confirming my worst suspicions. I might as well be watching the heads of my dead friends tumble from the parcel.

*How many? How many packets of this garbage is Rete responsible for?*

Possibilities and conspiracies fog my brain. Rete's worked for Maggie a long time. Learning her distribution channels. Meeting her contacts. But even so, he couldn't switch over to applejack so soon after she went missing.

Way too late, I've finally put the pieces together, and I don't like the picture they form at all: *Maggie's been dealing applejack this whole time.* The realization hits me with a dull thud.

I set the drugs aside and grab a clean shirt, my bandaged forearms aching slightly with every movement. Bending down to retrieve my sneakers, I jump when Vee speaks.

"Going somewhere?" She's propped up on one elbow, eyes and nose still red from crying. Worse, she looks concerned. About me.

*She thinks I'm hiding things again.*

I hop once, slipping my sneaker on as I cross to sit at her side, the other shoe still AWOL. "I wanted to surprise you with a decent breakfast after our long night. You've had enough protein bars to last a lifetime."

"That's it? Just food?" She touches my cheek, suspecting something but trusting that I'll tell her.

"I found something in that parcel." I don't need to say what. She's already figured it out.

"You've got your proof. Rete is dealing applejack." When I don't answer right away, Vee pushes the hair out of my face, knowing there's more. "Micah?"

"Not just Rete," I tell her. "Maggie, too."

That one surprises her. "So where do we go from here?"

"How about we discuss that over pancakes? I'll bring some back." I lean forward and kiss her deeply, hoping to reassure her. Breaking it off, I brush her lips with mine as I say, "Vee, about yesterday, I'm so sorry—"

Two fingers slip between us as she silences me. "Stuff it, love. I know. I just . . . I'd be fine if we never ever talked about it again. And as long as you're not going to do anything stupid, we're good. Are we good?"

I nod quickly, stuffing my foot in my other shoe. "I promise. Just a quick breakfast run, then we figure out what comes next. Together."

"Okay, go. But get back here lickety-split. This blanket's a poor substitute for warm boy."

I smile, heading for the tarp.

"Hey," she calls out, tossing me the Brights when I turn around. "Just in case."

I slip them into my pocket. "Back in a flash."

And I'm off, climbing down the familiar stonework and making my way onto the streets of the Odeaglow, my only companion the steady hum of Cyrene.

There's plenty on my mind en route to the stimshot spot two blocks over. *Too many near misses. We need a plan, and soon, before somebody finally pins us down and puts an end to this.*

So where *do* we go from here? With the drop aborted yesterday, we can add His Majesty and Rete's thugs to the ever-growing list of people looking for us, since I doubt Rete'll tolerate a courier kicking the crap out of a client. *No matter how much that client deserved it.*

Rete's applejack parcel is still back at the warren, too. Evidence, six months in the making. Something inside me cries out "Keep going!" Demanding justice for Zane and Rina, Trav and Bryn. My mission.

*Can't get my vengeance against the dealer, but I can still take out Rete and part of the applejack trade.*

Sounds good, but what about Vee? Going kamikaze to bring down the dealers made sense when it was just me . . . but she could get hurt. *Killed.* If the thugs don't get her, then the greyfaces might, shuttling her right to her ivory tower, Corporate's pet back home safe and sound.

All these months, every moment has boiled down to two choices: stay or go. It always comes down to stay or go. Stay with Vee, keep her safe, make a life with her, or go after Rete, the dealers, every tab of applejack in the city.

*When you put it like that, the choice is easy.*

I order some breakfast sandwiches and a stack of pancakes to go, then pour two cups of the high-octane stuff, grabbing little packs of creamer for Vee and a few sugars for me.

So now that Rete and the 'jack dealers are out of the equation, the game changes. It's still stay or go, but if we stay, we take on everybody. If we go, we have everything Vee left behind waiting for us outside the Wall. Not to mention Corporate's impressively long reach.

As I head back to the warren, my eyes drift toward the horizon, knowing it's a holographic forgery. Running my eyes up and down, I spot it: the thin seam between the real sky and the projection. The top of the Wall. All the parkour training in the world won't let you climb that high.

*But you don't have to go over. People leave all the time. I got in, I can get us out. We'll find a way. Fuck Cyrene and the drugs and the hum and the thugs and the nanotech bullshit and everything else bottled up here. I'm gonna get Vee out, leave all the bad memories behind and just go. Those gangland fuckers won't be everywhere. We'll find a place to start fresh.*

Bag in hand, I head for home. Home and the girl who makes every second worthwhile.

# V

Micah's side of the bed is still warm, so I slide into it with an all-over shudder. Not just because I'm cold. It's taking every bit of effort to stay focused. Present. I feel like a little kid who knows damn good and well that there are real fucking monsters under the bed. But as long as I stay away from the edges, nothing can grab me and drag me under. Not the memories of the past. Not my fears for our future.

I glance at the tabs of applejack taunting me from the floor.

*Rete's a dangerous little fucker. If Micah keeps going after him . . .*

*No. It'll only end up with Micah dead in an alley. I have to convince him to let Rete go. To let it all go.*

*Except I don't have any idea if he* can *let it go.*

I squeeze my eyes shut and try not to let the panic swallow me whole. The familiar reminders of Micah offer up small measures of comfort: his blanket, wrapped around me; the clean shirt I'm wearing off the top of the laundry stack; the gentle weight of his silver chain hanging around my neck. I twist my fingers around the links of his necklace and try to relax—

Something lands atop me, and my eyes fly open. I'm expecting a paper bag of food and Micah smirking at me from the door. Instead, there's Little Dead Thing, bedraggled, wet from end to end, a sorry scrap of fur and bonier than usual. He looks like he's swept every inch of the city, looking for me.

"Holy shit, baby, have you been roaming this whole time?" Guilt-stricken, I scoop him into my lap and try to dry him off. Yowling a protest, he settles against my legs with his ears flattened, eyes narrowed to slits. He follows that up with a hiss at nothing. "Why the hell did Sasha let you out of the Loft . . . ?"

*Shit. Sasha. And Jax.*

I haven't spared many thoughts for them lately.

*They're probably worried sick by now . . . I think. Unless they're relieved that I bailed on them—*

The rhythmic rotor-whirr of helicopter blades interrupts me. Moving the cat to one side, I run for the door and peer out, hoping against hope that the chopper will fly right past the Arkcell. Instead, it heads straight for the bridge, banks hard at the last second, and circles around to come at me again.

*No.*

No time for shoes and no time for Little Dead Thing. I have to put as much space between me and the warren—and Micah—as I can. This time, I know it's not a drill. This time as I climb down, there are incoming sirens as a soundtrack.

I jump the last five feet and take off at a run just as the first black SUV screeches in. I've already worked up some speed, and I'll be fucked if I stutter to a halt now. Pushing harder, I manage to plant my right foot on the front tire, pop up, and land on the hood. My ass hits metal and I slide the rest of the way across, dropping to the ground on the other side.

*Thanks for the lessons, love.*

Hair in my eyes, I hitch in a breath and keep running. Behind me, I can hear the Facilitators already bailing out of the first vehicle. More dark cars are heading my way at top speed. The second slams on its brakes, steering into the turn so that it stops in front of me. The third boxes me in from the right.

*Keep moving, Vee. Don't fucking stop.*

I break left, a stitch in my side, the pain in my chest low and slow but gaining on me. Rocks and bits of jagged concrete rip up my bare feet, but I ignore it. One fleeting look over my shoulder and I see at least a dozen uniforms swarming after me. My only exit option now is a pile of rock and demolished concrete. My thighs and arms start to burn before I'm even halfway to the top.

"Be careful, you shitheads!" I hear Damon yelling somewhere below me; that's all it takes to slam me back into high gear. Something pings off the rocks to my left. A second *thwip!* of air brushes past my arm.

*What the hell? They're* shooting *at me?*

Matching pinpricks of pain hit me. Reaching back, I feel needles sticking out of my skin. Three seconds after that, nothing from the neck down belongs to me anymore, and I go down like a prize hunk of meat. My forehead glances off a rock. Unable to catch hold of anything, I slide several feet before coming to a stop.

All I have left is my voice, so I close my eyes and start to scream with every bit of strength left in me. Hoping Micah will hear it. Hoping he'll stay the fuck away.

# M

I hear the bustle of activity before I see it. The oppressive battering noise of a helicopter, screeching tires stopping short on asphalt. As I sprint down the alley and onto the street, the bag of food slips from my hand.

*They've found us. Oh sweet fuck they've found us.*

An army of Facilitators pours from several vehicles, well-armored thugs in Kevlar and black charging in all directions, cutting off any chance of escape. And Vee, magnificent Vee, gives them fresh hell, running circles around them, sliding across the hood of an SUV, and making it halfway up a wall of broken concrete before she collapses to the ground.

*Darts. Must have been. Cowards.*

Too many to attack. Too many to dodge. They're everywhere, swarming over the bridge and the warren and the riverbank. Still, my Brights are in my hand as I march across the street, only a few blocks separating me from the disgusting paramilitary fucks pulling Vee to her feet and taking directions from that suit-wearing asshole.

Vee said not to do anything stupid—apparently a mantra of the women in my life—but letting them take her is the stupidest thing I could ever do. Pushing my way through a gathering crowd of onlookers, I'm ready to rush everything Cyrene Security can throw at me.

And then I stop, cemented in place as Vee screams at the top of her lungs, shrieking with everything she has. I can't make out what she's saying, if she's saying anything at all. It's agony to watch her being manhandled, but I'm powerless. And as the thugs bundle her off into a waiting limo, I realize what she's doing.

She's *saving* me, singing without singing to keep me from throwing myself into the fray in a futile attempt to rescue her. I stand there, stock-still, loving and hating her for it.

Her voice echoes off the walls of the urban canyon as the Facilitators tear down the tarp hiding the warren. White flashes of light document what they find before they start tossing things down to the ground below, to be shattered and scattered against the unforgiving stone. My cot. My lamps. Lara, dashed against the rocks, her neck broken and hanging off to one side, her body in splinters.

Vee's scream fades as the limo speeds off with my darling girl inside. The second I can move again, I launch myself down the street, leaving any onlookers in the dust.

*I know where he's taking her. I need to know she's okay.*

With just the clothes on my back and her name written on my heart, I run.

# V

The back of the limo is eerily silent, save for the pinging of Sasha's laptop. *She helped Damon find me. Somehow.* My gaze drifts to Little Dead Thing, scrunched into a corner of the car, ears still flattened, tail twitching.

Kicking out with my bare foot, I nail the laptop so hard that it goes flying from Sasha's hands.

"You *bitch—*" is all I manage to get out before she fires back a wholly unexpected "Fuck you!" at top volume.

Sliding to the floor, she drags her borked toy into her lap. I was hoping it would explode into as many pieces as my broken heart, but other than a cracked screen, it's functional.

That doesn't take the edge off Sasha's venom. "Shoot her with another dart, Damon, or I swear I'll punch her in the face."

This isn't the little pink butterfly of a girl that I left behind. Somewhere along the line, Sasha shed that persona like a cocoon. Everything is hard angles and angry edges, down to the stabbing lines of liquid liner around her eyes.

"She doesn't need another one," Damon says, fingers finding my wrist to take my pulse. I jerk away, but a second later, his hand is on mine again. "The immobilizer reacts to any increase in her heart rate. The more she fights it, the harder she's going to crash. I doubt she'll have enough energy to walk into the Loft under her own power."

"Tell that to my laptop," Sasha snarls, sliding back into her seat.

"Stop talking like I'm not here." The demand is slurred. Except for that shot of moondust at the Pyxis, I haven't had anything in my system since detoxing off the applejack. With my racing heart moving poison through clean and eager veins, the tranqs are hitting hard. Slumping into the corner of the seat, I can feel my bones melting out from under me. "The fucking cat is wired to find me, isn't he, Sasha? He's a goddamn homing device."

"Has been since Day One," she answers, the words like chips of ice. "Damon's idea, and I rigged it up. Still took a while to track you down." She pauses, her hands fidgeting away. "Too long."

Damon settles next to me, helping me stay upright with the firm application of his palm to the nape of my neck. "It was a fail-safe. In case something went wrong. In case your nanotech burned out, and we couldn't find you."

His fingers trail over the exact spot where the darts landed, and I can feel my pulse kick in my throat. I'm looking right at him, but all I can see is—

*Black undershirt. Baggy jeans. Fresh ink.*

I suck in a breath. "Damon, stop."

Instead, he leans closer, his breath warm in my ear. "And that's exactly what happened, isn't it, Vee? The thrum-collectors overloaded and glitched you right off the grid. You passed out, and some obsessed fan got his hands on you in the dark, right? Somehow got you all the way out of the Dome and away from everyone who knows about you. Cares about you. A psychotic kidnapper who held you hostage while we scoured this city from top to bottom."

*I know what you did.* But he doesn't let me say it, pressing his thumb against the tiny holes in my skin. A sharp arrow of pain shoots up the back of my neck, and I gasp. Trying to pull away from him only earns me another look of mock concern.

"Corporate's been riding my ass since the second you went missing, Vee." One hand still clamped down on me, Damon pulls his phone out with the other. With a few swift strokes, he dials a number and tells the person at the other end, "Roll it." Then the charming-as-fuck smile is back in full effect. "Everyone's going to be thrilled to hear we've found you, safe and sound."

*I know what you did.* "They aren't going to hear that from me."

"They already are." He holds up the phone, just out of reach—look but don't touch. Someone with my hair extensions and my face paint is giving an interview, all wide eyes and little gasps of breath . . . and my voice.

"It was terrifying," Not-Vee says, playing every angle, enjoying her moment in the spotlight. "I can't thank Cyrene Security enough for their tireless efforts to rescue me."

The camera cuts away to Micah's ID photo and description. The newscaster runs down every detail.

*Which means they didn't catch him. Not yet, anyway.*

I twist my finger around his silver chain, drawing it tighter against my skin.

*Be smart, love. Get out while you still can.*

# M

It's already all over town. I hear the snippets of reports from vidscreens as I fly by, touting the spectacular rescue by Cyrene Security's finest. I stop to watch it only once, when I catch a glimpse of white face paint and black lips.

Vee, in full Sugar Skulls gear, singing the praises of her saviors and denouncing the monster who held her captive. She pauses for a sip of water, offered by someone offscreen.

*Wow, she's good. She is really good.* The inflections, the word choices, the gestures. It's immaculate.

*But she's not Vee. Not in a million years. I'll never make a mistake like I did at the Palace ever again. Stage gear, makeup . . . Hell, put her in a gorilla suit, and I'll know her by instinct alone.*

The ruse works on the populace, though, whipping up plenty of antikidnapper sentiment to make hiding even harder for me. I slip away during the report and resume my run, forced to avoid my usual routes, detouring around greyface patrols and crowds glued to the vidscreens. It's taking longer—too damn long—to get anywhere, and frustration builds up in me like fatigue.

*Calm down. Focus. This isn't about you. This is about her.*

Halfway across the Odeaglow, I hear, "Hey, there he is!" *Fuck.* I glance back and see six kids in tracksuits hustling toward me, followed by an interested greyface. I don't know if they're more scavenger hunters or just enthusiastic bystanders. Either way, I'm gone.

They're fast, no denying it, but they're rookies when it comes to this stuff. I lose two of them with quick hops over chain-link fences, and two more are scared off by the static electricity of the pylons when I duck into the glass-globe power substation. Back out on the street, I clothesline another with my arm when he steps out from an alley.

The last one, a brown-haired girl with a nose ring and a serious snarl, keeps the chase going. Fast as all hell and determined as fuck, she leaps onto my back, knocking us over a trolley-stop bench. We both hit the ground rolling, my ribs protesting the impact.

She's up first. "Stay down, asshole! You'll pay for what you did!" She stomps down, and I pull my hand away just in time.

On my feet once more, I duck a wild swing from her, waiting for my chance. When she wings another haymaker my way, I brush my Brights against her arm. She tenses up in shock, and I catch her before she hits the ground, laying her down gently before taking off again.

There's no sign of the greyface. *Probably checking on the kid I wrecked.* But I'm wasting time losing the volunteer Micah-hunters.

At least I'm a little closer to my destination. There's only one place he'll take her, one place he can control her utterly.

I make tracks for the Carlisle Building.

# V

Sasha storms into the elevator ahead of us, keying in the code for the penthouse and staring steadily at nothing. Every button that lights up carries me closer to a very luxurious prison. When the elevator pauses three floors from the Loft, I stiffen, wondering if I can bolt as the doors slide open—

"Don't even think about it," Damon warns, jamming his thumb down on the override.

He's right. Even that tiny bit of hope raised my heart rate, and it's playing kissy face with the immobilizers. I slump against the wall, clutching the wooden railing, not trusting either of them to catch me if I faceplant.

I'm shaking hard by the time we reach the top floor.

Damon clamps a hand down on my arm and hauls me through the foyer, barking at the people scurrying out of his way like roaches. "Are they set up yet?"

"Ten, maybe fifteen more minutes—"

"Make it five." He steers me to a new couch—stiff black leather—and drops me onto the cushions. Sasha stalks off toward the studio space followed by a yowling Little Dead Thing. The cat doesn't spare me a glance. Just another betrayal.

*I know what you did, Damon.*

"What are you going to do?" I'm not sure if I'm asking for me or for Micah. It might not matter, either way.

"What I always do, Vee. Try to make the best of whatever clusterfuck you've ignited and tossed into my lap." Damon doesn't bother to look at me, preoccupied with reading another set of messages on his phone. "Apparently, the team found a lot of drug paraphernalia in that charming little hideout of yours. More than even Jax would consider 'recreational.'"

Damon holds out the phone to me, and pictures of the warren slide over the screen. My throat closes up as I witness the step-by-step destruction of Micah's safe house, finishing with the ripped envelope and the little green tabs that have caused so much pain.

"No one outside Corporate knows what really happened at the Dome," Damon adds, "but the higher-ups aren't happy about the applejack."

"They aren't happy about the fact that it almost killed me, or that you were the one cramming it down my throat?" I'm not going to pull any more punches with him. "Just get to the goddamn point already."

"The point is, now that you're back where you belong, it's my responsibility to bring in the scumbag street dealers who almost killed Corporate's little songbird." He shifts his weight from one foot to the other, and I wonder how long I have before he pounces. "We're zeroing in on the runners, too, but I think you can help me with that, can't you?"

"I am not," I say, very deliberately, "helping you with *shit*."

He indulges in a short, mirthless laugh. "You might spare a moment's consideration for your boy toy. The dealers are no doubt very pissed off about the applejack in his little dungeon. Did he screw up a delivery? Or just steal it outright? You better tell me where they are *and* where Micah is, so I can find him before they do." Damon gives me a moment to let that sink in before he continues. "I want him alive. Can you say the same for them?"

It's a nice speech, but I can all too easily picture him hurting Micah. *And enjoying it.* Unfortunately, I know what Rete and his goons will do, and I have some chance of influencing Damon. *So it's the lesser of two evils, for now.*

I start reeling off addresses, hands clasped in my lap, eyes trained on the fire burning in the hearth. The Sugar Skull Vee glares down at me from the photo above the mantelpiece, fucking disgusted that I'm cooperating with him. Damon shunts information and orders over his phone; with every keystroke, he's standing straighter, taking up more space, until I'm backed into the corner of the couch and can hardly breathe.

Empty, guts spilled, I fall into silence. He sends out the last message and then finally looks up at me. Through me.

Three words. Not the three words I so desperately wanted to say to Micah, but they're all I have left. "Don't hurt him."

Ignoring me, Damon snaps his fingers at a passing assistant. "Brandy."

I close my eyes for a second, knowing when he goes old school with his liquor, nothing good follows. Three more words. "What now, Damon?" I'm pretty sure I know the answer already, but focusing on the horrible shit about to happen to me takes my mind off the horrible shit that might be happening to Micah this very second.

Damon receives his drink and unbuttons his jacket. One sip later, he sits next to me. "We have to get you back on the grid, Vee. You're of no use to anyone as long as you're freeloading."

"Fuck that noise," I say, not wanting to meet his gaze but unable to look away. "I've put more than my fair share into this place—"

"Right up to the second you blew those thrum-collectors at the Dome." He takes another sip, eyes locked with mine over the rim of the glass. "Just to save *him*, unless I'm much mistaken."

When I refuse to answer, Damon tilts his head at me. "Do you recall the night we met? That night at Moonship & Stardust?"

"Yes." *I remember almost everything.* But my past is the only card I have up my sleeve. I can't play it just yet.

He loves telling this story, so it doesn't matter if I remember or not. "I was out scouting," he murmurs, cradling the drink in his hand. Gently. So gently. "Everyone at Corporate was slobbering over the idea that we could take Cyrene beyond self-sufficiency and start selling energy. While they dicked around in their offices and labs, I was roaming the city with a portable thrum-meter, hunting spikes in output." He leans forward now, gaze boring into me. "Came into the bar at the end of another long day of finding squat. Walked right past you, sitting on a table and absolutely nothing to look at. But then you started trading songs for drinks. I must have sat in the booth behind you for the better part of an hour, pinned to my seat while you held court. A single high note burned out the damn thrum-meter. The second you let up and I could think again, I saw my chance."

I know this script. "You sent over your card. It came with a shot of Pennyroyale."

His hand tightens around his glass. "And that should have been it, Vee. That should have been our 'once upon a time' beginning."

There's nothing I can say that won't light his fuse, but even my silence sparks his temper. He cocks his arm back and hurls the brandy snifter at the hearth. I don't even get the chance to process the shattered glass, the splashes of liquor that cause the flames to flare up, before he's got me by both arms.

"Was it worth it?" When I bite my lip instead of answering, he shakes me again. "You almost fucked everything, *everything* to the wall—"

"They're ready for her," someone interrupts, and Damon's dragging me down the hall before anyone can say anything else. Rage boils out of him, hot and unforgiving.

"Stupid. So fucking stupid." Another shake. "Your goddamn nanotech is shut down, Vee. Then you ran off to bang some guy who glitched off the grid months ago. Do you even realize what that could mean?"

Suddenly, I have to consider something other than his fury.

*It means I could be pregnant.*

All of our worrying. Dreaming. *And neither of us realized . . .*

Damon pulls me into the guest bedroom and slams the door shut with a hollow bang. Wall-to-wall mirrored panels wink in the harsh white light of six halogen lamps. Everything else was cleared away to make room for a bank of computer equipment. A metal table. A cart loaded with injectors. Gauze. Vials of drugs.

"Scrub her out," Damon says, handing me off to a burly orderly almost twice my height and weight, like I'm nothing more than a packet of applejack trading hands. "Scrub *everything* out."

The attendant pauses, holding my arms to my sides. "Her file doesn't say anything about a mind-wipe. Just the reboot—"

"Mind your fucking business and do your job."

The guy scuttles off, probably to retrieve some piece of equipment; this is the only chance I'll get.

"Why don't you take your jacket off, Damon? Roll your sleeves up and get comfortable. This is gonna take a while."

His eyes cut straight over me, narrowing with sudden suspicion. "What the hell is that supposed to mean?"

This time, the memory gun is pointed at him, and I'm more than happy to pull the trigger. "It means I remember the house." *Bang.* "I remember the gang initiation." *Bang.* "I remember the *rapes.*"

One more bullet in the chamber.

"I remember you . . . waiting your turn."

Forget shooting him; Damon looks like I slid a knife between his ribs and twisted. "That's the trouble, Vee. Eventually you remember *what* happened, but you never remember the *why.*"

*He doesn't look surprised. Shouldn't he look more surprised?*

Damon shrugs out of his jacket, folds it carefully in half, and lays it across a chair. Removes both his cuff links and drops them with twin *plinks* on a side table. By the time he starts rolling up the first sleeve, the tears are burning my eyes; long before he's done with the second, they're coursing down my face. There they are: the skulls, the daggers, the roses, the gothic lettering I thought I'd imagined. I shake my head, trying to look away, unable to escape the hollow socket-stare of his tattoos.

"You always came back to the house," he tells me. "Three months. Six. However long you'd last at the new foster home, you always circled back to that empty house. It was your parents' rental. Probably the only place you ever thought of as home. Neighborhood really went to shit over the years, with the 'bangers moving in, and I was just the dumb asshole a few doors down who brought you food and blankets and whatever else you needed before CPS tossed you in a car and hauled you off again."

Can't swallow. Can't *breathe.* As Damon talks, the kaleidoscope shifts, fragments tumbling so that I catch snippets of a yard, a rusting fence—

And him. A younger, happier version of him. A chance meeting in the twilight. A clumsy peanut butter sandwich in a plastic bag. A sleeping bag that had seen better days but smelled like his drugstore aftershave when I unzipped it.

"We were supposed to make a go of it in LA," Damon says. "Your voice. Me getting you the gigs you needed. I just couldn't figure out how to keep you out of the system. Keep you with me long enough to make it happen." His eyes are too dark to read when he adds, "Joining the gang seemed like the best bet. Muscle to keep Child Services away, money to get us started."

When he takes a step toward me, I stand my ground, refusing to back away from him. "And after that? When those guys were taking turns with me on the floor? That still feel like the best bet you could have made?"

There it is again: the look like I've stabbed him right in the heart. "I wanted to stop them, Vee. Swear to god, I tried. But it was that or them killing us both."

*I wanted to die. Maybe that was enough.* "How did I get to the hospital?"

"I carried you there." His hand keeps opening and closing, like he can't make up his mind if he should punch something. "Found you a gurney in the ER and bolted, because I was covered in your blood and new ink. Leaving you was the hardest thing I've ever done, but they would've taken one look at me, called the cops, hauled me off to jail. By the time I got cleaned up and came back, they were transferring you to Cyrene's medical facilities. So I made damn sure I was head of the line when the next batch of recruits got in."

"So you could stalk me."

"So I could *protect* you. So that I could make things right between us. So that I could take care of you the way I used to take care of you before everything went to shit. So that I could give you everything I couldn't fucking give you *out there*." Damon reaches forward and snags Micah's chain with one smooth finger. "I'm going to decorate you with platinum," he says, his sudden quiet tone ten times as frightening as his fury. "Diamonds." One swift jerk, one flare of pain across the back of my neck, and he's holding the broken gift in his hand. "We are going to start over *yet again*, and maybe this time you won't fuck it up."

My legs go out from under me as I cry out, "Give it back, Damon! God . . . just, please. Give it back—"

"No point, Vee. You're not going to remember his name when you wake up, much less the fact that he gave you this two-cent piece of shit." Damon's hand clamps shut on the necklace. "Do you understand?"

Med techs flood into the room as I start to scream. "Give it back to me, goddamn it, Damon, or I swear I'll kill you!" My threat rattles the windows in their panes. "Do *you* understand? Fucking! Kill! You!"

The immobilizers are already betraying me when the techs pin me to the table and shoot tranquilizers into my arm.

"Give it back!"

The dark reaches for me, but it's Damon who smoothes my hair out of my face. Damon pressing a single kiss to my forehead as I shriek myself unconscious.

# CHAPTER SIXTEEN

## M

I don't even make it as close as the chain-link fence this time before I'm turned back by greyface patrols. The Carlisle is locked up tight, with fully geared and plainclothes guards maintaining a block-wide perimeter around the building. The message from Damon is loud and clear: *You know where she is, but you can't do a damn thing about it.*

*Maybe not, but I can at least try to check on her.* I turn back and book it to the Clocktower, easily sneaking in and working my way up level by level until I'm inside the cavernous clockwork mechanism itself. Soon enough, I'm perched on one of the maintenance platforms, looking out over half the city. But only one building has my attention. One suite. One window.

The living room is empty this time, save for a few wandering guards assigned to remind Vee that the songbird is once again caged.

Suddenly, she cries out. I don't know if there's a skylight open somewhere, or the sheer sonic assault is rattling the glass in its frames, but the building practically vibrates as she shrieks, a piercing howl from deep within her that shakes me to my core. This isn't a warning, or a defiant battle cry. This is fear given voice. This is terror. I don't know what they're doing to her, but I can imagine, and that's even worse than knowing.

*I put His Majesty through a table for less. Damon, you're gonna suffer for every moment she suffers. I will fucking end you.*

Fury surges within me like lava, threatening to erupt, and I clench my fists to keep it tamped down. I can't get my hands on the suit, but there's someone deserving of my rage that I *can* put my hands on.

*Rete.*

His Majesty was in no shape to follow us back to the warren, and after the debacle at the Dome, he wouldn't dare call Damon. But he could have called Rete. Rete could've had Ludo trailing us at any point over the last few days, he was so paranoid about the Rivitocin. All he would have needed was a ballpark location, and Damon swept in like a hurricane.

*I owe Rete a visit. I was gonna leave, let him take his chances with Corporate. But not now. Now he's mine.*

Vee's screaming fades to silence, horrible silence, and it's a punch in the heart.

*Damon wouldn't kill her, she's still too valuable to him . . . But he could easily hurt her until she passed out.*

They say there's a certain point where your rage plateaus and you can't get any angrier. Instead, everything inside goes cold and you feel very, very calm. I had no idea that was true until this very moment.

I give the Carlisle a last look, hoping for a glimpse of her, but there's nothing, nothing at all. *I'm coming, Vee. As soon as I figure out a way in, I'm coming, even if I have to make your lyrics come true. Even if I have to burn this city to the ground.*

Nobody hassles me on the way to the warehouse, lucky for them. My fury accompanies me all the way to Rete's, and before Fire Plug even has the garage door up past his waist, I roll inside and tag him in the balls with my Brights. He collapses like a demolished hotel, and I'm on my feet in an instant.

Scrappy charges toward me, only to be cut short when I kick him hard in the knee, hobbling him. I follow it with a jab to the throat, and he seizes up from the shock before one good shove sends him to the floor with a thud.

I turn to Rete, who stares at me slack-jawed and abandons his search for something, anything to defend himself with. *Expected these two to handle security for him. Anyone else on the payroll must be out looking for me or making runs.*

I stalk toward him. "You sold us out, you spineless sack of dogshit."

"Whoa, man, I don't know what you're talking about." He's quick to put some distance between us, weaseling between the wall and a stack of plastic-wrapped crates.

I shadow him, not letting him out of my sight for a second. "You saw the vid-alerts. You tried to take her and score some nice reward credits for yourself."

Keeping his hands up, palms facing me, Rete's cool façade finally falls to pieces. "Hey, you attacked a customer. You're a liability. And I didn't tell Adonis to grab her. That was his own thing. Everybody takes what they can get—"

"What we got was raided this morning, *and they took her*. So now, I'm taking it out on you." I grab a chair and hurl it over the crates at him. He ducks, and it crashes against the wall.

Closing the distance between us in two steps, I grab his shirt and slam him against the wall, too. "I'm taking everything out on you." Three shots, right to the eyes. "Peddling the shit that killed my friends." Two jabs to the gut. "Calling in those fucks who took Vee." Planting my forearm against his throat, I press down, watching his eyes bulge as he twitches.

Out of the corner of my eye, I see Fire Plug and Scrappy getting back to their feet. *Fuck. The charge must be going on my Brights.*

Rete takes advantage of my distraction and shoves me with everything he's got, making a break for it out the back door. I scramble over the smaller crates and give chase, following him out into the sunlight and down the alley.

*Asshole is faster than he looks.* Rete dashes around the corner, hoping to lose me in the endless rows of storage garages, but he's not getting away that easily. Down one alley, up another, we race like rats in a maze made of corrugated steel and concrete. Around another corner, I'm nearly decapitated by a piece of pipe sitting at neck height. I duck, and my feet slide out from under me as I skate across the asphalt.

*Whoa, where the fuck did that come from?!* Down the next alley, there's a pipe at shin height, perfect for tripping pursuers and breaking legs. Rete's obviously been busy the last few days. *The bastard already had an escape plan.*

Movement up ahead, and I race forward, my eyes peeled for any other nasty surprises. As I round the corner, Rete's waiting in the shadow of a doorway, and he cracks me in the chest with something. A bat or a piece of metal, not sure. All I know is, it fucking hurts.

He hits me again, under the arm, and I feel my rib break in two with the blow. I cry out, hugging my chest as I fall to the ground. The wind goes right out of me, and I gasp for air. Rete doesn't give me the chance, kicking me in the face and damn near breaking my nose.

"Fuckin' making me run! Cocksucker!" I only now realize he's sucking wind badly. I try to roll onto my good side, but he shakes the length of pipe in his hand at me as a warning. "I don't know anything about your friends or you getting raided. Boo-fucking-hoo. One less fuckstick dealing on my turf? Looks like I did the place a favor." He jabs me in the chest with the pipe to grab my attention. "I don't know shit about you, 'cept Maggie was protecting you. Fat lot of good it did her. Hell, I didn't even know about the Dome thing 'til yesterday."

With my ribs screaming at me and my vision blurry, I find little comfort in his words, seeing as he's a fucking liar. I try to get to my feet, but Rete's ready and smashes me in the back of the leg with the pipe. Not hard enough to break anything, but plenty hard enough to drop me again.

Fire Plug and Scrappy soon arrive, and Rete gladly lets them get their licks in, too. "Payback time, loyal minions. Have at 'im!" And they do, with gusto.

# V

The first thing I notice is how soft everything is: the sheets, the pillows, the light. Sunshine bathes my room, more delicate than anything achievable with glass and wiring and electricity.

I have the sense that everything should hurt, but it doesn't. I'm floating. Free-falling. It's only as my body's systems come back online that I recognize muscle fatigue. IV lines dangle from the rack next to the bed. The thrum monitor spikes the second I move.

*Back on the grid. They had to reboot my nanotech again.*

My throat is stripped raw, like I've been crying in my sleep. My eyes are swollen and puffy. And reaching up, my fingers find two pinpoints of dull pain on the back of my neck.

*Immobilizers? Someone said something about shooting me a dart?*

I reach up again, this time seeking silver reassurance that's no longer there.

*Micah.*

Every memory of the last few days slams into me like one of Damon's black SUVs. Unable to breathe, I struggle to sit up. Someone slips an arm around my back. It takes precious seconds to realize it's Jax.

"Shh, Princess. They're right down the hall. Damon's out there with half of Corporate."

She presses a cup of water to my mouth, and I manage to get a few sips down without choking. I cling to her, unable to remember ever hugging her before, outside of promo shoots.

*Always keeping everyone at arm's length. Never sharing anything with anyone because there was nothing* to *share before now. Empty. I was empty before.*

Jax's somber expression and her uncharacteristic silence untie the knot inside me. The highlight reel version of *The Me and Micah Story* comes out in a hoarse whisper. By the time I'm done, her eyes are huge.

"Shit, Vee, that's fucking insane. I'm impressed."

Backed up against the headboard, I lean forward until my cheek presses against my knees. "Thanks, I think. If it wasn't for Sasha—"

"You're gonna have to cut the kid some slack," Jax says. "Damon's gone completely fucking rogue. He's not telling Corporate half the shit he's pulling now. Sasha and I have been on fucking lockdown and can't get a message in or out. He had Little Miss Cherry Tart picked up and 'indefinitely detained' on some bullshit charge. He told Sasha to activate the tracker unless she wanted to start getting her girlfriend's appendages delivered to her every hour on the hour."

"Damon wouldn't . . ." I trail off, uncertain as to what Damon would or would not do to get exactly what he wants, especially if he's taken the Redheaded Mini hostage.

Jax abandons the bed to dump what's left of the water down the sink, then pours me something stronger from a brilliant blue bottle sitting on the side table. Handing me the cup, she takes a pull straight from the source. "Sasha didn't believe him, either. Took a gift-wrapped ring finger to change her mind. There's some creepazoid who keeps pinging Damon's phone. That's the guy who did the slice-and-dice. He sounds like a sadistic motherfucker."

My stomach twists into a knot again, and the thrum monitor rises in response, but Jax isn't done. Not by a long shot.

"He followed that pretty present up with a letter from her parents, asking why their bank account had been emptied out." Another long pull from the bottle as she shoves her hair from her eyes. "The kid's only human, Vee." She looks me over with ill-concealed sympathy. "And love fucks everyone up, doesn't it?"

"Yes." *But I shouldn't know that. Shouldn't remember that—*

Damon's voice cuts through whatever else I might have thought or said. "Call me when it's done" drifts through the door, followed by the sound of footsteps.

Reaching into her pocket, Jax shoves a body-warm length of silver chain into my hand. "Hold onto that, Princess. You're gonna need it." The moment Damon opens the door, she bounces off him with a cackle of maniacal laughter. "You gotta try the blue shit. It's unreal." With hoots and giggles, she stumbles down the hall, leaving me to wonder how much of her usual antics have been for show.

Damon closes the door behind her, his steady gaze locking on to me. "I think you'll be happy to hear they didn't find anything unusual in your scans."

*Meaning I wasn't pregnant.* I have to force back tears, to get a grip on the emotions threatening to spill out of me. Every second of our previous encounter burns through me like applejack, and the thrum monitor spikes with a loud whine.

"If you meant to clear out my brain, it didn't go very well," I finally say.

"Had a chat with Corporate, and we decided it wouldn't be wise to subject you to any unnecessary procedures or further trauma." He strolls across the room, hands tucked in his pockets.

"Unnecessary? But I thought . . . You let me believe . . . that I had to get mind-wiped every time they rebooted me."

"It helps clear the slate, but no." Damon pauses at the bank of medical equipment, eyeing the thrum monitor.

"Then why?" When he doesn't answer, the questions snowball. *I know that I asked for the first one. Wanted to start fresh, if I pulled through. So why all the other mind-wipes?* As I go cold inside, I can see my thrum levels dropping, the tiny green line fading. "I started remembering, didn't I?"

"Yes."

"How many times?"

He hesitates before answering. "Five. Two solo careers and three bands, flushed down the toilet before I ever got you on a stage. There's too much at stake this time to start over again."

*Which is why I'm still* this *Vee. With the memories.* All *the memories.*

I pull my knees up and try not to think of Micah just yet. Not now. Not with Damon looming over me. Jacket off, shirtsleeves rolled up, he has nothing to hide anymore. "It was your tattoos, wasn't it? They'd trigger me, and you'd have me wiped."

"The first time, yeah. We'd just landed the Corporate contract. Went out to celebrate at the Chroma Room and then a suite upstairs." He's got his eyes closed, reliving some piece of my past that he's stolen. "I pulled out all the stops: over-the-Wall champagne, room service, silk sheets. Blindfolded you and we made love for *hours*. It was like every dream we had was finally coming true." Then I get the full force of his gaze on me. "You were mine."

*Except that wasn't me. That was some other girl. Some other Vee who's as dead as Bryn is.* "I guess the only problem was that you couldn't keep me blindfolded forever."

A muscle in Damon's jaw flexes when he grits his teeth. "The second you got a look at my arms, you freaked. Full-blown panic attack. The screaming brought security guards, but I got you sedated and back to the medcenter without having to answer too many questions. After that,

I was careful to keep them covered, but it's not like you were trying to get my clothes off."

So much bitterness in his voice; some other person might muster some sympathy for him. *But not me.* "If they were such a liability, why not have them removed? You had mine lasered off."

That provokes another flash of anger. "Cleaning up your arms was Cyrene's call, not mine. Part of the reconstructive surgery after the attack. Fucking Corporate erasing me from your life." He rubs one hand over his arm. "I couldn't take mine off, Vee. They were *all I had* from outside. The only remnant of *us*. And I hoped that one of these days you'd remember who I was and everything I did for us and be happy. Be grateful. But every fucking time, the answer was no. Your mind, your body just kept right on rejecting me, even if the meltdown was triggered by some other guy's ink." He pauses, looking down at his arms. "But the good news is that we won't have to worry about shit like that ever again."

"We won't?" And I know I'm not going to like the answer even before he smiles.

"No. Because we're back at 'once upon a time.'" Pulling a long velvet box from his pocket, Damon opens it to reveal platinum and diamonds. The kind of jewelry that should say "I love you" but instead screams "You belong to me." Damon holds the necklace out, one eyebrow up. "As promised."

I have to find the strength to smile. Have to play along. "It's gorgeous."

"Put it on." Not a request.

Somehow I manage to tuck Micah's chain under my pillow, freeing up my hands to obey. I barely feel the links against my skin, but they sit there all the same, like hands spanning my neck. It's delicate, for a collar. Time to manufacture a new Vee, one who'll say all the things that he wants to hear.

"Thank you, Damon. For the gift. For understanding. For . . . forgiving me. I'm not sure I deserve any of it."

"You don't. Not yet, anyway." He disappears into my closet for a few minutes and emerges with a red silk dress. "Go take a shower. Put that on and make up your face. Your benefactors are down the hall, each expecting a personal thank-you for your glorious rescue." Striding back to the door, he pauses at the threshold. "Leave the necklace on."

"Of course." My tone is already brighter, my chin tilting up. I know all the lyrics to this song. "It's the very least I can do."

# M

Rete supervises as his boys dismantle me piece by piece, opting to observe rather than involve himself or his rib-cracking equalizer any further.

Fire Plug sticks to the upper body, cheapshotting my cradled ribs and muttering about Vee as he pounds my face in. "Little fuckin' bitch," he spits.

"Takes one to know one," I reply, not regretting it for a moment, even when he steps on my wrist and I hear a sickening pop.

Scrappy prefers the all-over approach. Whatever company made his shoes will have free advertising on my skin for a while to come. Eventually, I lose myself in the pain, my thoughts drifting back to the raid on the warren.

*If it wasn't Rete, and it wasn't His Majesty, how did they find us?*

Rete mumbles something I can't make out, and I realize the beating has stopped, but my eyes refuse to focus, leaving me squinting at colored blobs on a blue backdrop. My mind immediately shifts to Vee.

*Is she all right? Those screams . . . God, Vee, please be okay.*

I hear footsteps approach, and several hands jerk me to my feet. Everything goes white with pain for a moment. My legs can hardly support my weight, and it feels like I'm being stabbed in the side with every breath. "What's . . . what's happening?" I suck air as best I can, but my busted rib makes it hard.

Rete, chipper as ever, replies from somewhere behind me. "Can't let them beat you to death in the street, pigeon. Got a few questions for you that require some privacy."

By the time we're back inside the warehouse, my vision clears enough for me to look around. I don't recognize the guys on either side of me—one squat with a bright-red Mohawk, the other lanky and chewing something that reeks—but they must be Rete's newest recruits. Ludo waits in one corner, so damn smug. After the shrill rattle of the door slamming shut, Scrappy limps into view, cracking his knuckles and smiling at me. He slugs me in the gut before I can ask how his knee is.

I gasp and slump forward, the new arrivals barely keeping me vertical.

"How many are in your crew?" Rete's voice echoes off the cinder block walls. Even with four guys between us, he keeps his distance.

"I don't have a crew. Just me." Scrappy looks off to one side for confirmation, then hits me again, and I double over. Ludo jumps excitedly with every shot, like he can't wait for his whack at the piñata.

"Oh, Micah, play ball, will ya? At least cough up Maggie's other source for 'tocin. There must be one. No way you could've kept yourself going with what you've taken in the last week or so. Come on, chum, no need for the hero routine. Give me a name, and we can start making nice-nice."

He waits for me to reply, but I don't waste the breath. *If shit-for-brains wants to waste time chasing shadows, he's welcome to it.*

Scrappy reluctantly steps away, and Fire Plug takes his place, now holding the metal pipe. Rete finally slips into view, and he looks up and down the length of pipe before turning to me. “I guess it really doesn’t matter if you’re running your own crew or not. After that stunt with one of our best customers yesterday, I need to make an example of you. Anyone on your payroll will either quit or fall in line. Such a pity your little punk rock paramour will have to wonder what happened to her fair-haired kidnapper.”

He nods and Fire Plug cracks me in the thigh, obviously still enjoying himself. Joke’s on him, though. The pain in my ribs is so bad, I barely feel it.

Rete takes the pipe and leans close, lifting my chin with it, locking eyes with me. “Say hi to Maggie for me,” he whispers. He pulls the pipe away, and my head slumps back down. All I can see is the concrete floor, covered with a rusty stain. Must’ve kept it hidden with deliveries the last few times I was here.

Not rust. Blood. Stained with blood. Way too much to be mine.

*I wonder what he did with her body.*

I hear Rete hand over the pipe to someone who slaps it against his palm. “Go ahead and finish him off.”

There’s a pause. I can picture him winding up to smash my skull in.

*I’m sorry, Vee.*

I feel the shock wave before I hear the explosion, as the garage door is torn from its tracks and hurled across the room. Mohawk and Chompers abandon me for Rete, and I hang there in the air for a second before collapsing to the ground.

“Everybody freeze!”

My head bounces off the cement and everything blurs again, but I can see black-suited security pouring through the door, rounding people up and firing off the occasional tranq dart.

A Facilitator kneels in front of me, the barrel of his dart gun aimed straight at my chest, and through his visor, I see him staring at me. He turns and shouts over his shoulder, “He’s alive. Bring him in!”

I have one last thought before I'm hoisted up and the pain finally takes me:

*How did they find me again?*

# V

Not-Micah. I'm cornered by the blue-eyed, blond-haired Micah doppelganger from the night of the VIP party. Well-dressed, charming, and very, very interested in hearing every detail of my perilous week spent at the mercy of the fugitive drug runner.

"That must have been very hard on you." He hands me an unidentifiable cocktail, his fingers tracing my bare, perfumed wrist. "I know everyone is so relieved Damon tracked you down." Not content with simply lingering, his hand slowly slides up my arm.

I can smell his cologne, along with ten other kinds of product he must have bathed in before coming here, and close my eyes for a split second.

*Be charming, Vee. Make nice with the other kids on the playground and maybe, just maybe, it will help Micah out.*

But every second I'm forced to spend in this guy's company is another needle under the fingernails. He can't know that he's turning my stomach, the poor bastard.

Damon does, though. Standing two, maybe three feet away, he's the picture of studied nonchalance. One hand in his pocket, the other holding his phone. Enjoying himself more than a little at my expense. No doubt he figures I owe him this much. Maybe more.

*Quite a lot more.*

"Parts of it were absolutely terrifying." True. Escaping the Dome. Seeing our ID photos on the vidscreens. Remembering that I was gang-raped and left for dead . . . "But I'm here now. Safe and sound—"

Damon cuts in, smooth as cream. "Terribly sorry to interrupt, but our songbird is due for another pick-me-up. Excuse us a moment, please?"

Not-Micah doesn't look happy with this turn of events, but he can hardly say so. "Of course." He kisses my hand like he's folding over a page in a book he wants to read later. "But don't stay away from the party too long."

Damon replies for me. "No, of course not." One predator snarling at another, but this one's bigger, and he marked his territory a long time ago. "Quick as we can."

In short order, we're in my bathroom and Damon's administering a vitapep shot just behind my ear. That's the first punch. The second comes when he says, "We've got Micah in custody, along with all his drug-running buddies."

I take a step back, my ass bumping against the marble counter. "He wasn't running the applejack, Damon, he was trying—"

"Do you think I give two shits what he was trying to do? I don't need to pin anything on him, Vee. Thanks to your timely contribution, we grabbed most of the outfit in one fell swoop, and Corporate can do whatever they want with them. All I care about is the credit." He sets the injector down on the counter and leans into me, so I don't miss a word. "They broke your little toy good before we got there. Do you want to see the pictures that just came in?"

"No." My voice goes flat. "No, I don't."

"Makes for very interesting viewing, I promise." Damon dangles his phone in front of me. "You're going to keep up the charming routine tonight, or I'll have your bedroom wallpapered with these, is that clear?"

"Yes." It helps to imagine sticking my thumbs into his eye sockets as deep as they will go.

"We're going to get him cleaned up," Damon continues. "Just enough to see if we can suss out why he's not the vegetable Corporate anticipated. I would have liked the pleasure of cracking him open myself, but we don't always get what we want, do we?"

Cold all over. I haven't been this cold since the night of the Dome concert. *I already told you that I'll kill you, Damon, and that was over a necklace. Do you understand what I'll do to you if you hurt him?*

"Just in case you were thinking about doing something stupid, let me assure you that something very fucking unpleasant will happen to him every time you don't cooperate." He runs his hands up my arms, letting them come to rest on either side of his necklace. "That little punk threatened my career and put his hands all over *what's mine.* I want you to remember *that* every time you consider using that beautiful mouth of yours to say anything other than 'Yes, Damon.' Take a guess. One little guess what I'll do." He shifts one hand over to trace my upper lip with his thumb. "And then multiply that by a hundred." He leans in to kiss me, his mouth still moving against mine when he adds, "And if you really piss me off, I'll have him scrubbed so he won't even remember your name."

I hold very, very still, afraid if I so much as blink that I'll fly into him, shred him into nothing.

"Ready to go back downstairs?" he asks, the first question on the test.

"Yes, Damon."

"Perfect." One more kiss and he tucks my hand under his arm. "Keep it up."

# M

I hit the gurney and jolt back to full consciousness. The low thunder of rolling wheels vibrates up the metal frame. *We're moving.*

The fog lifts, pain bringing unexpected clarity. *Keep your eyes shut. Reveal nothing. Assess the situation.*

My ribs throb angrily, demanding my attention. Instinctively, I want to reach for them, but I clamp down on that thought before moving a muscle. My left wrist is sore as hell, like something's pressing on it. The weight on my ankles confirms my suspicions. *Restraints. Lovely.*

There's something else, a hint of cold metal in my forearm. *An IV?* Can't tell if it's fluids, antibiotics, or tranquilizers.

There's a bump as we hit a set of double doors and push past them. Flashes of white light cross my eyelids as fixtures pass overhead. I crack one eye open and peer around, spotting at least four lab coats moving in tandem with the gurney, one of them already jotting notes on a datapad.

"Subject awake and responsive to stimuli, probably regained consciousness several minutes before apparent ocular movement."

*So much for the element of surprise.*

With my cover blown, I try to open the other eye and look around, but it's swollen shut. On my good side, I can see white walls, pristine almost to the point of nonexistence. The only lab coat paying me any attention is Datapad, a thirtysomething, eager-to-please tall drink of nothing.

I meet his gaze. "So, this way to the dissection room?"

He nervously snorts with laughter, then looks around ashamedly. "Oh, I'm not at liberty to say where you're headed, si—" He cuts himself off before calling me sir.

My lip, now fat from Fire Plug's attention, protests every time I speak. "Are you at liberty to answer questions?"

"That would depend greatly on the question, I should think."

That's an answer. Good start. "I heard screaming coming from the Carlisle. Is Vee okay? What did they do to her?"

He looks confused and starts stammering, "I have no—Oh, I mean, I'm not at liberty to say."

*Fuck.* Maybe whoever he's taking me to will be able to answer that. This is a glorified delivery boy. Takes one to know one.

I clam up for the rest of the ride, down various halls bleached within an inch of their lives. Finally, two big double doors and a soft beep later, I'm there. Wherever there is.

Datapad pulls an injector from his pocket and tags me in the neck. Tranquilizer, same double dose they hit me with the night Vee and I crossed paths at Hellcat Maggie's. *Not much of a learning curve there, fellas.*

Things get a little fuzzy around the edges, but I'm still lucid for the transfer to the exam table. They're not taking any chances, so the entire top of the gurney comes off and sits on the table, then they remove the side slats one at a time, slipping the magnetic restraints into designated slots on the table itself. They slide the gurney top out from under me and leave me on the slab, ready to be sliced up like a birthday cake.

The other three lab coats hightail it out of there, and Datapad follows after making a few final notes on his namesake and leaving it on the lab table. As he walks toward the double doors, I start fighting, my arms jerking and legs kicking, ignoring the pain in my ribs as I slam my body against the table, but the restraints don't budge.

"Hey, hey! You can't leave me here! Not like this!"

He continues through the doors without breaking his silence. I yell for help as long as the doors are open, and for a while after, but no one comes. Taking a shallow breath, I stop thrashing long enough to look around, hoping for something, anything that'll get me out of these restraints. But there's nothing within reach. Cabinets are against the wall and locked up tight. Except for the datapad, the table nearest me is spotless.

Then I hear footsteps from behind me. Someone's been standing there the whole time. Silently. Watching. There's a gentle click of plastic on metal as whoever it is picks up the datapad and stylus. "Hello, Micah."

The speaker steps into view, but despite the sharpness of the light, my eye refuses to focus on him. I'm only vaguely aware of the lab coat, the close-cropped hair, the slow, measured walk. Instead, I keep seeing a tank top and track pants, hair shaggy on one side and shaved on the other, always in motion. Like my mind can't reconcile the two.

*This is insane. This is impossible.*

I finally find my voice. "Trav?"

# V

With platinum and diamonds a constant reminder of what's at stake, I manage to keep my rage at a slow simmer for the rest of the evening. Damon's uncharacteristically jovial, taking celebratory shots of Pennyroyale with a group of Corporate execs. It's obvious they're congratulating him on a job well done, and watching them fawn all over that psychopath slowly but surely unravels what's left of my composure.

Guests start to wander off after midnight, headed out to the after-party. Of course, Damon's booked it at the Chroma Room. Not-Micah has had his arm around me for the last hour or so, convinced he's going to get a romp in the funhouse when everyone else is gone. The joke's on him when I peel him off like a coat and maneuver him into the foyer.

"Going down, are we?" Half a dozen drinks have made him bolder, and his hand is sliding south as fast as he can manage. "Your room might be more comfortable."

Nothing about him reminds me of Micah anymore. Not a goddamn thing. I'm not sure how I ever could have mistaken one for the other in the first place. "Not tonight, I'm afraid." *Not ever.* He's lucky to get a coy wave of farewell instead of a knee to the balls.

The moment the elevator doors close on him, Damon steps into the space left at my side.

"Disgusting little shit," he observes. Despite all the drinking he's done, the only telltale sign is the faintest whiff of alcohol on his breath.

"I couldn't agree more."

"You handled it well enough." His hand finds the small of my back when he adds, "I'll have the car brought around. We need to put in an appearance."

I slant a look at him, but all I say is, "Yes, Damon."

He stifles a sigh, pressing a fist against his leg until his knuckles crack. "I was pissed, Vee. I shouldn't have said that."

*You shouldn't have said a lot of things. I might have burned the city to the ground, but you took out all the bridges on your own.* "No apologies necessary." *Because it's a total waste of oxygen.*

"Good to hear." His arm snakes around my waist, and he pulls me close.

"Corporate tell you anything that I should know?" Somehow, I keep my tone light, my body relaxed. "You all looked awfully cozy tonight."

"Picked up on that, did you?" He reaches up and loosens his tie. Undoes the top button on his shirt.

*Like he's fucking home.* Suddenly, I'm made of ice. The small breath I'm able to draw is laced with the starch from his shirt, the light application of cologne he never forgets after shaving. I feel like I am choking on them.

"They agree that it's better for everyone if we're together." Damon doesn't mention Micah, but I can tell the exact second that he thinks of his competition. The muscles in his arms and shoulders bunch up as he dips lower to put his face in front of mine. His hands are in my hair—

*Don't scream, Vee. Keep your shit together.*

—and his forehead meets mine. "This is how it was meant to be."

The old Vee, the one before Micah, would scream. She would claw and screech and savage him to pieces. Instead, I get very, very calm. "I'm tired of fighting you, Damon."

"That'll make it easier when I move in." He smiles. Another test. He's waiting to see what I'm going to do, what I'm going to say.

"The sooner, the better, I think. I vote we skip the after-party so you can go get your suits. I'll clear out a spot in my closet."

He backs off enough to laugh. "I already sent out a couple guys for that stuff. There are a few things in my office I need to retrieve myself." Another pause, another assessing look. "I need an hour, maybe two."

I cross to the couch, picking up a glass along the way. Fresh off the nanotech reboot and full of fucking vitamins, I've been setting drinks down on passing trays all night. Now I only pretend to take a sip from the cup, barely letting the liquor touch my lips.

*Need to keep my head clear.*

I take a seat and curl my legs under me, red silk on black leather. "I'll be here."

"Of course you will. With two squads of security, so don't get any ideas, all right?"

Putting an arm over my head, I slide down into the sofa just a bit, giving him a really good view of what he's locking up. "I'm going to have another drink."

"Seriously, Vee, behave yourself."

"Not my specialty," I tell him, "but we'll see what I can manage by the time you get back."

*Also not a lie.*

He turns on one heel and marches out, barking, "Lock it down!" into his phone.

As soon as the elevator doors slam shut, I head down the hall toward Jax's room.

# CHAPTER SEVENTEEN

## M

Trav studies me, as if he can't believe I'm here.

I know the feeling. "Trav, oh my god. What happened? What are you doing here? Where have you been? What's going on?"

He ignores every question, locking my head in place with more magnetic restraints. I'm so stunned, it takes a few minutes before the million-dollar question occurs to me. *If he somehow survived . . .*

"Trav, what about Bryn? And Rina, and Zane! Did they make it too?" For the first time since waking up on the gurney, hope blossoms in my chest.

The heat radiates off his skin as he leans close. "All dead. It's just you and me."

He has the same determination, the same will and drive that I remember. But now there's a coldness in his eyes. "Trav, wh-what happened to you? I mean, after."

He casts a long look my way as he replies. "A full neural reconstruction. Or damn close. The first they'd ever performed. Everything they would've done to you, if you hadn't been in worse shape than me." Every syllable is dispassionate and professional as he gives me the once-over. "Or so they said."

"You don't think—"

"That you faked brain damage and a coma just to screw me over? No, I don't think that." He pulls back for a moment, still physically close but miles apart in every other possible way. "You lucked out. I got the exploratory brain surgery, the poking and prodding to see how I managed to survive. They zapped me with so many microamp pulses, I wasn't sure if they were gauging my responses or trying to make me dance."

Not an ounce of humor in his voice, just the cold recitation of the words.

*How badly did the applejack burn him out? If it got too deep into his nervous system, he might not be able to show more emotion than that . . .*

"But I'm glad. They did what they had to. To bring me back, to rebuild motor functions. I couldn't even talk at first." He pauses, as if he's out of practice speaking aloud. I would know, I suffered from the same affliction until recently. "You know when people do things that hurt you, and they tell you it's for your own good? This time, it actually was."

Trav hooks me up to all kinds of monitoring equipment and taps away on his datapad, syncing it up to the monitors. Suddenly he changes tack, his hands going still. "You've been off-grid for a while now."

"Ever since the coma, yeah."

"They had to map my neural pathways to chart how much damage the applejack had done before they could reintroduce my nanotech. So for a week, I had physical therapy outside during my recovery, and I heard this . . . white noise all around me. Only when I was outside, or working with a window open."

*The hum.* "Yes, I hear it too! Always. Ever since I came back to Cyrene." *I thought I was the only person in the whole damn city who heard it.*

He nods slowly, eyes glazed slightly as he reminisces. "It stopped when I went back on the grid, after they repaired the worst of the scarring. My doctors said the . . ." He searches for the right word.

"I call it the hum."

"Okay. My doctors said the hum was a form of tinnitus after the overdose, and that it would fade. But you've been hearing it for months."

"It doesn't fade, but it does settle into the background after a while. Took some getting used to."

"I can imagine." He's interrupted by a beep on the datapad. His eyes scroll across the screen as he reads. "I take it Genevieve didn't report hearing anything while she was off-grid?"

I'm thrown off by the swerve in topic. "I . . . don't know who that is."

"Black hair, hazel eyes, 1.65 meters tall." Trav's gaze flicks across the information on the datapad in his hand. "Professional singer. Prone to antisocial behavior and antiauthoritarian outbursts. Recent recipient of unorthodox treatment for an adverse reaction to applejack. Kudos to you for pulling that off, by the way."

*Genevieve. Another thing she doesn't remember.* "Her name is Vee. And no, she didn't hear it. What else do you know about her?"

"A lot. Tough girl. Resilient. Problematic nanotech. Tendency toward hysteria during preparation for memory revision procedures."

I tense up and push against the restraints with everything I have. "No, please, tell me you didn't mind-wipe her."

Trav looks almost disgusted by my words. "You'd be fine with her carrying that pain around every second of every day? In her shoes, wouldn't you want to leave the past behind? The blood, the brutality, the waking nightmare. All that suffering, gone in an instant. It must be so peaceful, starting over. A gift, really." He hesitates, catching himself.

*That didn't answer the question. Is he toying with me?* Worry washes over me. Releasing the breath I've been holding, I wince as my rib reasserts itself into the conversation.

Reaching up, Trav activates the microphone to start the "official" exam. "Subject C-15 appears to be in quite a lot of pain. Unfortunately, the subject remains awake after multiple doses of tranquilizer, and I suspect any pain meds on hand would have the same negligible effect."

He clicks the mic off for a moment. "You're going to feel every bit of this." Another click. "Before we scan the subject for any foreign implants, biotech, or other illicit body modifications, we need to get the lay of the land, as it were. Despite the anomalous—and quite miraculous—recovery from his previous misfortune, the subject has suffered some extensive nerve damage, and the severity of any impairment to brain function is unknown."

*Foreign implants? Biotech? Like I'm a spy, infiltrating the city for some rival company? They don't know why I came back to Cyrene, why I'm still walking around instead of weighing down a couch or bed at home.*

*But Trav must know that's insane. He knows me . . .*

*He used to, anyway.*

*What is all this? Is this for show? Is . . . is he on my side, after all?* I feel adrift here. Nothing to anchor me. *Not even my name.*

An assistant steps into view, and Trav points out something on his datapad. The assistant nods once and moves behind me. With my head and neck affixed to the table, my field of vision is limited. Right now, all I see is Trav, picking up where he left off.

"With such significant scarring in the brain tissue, our less invasive scans will prove ineffectual. We'll have to employ more direct methods before we can proceed any further. Fisher, I'll make sure the braces are secure. You get the drill."

I writhe, jerking my arms and legs with all my strength, but the restraints don't budge. "Trav, stop. Please! You can't—"

He purposefully steps over to me and slaps a thick adhesive patch on my neck. It stings like a dozen hornets striking at once, and I go silent, lips moving but no sound coming out.

"There we are. Mechanical paralytic. The barbs work directly on the muscles themselves, no chemicals necessary." He examines the brace holding my head in place. "Means no more outbursts to distract us from our work."

I'm still screaming, screaming for all I'm worth, but no one can hear me. No one at all.

# V

I'm ready to unload the entire plan on her, but Jax is on board before I get three words out of my mouth. Leaving her rooting through her personal stash of pharmaceuticals, I detour through the kitchen.

Security is everywhere: in the hall, stationed at each door, blocking the service exit at the back. Taking a page out of Jax's book, I'm all smiles and giggles and flirty flourishes when I skim past Damon's private goons. They track every move I make, but that's the only response I get as I grab the necessary supplies from the fridge and head toward Sasha's room.

She avoided most of the party, pleading a headache and ducking out early. All the lights in her room are out, so it takes a second for my eyes to adjust. There's a huddled lump in the bed sniffling with misery, and I home in on that, peace offering in hand.

"Hey, sweetie." I peel the blanket back far enough to reveal her pitiful, tear-stained face and Little Dead Thing curled up in her lap. "I brought cookie dough."

She moves over with a miserable sort of gulp. All the fire burning her up in the limo has faded down to embers, smothered by the heavy air in the room, her memories of the Redheaded Mini, the torment of not knowing where she is or how she is or what will happen next.

*I can sympathize.*

The next thing I know, Sasha's crying her heart out against my shoulder. "God, Vee, I'm so sorry." Hiccup, cough, sniff. "I didn't want to do it, I swear . . ."

Appalled by the emotional fireworks, Little Dead Thing abandons both of us with a hiss. I put my arms around Sasha and let her get it all out, too fired up and focused on Micah to join her in a weepfest.

"It's all right," I murmur, patting her. "Jax told me what happened with . . ." *Shit. What's the Redheaded Mini's name? The girl lost a finger because of me, and I don't even know her name.*

"Callie." Sasha wipes her nose on her sleeve. "But you're back now, and Damon's not going to do anything else to her, right?"

Tearing off the foil seal, I break off a blob of cookie dough and eat it myself, trying not to choke. "No. Damon's probably done. For now." I pass her the package and lean back, letting that last thought spin cobwebs in her brain.

She frowns. "For now?"

"Until he wants something else from you," I explain, trying to swallow and silently vowing that I will never eat another chocolate chip anything ever again. "Corporate doesn't know he's up to any of this. What he's done to Callie. The fact that he's got Micah locked up, too, so that I never forget to behave myself. Once he's got something on Jax, he'll have all three of us sewed up in a pretty little package."

Sasha peers unhappily at the cookie dough, then sets it down, like she's lost her taste for it. "We have to get a hold of someone higher up the chain. Tell them what Damon's doing. They can help us get Callie and Micah out—"

"By the time we get a hold of someone at Corporate with influence, and they figure out who's lying and who's telling the truth, Callie and Micah could be dead." I swallow hard at the thought, then press forward. "I can fix this, Sasha, but I need your help."

She hesitates. *All it will take to end this is her saying no.* She doesn't even have to tattle to Damon, though that certainly would bring every bit of his wrath down on my head. When she starts to pull back, I grab her hands. My thumb finds a chunky piece of jewelry on her middle finger; the way Sasha gasps a little tells me it's the Redheaded Mini's ring.

*Probably the one on her damn finger when they cut it off.*

"We'll get Callie out." I press as hard as I can on the silver, pushing the tiny skull and crossbones into her skin.

She blinks once, twice, then whispers, "How are we supposed to manage that?"

I have to trust her now. Have to throw myself out of the nest. Fly or fall. All or nothing.

"I need you to help me make a few phone calls."

# M

It's not when the pain starts that scares you. It's when the pain stops. Even as the drill continues to whir behind you. And for a very long moment, you wonder if you'll ever feel anything again. When the electrodes and exploratory probes begin snaking inside, it's horrifying and reassuring all at once.

Describing their every action in excruciating detail for the official record, Trav and the assistant are hard at work behind me, like the monsters you know are lurking just out of sight.

*Or one monster you thought you knew.*

*It's been nine months since that night. Has he been here the whole time I've been running around the city? How soon did he know I was out of the coma? Why won't he tell me about Vee?*

*What's his role in all this?*

My jaw aches from silent screaming, and eventually I stop, unable to summon the energy to keep at it. Better to keep my efforts in reserve for an opportunity down the line. If one ever presents itself—

There's a ping, and Fisher stops to check his phone. "Your *guest* has arrived. I'll send him in." Trav nods slightly as he checks my vitals again. The whole time, his eyes refuse to meet mine.

The double doors open and shut out of view. "From street rat to lab rat. How fitting."

I don't know the voice, but I can guess. I see the pricey suit before the victorious sneer on his face.

He makes sure to approach me from my good side. He wants to savor this. "Well, what have we here? Huh. Micah. The survivor. The runner. The legend. The man who outsmarted every guard at the Dome." He leans over, ripping the paralytic patch from my skin. His breath stinks of mint, as if he's been sanitized. "You don't look like much to me."

*If he leans an inch or two closer, one bite will make him regret it.*

Trav replies before I do. "Damon, I have a great deal of work ahead of me. Determining Micah's viability for the project will take time. So if you'd like to see your cut anytime soon, make it quick."

*Viability. The project.* I shudder at how casual that sounds. *How clinical.*

"Oh, please, I gift-wrapped him for you. The least you can do is shuffle off and play with your chemistry set while I enjoy myself for two seconds." With a hard glare, Trav steps away, and Damon turns to me, smiling wide, triumphant. "Hey there, lab rat. Sounds like your old friend here will have to dissect you just to find something of interest.

You might be something special to this nutjob, but not to me. And certainly not to Vee." He licks his lips before continuing.

"I can't believe a piece of pathetic trash like you almost stole everything from me. Some delusional vigilante *clown* running around my city taking what's *mine*!"

He leans close, grabbing my throat. "Unacceptable!" He looks at the restraints pinning me down, reassured that he has control once more, and he composes himself. "It's unacceptable, so I put a stop to it. She's been scrubbed free of your filth, and you're nothing but a stranger to her now. Vapor. Dust in the wind."

*I refuse to accept it. Trav didn't say one way or the other. And even if it* was *true* . . . "No version of her has ever loved you, Damon."

He turns crimson, and I watch the rest of the professional façade collapse in on itself. A thug-gone-Corporate emerges. He punches me right in my broken rib, one shot like broken glass in my side. I cry out as everything goes white with agony.

"Damon." Trav surprises me by speaking up. "That's enough. I can't have you interfering with my research. You should be tending to your pet and keeping Corporate happy. I doubt they'd care to hear about how far you've gone to ensure these little victories."

*I can't tell if that was an act of kindness or Trav calling dibs on dissecting me like a frog in science lab.*

My vision clears, and there's Damon, making sure his suit is just so. But a slight twitch at the corner of his mouth tells a different story, one of rage barely contained.

"Fine. Good luck with your experiments. After the work I put in tracking this shitstain down, they better be profitable. And don't forget to wipe your toy clean when you're done with him." One last time, he closes the gap between us. "Don't worry, Micah. I'll take excellent care of Vee. She's all mine. Spend your last few moments considering that, lab rat."

Trav applies another paralyzer to my throat before I can reply.

The thought of Vee, vulnerable, confused, and in that bastard's hands . . . *Please be okay, Vee. Please be okay.*

After a beep acknowledging his security tag, the scumbag walks out, crisp and businesslike once more. And now my attention falls to the array of surgical implements and unidentifiable tools awaiting me.

Trav leans over and whispers in my ear, "That guy is a real asshole. He says you were running applejack. But after what we lost, you wouldn't. You couldn't possibly. Could you?"

I look at him with my good eye, unable to reply or shake my head, but hoping he'll see the truth.

His tone is halting, reluctant, as he continues. "I thought you were gone. They told me you wouldn't recover. But you did, and you've been here for months, doing . . . what?"

With the paralyzer on, I can't tell him about running down the dealer through Ludo, about getting in with Maggie and Rete and trying to trace the sources of applejack, about everything I've done for months. For him, for her, for all of us.

Even as I say it in my head, it sounds so small. So pointless.

"How long did it take you to forget us, Micah? How many days of palling around with lowlifes and diddling your popstar girlfriend?"

His words run through me like glacier water. And then, with the simple click of the mic, Trav is the picture of professionalism again.

"As our probes gather useful data in the background, we'll perform thorough scans and examinations in order to locate any recording devices present, either mechanical or biological." Trav tapes my eyelids open and draws a long needle, filling it with a nausea-inducing seafoam-colored mixture.

*Watching something awful happen and being powerless to do anything about it is becoming a recurring theme in my life.*

The needle inches closer and closer, looming over me, big as life, before finally plunging forward.

# V

Coming out of Jax's room for the second time, I run into the same dink from the pre-Dome party. Damon's right-hand guy is a fucking wall of muscle, and even a well-tailored suit can't disguise the fact that he's got no neck.

*And aviators? Past midnight? Sure sign of a complete douchebag.*

He doesn't know it yet, but he's Phase Two.

"Enough running around for the night," he says with a grunt, nudging me in the direction of the stairs.

"Damon's orders?" I grin up at him, trying to sound playful. "You realize I've only seen you once or twice without these glasses?" Scrunching up my nose at him, I make like I want to push them back.

He reaches for that wrist while my other hand slaps a level-nine sedative patch under his jaw. Down he goes like a sack of rocks, and I smack a second snooze button on his cheek. By the time I reach into his coat pocket and locate Damon's backup phone, he's full-out snoring.

"Pleasant dreams, asshole," I mutter.

Jax bounces into the hall carrying two bags loaded with supplies. "Holy shit, it worked."

"Told you it would." I step over Mount Fucknuts and head straight for the studio. Sasha's already got an impressive bank of equipment up and running. Two glowing pinpoints of light indicate that Little Dead Thing is curled up in the corner, scowling at all of us.

Sasha's just as focused, her gaze never straying from the glowing blue light of the holographic displays hovering in front of her. "Everything's ready to roll." She hands me the vocal modulator from Damon's bullshit fake-Vee PR stunt.

I fit it into my ear and adjust the mouthpiece. "You wrote an override program for the city vidscreens?"

"Yup. It'll go live as soon as we're ready." Sasha leans back far enough in her chair to flash me a smile. Some of that fire she had in the limo has returned.

*Good damn thing, too, because this is going to get very hot very quickly.*

Damon's backup phone is linked to every account he's got, so it doesn't take me long to sort through his incoming messages. Pictures of the warren that I've seen already. Pictures of Micah that I have not. My stomach clenches at the sight of his face, bloody and swollen, but I thumb through the folder until I find the address.

I was expecting a holding cell in a detention facility, but he's in the fucking medcenter, and not for 50 cc's of TLC, is my guess. Callie's there, too. In case Damon needs more leverage over Sasha.

Trying to keep a lid on the medical horror show running through my head, I hand the phone off to her. "Dial out for me?"

She plugs the phone into her mini-grid, calls up a vocal sample from one of Damon's outgoing messages, then fires off a finger-pistol at me.

When the person on the other end of the line picks up, I use Damon's voice to bark out my order: "Bring the car around." He starts to protest, but I yell over him, "Yes, jackass, I know I'm inside one already. Bring the other goddamn car around."

*Hold on, Micah. I'm coming for you.*

# M

Trav gives me a series of injections designed to reveal any subdermal biotech or microscopic recording devices. My vision blurs, tinted blue for a few minutes by a chemical eyewash that burns like hot sauce.

With my eyelids taped open, I can't help but watch Trav throughout the tests. He keeps his expression neutral, hardly looking at me at all. I'm a lab rat pincushion. Subject C-15, nothing more.

But after those whispered questions, I can't help but see something in his eyes. Resentment at my very existence.

*I'm starting to prefer being Subject C-15 to being Micah.*

He activates the mic as he reviews the results of his chemical trace tests. "Preliminary examination reveals no sign of biological or artificial technology in the eye, ocular cavity, or in any subdermal tissues so far. Fisher?"

The assistant reappears with datapad in hand and points to several spots on the screen. When he catches me watching them, he frowns slightly, offering a look of pity before turning away.

Trav resumes his analysis. "No sign of biotech or other foreign material in the brain tissue." He gives the full scientific spiel to the microphone, explaining how the overdose charred my neural pathways.

*No wonder Cyrene's best chemical treats don't affect me anymore.*

His last statement sticks with me: "The thalamus remains virtually untouched, so his ability to feel pain is unimpaired."

At that moment, I swear the barest hint of a smile crosses Trav's face. A smile colder than applejack withdrawal.

"As expected, the subject's responses bear a strong resemblance to my own, recorded nine months ago. Higher-than-average tolerance for pain, heightened ability to regulate the body's reaction to adrenaline. Changes well complemented by the subject's naturally impressive coordination, balance, and reflexes. And the abnormally fast metabolism that marginalized the applejack's effects just enough to stave off death."

My mind drifts back to better times with Trav. *Training together, running the obstacle course, making the city our playground. Brothers in everything . . .*

*Until they sent me home in that coma, and kept him.*

*Did they make him a monster? Did I?*

In my reverie, I've missed some of the science talk. I focus on Trav's lips as he speaks. "We will now proceed with a full sweep, reintroducing nanotech and returning the subject to the grid."

Standing up, he wheels over a horseshoe-shaped device with regularly spaced injectors, which he attaches to the braces holding my head in place. Trav removes the paralytic patch again, leaving my neck raw from the adhesive. "How you holdin' up?"

Wetting my lips, I slowly reply, almost begging. "Trav, please—"

The device locks in place with a resounding click, and he steps back, expression chillingly blank. "Now, this may sting a bit. Your body's been without nanotech for a long time, so the reintroduction might be a bit . . . aggressive."

This time, he doesn't get the paralyzer on before I start screaming.

# V

The costume change is ridiculous but necessary. Shedding my party dress like a snakeskin, I throw on head-to-toe skintight black lace, clip in some fire-engine red extensions, and manage full face paint in less than five. Jax and Sasha are dressed to match in even less time.

*To hell with the styling team.*

"I locked Little Dead Thing in my bathroom," Sasha says, hefting the digital broadcasting console. "He's been through enough for one day."

Jax snorts so that I don't have to. Carrying her minipharmacy and the injector that Damon thoughtfully left on my bathroom counter, Jax hands over one of her precious haptic gloves, the neoprene peeled back to expose a serious amount of wiring. "That's the best I could do in fifteen minutes. The insulation's compromised now, so be careful."

"Got it." I pull on the glove and wrap Micah's broken chain around my knuckles to maximize surface contact. Holding everything tight, I run a half-second test on my leg with the improvised Brights, which hurts like holy fuck. A few minutes later, I can move enough to consider a jailbreak.

Adjusting the vocal modulator, I wait for Sasha to patch me into the security circuit. When she gives me the go-ahead, I borrow Damon's voice again. "Everyone to the back alley of the building. There's been a breach at the loading dock."

I hear the message relay down the hall out of six different radios. As one, the guards stampede for the service exit at the back of the Loft.

"Let's go." I lead the way down the hall, trying to keep my breathing and my heart rate in check. Trying to play out every possible outcome of our mad escape.

*No one better get between me and that limo.*

We've reached a dead run when the front door opens just ahead of us. Damon steps into the foyer, a bottle of over-the-Wall champagne in his hand, a smile playing about his lips.

Then he catches a good look at my face and starts to sputter. "Vee, what the hell—"

Barreling into him at a million miles an hour, I take him down in a tangle of arms and legs. The bottle hits the floor and detonates, spraying the walls with sparkling wine. His head bounces off the marble, but he's still trying to sit up, to reach for me. Profanities stream out of both of us. I get my hands on his neck this time, not the other way around, shoving my Brights into the soft spot under his chin. They discharge with a series of hisses and pops, and the next thing I smell is barbeque. Damon falls back again, out like a light.

I slide off of him, panting, cradling my burning hand against my chest as I eye the livid stripe of raw flesh under his jaw. "That's for getting in my way."

Without comment, Jax tags him with a dose of elephant tranq, courtesy of his own injector. When I'm able to move again, I cram the diamond necklace into the pocket of his coat with my good hand before turning back to the girls.

"Come on."

Jax steps over him and follows me into the elevator. Sasha hesitates, looking as if she'd like a little payback for everything she's been through. A better person than I am, she detours around him instead of stomping his face in.

"Going down," Jax says cheerfully, jamming the lobby button with her thumb.

Next stop, Mercette Park.

# M

I break out in a cold sweat as Trav bombards my body with the nanotech. I can feel it pouring into me, millions of atom-sized ants crawling around my brain. My arms and legs twitch as it triggers spasms and synaptic misfires. It bites like freezer burn screaming through my veins.

*This might be it. After everything, this might finally break me apart and finish the job.*

Shutting my eyes so hard that I pull the surgical tape free, I push back, push back against the nanotech and the memories and Trav's return and everything malignant in the whirlwind of my mind. I force it all back, until all I hear, all I feel is a single, constant tone, like the flatline of an EKG. But it's not the end. It's the beginning.

Vee's first note, the one that lit the fuse way back at Hellcat Maggie's. Still resounding inside me. Her voice. Her life. *My life.* I grab it tight and refuse to let go.

On the periphery of my mind, I sense a release of pressure, a weight lifted. I slowly trickle back to full consciousness, opening my eyes in time to see Trav wheeling away the horseshoe apparatus.

My body pulses with pain from a thousand spots. *Aggressive nanotech . . . No shit. Those little bastards tore through me like a herd of cattle.*

Fisher joins Trav as he analyzes the readout. From the up-and-down movement of his eyes, I'm guessing it's a playback of either my heart rate or my brain activity during the attempted nanotech reboot. Pointing to something on the datapad, Fisher can't get a word out before Trav shuts him down.

"Take five minutes. I need to figure out where we proceed from here."

His assistant nods and heads through the double doors.

"I'm so close, Micah. So fucking close, and you will *not* stand in my way." Trav stares me down for a moment, daring me to oppose him.

But I wouldn't know how. *I'm not even sure why he wants me back on the grid in the first place . . .*

He stares at the datapad, his eyes ricocheting from point to point, mumbling to himself. I hear phrases like *nucleus accumbens* and *neuronal variance*, but none of it means anything to me. Then his eyes light up. And for the briefest moment, he's the old Trav again, exhilarated by solving a problem, conquering an obstacle, getting a look of approval from Bryn.

Part of me, some small part that remembers and loves the Trav I knew, wants to encourage him, to see him succeed. Trav peers close, meeting my gaze. And I search his face for any sign of my old friend.

When Fisher returns, Trav has him call for more equipment while doing some quick calculations on the datapad. "We'll need a secondary conduit for increased output. I'm talking about a constant flow. No more measured doses of nanotech. We'll plug him straight into the wall like a fork in the socket."

As Fisher makes the necessary preparations, I can feel the electrodes and probes sliding from my skull. Trav steps away, cradling a modified aerosolizer in his hands. It looks like an ink-black pyramid, with output jets on four sides and a small reservoir in the center. There's the tiniest puff of air from one of the jets as he puts it back down on the counter.

And as worn out, as burned out, as confused as I am, I finally know something for sure. Trav's not on my side. No matter how much I wanted to believe it, he's not. He can't be.

Because I can smell it. I can smell the rotten cider stink from here.

# CHAPTER EIGHTEEN

## V

By the time we hit Hawthorne Street, every vidscreen in town is flashing the announcement:

**"NIGHT OF THE DEAD" PARK CRAWL**

**FREE CONCERT BY THE SUGAR SKULLS!**

**PAINT YOUR FACE AND JOIN THE FAMILY!**

We put the tinted window up between us and the driver so he doesn't realize his orders didn't actually come from Damon. Sasha's keystroking as fast as she can, hacking into the citywide speakers using his phone as the intermediary between her laptop and Cyrene's broadcasting system.

"Almost there," she mutters, fingers flying.

"Keep at it," I tell her. "None of this is going to mean dick if we can't go live—"

"Shut up, then, and let me concentrate," she snaps back, her thumb brushing over Callie's silver ring before she resumes typing.

Jax tries to get a better look at my injured hand. "Shit, Vee, you burned yourself a good one there."

Sparing a glance for my blistered knuckles, I surprise myself by grinning at her. "It was worth it."

"Yeah, you dropped him like a pro, Princess," Jax says. "Remind me not to piss off this new Vee, all right?" With a glance at Sasha, she adds, "You, either."

Sasha laughs but doesn't look up from the blue glow of her digital displays. "Just don't get between me and Callie, and you'll be fine."

I know exactly how she feels. Rewrapping Micah's silver necklace around my hand, I count off the links, every one a promise to him. *If they've hurt you, I'll pay it back a thousand times over, love.*

"Got it!" Sasha crows seconds before every speaker across the city crackles to life. Given that one in the morning is when a lot of the die-hard shenanigans commence across Cyrene, kids are pouring into the streets in droves. All of them wearing leather and lace and tatters. All of them ready to raise a little hell.

*Time for Phase Three.* Slipping on my wireless earpiece and adjusting the mic, I nod to Jax. "Open it up."

With a sinfully satisfied smile, she opens up the sunroof and I boost myself into the moonlight. Almost immediately, screaming fans surround the limo, each of them wearing a different version of my face.

"It's the middle of the night, you kinky little motherfuckers. Why aren't you in bed?" They all laugh as the car loops slowly around the park, gathering everyone converging on the green square. "How are all my pretty little dead things?"

They roar their answer. I have to give them credit. For all their blistering enthusiasm, they're keeping enough distance to allow the limo to pass through the streets, falling in behind it, my own personal undead army.

Somewhere below me, Jax knows it's time to give them what they want. Using her mini-ironing board mixer from the mall concert, she shoots a spiral of notes from here to eternity. After the second pass around Mercette, I jump into the song and the car rolls toward Richter Park, gathering strength like a storm.

# M

The first try nearly tore me apart; this one shatters me instantly, roaring like a hurricane and battering me from all sides. Every inch of me is on fire as a flood of nanotech pours in. It's a jailbreak, throwing open cell doors and unleashing everything the applejack overdose stole from me. Dead neurons flare back to life, and I feel it. The pain in my ribs explodes, and tears stream down my face.

Nine months of emotion crash into me like a wrecking ball. Memories well up, fresh and revitalized, magnified a thousand times, begging for a chance to be felt for real.

Vee and I kiss, and my heart swells three sizes like the Grinch's.

Venomous spikes of despair and joy and fear run me through as Bryn's death and Trav's reappearance wrestle for my attention.

Old scars and new feelings, agony and delight . . . I drown in it, the ultimate sensory clip show.

When I can bear to open my eyes, there's no sign of Fisher. Instead, I see Trav slipping on a full rebreather, holding the aerosolizer, and watching the datapad intently for updates on my condition. He's almost giddy.

And I realize he's counting down. Waiting to test his new and improved applejack on me.

"Think of it, Micah. No more deadly tabs and inconsistent doses! No more burnouts! No more deaths! Just white-hot highs and a massive boost in thrum!"

The full weight of his betrayal cuts me to the quick, like a drill bit to the heart.

That's why he needs me on the grid. I'm his guinea pig. His test will either kill me or make him a millionaire.

*Either way, Trav wins.*

# V

The music rolls ahead of us, thumping bass barreling down the street. It sweeps up everyone in its path like flotsam; by the time we hit Raskin Park—our final stop—the crowd has tripled in size. If I had to take a guess, at least half of Cyrene's under-21 population has us surrounded, and they're messaging the other half to come join us.

They're not the only ones burning up the Cyrano network. An incoming call almost knocks us off the broadcast system, but Sasha manages to reroute it through her laptop.

"That was unexpected, Vee." Damon's voice, softer than expected. *Damage control mode.*

Jax loops in the chorus of "Little Dead Thing" so I can cover the mic and purr, "I guess your security team found you taking a nap on the marble? How's your neck feeling?"

"Vee, we can fix this. If you pull the plug and get your ass back here, I can explain—"

"I'm sorry, this is a *terrible* connection. Apparently there's some huge park crawl concert going on right now—"

"You kept going back to that house, Vee. Hoping your family would be there, waiting for you."

Goose bumps ripple down my arms. I thought my past was *my* card-up-the-sleeve, but it turns out that it was his, too. "So fucking what?"

"So, I know where they are, Vee. I can take you to them—"

I signal to Sasha to end the call, and the line goes dead. Both the girls stare at me, but I don't want to explain, *can't* explain that a few simple words were somehow the cruelest thing he's inflicted on me yet. So I shake the curls out of my face and jab a finger at the equipment.

"Don't stop, damn it. Stick with the plan!"

Sasha immediately starts broadcasting a live feed of our impromptu performance to every screen in the city. Jax gets in my face with a palm-sized vidcam, which she then pans over the crowd. Every time they see themselves, their energy levels spike higher. Instead of forcing the car to a crawl, the crowd pushes us along with screams and snippets of songs.

It's building, this lovely apocalyptic juggernaut, and now that we've turned down Dover, I'm aiming it straight at the medcenter.

"You asked for plenty of advance notice the next time around. Are you ready to riot?" I ask under my breath.

Jax swings the camera back to me with another huge grin. "Five minutes more, and I could have managed grenades."

*I don't need grenades. It's time to set off some dynamite.*

Out of old material, Jax uses her unmolested glove to cue up a new heartbeat, the hand holding the camera never wavering from my face as I light the match.

Red hot wires jack up my soul,
They want to think they have control,
Inferno starts with a single candle,
Power's too much for them to handle.

Fuck the thrum, screw the grid.
Lick the sparks, eat the dark.

All the pretty undead things
Wear silver necklaces and rings.
We're coming for you, one by one,
Your perfect satin knot's undone.

Fuck the thrum, screw the grid.
Lick the sparks, eat the dark.

By the time I hit the second chorus, the crowd is singing along. This isn't like the Dome. No mayhem. No wanton destruction. The boys and girls out to play don't splinter off down the side streets; they're with me, heart, body, and soul, waving their middle fingers at Damon, at Corporate, at Cyrene. Banshees, every last one of us, and we're going to make them hear us.

Even if we have to take down the city to do it.

The first of them runs up against the metal gate blocking the entrance to the medcenter. Hands grasp chain-link, rattling it like a necklace of chicken bones.

Fuck the thrum, screw the grid.
Lick the sparks, eat the dark.

More hands, more weight, more undead howls from all the face-painted sugar skulls, but they need something more.

*They need me.*

Boosting myself out the top of the limo, I slide down the windshield and take three running steps down the hood. Launching myself into the crowd, I trust them to catch me, just like they did at the mall. Riding the energy currents, I end up at the fence. Two of the tallest guys offer up their shoulders, and after that it's a quick scrape over paltry razor wire. I cut up the hand not wearing the glove, but fuck it.

*What's a little blood now?*

I land on the other side of the fence in time to tag a security guard headed for me. The Brights shock the shit out of me again, but it's nothing compared to the adrenaline pouring through me, and everyone roars when he hits the concrete. I was almost expecting to run up against an army's worth of Facilitators, but Damon hasn't had time to scramble his backup.

*Better make my move.*

Jax loops the new song around to play again, ghost-voicing me and adding some nice reverb on the back end; normally Sasha would do this, but she's busy organizing the tech side of our little revolutionary diversion. The music makes for the perfect soundtrack as I run to the empty security booth, punch every button, set off sirens and rotating red lights. Finally the front gate swings open. The crowd pours in, chanting, "Screw the grid!" They head straight for the front doors, battering against the glass like zombies in search of brains.

I bolt for the side entrance, hearing glass shatter seconds before Sasha manages to cut the power to the building. Security system fucked six ways to Sunday, the side door swings open, and the only thing between me and Micah is a million miles of pitch-black corridor.

"Lick the sparks," I mutter as the nearest emergency light crackles on, green instead of the usual orange. "Eat the dark."

# M

I scream myself hoarse, and then I scream until I can taste blood, but it has no effect on Trav. He's wild-eyed, practically foaming at the mouth, waiting for whatever sign he needs to activate the aerosolizer.

"We'll test every batch on you first! Perfect quality control!" Trav's hands are shaking slightly, from adrenaline or excitement or rage or all three at once. "How fast did your love for Bryn fade? How soon after you woke up were you fucking whores like your little singer? Was Bryn's body even cold yet, you piece of shit?" He's ranting now, spewing every vile bit of misery and anger he's bottled up over months and months. Each word lands like another vicious jab to the ribs.

With the nanotech surging through me, I'm a raw nerve. I can't resist, I can't fight. I just feel. I've completely trashed my voice with my screaming, but I still manage to choke out a few words: "Trav, I'm sorry."

He drops the datapad, grabs my face hard, and stares into my eyes. "You're sorry?! You ruined my life, you took her from me, and you're sorry?" He lets go of me, and I can feel bruises already forming from his fingertips. "If you were really sorry for what you did, you'd be dead. You should have saved us all the trouble and just killed yourself—"

The window suddenly crashes inward, bits of frosted glass tinkling to the floor, the subdued after-hours glow of a Cyrene high-rise now visible. *We must be a few floors up.*

And slipping through the myriad cracks, there's chanting, over and over.

> Fuck the thrum, screw the grid.
> Lick the sparks, eat the dark.

Trav turns his attention from me to the window, glaring through the spiderwebbed glass at the street below.

Fisher bursts through the double doors. "Sir, there's a mob outside. Security will be here in a few—"

"I'm fine! We're almost there. Give me five more minutes. If I need anything, I have my panic button. Now go."

The assistant glances at me before leaving, obviously spooked by more than the noise outside.

Fuck the thrum, screw the grid.
Lick the sparks, eat the dark.

That single note, that tone resonating inside me, is bolstered by one particular voice in the crowd. Her voice emerges from the frantic pitch and leads the sonorous charge.

Vee is okay.

She remembers me.

And she raised an army with just her voice.

Trav stares out the window, looking without seeing. "A rescue mission. How sweet. You did the same thing for her, didn't you? At the Dome."

I try to nod, but my head is still locked down by the restraints. "Yeah." *Using some of the know-how you taught me.*

"Smart enough to save her but not us, right? Not Bryn?"

*He's still there. In the alcove. He lives there every day.* "I couldn't move, Trav. I couldn't do anything."

"I watched her, Micah. I watched her die, and as she died, she reached for you. For fucking you. And you just sat there. I reached for her, with everything I had. Just fingertips away." Angry tears streak down his face.

The nanotech races through me, dozens of doses. Hundreds. It's hard to think. Hard to focus.

*I wonder if I can still reach him, the man who loves Bryn, even now.* "She . . . she wouldn't want this for you."

He rips the rebreather from his face and hurls it across the room. "You don't know the first thing about what she wanted! She wanted *me*. She came to me with open arms. You had to chase her down to get her to notice you at all." Taking a deep breath, he carefully puts down the aerosolizer. "You don't know shit, Micah."

*Keep pushing.* "I know she was better than this. Better than stupid, petty revenge."

He punches me in the stomach, a hammerblow that knocks the wind out of me. "Stop talking!"

Two voices battle in my head. Trav and Vee. Trav's bitterness, his fury, versus Vee's passion, her strength. I wrap myself in her words like ablative armor, whispering "Fuck the thrum, screw the grid. Lick the sparks, eat the dark."

"Shut the fuck up, Micah! No more hiding behind Bryn and your whore and your lies and your bullshit and—"

"Fuck the thrum, screw the grid. Lick the sparks, eat the—"

Everything goes dark. Displays and monitors, Trav's datapad, the lights—all gone. The relentless nanotech assault stops. I plummet back to earth, exhausted, burnt out.

*Vee. Saving me again.* It's silent, except for my voice chanting the verse over and over as the emergency lights kick on.

Trav stares at me in disbelief. "No. No! Not again. You are not getting that fucking lucky again." He grabs the aerosolizer off the table, and for a long moment, I believe he's really going to dose us both with it.

But then he just stands there, clutching it tight in his hand. He cracks his neck, listening to the crowd outside.

*He always did love the noise of a crowd cheering him on.*

His shoulders fall slightly as the tension bleeds away. He puts the black pyramid down calmly. "There's no sport in doing it that way." Reaching into his lab coat's pocket, he removes a circular object. *The panic button.* He places it next to the aerosolizer.

"You know, I've got about two minutes before the magnetic charge on those restraints dissipates and you're free. I could spend that time beating the unholy shit out of you, Micah. I'd like that. I'd love that." He strips away the lab coat next, and the dress shirt underneath, leaving him in an undershirt and slacks. He's not quite in the same shape I remember. Less lean, but obviously he's kept active.

And he's still in much better shape than I am right now. However much he's changed, he's still a competitor. He's still competing with me.

*Maybe I can use that to buy me some time until the restraints unlock.* "But you won't do it that way. No challenge, no glory. Right, Trav?"

"I knew you'd get it." He taps his nose as he walks around the operating slab, stretching, loosening up his joints. "I'll tell you what, Micah. Your little fuckslut is gonna be in the building soon. You want to see her again? All you have to do is go through me."

A moment later there's a series of clicks: five sets of magnetic restraints shutting down in a nanosecond. Sliding off the slab and onto the floor, I'm wobbly but standing. Free.

Trav stands between me and the double doors, practically baring his teeth at me. "Come on, killer. What's it gonna be?"

## V

The trouble with the plan is that there isn't one beyond *get to Micah*. Every time I've been in the medcenter, it's been for a reboot. Spectacularly spaced-out and kept in a private room until I got transferred to a recovery spa, I wasn't exactly drawing up blueprints and mapping out the air ducts and whatever else a spy or supersoldier would have done to prep for a situation like this.

It's only now that I realize the building is fucking huge, with hundreds of rooms and miles of corridors.

*And Micah could be anywhere.*

I try to stop myself from thinking that Damon had him wiped already. That all this could be for nothing. That I could get to him, and he'd say, "Who the hell are you, you crazy face-painted freak?"

My stomach clenches up at the thought.

*Hang on, love.*

I check every room along the first hall, but they're vacant. Nothing fucking creepier than a bunch of crypt-empty labs, metal tables glowing pale green, cabinets stocked with every sort of pill and powder and drug . . .

*And needles, Vee. Get your head out of your ass and start thinking on your feet!*

Detouring into the next room, I burn through precious time loading two injectors with high-caliber sedative. Before I can do more than that, my earpiece crackles.

"There's trouble coming at you," Sasha whispers from back in the limo. "Three teams of Facilitators in the parking lot and two more blocking the car. Special ops are—"

The side door slams open. Security pours in, tranq guns raised. I duck back into the lab and flatten myself against the wall. When their radios crackle and hiss, I hear Damon reaching for me again.

"She's somewhere in the goddamn building. This isn't fucking rocket science! Just find her before she gets to Level Three."

*Only one thing he doesn't want me to find, so now I know which floor Micah is on. Thanks for the heads-up, jackass.*

My options now: let them take me or start running. And I know what Micah would do.

"Sasha, get rid of the emergency lighting, if you can," I whisper, sliding one injector into the waistband of my pants and hoping I don't shoot myself in the leg. The other one stays in my left hand, while I tighten my grip on my Jax-hacked stun-knucks.

Footfalls approach, but they're pausing to clear every room along the way. Across the hall, a stairwell glows green. Listening to the boots getting closer and closer, I wait for my chance.

*Get it done.*

As if on cue, the emergency lights cut out. I launch myself up the stairs, taking them two at a time while the Facilitators reach for their flashlights. By the time the first narrow beams cut like scythes through the darkness, I'm past the first landing and almost to the second floor.

"She's headed up! Move! Move! Move!"

*Heeled boots against metal grating.*

They charge up the stairs behind me, but the bigger problem is that the door with the modest number three stenciled on it opens up before I can reach it. Twin greyfaces aren't expecting me to leap against the heavy metal, slamming it shut in their faces and, judging by the howls, catching at least one of them by the fingers.

*Going to have to go up to get down.*

One more flight. The fourth level of the building looks clear for the moment; everyone's probably down on three, swarming into Micah's room, surrounding him like vultures. I bolt the door shut behind me and check everything—sedative injectors, Brights, my heart rate, my breathing—and try to look before I leap. The urge to keep moving almost swamps me.

Then the lights kick back on, the same ghostly green as before.

"Sasha!" I hiss into my earpiece. "What the fuck?"

Jax answers instead. "She bailed out two seconds ago and joined the crowd. I think she's going after Callie."

"The goddamn emergency power is back on!" At the far end of the hall, I can hear the elevator cables whirring. *Shit.* "Tag it off again."

"No dice, Princess, I already tried. Hang tight. I'm coming in." Then Jax is gone, too.

*Fuck me.*

The indicator at the top of the elevator counts off the levels, passing the second and third floors, then pinging when it arrives at the fourth. The doors slide open, and three Facilitators step off. I don't have any long-distance weaponry, so I have to wait in the doorway, biding my time. They're ambling along, not exactly on high alert while they bitch amongst themselves.

"I put in for the overtime, but the fucker denied it. God, that guy is a dick."

"Just a cleaned-up street punk. If he doesn't get this whole situation under control soon, his ass is toast."

"Yeah, well maybe we should let Miss Hotpants find her boyfriend and take off into the blue yonder—"

They pass where I'm standing, which gives me the chance to shove the first injector into the back of Overtime's neck. He's down before he can finish his thought, and I sweep the Brights over his buddy's face as he whips around. Both of us hit the floor.

Number three's tranq gun goes up as she shouts, "Get the fuck down!"

"I'm not sure," I wheeze, "how much more 'down' I can get."

She shuffles forward, shoving the barrel under my chin and using it to tip my head back. When the beam from her flashlight passes over my face, she pops off with, "Shit, it's you." Then she's reaching for her radio.

"Yup, it's me." Right hand still recovering, I have to pull out the second sedative shot with the left.

Summoning backup that will end our little rebellion here and now, she stops long enough to snarl, "Don't fucking move."

"You first." I fire the injector into her leg. Unable to reach any bare skin, I have to hope enough of it gets through her pants and into her system. Must have, because she staggers back, slams into the wall, and slides down.

It takes a few minutes to find my feet again, but I liberate two of the tranq guns from my newfound friends and head straight into the elevator.

I press the button for Level Three.

*Going fucking down.*

# M

Trav waits. He's tensed, ready to pounce on my first step, my first swing, my first mistake. Patient and tactical. At least that hasn't changed. He always let the challenges and the rewards come to him.

*Bryn included, I guess.*

Today's no different. He knows my window of escape is closing, and he has all the time in the world. "You can't hide, you can't outrun this, Micah. Grow some balls and get over here."

When I step around the operating slab, his arms flex in response, like he's champing at the bit to unleash them on my already battered body. The lights cut out, and I check the back of my freshly shaved head to make sure Fisher patched me up okay. It's tender, but I won't be leaking brain all over the place.

*Good. That's the last thing I need.*

"I don't want to fight you, Trav," I plead into the darkness. "This isn't a race, or a game, or a competition. This is fucking real. Please just . . . get out of my way and let me go find Vee."

The power kicks back on as he steps forward, anger showing for the first time since my restraints fell away. "No. You don't get off that fucking easy."

One hard shove, harder than I expect, slams my lower back against the slab. My ribs twinge, and I grit my teeth. *He's stronger than I remember.*

"Fight me, you coward!" Trav grabs my shirt with one hand and punches me across the face with the other, reopening some of the wounds from Rete's beatdown. "I didn't get that satisfaction from the dealer. Couldn't get my hands on you, so I went after him." Another stiff punch, right to my swollen eye. "After I was all healed up, it took a week or two to find him. And then I couldn't exactly beat the shit out of him and make it look like an overdose, could I?"

*No wonder I couldn't track down that scumbag.*

I raise my hands up to ward off more blows, but Trav brushes them aside. He lays into me with two more thunderous shots before bunching up my shirt in both hands and shaking me.

"Man the fuck up and fight me!"

When I shake my head no, some of my blood spatters onto his tank top. Trav roars and swings at me again. I barely duck the punch, planting two hands on his chest and pushing him away for a moment. Rolling back over the slab, I put the table between us, and he slams his hands against it.

"It doesn't have to be like this," I say. "Just stop!"

He jumps up onto the slab, charging toward me.

*He won't listen, won't even consider it.* I whip around the other side as he lands. *He's stronger, but not as agile as he used to be.*

And now there's nothing between me and the exit. Making a break for it, I crash into the double doors full force, finding out the hard way that they're locked. I ricochet off them and tumble to the floor.

"Not that easy, killer. You need a security tag to get out." Trav crouches over me, grabbing my head with both hands and slamming it against the floor. "You're gonna fight me, Micah, or I'll smash your skull in."

Even with one eye swollen shut and the other blurry from the impact, I can see the truth etched in his face. I believe him. "Don't make me do this, Trav. Please."

"Why not? I made you do everything else. I made you better. You trained harder, ran faster, and took bigger risks because of me. You wanted to *be* me. To have what I had. You didn't love Bryn. You just wanted her because I had her. Good thing she died before she found that out."

Thoughts of Bryn flash through my mind: the mischievous smile after our first kiss, the soft moans she made when we snuck away from the group at Maggie's or Solfetara's.

Trav bounces my head off the linoleum again, jarring me back to the present. "Come on, Micah. That little bitch is out there somewhere, looking for you. Don't you *love* her? Don't you even care?" Baiting me. Trying to make me angry.

*It's working.*

I knee him hard in the back, and he arches in pain, just enough that I can throw him off me and roll onto my hands and knees. When I check the back of my head again, it throbs, but there's no blood.

As I stumble to my feet, Trav is waiting for me, grabbing my wrists and pulling me to him. He drives his knee into my gut, and I drop to a crouch, desperate to get my air back.

But all I can think about is Vee.

*Out there, fighting, searching for me. Let Trav have his bitterness, his memories of Bryn. I have more than memories now. I have Vee.*

I spring up toward him, burying my shoulder in his stomach and hurling us both through trays of supplies and into the wall. As we fall to the ground together, he slams his elbow down between my shoulder blades, and I see stars.

Rolling away from him, my hand bumps against something on the floor . . . One of the magnetic restraints. I grab it as I duck a wild swing from Trav and smash the metal loop into his skull.

He falls to his knees, clutching the side of his head. I kick him in the chest, and he rolls to the ground. Once he's down, I can see some blood welling up beneath his fingers.

Staring at the blood on the metal loop in my hand, I'm barely able to keep from throwing up. I crouch down next to Trav, lying there among the scattered injectors and surgical tools. He swings at me blindly with one hand, still holding his head with the other. Pinning his arm down, I stare into the teary, manic eyes of my friend.

"Go on then, killer. Finish me off. Finish the job!" He spits out every syllable.

*I will, Trav.* "I'm so sorry. For Bryn. For everything. For this."

I pick up a sedative patch from the floor and slap it on his neck before he can respond. He struggles for a moment, and then his eyes close. His last words before unconsciousness takes him are "I hate you, Micah . . ."

"I know. I do, too." I slowly stand up—battered, bruised, and heartbroken—and grab Trav's security tag from his lab coat. Quickly rummaging through various drawers, I scrounge up a stun baton. Fully charged.

Passing through the double doors, I stumble into the corridor. One deep breath later, I'm moving, realizing I have no idea where to go next. The elevator in the center of the hallway dings, and I'm about to run, hide, anything to give myself a little more time to find Vee.

The doors part, and twin tranq gun barrels are the first thing I see. Trigger fingers clench, then hesitate. The barrels dip slightly, and I see her face, streaked with white and black war paint. Even in the hideous emergency light, she's radiant.

I lower the baton, thumbing it off as I stare. The crushing weight of every kick, punch, injection, and accusation from the last day crumbles and blows away.

*If I'm hallucinating, if this is the angel I see before I die, I'm okay with it.*

I reach for her with open arms.

# V

One second I'm ready to shoot in the face whoever's between me and Micah, and the next his arms are sliding around me.

"You're here," he murmurs, his face buried in my hair. "You saved me again."

I get fleeting impressions of his hands on me, his cheek pressed to mine, his ragged voice in my ear. Someone shaved his fucking head, and god only knows what else they did to him before I got here. My heart kicks in my chest, but I don't get the chance to do anything, to say anything before the elevator opposite us pings.

Micah twists around, his instinct to act as a human shield kicking in. "Stay behind me."

"Like hell."

*Have to move. Have to run. This is our last chance to get the fuck out of here—*

But the doors slide open, and it's Game Over. Four Facilitators step out wearing Kevlar chest plates and helmets, guns raised. Not tranq guns like mine, but actual M16s. The kind that fire real fucking bullets and tear open big messy holes and leave lots of blood on the floor. Every barrel is thoughtfully capped off with a matte black suppressor so they won't blow out our eardrums when they shoot us. Electronic sights partially obscure their faces, but I can tell they won't hesitate to pull the trigger.

Damon steps out next. His jacket and tie are gone. His shirt is unbuttoned at the collar and the sleeves are rolled up, but none of his tattoos are as vivid as the burn mark I left on the side of his neck.

*Give me even half a chance, Damon, and I'll make it a matching set.*

Seeing the look on my face, he goes very still, gaze roaming from my sugar skull paint down to my purloined weaponry. "Drop everything."

The request is punctuated by the pounding of boots down the hallways and the arrival of more special ops. More than I can count. We're hemmed in, nice and neat.

"Vee." It's all he says, all he has to say: A reminder that he's waiting. That he gave me an order. That my job is to say "Yes, Damon" and obey.

I drop both the tranq guns. They hit the floor with a clatter.

"The glove, too." Damon hasn't moved an inch, but if he had a tail, it would be twitching by now.

As I uncoil the length of silver chain from my knuckles, my eyes never leave his. I slide the broken necklace very deliberately into my bra before peeling off Jax's wrecked haptic glove. The second it's gone, I feel panic rush through me.

*There has to be a way out. Back down the stairs. Get lost in the crowd. Fuck, Vee, think.*

But it's a suicide mission, with Micah first in line to die. He's still between me and everyone else, refusing to budge, stun baton at the ready.

"Drop it, or she's dead," Damon says. Calm. Vicious.

Micah's shoulders tense up, as he considers the threat. I count the moment off in heartbeats; between the second and third, the baton bounces off the floor and away from his feet.

Damon jerks his chin in our direction. "Now move away from each other."

Neither of us budges.

*They're going to have to pry me off of him.*

I step up behind Micah, slide my arms around his chest, press myself against his back. He's sweated through his shirt more than once, so he doesn't smell like detergent anymore. Hell, he doesn't smell like anything but fear and pain. But this is the last chance I might have to hold him, and I take it. For a split second, I can imagine we're back at the slow jams club, just us and the music and the dance floor. The perfect night. The perfect moment.

In the dead silence, I stand on tiptoe to whisper into his ear, "I love you, Micah."

His every muscle clenches in response. He covers my hands with his own. "I love you, Vee."

I hold him tight, words failing me.

Micah looks at me over his shoulder. "Always you. Only you."

Damon's rage boils over. "Grab her and shoot him—"

Somewhere down the hall, doors slam open in quick succession. Radios start to crackle with warnings, but the chants of "Fuck the thrum, screw the grid!" drown out everything else. The noise is unbelievable, bouncing off the walls, the ceiling, accompanied by the screech of metal and shattered glass. The countless Facilitators surrounding us whip around to face the new threat: Jax charging down the hall like some kind of Valkyrie, leading an army of energy-high little dead things. Somewhere along the way, she's picked up a foot-long blade, the swingarm off an industrial paper cutter, by the looks of it.

For the first time, Micah seems genuinely surprised. "Here comes Trouble."

"Get to Vee!" she yells, hair streaming over her shoulders. "Save the Princess!"

Still singing, they surge forward, armed with pipes and knives and Brights and pointy makeshift weapons they've twisted off gurneys and railings.

"Tranqs only on them! They're civilians!" Damon orders.

The first row of Facilitators starts spraying the crowd with darts, but the chanting overrides the drugs, and the kids plow into the nearest guards.

"Get the one in the middle!" a familiar voice shouts from the right. I twist around in time to see Sasha flying in from the other side, tranq guns in both hands, followed by another crowd of rampaging fans. Matching her step for step, the Redheaded Mini is looking a little less pretty and a lot more pissed off, right hand bandaged but her left hand clamped down on a glowing shock baton.

"The one with the fucking tattoos!" Callie calls out to the horde at her back. Taking out the nearest goon, she heads straight for Damon, looking for payback and then some.

The balance is tipping, tipping slowly in our favor. I can feel it in the frisson of energy all around us, in the shrieks of the little dead things, and in the thuds of security hitting the floor. But there are still guns trained on Micah, on me, and all it's going to take to finish this the quick-and-dirty way is for Damon to give the order.

The special ops know it, too. Their eyes never leave us, but the closest one asks, "Do you still want us to shoot him, sir?"

I ease around Micah, putting myself between him and the imminent bullets. "You'll have to shoot me first. And then"—tipping my head toward the crowd fighting their way to us—"maybe half this crowd. That's going to be hard to explain to Corporate, isn't it?"

I wait forever for Damon's answer, trying to remember how to breathe. Jax is ten feet away; Sasha maybe twenty. The girls' sugar skull faces are studies in glee and murder, respectively.

He actually has the balls to hold his hand out to me. "Vee, make them stop. You and I can fix this. We—"

Over his shoulder, I can see my face reflected in the shiny gold surface of the elevator doors, an angel and a demon all at once. "I told you before, Damon. There is no fucking *we*. You're clinging to that idea so hard, you can't see that the girl you want is gone . . . if she ever really existed in the first place."

He looks every bit the street thug when he spits out, "So that's it, huh? I'm nothing to you. Your family means nothing to you?"

"Not if I have to trade it for what I have right now. What I'll have tomorrow morning and every morning after that." I glance around at the crowd closing in from both sides, the Facilitators eyeing the elevators.

Damon's once-steely gaze searches my face for guideposts long gone. After riots and blackouts and declarations of love at gunpoint, he finally looks uncertain. "I would've given you everything."

"Except the freedom to be who I am. To become who I was meant to be. Because you were afraid that person might not love you." I make sure I'm looking him right in the eyes when I add, "You were right to be afraid."

That's when he flinches. His shoulders slump, and through a rushing crackle of white noise, I hear him give the order to lower the guns.

Lacing my fingers through Micah's, I pull him as close as I can and murmur, "I think it's time to renegotiate my contract."

# EPILOGUE

## V

*Another concert, another corset.*

The dressing room scene is the same as always: total chaos. Face already painted, I get laced into a black satin waterfall. Little Dead Thing scowls at everyone from a cushion in the corner. Jax twirls new waist-length colorshifting hair extensions like a stripper on a good night. Sasha's having some issue with her laptop. Glaring at the screen, she's reduced to tears that somehow magically evaporate the second Callie appears in the doorway.

"Ten minutes," the Redheaded Mini warns the rest of us.

Damon might have blamed the worst of his manager-gone-wild excesses on Trav, but Corporate didn't exactly buy it once they heard my side of the story. That should have been that, but Damon still had cards up his sleeve, all aces: the upper-echelon investors he'd cultivated, several bigwigs on the board of directors with more greed than common sense, and last but not least, the Sugar Skulls' contracts. Negotiations to remove the tumor in our midst took longer than I liked, but I'd expected nothing less. Of course Damon would go down swinging. Corporate finally agreed to let him stay until the "Night of the Dead" damages were paid back in full; the second I hit the stage tonight, he'll be escorted out of Cyrene and shuttled off to his shiny new gig in a second prototype city.

Sensing the need for someone to run interference, Callie stepped in to handle things. Pretty diplomatic, given what Damon had inflicted on her, but Corporate was just happy she wasn't going to sue them. It doesn't hurt that she has a definite knack for prepping for shows, managing PR, and dealing with all the details. Bonus for everyone that her flavor of capable is laid-back, it's-all-good. Like right now, she manages to assess the status of our costuming and Jax's mood even as she crosses the room to help Sasha with whatever coding snafu is holding her up.

"The new thrum-collectors are all online and working without a hitch." Callie gives me a sidelong glance and the merest flicker of a wink. "Let's see if we can keep it that way, okay?"

"Hey, I haven't tested them nonstop for a month just to blow them out now." Truth be told, tonight's concert really *is* the test of what the new tech can handle—*or not handle*—under the combined pressure of my voice and the crowd's energy. Trying not to let my nerves eat me alive is getting harder by the minute, especially as I wait for word from Micah. I run my fingertips over the electroluminescent wire threaded through the front of my corset. Right now, it's glowing pale violet.

Jax notices, of course. "You should take a handful of something and calm the fuck down."

"It makes you nervous that I'm off all the chemicals, doesn't it?" Social drinking is one thing, but getting all hopped up on sky-candy isn't something I do anymore. *Not after the applejack. Not ever again.* "Why don't you take extra pills for me? Might improve your mood."

"It's completely unnatural for anyone to be high on life, is all I'm saying."

Callie snorts out a laugh as her arms wrap around Sasha. "Shoot a note to your mom and dad. Payment for the month should have gone through, no problems."

"Oh, good." When Sasha closes the laptop and leans back, the crease in her forehead disappears. Her sigh of utter contentment brings a tiny ache to the back of my throat.

"You two are absolutely fucking nauseating," Jax observes, sitting on a stool and swinging her legs so the toes of her boots scrape against the floor. "Keep it up and I'm gonna Technicolor yawn all over this place."

Callie's earlobes flush bright pink under her piercings, but Sasha responds by turning around far enough to plant a serious kiss on her. Setting the laptop aside, Callie grabs Sasha by the wrist and tows her from the room, tossing "We'll be right back" over her shoulder.

"Seriously? Eight minutes to curtain and they're gonna squeeze in a quickie?" Jax scowls at the ceiling. "I need to get laid. What do you want to do after the show, Vee? Up for playing wingman?"

The dresser ties off my laces and gives me a gentle pat. I can't sit, so leaning against the wall is as relaxed as it gets for now. "I don't think so. Not tonight, anyway."

"You always have plans," she grumbles. "All of you have abandoned me in my hour of need."

"You've gone a whole hour without?" I smile. "Back at the Loft after the show. Whatever you pour out, I'll drink, all right?" I get my earpiece and mic situated, wishing that I had Micah's arms around me, that I was the one stealing kisses and more before the show. "In the meantime, let's get our asses onstage."

"At least it's the end of the Indentured Fucking Servitude Tour. This bitch needs to get paid." Flashing a grin at me, Jax is already halfway out the door. Despite having the wrack-and-ruin from the park crawl riot stuck on the Sugar Skulls' tab, she's still reveling in the glory of leading a zombie army. Some days she threatens to do it all over again, just for shits and giggles.

One corridor and a set of stairs later, we're in the red-lit wings. "If the collectors don't blow."

Sasha joins us seconds later, adjusting her clothes and running her fingers through her disheveled hair. "What did I miss?"

Jax nudges her hard. "Something about blowing. Unless you squeezed that in, too."

"Shut up," Sasha tells her without any real heat behind the words.

We hit the stage, following the paths of yellow glow-tape to our respective marks. Amber lights fade up and crimson sparks rain down on the stage as vidscreens all over the Dome sizzle to life.

"Take it easy on the first few songs," Callie tells me through the earpiece. "Ease them into it, all right?"

A nod of acknowledgment, and then we launch into "The Morning After." Jax hates my newest song, preferring riot-inducing riffs to celebrations of love, but when I'm singing it, I can close my eyes and picture Micah that very first morning in the warren, the way his hair fell into his eyes, the way he held me even when sleeping. He's with me, even when he's not with me, every time I sing this one.

After that, it's a slow build to "Revolution." Corporate still doesn't like it, but the recording sold an epic number of downloads the day after the park crawl, so they ignore the lyrics as best they can.

The audience loves every word. By the second verse, they're screaming along with me.

> All the pretty undead things
> Wear silver necklaces and rings.
> We're coming for you, one by one,
> Your perfect satin knot's undone.

Fuck the thrum, screw the grid.
Lick the sparks, eat the dark.

One hand reaches up to touch the silver necklace hanging around my throat, and I drive into the chorus again, pushing the words, spitting the lyrics, sending the crowd into a screaming frenzy. They're high on vaporized moondust; by the time we've looped around and sung the chorus a third time, I can feel the breaking point, the glass ceiling just over my head.

One more time, and I bump into it again, but it doesn't break. The thrum-collectors hold, whisking away all the energy safely into the grid.

*The grid. I pushed as hard as I could, and I'm still here. Still on it.*

*This nightingale gets to stay in the nest.*

Not a cage anymore. You can't build a cage out of music and light and—

*Love.*

The electroluminescent wire lacings on my corset colorshift from violet to blue.

*Perfect timing.*

I close my eyes, take a breath, and transition to "For You."

What would I give for just one taste of you?
What would I trade to fall straight into you?
I would burn this city to the ground.
Down, down, down to the ground.

# M

*Okay, she should've seen the alert by now. Time to record. Hold on, gotta center this in the frame.*

I zoom in with Jax's mini-handheld vidcam as a pair of Facilitators in full gear escort Damon to the waiting town car. No crowds, no fanfare, no farewell party from Corporate. The contracts are signed and thumbprinted; it's time to wrap him up and send him packing.

I track him, moving from rooftop to fire escape to balcony, running the intricate maze of the Odeaglow while keeping the car in my sights. Finally, a section of the Wall parts like a curtain, and the car is gone, taillights fading from view.

*It's done. She's finally free.*

I shut off the vidcam and wirelessly upload it to Sasha's private server. She'll have the video polished and ready for everyone later tonight. After today's show, seeing Damon transferred out of town will be the icing on the cake for Vee. No more threats against her, no more mind-wipes or power games.

*No more boogeyman hiding under the bed.*

As the curtain closes, I glance upward at the Wall. The best playgrounds have fences, and right now, it's our staunchest ally. Keeping us safe. Keeping our enemies out. Those projected blue skies are more welcome than ever. New chapters and all that.

I've got hours to kill before the Sugar Skulls are done performing, so I stop by one of the local security offices en route to The Warren. Wanting to make sure I stayed in Cyrene—even another set of clean scans at the lab didn't temper their espionage paranoia much—Corporate offered me a gig I couldn't refuse: freelancing with the Facilitators, sealing the city up tight and preventing anyone from sneaking inside like I did. After all, who better to help you secure the place than the guy who already beat the system?

So now, instead of ducking shadows and patrols, I spend my days running to ground every dealer I can find. In exchange, I get the resources and the freedom to finally do what brought me back here: rid the city of every last tab of that poisonous shit.

We're off to a good start. With Rete and his people already in custody, the majority of in-house cartel activity dried up. The pipelines are closed, and reports of applejack use are dwindling, though we still have no idea what over-the-Wall group was manufacturing it in the first place.

We brought a runner in yesterday, and as she was hauled off, I thought about Trav killing the dealer who started all this. In Trav's place, I don't know what I would've done. There was never a real plan after "find the dealer." I'd like to think I'm not a killer.

*But if Trav could do it . . .*

I don't suppose it matters much now. Trav vanished from Corporate custody a few days after the "Night of the Dead" riot. No sign of him anywhere in Cyrene for weeks now. Him or his new applejack variant. My friend, gone as suddenly as he reappeared. His anger, his bitterness, his hatred, etched into my memory as clearly as his name on my skin. Our meager good-byes at the medcenter hardly enough for either of us.

After checking in with Cyrene Security, I make a quick supply run at the home improvement shop not far from Maggie's club.

No, not her club anymore. It's already in renovations for the new owner, same guy who redid Moonship & Stardust a while back.

They offered the space to me, but I couldn't take it. I gave them the whole spiel about it being too big and not the right layout for The Warren, but truth be told, it would never feel like mine, new floor plan or not. It'll always be the Hellcat's, if only in spirit.

Last week, Rete gave up the location of her body, confirming my darkest suspicions. I barely recognized her. I know she misled me and trafficked in some serious garbage, but she deserved better.

*We all did.*

Shuttering those thoughts for now, I make tracks to The Warren to continue getting it ready for tonight.

*I swear, it's easier to meticulously weave lengths of copper than it is to install this high-end lattice shit just to do the same job. But if that's what it takes to ensure the place is totally off-grid, it's still worth the effort.*

Once the final piece is secured to the walls, I step back and admire my work. There's a long way to go before The Warren is up and running, but this is one big step closer to the finish line.

I dash over to the gym a couple blocks down and grab a shower, scrubbing away the grime and sweat from the day's labors. My hair is growing back, but I'm still careful when washing it, tracing the myriad scars left from my time in the lab. No nanotech to heal me up. Even Trav's best efforts couldn't plug me into the grid for good. The hum's not going anywhere.

I dry off, dress, and make it to the club just in time to sign for the first delivery of over-the-Wall spirits to enhance the bar's selection. Corporate has agreed to look the other way on a few minor indulgences in exchange for my continued silence about what I endured at the medcenter. Amazing the leverage potential negative PR confers.

After stashing the cases of liquor in the back storage room, I quadruple-check my improvised stereo system, since I've already gone over it three times today. *Gotta make it perfect. She deserves perfect.*

I hear Vee sneaking up behind me while I tinker with the bass and treble settings. *Let her think she's got the drop on you.* Her hands wind around my waist, and I can sense her vague disappointment when I don't leap out of my skin in surprise. Instead, I tilt my head back as she kisses my neck and murmurs, "Hello, love."

I turn around and kiss her properly, pulling her body to mine, noticing that she's traded her stage gear for something soft and tantalizingly short. My lips reluctantly break from hers as I whisper, "How was the show?"

"Another glowing success. No blowouts, no blackouts, and only the regular burnouts in the crowd." She reaches up to twist her fingers in the collar of my shirt and pull me a few inches closer. "And just what have you been doing with yourself while I was gone?"

I give her my best smile as I walk her around the club, showing her the little touches that occupied part of my day. Once all the pieces are in place and we generate some positive word-of-mouth, The Warren will be our slice of underground paradise.

By the time I've got her in the center of the room where the dance floor will be, she's seen so much that the lighting I've jury-rigged escapes her notice. Ditto for the remote in my hand. I dim the lights and cue the music as I draw her close, and she smiles, a radiant, intoxicating smile that makes a peasant feel like a king.

My hands find her waist as she drapes her arms over my shoulders, and we slow dance to the simple strumming of the song. Her eyes light up with recognition, and I answer her question before she asks. "Had a little help from Sasha and Jax. Recorded it yesterday."

"On the new guitar?"

"Her name's Sofie, thank you very much."

"Good thing I'm not the jealous type." Vee kisses me, just for a moment, before retreating to arm's length. I stroke her cheek as she croons along with the recording of me playing.

> You came in through an unguarded window,
> Finding me alone in this dark and empty space,
> Creeping through my every waking thought,
> Quiet as a mouse, and vibrant as the chase.

I still tense up as the electric shocks of her voice roll over me, totally and utterly hers for the duration of the song. It's a concert for one, and I sway with her, following her every lilt and half step.

As the last note slips from her lips, I hug her tight and we just stand there, lost in a stolen moment. Eventually, Vee breaks the silence. "They're expecting us back at the Loft."

I nod. "Game Night, right?"

Her face pressed hard against my chest, it takes her a second to answer. "If Jax wants to play Full-Contact Rock-Paper-Scissors again, I need you to watch my back . . ." The words trail off as she concentrates on her breathing, like we've practiced: one count in, two counts out. Two counts in, four counts out.

The last time we played, I'd gotten distracted trying not to step on Little Dead Thing in the middle of a skirmish. Jax had tackled Vee, pinning her to the couch and triggering a full-blown panic attack. With every day that passes, Vee's remembering more and more of her time before Cyrene, her time in foster care. The neglect. Bad nights on the streets, in abandoned houses.

Every time she edges toward that dark place, I pull her close, just to remind her that she's here, with me. Not alone. Never alone.

Counting Jax, Sasha, and Callie, we're five against the world. *Again.*

I run my fingers through the silky waves of her hair. "I'll always have your back, Vee. I just wish . . . I wish it hadn't come down to forgetting me or remembering all that."

The smile she gives me now is tentative, wavering like water, but the words are strong. "I choose you, love. I'll take the bad with the good as long as it means that I have you."

My fingers brush over her silver necklace as I smile. "Forever, love. I'm not going anywhere." Taking her hands in mine and squeezing them in reassurance, I leisurely lead her toward the back, past the stacked-up crates and beyond piles of building materials. "I do have one more surprise for you."

I open the reinforced steel door labeled "Authorized Personnel Only," and she laughs with delight as she takes in the miniature pad I've set up on the sly. There's a double bed and a stack of pillows to lounge on. Rose petals on the bedspread, candles bathing the room with warmth.

"I know it's even smaller than our old love nest under the Arkcell, but I figured if we ever need an escape for a night—"

"It's going to be a lot more often than that." Closing the door behind us with a definitive *click!*, she has me by the belt loops again. This time, I don't mind it in the slightest, especially since she's steering me straight toward the rose petals. "As nice as the Loft is, it's a little like a fishbowl. A lovely . . ." Kiss. "Well-furnished . . ." Gentle bite to my lower lip. "Fishbowl."

"And this is just for us." I run one finger along her jaw and down her neck, my lips inching closer to hers with every syllable. "No intrusions, no cameras, no bullshit glamour or artifice. Just our words, our thoughts, our music. How does that sound?"

"Like a love song," Vee whispers. "It sounds like a love song."

# ACKNOWLEDGMENTS

To our literary agent, Laura Rennert, who puts Micah to shame when it comes to delivering the goods. Thank you for finding a home for Micah and Vee's story.

To the Skyscape team: Miriam Juskowicz, for being the first real investor Cyrene ever had; our editor, Robin Benjamin, for helping build the city and making it run; and our copyeditor, Ben Grossblatt, who outperformed our nanotech when it came to finding every bug and flaw in the system. You can all have ten minutes in the zero-g room at Sarabande, our treat.

And to Nicole Brinkley and Dave Olsher, for offering fresh perspective when it was most needed.

From Glenn:

I have an endless cavalcade of people to thank, only because I am blessed when it comes to both support and encouragement.

To everyone who picked up this book and read this far. Thank you for taking a trip into a peculiar alternate future with us. Hopefully a few of you woke up on Jax's floor with a story to tell.

To my siblings, nephews, and nieces. Thank you for making my world a more colorful and adventurous place. Thank you for dragging me out of my head from time to time. Also, to my nephews and nieces, you shouldn't have read this. There were lots of swears.

To all of my workshop pals, to the members of the HWC, to all the hilarious and creative folks I've met on Twitter, to my fellow FFBs—Dan Angell, Heather Clawson, and Amanda Wils—and to everyone on OpenDiary and ProseBox who ever took the time to read my scribblings and share your thoughts. Thank you for making me a better writer, for critiquing (and haranguing when need be), and for reminding me to cool it with the adverbs. Seriously.

And finally, to Lisa. Thank you for being the best writing partner I could ever ask for. Thank you for your laughs and your "Oh I LOVE that's" and for all the times you took those extra five or ten or twenty minutes and helped me find the right words. Thank you for keeping it conversational. Thank you for that first email, so long ago, asking what I knew about guitars and if I'd like to be the bass-playing boy in your weird fictional goth-girl band. Thank you a thousand times for a thousand different gifts.

Let's do this again sometime.

From Lisa:

*(sweeping up the tickertape from Glenn's Parade of Thanks but refusing to clean up after the elephants)*

First and foremost, thank you to the readers. There was a tiny hop in style from the theater series to the steampunk novel, and then a massive leap to this near-future not-dystopian. Thank you for making that jump with us.

To my family. Over the course of this novel's publication cycle, I've watched my daughter turn into a preteen, my baby turn into a preschooler, and my nephew join our motley crew. The kids, as well as my husband, mother, sister, and family-by-marriage, are the life and light that make the daily trudging worth every second.

To the loyal supporters, the faces that turn up at the signings, book launches, and conventions; the online enthusiasts; Patreon patrons; and Dress Circle members Cat Healy and Rose Elizabeth Pedersen. Your kindness, generosity, and love of reading never cease to amaze and delight me.

And last but certainly not least, to Glenn. For answering that first email with "I'm in. Let's do this thing." For all the hours on the phone. For the jokes you had to explain. For knowing where the hyphens should go. For taking all the notes I shoved at you with good grace even when the hour was impossibly late. And for hanging in there until our weird word baby found a home. It's been a joy and a pleasure to go on this journey with you.

Yes, we really should do it again.

# ABOUT THE AUTHORS

When not working on puzzles for Penny Press or writing about them for PuzzleNation, Glenn Dallas is an author of short stories and at least half of one novel. After appearing in the acknowledgments of several outstanding novels, he looks forward to returning the favor in the future.

Lisa Mantchev is the acclaimed author of *Ticker* and the Théâtre Illuminata series, which includes *Eyes Like Stars*, nominated for a Mythopoeic Award and the Andre Norton Award. She has also published numerous short stories in magazines, including *Strange Horizons*, *Clarkesworld*, *Weird Tales*, and *Fantasy*. She lives on the Olympic Peninsula of Washington State with her husband, children, and horde of furry animals. Visit her online at www.lisamantchev.com.